NO ORDINARY LIFE

HARRIET KNOWLES

ISBN: 9781091227323

CHAPTER 1

The late summer sun was still high above the horizon as Elizabeth Bennet began to pick her way through the meadows above Shenley, her empty basket swinging from the crook of her arm.

She sneezed suddenly as the basket brushed against a clump of tall Michaelmas daisies, and the pollen blew around her in a cloud.

Laughing, she broke into a run to avoid breathing in too much more of it and sneezed again.

She was pleased to be away from the parsonage, and shook her head in dismay as she acknowledged the thought. But she was proud of her honesty and wouldn't deceive herself.

Since her marriage, Jane had become — boring. It hurt Elizabeth to admit it, and she was angry with herself for not being able to accept it.

All her life, she and Jane had been constant companions and confidantes. Jane had been Elizabeth's unstinting source of encouragement as she listened to her hopes and dreams of the future, listened to her sister tell her what she'd learned as she studied her newest passions.

But Mama had become increasingly anxious as her five daughters grew older. There were so few gentlemen in the area, so few chances for her daughters to make a good match.

Elizabeth had watched in dismay as Mama cast around increasingly desperately.

She blinked as she made her way into the shadows under the trees, and picked her way a little more carefully.

There was a sudden splash in the small stream and Elizabeth, distracted, bent to see if she could see the small fish that must have snapped at the surface.

A few minutes later, she realised she still had a long way to go to be home in time for dinner and straightened up.

Her eyes were adapted to the poorer light now, and she looked round as she hurried up the path. At least Shenley was not too far from Longbourn and she carried food over to Jane at least twice a week.

She snorted inelegantly as she considered Jane's predicament. When the new clergyman had arrived at the living at Shenley, Mama had brightened up.

"He is a true gentleman, Jane! His mother is a Lady!" She'd fanned her face, florid with excitement. "Mr. Peter Lawrence. His grandfather is the Earl of Harston, you know." She leaned forward. "His wife would move in the highest circles, once she was part of that family. And Shenley is so nice and near to Meryton."

But Mr. Lawrence was the younger son of the family, and, as Lady Emma had married rather below her, his father was not wealthy.

Elizabeth hadn't believed her mother would pursue him for Jane, once she had determined how poor his prospects were.

But she'd been mistaken. The war with France had been ferocious over the last few years, and young men were being lost at a terrible rate. Elizabeth knew several families who had suffered losses.

Mama had not been able to comprehend the grief of losing a son, and would not have to. Her grief was all about failing to find suitable husbands for all her daughters, and Mr. Lawrence was definitely from the right sort of family. It was a pity he was the younger son, but with a war on, the situation might yet change; and, even as a mere clergyman, he would be able to provide for his wife.

Elizabeth had been mortified as Mama spoke about her quarry perhaps becoming an only son, and hoped fervently that he would not get to hear about it. At least Shenley was far enough away that she need not be embarrassed about it for long, when it was all forgotten.

But it wasn't forgotten. No other suitable gentleman presented themselves as quarry, and Mama was relentless.

Elizabeth stopped at the brow of the hill and watched a litter of fox cubs tumbling and play fighting in a small clearing.

She had never believed it would actually happen.

"You can't marry him, Jane. You can't!" She had swung on the bedpost of Jane's bed, and watched her brush out her long blonde hair.

"But, Lizzy, why not? He is a kind gentleman, and his position means he can afford to marry." Jane looked at her through the glass. "He is kind and respectful. And if Mama and Papa wish me to marry him, then I should be properly dutiful and I can't say they'd be wrong."

Elizabeth ran down the hill, stopping to pick a selection of woodland flowers. They'd make a nice change from the familiar garden ones on the dinner table tonight. But Jane had now been married for two years; and Elizabeth knew that Mama was beginning to cast a calculating gaze on possible matches for Elizabeth herself.

She decided to call at Lucas Lodge. Charlotte would listen to her.

"Mr. Lawrence is so foolish, Charlotte! Why won't he let Jane do anything? Apart from parish work and making sure the house is run well, she just has to sit there with that endless embroidery." Elizabeth sat opposite Charlotte, the cup rattling on the saucer in her hands. "She won't even read the books I take her unless he approves!"

"Oh, Lizzy, please don't get so agitated. Not everyone is the same, and Jane seems quite content with her life." Charlotte smiled gently at her. "Mr. Lawrence really wants Jane to be a lady and is trying very hard to provide for her."

Elizabeth sniffed. "Mama was wrong to put so much pressure on Jane. She was only one-and-twenty, not at all past marrying age …" she stopped suddenly, realising that Charlotte was already seven-and-twenty, and might consider herself too old.

She changed the subject quickly, embarrassed

that she might have distressed her friend. "But Jane and I used to talk so much when we were younger, about how we would only marry for love, how exciting our lives were going to be when we found a gentleman who not only loved us for us, but appreciated our minds and lively intelligence as well." She looked at her friend. "You and I used to talk like that, too, Charlotte, didn't we?"

Charlotte smiled. "We did, Lizzy. But we were children then, and our hopes and dreams were not very realistic." She reached over and offered Elizabeth the plate of pastries. "Jane is content. Her husband is kind and respectful to her, and they are not destitute. That is all that we really have a right to hope for in the future, Lizzy. I hope you do not make Jane restless or discontented."

She leaned forward. "I am sure that once she is blessed with children, she will find her life very fulfilling."

Elizabeth stared at her. "Perhaps you're right, Charlotte." She forced a smile. She would not say what she really thought, not for anything would she upset her friend.

She began the last mile home, thinking what had been said — and what she had not said. Did Charlotte really believe what she had told her? Or was she, too, hoping for more out of her life than such a humdrum future?

Perhaps everyone kept their hopes and dreams secret for fear of having them dashed by scorn. Elizabeth knew she could never tell her mother how she felt; Mama would not be able to understand.

She smiled to herself. Papa would understand. He knew what she was like; he delighted in her quick mind and lively curiosity. His library was undoubtedly more varied and learned than perhaps it would have been, had Elizabeth not wished for so much variety to read.

Her pace quickened, she was enjoying reading about the great work of the Dutch scientist, Van Leeuwenhoek, in the last century. He'd been a mere draper, but had studied science and made great discoveries, too.

She felt an affinity for the man; he'd not been satisfied with his family trade, and he'd achieved something with his life.

Then she sighed. What was the point of reading about it? As a man he'd been in control of his own life and been able to finance his research, grinding and polishing the lenses that let him look into the microscopic world.

Elizabeth knew she could never do anything as profound with her life, the opportunities for ladies were not the same. But she would never let someone look down on her, never let them think that as a female, she must be foolish and empty-headed.

She was proud of her intellect, proud of her sister. proud of the things she learned, proud of who she was. But she would not like to distress her friends and her sister. Perhaps she ought to keep her opinions to herself.

CHAPTER 2

*E*lizabeth spent the next morning in Papa's library; her eyes on the text, and pen and paper beside her. But she could not concentrate today. The lines of print jumbled in front of her eyes, and her mind wandered. Had Van Leeuwenhoek actually achieved happiness and felicity in his own life? Perhaps there was something to be said for trying to be satisfied with one's own condition and situation; rather than being discontented with things that could never be.

"That's a heavy sigh, Lizzy." Her father's voice sympathised from the depths of his favourite armchair. "Why not take a break for a moment and join me? We could ring for some tea."

"Of course, Papa." Elizabeth pushed the book away. She rang the bell as she joined her father, and ordered tea. Then she sat on the edge of the chair opposite her father.

"You're not your usual self today, Lizzy." Her father smiled gently at her. "Do you wish to share what troubles you?"

Elizabeth took a slow breath and forced herself to relax. She pushed herself back into the chair and tried to make herself appear untroubled.

"It is nothing, Papa. I am just — thinking about a lot of things."

He glanced at her. "I wouldn't say it's nothing, Lizzy. I suggest you are deceiving yourself."

Her lips tightened. She knew from his smile that he used his words carefully, deliberately, because she'd told him in the past that she would never wish to practice self-deception.

But he was right. "I suppose you're right, Papa."

"You're often like this when you've visited Jane, aren't you? It can be difficult to keep the same intimacy and sense of companionship when one person in a friendship has moved on to something different."

Elizabeth felt despondent. "I suppose so, Papa. But it's not that — at least, not just that." She glanced out of the window, seeing the little scudding clouds high in the sky.

"I am just surprised and perhaps a little discomposed that Jane seems to be so different. I thought she was like me, interested in so much and yet now she seems less interested in learning new things." She wondered for an instant whether to say the next thought. "And she wishes to get Mr. Lawrence's opinion and permission for everything, too."

Papa glanced at her, but didn't say anything while Sarah carefully carried in the tea tray, setting it on the only part of the table not covered in books and papers.

Elizabeth had a sudden thought; she was fortunate to have been born the daughter of a gentleman. As a serving girl, she would have had little chance to educate herself.

"Well," her father's voice drew her attention back to the conversation at hand. "I'm thankful to hear that Jane seeks her husband's approval when necessary. Marital harmony is a great blessing, Lizzy." His lips twitched.

"You will discover that in your own good time. But Jane has had much new to learn. Running a household, and managing the money one is given to do so, can take a great deal of a lady's energy when she begins to keep house in her first home."

He raised his hand as Elizabeth drew breath to interrupt. "No, please let me finish, Lizzy. I know you wish to say that Jane has had ample time to learn such things, and perhaps she has. But people do grow and change, and that might lead to new hopes and dreams."

There was some sympathy in his eyes. "Do you think Jane is content with her life as it is now?"

Elizabeth nodded reluctantly. "Yes, Papa."

"And I am sure your wish for her is that she be happy and not discontented with the choices she has made?"

Elizabeth looked over at him. "Yes, Papa," she repeated.

"Well, then. I'm not saying you must let go of your own hopes and dreams, Lizzy. I am delighted and proud of the quality of mind and curiosity that has got you this far in building your knowledge. But I know you have loved Jane dearly as your sister, and I hope you do not resent her for choosing a different path to you." He reached out and took her hand.

"You can still be good friends with Jane and respect her choices as well, Lizzy. But until you accept that she's changed, and stop trying to keep her the way she was, then you will always be unhappy about changes that are always going to happen in life as we all grow older."

Elizabeth rose to her feet. "Thank you, Papa. I will think about what you have said. And now, I will pour our tea."

"Good." Papa stretched his legs out comfortably.

"And over tea, you can tell me what you have learned about Van Leeuwenhoek."

Elizabeth reached for the twine as she bunched up the lavender stems to dry in the flower room that afternoon. Kitty smiled at her and handed her the scissors.

"We've done well today."

"We certainly have, Kitty." Elizabeth lifted the stems to her nose. "It was good to pick them so early this morning; they've a very strong scent."

Kitty finished tying her bunch and reached up to hang it from the hook above her head. Then she reached over to her basket and collected more stems.

"How was Jane yesterday, Lizzy? Are you still concerned for her happiness?" She began placing the stems into a neat bunch.

"Well, there is little new, Kitty. But Papa asked me about it this morning and he had some advice for me that has made me think."

Her sister's eyebrows rose. "It's not like you to take unpleasant advice too much to heart, Lizzy." She smiled knowingly, and Elizabeth laughed.

"You're very good for me." In a way, her sister had become her new confidante since Jane had married, and Elizabeth wondered if she would ever have appreciated Kitty's wry sense of humour and outlook on life if she had stayed close to Jane.

"Well, Papa said to me that I was discontented because I was trying to keep Jane the way I wanted her to be and not the way she might wish to be now." Elizabeth hadn't known that was what she had been doing until it had been pointed out to her.

Kitty's hands stilled. "That's an interesting comment," and she looked up. "How did you feel about it?"

Elizabeth sighed. "I just said I would think about what he'd told me. I didn't want to say something I might regret. But now I feel even more despondent. Looking back on what was said, the whole conversation seems to me to imply that once I am married, I am going to find ordinary things interesting me and just turn into another lady who keeps the household running." She loosened the twine a little around the stems, almost as if the poor flowers could feel pain.

"Don't frown like that, Lizzy!" Kitty laughed and reached over to Elizabeth's basket for more flowers, having finished hers. "I can't see that you will ever find a gentleman who in your eyes is worth marrying, so you have no prospect of becoming ordinary."

Elizabeth dropped her bunch of flowers. "You think I will never marry?"

"I didn't say that," Kitty said equably, reaching over to pick up the flowers and tying the knot. "I said you will think no gentleman is worth marrying, and that is entirely different."

"How is it different?" Elizabeth grumbled, putting the twine and the scissors in the baskets and placing them up on the shelf.

"Why," Kitty glanced at her, "you can make the choice yourself." She laughed. "Just make sure you do not frighten the gentlemen away. If you appear too clever, they will be afraid of courting you."

Elizabeth turned back from the doorway. "Such a gentleman will certainly not be my choice of partner in life!"

"Well, you know, Lizzy?" Kitty caught up with her. "I think there are things you could do to make ordinary things more interesting to you and help others at the same time." She shut the door carefully behind them.

"As an example, you're interested in botany and things. Why not research the making of tisanes and tinctures? You could write them up and encourage Jane to grow and dry herbs from her own garden. Mr. Lawrence could not object to that, I'm sure."

Elizabeth stared at her. "But Jane knows about that already."

"I'm sure there are new things, different mixtures you can find out about by studying new texts." Kitty moved towards the drawing room. "I'm sure Jane would appreciate your efforts."

Elizabeth gazed after her. She wondered if Jane would be interested. At the moment she seemed far more concerned that she showed no signs of being with child. After more than two years, both Mama and Jane's mother-in-law were beginning to make pointed comments. Elizabeth shook her head sadly. Worrying about it was not going to make Jane any easier in her mind.

Perhaps it would be worth researching the topic. She went thoughtfully up to her room. She could certainly look at the subject. Van Leeuwenhoek could wait a few days.

CHAPTER 3

*D*arcy looked up at the knock on the door. He frowned. "Enter!"

The footman opened the door. "I am sorry, Mr. Darcy. I know you gave instructions that you were not to be disturbed, but Miss Darcy insists upon seeing you."

Georgiana didn't wait to be permitted entry, but flounced rudely in past the servant.

"William! Why do you always hide in the library? I wanted to talk to you!" She glared round the room before stalking to the armchair next to the fireplace. The fire wasn't lit as the weather was unseasonably warm this year, but Darcy pushed himself to his feet to join his sister. He glanced at the footman.

"Thank you, Stephens."

The man bowed and shut the door quietly behind him.

Darcy stifled a sigh and crossed to the chair opposite Georgiana. "Well, Georgiana? What is the matter?" He forced an affectionate smile to his face, although he didn't feel like smiling.

Georgiana had changed so much since she had first been sent to school in London when their father died. And even more so since Darcy had brought her back from Ramsgate. Her time there had spoiled her, made her think she was quite grown up, and she was far more petulant than she had ever been.

"William, I want you to send Mr. Laidlaw and Mr. Mercer away. I don't need them — I don't need to learn all that silly science, or about the wretched wars." Georgiana tipped her head up. "I need to be seen around town, visiting galleries and going to concerts." She bent a glare on Darcy.

"You should be taking me out more often."

Darcy was unable to prevent his eyebrows lifting, but he forced a mildness to his tone. "And how would you occupy your time on those occasions when I cannot take you about town?"

She gave him a slightly scornful glance. "I will practice my pianoforte playing and improve my skills on the harp. These are skills which I can show off in public and catch the attention of a suitable gentleman, since you feel my choice wasn't right."

She tossed her head. "Everyone says how handsome I am, and how very accomplished already." She sniffed. "And with my fortune, I am certain to attract a very suitable husband — even to your stringent standards!"

Darcy failed to stifle his sigh. "Georgiana, you are not yet sixteen. Not only will Cousin Richard and I not permit you to marry before you are eighteen at the very earliest, we are in agreement that you will not come out until then, either."

As her expression darkened, he shook his head. "You will not. You have been at school for nearly five years, and what have you learned?"

Georgiana looked furious, but she pressed her lips together and glared at him.

When it was obvious she wasn't going to answer, Darcy tried a different tactic. "You're a very intelligent young lady, Georgiana. Much more so than many of your age. But I do think the school has not served you well if you think that a pretty face and a fortune are enough to secure a happy marriage."

The flash in her eyes told him it was the wrong thing to say. He tried again. "You must work hard so that you're able to converse with knowledge as well as intelligence. Most of those young men in society are stupid, told only that they must marry a lady of wealth to support them." He leaned forward.

"Georgiana, you will never be happy with a man like that. You're lovely and clever, and need a gentleman who is fully your equal." He tried to see understanding in her expression. "You're my beloved sister and I would not care to see you unhappily married."

She jumped to her feet. "No! You and Cousin Richard would rather see me not married at all!" She whirled round. "You've not managed to find anyone, either of you! I won't be held back like that!"

He rose to his feet too, wondering how he'd gone so wrong. "Georgiana, I am only eight-and-twenty. There is plenty of time …"

"But not for me!" Tears of rage spilled down her face. "Do you not know how ladies laugh at other ladies who are past marriageable age? How being unmarried at even two- or three-and-twenty show how you have failed?" She marched to the window, anger in every inch of her back.

"Georgiana, dearest sister, I am sure you must be mistaken. But, I have listened, and I understand what you're asking of me, and before I accept or refuse your request, we will go together and ask Aunt Alice her opinion. As a lady herself, she will be able to say whether or not your apprehensions are well-founded." Darcy thought it was a good idea. Richard's mother was a kind and gentle lady, and had been a mother figure for Georgiana when they had first lost their mother.

"But she's old! She won't understand!" Georgiana wailed. "Things are different now to how they were then." She pulled out a scrap of lace handkerchief and dabbed at her eyes.

Her look was beseeching. "William, it's so dull, learning all those things. And at school we never had to study like that, either."

Darcy took a step toward her and took her hand. "Georgiana, I understand. Perhaps we need to consider how to find something that will interest you, that will have a meaning in your life." He hoped he wasn't making things worse.

"But only practicing the things that will attract a husband — why, what will you do after you are married and don't need those accomplishments after all?"

She pulled her hand away from his. "You aren't even trying to understand! Ladies want different things to what gentlemen want, and you can't make me think like a man!" she spun round and ran towards the door.

"I don't want …" Darcy felt winded. He seemed to lose all the arguments with Georgiana on these occasions, he couldn't keep up with her thinking.

He watched as she hurried up the stairs towards her private apartments. He must think of what to say to her at dinner this evening.

Somehow she needed to know how much he cared that she was curious about the world around her, how it might affect her life, and that of her family and their future.

How he despised the empty-headed simpering of the young ladies he met at balls and dinners; and how little they seemed to know of what was happening in the world and the many exciting discoveries being made. Even many of the young men newly up from Oxford and Cambridge seemed to bear no comparison to those he had known when he was there.

He shook his head, and rang the bell. "Coffee," he ordered tersely when the butler entered, and dropped into his armchair while he waited.

Perhaps he should ask Richard to come to dinner more frequently — maybe even this evening. They could include Georgiana in their conversation on current affairs and literature. It might help her to see that stimulating conversation could be interesting and diverting.

He sighed. How he wanted Georgiana to be intellectually curious, for her mind to be as engaging as her beauty and her accomplishments. And how much he wanted her to wed a gentleman who would value all these things in his wife, a wife who could nurture such liveliness in their children.

He nodded his thanks at the footman who set the tray on the table beside him, and breathed in the aroma of the finest coffee.

He frowned. How much more he desired to find such a lady himself, a wife who desired and valued the opportunity to learn new things, a wife who would encourage their children to be excited about knowledge and skills.

He shook his head despondently. It was only in the last year or two that he had begun to feel the need to settle, to marry, and to ensure the succession of Pemberley. But not one of those dull, fluttering girls in society could even remotely achieve what he wanted — needed — in his wife.

He pushed himself to his feet and went to his writing desk to pen a note to his cousin to join them for dinner. Richard's presence would be good for him and Georgiana.

He handed the finished letter to the footman outside the door and returned to his coffee.

He was sorry now that he'd accepted Bingley's invitation to his new estate. He would need to leave the day after tomorrow and might be gone some weeks.

Still, it would do Georgiana some good to attend

to her studies properly, and her new companion was an excellent woman.

Perhaps she might like to go and stay at Matlock House with Aunt Alice and Uncle Henry. Cousin Richard was there, and Cousin David's family called quite often. Georgiana liked their children.

He smiled, he would ask Richard before mentioning it to Georgiana.

CHAPTER 4

*C*harlotte carried the cup and saucer in carefully. "Here you are."

Elizabeth glanced up. "Oh, thank you, Charlotte!" She pushed aside her notebook to make room on the table, and Charlotte placed the tea down, glancing at the tiny text and closely printed lines of the leather-bound volume that lay on the table.

"Goodness me, Lizzy! Whatever do you find of interest in there?"

Elizabeth glanced up and smiled at her friend. "I have you to thank for the opportunity to come here to your father's library." She glanced round. "I agree with you that it's not extensive, but Papa doesn't subscribe to this periodical, and I find something of interest on almost every page."

She pulled it towards her. "Look here. There's a whole page from a correspondent on a proposed Bill to register births and deaths properly, with enough detail, so that one may be certain of one's family and it also proposes that the details not only be kept in the individual parish, and thus at risk of loss or even failure to complete the register by an indolent clergyman." She turned the page back. "And here's a description of the work to save Canterbury cathedral. I only wish there was an illustration, it's hard to imagine it from the description."

"So what's this volume called?" Charlotte didn't sound very interested, but she had asked, so Elizabeth turned to the frontispiece.

"The Gentleman's Magazine and Historical Chronicle," she read out. "It's a wonderful collection of letters he's been sent on every subject under the sun, it seems." She smiled down. "Some of the letters I pass over very quickly as being too staid even for me. But look!" she leafed quickly past the preface to the closely printed page of contents. "Later on, there's an article on a new system of physic, and an essay on the art of flower painting." She smiled mischievously up at Charlotte. "Even you can't disapprove of that!"

Charlotte bent over the page. "Place of Athelwold's death mistaken by ..." she peered closer, "... Hutton." She laughed. "I'm not in the slightest inclined to follow your example. But I wish you all the enjoyment you seek." She stood up. "I will talk to you later, perhaps, when the light is too poor to read longer."

"Of course, and I'll look forward to it." Elizabeth smiled brightly at her friend.

"Yes, I want very much to talk about the new tenants at Netherfield Park." Charlotte eyed her. "They'll be coming to the assembly, of course."

"Ah, well." Elizabeth smiled. "I suppose I can always come back and read the rest another day, can I not?"

Charlotte laughed. "Let's go through to the sitting room, then. Maria has much of the news to tell us. She saw the gentlemen riding through the town yesterday."

Elizabeth raised her eyebrows. "More than one, then?" She carefully closed the book and put it back on the shelf, before picking up her notebook and cup of tea and following Charlotte out of the library. More than one gentleman — Mama would be beside herself with excitement.

"So, tell Lizzy what the gentlemen looked like, Maria," Charlotte urged her younger sister.

Maria turned to Elizabeth. "Oh, they were so

handsome, Lizzy." She clasped her hands together and sighed. "But they were so different, it's hard to believe they might be friends."

Elizabeth laughed. "Well, if they were both very handsome, then they must be somewhat alike, for society's view of handsome does not allow for much difference."

Maria looked at her earnestly, not noticing the teasing tone. "Oh, no! Why, they were both handsome, to be sure. But one gentleman had such an open, cheerful countenance. He smiled upon everyone as they rode through the town." She raised her eyes. "When he looked at me, I thought I would faint away." She leaned forward. "He wore a blue coat — so finely tailored. It must have cost a great deal."

Elizabeth waited a moment. "So you prefer the smiling gentleman. I suppose the other scowled and looked exceedingly proud?"

"Why, no, Lizzy! He didn't smile, but he wasn't scowling at all." She looked pensive. "He was certainly very handsome; so if he is proud, I am sure his pride is not misplaced. No, he looked as if his thoughts were far away, as if he wasn't really looking at anyone."

She looked pensive. "But his looks showed enormously good breeding. I am sure he is of an old and wealthy family. His clothes were immaculately made and both rode such fine horses." She sank back into her chair with a sigh of longing.

Elizabeth laughed. "So you will no doubt make great efforts to appear lovely at the assembly, then, Maria?"

"Of course!" Maria looked shocked. "And so will you, Lizzy — we all will." She heaved an enormous sigh. "Why are they here now, when I am too young to catch anyone's attention?"

"It's a great pity, Maria. But when you're of an age to catch a young man's eye, there may be an even more handsome gentleman riding by!" Elizabeth stood up. "Thank you for telling me about the Netherfield gentlemen. If you'll excuse me, I will go back to my books before the light fades too much."

CHAPTER 5

*K*itty looked up from her book. "I think we have visitors, Mama."

Elizabeth looked up, too. She wasn't really reading, her eyes still felt tired from reading the tiny print in Sir William's periodical the previous evening, but she would never tell anyone.

But, by pretending to read, she could stay clear of the conversation, her mother fretful that Jane was still not with child, and that the Bennets had not been invited to visit Lady Emma's home. Elizabeth smiled to herself, Mama wished so much to be able to boast about her connections. Jane had called this morning and was sitting beside Mama, apparently content to listen quietly.

"Oh, it's Charlotte and her sisters — oh, and John Lucas, too!" Kitty was at the window.

"How lovely." Elizabeth rose to her feet. "Mama, should I ring for fresh tea?"

"Oh, yes, dear, you know what to do." Mama waved her handkerchief vaguely, and Elizabeth nodded, smiling.

"But what is John Lucas carrying?" Kitty was still peering out of the window and Elizabeth went over to her to glance out as well.

"Oh, you're too late, sorry, Lizzy. They've just gone round the corner." Kitty let the edge of the curtain drop.

"Never mind," Elizabeth shrugged, "we will find out soon enough."

She greeted Charlotte affectionately and dipped a small curtsy at John Lucas. He was only three years older than she was, but since being sent to sea as a midshipman at the age of twelve, he'd grown up and looked much older than his years.

He greeted her gravely. "It's good to see you, Miss Elizabeth." Then he turned to her mother.

"Good morning, Mrs. Bennet. You're looking remarkably well today."

His manners were exceptional and Elizabeth smiled reminiscently. The two families had been inseparable when they were younger — she remembered getting into many play fights with John and his elder brother Edwin when they were younger. She was a little embarrassed when recalling them now; she had fought with fervour and ferocity when she disagreed with something, and yet, here was John, older and more serious, with eyes that had seen terrible things in battle. Yet he was polite and respectful to his sister's friend.

She smiled more genuinely at him and turned to pour the tea. "So, do you have long for your leave this time, John?"

He accepted the cup from her. "Thank you. No, I'm afraid not. I have less than a week, as I am posted to another ship."

Elizabeth raised her eyebrows. "I believe that means a promotion? If I am right, then may I offer my great congratulations?"

He was still young enough to flush with embarrassment, and she hid her amusement.

"Yes, Miss Elizabeth, thank you. I am promoted to Lieutenant on the Hibernia." His eyes lit up. "She's quite new, a three decker of one hundred and ten guns."

Elizabeth smiled at his enthusiasm. "I cannot think but it must be very well-deserved, John." She offered a plate of pastries. "And such early promotion; it is not long since you reached the wardroom."

He smiled, and took a small tartlet. "Thank you." His eyes met hers. "Thank you for the compliment, but of course, promotions come thick and fast in wartime."

Elizabeth couldn't prevent a grimace. "I'm sorry, I ought not to have been so thoughtless, John."

He shook his head. "When I come home, none of it seems real, either." He smiled and waited for her to sit down before sitting down close to her.

"So, Miss Elizabeth. I hear from Charlotte that you spend much time in furthering your learning." He smiled. "I wouldn't have expected anything else."

She laughed. "Yes, I'm always curious, especially for things that I ought not to be." She knew her eyes danced. "Kitty says you were carrying something, but she couldn't tell me what it might be."

He laughed, too. "I was certain you wouldn't rest until you knew what it was." He carefully put down his tea on the table. "Excuse me for a moment." Elizabeth watched him as he left the room, wondering what it could be.

As he came back through the doorway, she saw he was holding a long tubular case, plain black, with a simple looped handle. Her heart speeded. It couldn't be …

He sat back beside her. "I know it wouldn't be proper to bring you a gift, Lizzy, so this is on loan to you for as long as you can find a use for it. I have another, and it might be that you will like it."

She took the case carefully, and took off the end

cap. Reverently, she drew out the telescope. "Oh, John! What a wonderful thing to bring me!"

He looked slightly uncomfortable. "It is not a very good one, I'm afraid. These Navy issue telescopes are not very good at catching light, so it will be no use to you after dark for any astronomy. But it will be adequate to see the moon at dusk, and of course, it will bring distant parts of the landscape, and animals, into view."

Elizabeth examined the instrument in delight. "I cannot believe how long it is, John. Why, it must be a full yard long, even though it is still closed."

He nodded. "I think I must have been quite a sight from the decks at twelve years old." He laughed. "I would have to swarm up the rigging carrying the telescope, hold on tightly, open it, try and find the other ship in the distance and hold it in the sights, even though the ship is rolling in the swell, and then shout down whether it was an enemy ship or a friend."

Elizabeth stared at him. "It sounds very difficult — and dangerous."

He smiled. "I think it is. But I am taller now, and stronger. And, of course, the captain will only send a lieutenant if there is some doubt over the midshipman's report."

Elizabeth opened the telescope. "How could you possibly hold onto the ropes and hold this steady enough to see through it?" She measured it with her eye. "What is it? Four feet long?"

He nodded. "You have a good eye, Miss Elizabeth. Fully open, it is forty-four inches." He smiled. "And holding it up to the eye is even harder."

She glanced round, there was enough room, and she held it up and looked through it. "I can't see anything."

John Lucas laughed. "No, it is no good indoors. You need to take it out into the fields and look at something at least a quarter of a mile away. I can tell you, you'll be amazed how close things will seem then." He waited until she had brought it back down into her lap. "And when you're holding it, if the view is blurred, then you twist it, here, to bring the object into focus."

She stroked the dark, polished mahogany tube. "Thank you so much. It will make such a difference."

He smiled, embarrassed. "Try it out of doors with horses in a distant field, Miss Elizabeth. It will be a good way to get familiar with it."

She knew her eyes were shining. "Oh, but the moon is waxing full in the next few days, John. I will not miss the opportunity." She wanted to run into her father's book room. "Papa has an astronomical atlas, I believe. I will look at it this afternoon."

"Dusk," he said. "That will be the best time to

see the moon, when you can still see to walk outside, but the sun is well below the horizon." He glanced at it. "For proper study, you will need to get the carpenter to make some sort of stand and cradle for it, so it is held still for you, and leaves your hands free to make sketches."

Elizabeth nodded. "Thank you, I will ask Papa to arrange it." Reluctantly she put the telescope away in the black leather case, and returned her attention to the guests and general talk. But her eyes strayed often to it, and the possibilities of new study made her inattentive to mundane matters.

She noticed Jane in quiet conversation with Charlotte and Maria, and shook her head. Their discussion couldn't possibly be as exciting as the chance of new things to study.

As soon as their guests had departed, Elizabeth hurried to her father's library. Waiting impatiently for him to bid her enter after her knock, she smiled at him.

"Papa, might I borrow your astronomical atlas? John Lucas has loaned me a spare telescope he has, and I would like to look at the moon at dusk tonight."

Her father smiled at her enthusiasm. "Come and talk to me first, Lizzy."

She frowned slightly. "Is something wrong,

Papa?" She perched herself on the edge of the chair.

"Not at all," Papa shook his head. "John Lucas came to me very properly yesterday, to ask if it would be permissible for him to loan you the telescope, or if it would be better to give it to me, so that you would then have the use of it."

He looked thoughtful. "I hope you were not so overcome with enthusiasm to begin, as to be inattentive to your friends and family while the rest of the visit continued."

Elizabeth stared at him. "Of course I was not inattentive, Papa!"

"I'm glad to hear it, Lizzy." Papa sounded as if he was thinking carefully of what he was saying. "You're a clever girl, and you know that. But you have a life to live with the rest of the family and friends around you, and I wouldn't like to think that you might make them feel inferior to you." He reached out and patted her hand. "I'm sure you'll understand that you must be careful not to let your pride in your accomplishments show and cause hurt to people you love."

Elizabeth was speechless. "Do I do that, Papa?" She didn't — wouldn't — believe it.

He smiled at her. "Don't be dismayed, Lizzy. I just wished to warn you, so that you don't face losing the affection of your friends." He stood up.

"Now. You may take the book to your chamber tonight. But for now, go back to the sitting room, while Jane is still here. See if you can recover a little of the felicity you shared with her before." He smiled slightly. "I understand there is a forthcoming assembly to talk about and get excited over."

Elizabeth glanced at him. "But Jane won't be there. Mr. Lawrence is taking her to visit his mother in Duxford."

"So he is. I'd forgotten." Papa smiled at her. "Well, you might tell her that you will observe the new tenants of Netherfield so you can tell her all about it when they return."

"Yes, Papa." Elizabeth knew she would not get to look at the astronomical atlas until later. But he was right, she wouldn't wish to hurt anyone.

CHAPTER 6

*D*arcy scowled. A dance at some dreadful small town assembly room was certainly not a pleasant way to spend an evening. Abominably played music could be heard through the windows as he climbed down from Bingley's coach, and he waited as the other gentlemen, and then the ladies, joined him.

"Come, Darcy!" Bingley tried to encourage him. "You must cheer up and decide to enjoy yourself." He beamed at his friend. "I tell you, it will be much more entertaining for you if you have an amiable expression."

Darcy looked at him in amazement. "Decide to enjoy myself? Cultivate an amiable expression? Bingley, I think you've forgotten that it's me you're talking to." He tried not to roll his eyes.

Bingley shrugged. "If you feel that way, Darcy, then just don't try and prevent me enjoying myself. I can't for the life of me think why you agreed to attend tonight, if you feel this way."

Darcy followed the rest of the party into the assembly rooms, wondering why, indeed, he'd agreed to go with them. As the doors opened, a wave of noise hit him; the music almost drowned out by the noise of twittering women, and shrieking matrons. What had he come to?

As the first part of the party entered the room, there was a slight cessation in the noise, and Darcy glanced around cautiously. There were more people in the room than he had thought there might be, and, of course, a preponderance of ladies. That was common enough in wartime, of course, and it meant that Bingley would undoubtedly have partners aplenty.

A plump man hurried up and greeted Mr. Bingley self-importantly. Bingley then introduced his party, and Darcy discovered the man was the former mayor, recently knighted. He certainly seemed to think he was in charge of the proceedings.

He never knew how he was discovered, but he could already hear the whispers spreading round the room. *Ten thousand a year, and a great estate in Derbyshire!* He scowled, did they think he would become enamoured of anyone in this room? Especially having heard their avaricious whispers?

Bingley nudged him. "This way, Darcy. Sir William wishes to introduce us to a local family."

A voice floated toward them. "Oh, sister! Why did I set my dear Jane at Mr. Lawrence? Why? If only she had been here, she would certainly have won the affections of Mr. Bingley — such a wealthy gentleman — or even Mr. Darcy! She would be the most beautiful girl in the room."

Darcy suppressed a shudder as he followed Bingley. They were being led to the owner of the penetrating voice, and he closed his eyes for an instant in horror. A large, frowsy woman, whose eyes held a calculating expression.

"Mrs. Bennet," Sir William bowed cheerfully. "Mr. Bingley wishes to be introduced to you."

Darcy wished himself miles away, but his gaze was arrested by a penetrating look from the young lady standing behind the large woman. Slender and with very dark hair, she seemed quietly well-mannered, and he could not understand why she was with this woman. He listened to the introductions, and heard that this was Mrs. Bennet's eldest unmarried daughter. He heard far more than he wished to about the beauty of the eldest daughter, married to the grandson of an earl, and was unsurprised when Mr. Bingley intervened as she drew breath and asked Miss Bennet for the next dance.

She nodded acquiescence, and Bingley beamed at her, and extended his hand. Miss Bennet took it with a lively pleasure, although Darcy hadn't heard her utter a word. He thought the mother was about to speak to him and moved away hastily.

Prowling around the edge of the room, Darcy watched his friend dance with Miss Elizabeth Bennet. She was fairly pretty, he supposed, although her features lacked a certain symmetry of form. But she seemed full of a certain joyful happiness. He scowled again.

Bingley would undoubtedly become infatuated with her. He always did, if the girl was pretty enough, and especially if she was lively and danced well. This female fitted the bill.

He turned away, looking over the rest of the room. Why should he care if Bingley lost his heart again? He would be able to get him away to London before he made too much of a fool of himself. If the girl's mother was disappointed, then so be it.

He moved toward the fireplace and took a drink from a servant's tray. Leaning against the mantel, he surveyed the rest of the room. The inferior breeding and the vulgarity of so many of those attending were indubitable, but, in essence, the occasion was just like the top society ball. It was a marriage mart, that was all.

As the small troop of musicians struck up the next dance, he saw Bingley was still with Miss Bennet. Darcy's jaw tightened, his friend was being indiscreet. Then the hairs on the back of his neck stood up.

"Charles is being foolish again." The sound of Miss Bingley's voice in his ear explained the sensation and Darcy turned to her.

"Your brother may dance with whomever he wishes." He eyed her, he would need her assistance to get Bingley away from Netherfield and this girl. He tried to be more placatory. "Perhaps we might ensure he has business in London quite soon."

She smiled at his words. "We understand each other very well, Mr. Darcy." She waited expectantly, but he turned to look back at his friend.

If he had to dance with her, it would be at a time of his choosing, not hers. Fortunately, Sir William claimed her hand for a dance, and he was alone again.

He watched Bingley, and frowned. Certainly his affections were already stirred, and Darcy bit back his irritation. Why could not Bingley hide his feelings — or, better still, be more cautious in losing his heart at the first opportunity?

But, as he watched, he could not help observing

Miss Bennet. He had to admit to himself that she was certainly more worthy of his friend's feelings than many who had gone before. She had a certain flash to her eyes, and an impertinent air. Bingley was hanging off her every utterance, although on one or two occasions he looked a little nonplussed.

Darcy's lips twitched, he wondered if the girl was challenging Bingley's notions of what it meant to be a lady. If so, Darcy must definitely protect him. His friend needed a girl with a gentle, kind temper, one who might never challenge him.

He thought, reluctantly, that he'd better dance with her, try and find out her own feelings and if she might try and snare Bingley. He didn't think so, she appeared quite untouched by him, and he was offended on Bingley's behalf.

But he was too late. The dance had finished, and Bingley was coming towards him.

"Come, Darcy! I must have you dance. I hate to see you standing about by yourself in this stupid manner."

Darcy scowled, he would dance when he wanted to, and not before.

"I certainly shall not. You know how I detest it, unless I am particularly acquainted with my partner."

Bingley shook his head. "I'm happy I don't have your disposition, Darcy. I'm having the most wonderful time. Look, there is a younger sister of Miss Bennet — Miss Kitty, I think her name is. She looks very agreeable, too. Let me ask my partner to introduce you."

Darcy glanced round. The girl looked as vapid and insipid as all the others, he certainly wouldn't give her any hope whatsoever. He looked back and shrugged. "She is tolerable; but not handsome enough to tempt me." He glared at Bingley. "Go back and enjoy yourself, don't waste your time with me."

Bingley shook his head and departed, and Darcy became aware of a glare from further down the room. He looked round and was nearly brushed against by Miss Elizabeth Bennet as she pushed past him. He watched, uncomfortably, as she sat beside her sister, who appeared near to tears.

It seemed he had been overheard, and the comment he had made to put Bingley off his endeavours had distressed the young girl. What he hadn't expected was the embarrassment he felt that the older sister had heard him.

She was speaking in a low voice to her sister, and then glanced at him over the girl's bent head. He was totally unprepared for the spark of rage making her gaze dazzle memorably.

He turned away uneasily. He supposed he hadn't been very gentlemanlike, and he was sorry he'd been overheard. He remembered he'd over-heard her mother with all her embarrassing talk, but the comparison was not as consoling as he'd hoped. He wanted another drink, but perhaps he ought to keep his wits about him.

A few moments later, he saw Bingley dancing with the younger sister, who seemed much restored in spirits. He smiled slightly, if it had been the older sister's idea, it had been a good one, and he looked round to see if he could see her.

Her glare seared his neck and located her for him, and he watched her talking earnestly to an older, plain young lady. She still appeared to be incensed with the incident. He turned away, and grimaced. He would not wish to be the object of such an embarrassment. Still, it was done now, and could not be helped.

He heartily wished the evening over.

CHAPTER 7

*E*lizabeth walked demurely towards Meryton, wishing Mr. Collins would walk further away from her.

The odious man had come to visit them and Mama had encouraged him to believe Elizabeth might accept his attentions. As they walked, she tried to ignore what he was saying by paying Mary much attention, but was constantly interrupted by him.

She rolled her eyes at Mary, wondering that Mama was being so insistent that he singled her out. She knew, of course, that he intended to choose a wife from among the daughters; and that Mama was delighted at the thought was painfully obvious. In her eyes, the problem that he would inherit Longbourn would thus be solved.

"We're nearly there, now, Lizzy," Mary encouraged her, as their cousin puffed alongside them, undeterred.

Elizabeth smiled, and speeded up a little more. Kitty was walking behind with Lydia; walking in age order was preserved. But Mary was not usually conversational. She must be encouraged by Elizabeth having talked to her so much on this walk. Why did Mama not encourage Mr. Collins toward Mary? She would certainly accept him, to be the wife of a clergyman had always been her dream.

Elizabeth smiled slightly, allowing Kitty and Lydia to tug her towards the milliner's shop, hoping that Mr. Collins would talk to Mary.

She knew why her mother was pushing him to her. Mr. Bingley had called on her a number of times and Mama had eagerly awaited that he would make Elizabeth an offer.

But he had not. And Mama must think that if he saw Mr. Collins' attentions to her, he would be galvanised into making the offer that Mama wished for so much.

Elizabeth liked Mr. Bingley, but she thought his interests superficial. She hadn't been able to talk to him of the subjects she liked to study, Mama soon put a stop to that, and Elizabeth knew that she was often distracted in his presence. Her attractions would soon pall, she knew that. She smiled, she had spent a while encouraging Kitty to join their conversations — *she* would suit Mr. Bingley perfectly.

Many times when he called, he had been accompanied by Mr. Darcy, who seemed to be unaware — or uncaring — that his presence was uncomfortable to both Elizabeth and Kitty.

And she was disturbed by the scrutiny from Mr. Darcy. He always seemed to be looking at her.

But she was drawn from her reverie by her youngest sisters bouncing with enthusiasm.

"Look, there's Denny!" Lydia nudged Kitty. "If we cross the road, we will encounter them!" She set off impulsively, followed by Kitty.

Elizabeth smiled tightly at her cousin. "I must follow them and ensure they behave with propriety, Mr. Collins. Perhaps you might prefer to wait here with Mary."

"Oh, Miss Elizabeth, I have the highest opinion in the world of your excellent judgment in all matters," Mr. Collins bowed so deeply as to appear to risk falling over. Elizabeth bit her lip, it would be dreadful if she laughed. He didn't notice, however, and continued.

"But I must say that I will join you on this errand of rectitude. I daresay my young cousins may take a deal more notice of my reprimands than they may of you, who treats them with great sympathy."

Elizabeth shrugged very slightly, and set off across the road without answering. There was a very tall stranger standing with Mr. Denny, of handsome mien and gentlemanly bearing, she was curious to meet him.

The stranger and Mr. Denny both bowed as she drew closer to them, and she curtsied. "Good morning, Mr. Denny."

The officer bowed extravagantly. "Good morning, Miss Bennet." He turned to her sister. "And Miss Mary Bennet." He returned his beaming smile to Elizabeth. "Might I introduce my friend, Mr. Wickham? He travelled down from town with me yesterday." He smiled over at him. "He has taken a commission in the Wiltshire militia, so he will be all winter in town."

Elizabeth curtsied at Mr. Wickham. "Welcome to Meryton, Mr. Wickham." She looked at both gentlemen. "May I introduce our cousin, Mr. Collins?" She was unable to keep the coolness from her voice, but she knew her cousin would be unable to discern it, and wasn't sorry.

She stood and listened as Mr. Collins made a fool of himself to the gentlemen. If she had been anyone else, she might have been embarrassed to be related to him, but she was thinking of the previous evening, when the moon had waxed a little more, and she had seen the great dark circle almost complete — what Gilbert had called in his old sketches the *Regio Magna Orientalis*.

She wished she had a more up to date book. She smiled to herself. She must work more on Papa to persuade him to buy one for her.

With a start, she realised Mr. Wickham was smiling quizzically, and pulled her attention back to the present. They must have spoken to her, because Lydia rolled her eyes.

"Come on, Lizzy!" and she turned to Mr. Denny. "She's dreaming of her maps again!"

Elizabeth knew she flushed — *why do I care what Lydia thinks?* — but she would not wish to discompose a new acquaintance. She smiled; not at their first meeting, at least.

They strolled along, Mr. Wickham on one side of her, Mr. Collins bobbing along on the other.

"So, you were anxious to join Mr. Denny in the country, Mr. Wickham?" Elizabeth began the conversation.

The gentleman smiled. "It is very pleasant to move here, Miss Bennet. I hope very much to find myself in agreeable occupation as much as I have already found agreeable company."

"Indeed, sir, indeed!" Mr. Collins almost tripped over himself with enthusiasm to join in the conversation. Elizabeth sighed inwardly.

Mr. Wickham listened politely for a few

moments, before turning his attention to Elizabeth. "Can you elucidate what Miss Lydia meant when she said you were thinking of your maps, Miss Bennet?"

Elizabeth looked away, a little embarrassed. "I have been loaned a telescope, Mr. Wickham, and I'm enjoying observing the moon at dusk and comparing it to some old observational sketches of the moon's features."

She saw his astonishment in the lifting of his eyebrows, and considered, resentfully, that yet another gentleman would consider her to be an oddity.

It was a few moments before he responded. "It shows an uncommon quality of mind, Miss Bennet, to study the heavens. Have you been interested in it long?"

"Oh, no!" Elizabeth laughed. "I have only recently been given the opportunity by access to the instrument. Previously I was studying the life of Van Leeuwenhoek, the Dutch scientist. And before that, I was reading Homer in the original Greek."

"Cousin Elizabeth, I beg you do not singularise yourself in such a manner." Mr. Collins was scuttling almost sideways as he attempted to face her while walking alongside her.

She pursed her lips, she didn't want to be rude, but his stupidity amazed her. How did he think she might ever accept his attention if he belittled her like this?

"Look Lizzy! It's Mr. Bingley!" Kitty's voice, behind her, drew her attention to other things and she looked along the road, seeing the two riders walking their horses along the road.

As they drew closer, Mr. Bingley drew up, and dismounted. "Miss Bennet! How fortunate we meet today." He bowed deeply. "I am delighted to meet you!"

He beamed round, and Elizabeth introduced him to her cousin and the other gentlemen. She didn't look at Mr. Darcy, who stayed several yards away, on his horse. She wondered at the little flutter of nerves within her, at knowing he was undoubtedly observing her.

She just happened to look up at the moment Mr. Wickham looked over at Mr. Darcy, who also seemed to recognise him at the same moment. The others were engaged in conversation with Mr. Bingley, and there seemed a sudden stillness. Mr. Darcy went white, and his expression froze. Elizabeth glanced at Mr. Wickham, where a dark flush had spread over his features. He hesitated, then touched his hat.

She looked at Mr. Darcy, who failed to acknowledge him, reined the horse and walked off.

A few moments later, Mr. Bingley hastily bowed to her and remounted, following his friend.

Elizabeth puzzled over the incident as they walked on to Aunt Philips, the gentlemen leaving them at the door, and over tea, their aunt promised to send her husband over to ensure the invitation to supper the next evening was extended to Mr. Wickham.

"Oooh, Kitty! I bet he'll have his regimentals by then!" Lydia giggled.

CHAPTER 8

On Thursday afternoon, Elizabeth was happily looking through her notes of Van Leeuwenhoek. Now the moon was waning, and she was also sure the weather was about to turn cloudy. It was time to pack away the telescope for the time being.

Mr. Collins was proving more difficult to make a decision about; she was no longer able to obtain solitude and silence in her father's library. She smiled ruefully. Papa had given her a plaintive look yesterday when she had carried this textbook upstairs to her chamber. He knew very well why she was hiding, and she knew that he'd hoped for some peace and quiet himself.

However, it was nearly teatime, and she thought the officers might well appear. She smiled; rather more contentedly, this time. The invitations to a ball at Netherfield Park had been brought this morning by the Netherfield party, and there was great joy amongst her sisters. Even Mary harboured hopes for a dance with Mr. Collins, as he had expressed a wish to dance with each of them.

She hummed contentedly to herself as she put her notes in order. She was sure she'd be able to dance with Mr. Bingley and Mr. Wickham, even if she did have to tolerate the first two with Mr. Collins.

She hurried to her closet, would she wear the dusky rose gown, or the cream?

She heard her sisters' excited voices below, and drew a deep breath. She wondered if Mr. Wickham would regret having shared his story with her the previous evening at Aunt Philips. While Elizabeth could scarcely believe what he had told her, she was glad that she knew. She had begun to have disturbed nights, thinking about the direct gaze of the darkly handsome Mr. Darcy. Now she knew of his disrespect for his father's wishes, and his cruel actions to Mr. Wickham, it must be easier to push aside her thoughts of him — mustn't it?

"Lizzy! Lizzy!" Kitty called up the stairs. "Come down, Lizzy, the officers are here."

"Coming, Kitty!" Elizabeth called back down. She carefully put her dresses away in the closet.

Perhaps the rose would be nicest. Mr. Wickham would like it.

She hurried downstairs. It was on these occasions that she still missed Jane. Even though she had been married for two years, Elizabeth still remembered past occasions where she and Jane could sit quietly enjoying the antics of the rest of the family.

But she would still enjoy herself. Mr. Wickham rose to his feet as she entered the room. She blushed pink with pleasure at his bow. Such a handsome gentleman, and yesterday, he'd seemed really interested in her study of Homer's Odyssey.

She would try and discover more of what he'd studied at Cambridge if she could. There must be something interesting to learn.

Hill bustled in with the tea tray, and Sarah followed with the second, laden with pastries.

Mr. Wickham smiled at her and indicated a chair.

"Thank you," she murmured, knowing he couldn't actually hear her above the loud protestations of happiness from Mama and her two youngest sisters.

Mr. Collins was holding forth to Mary, who was listening raptly, and Elizabeth hoped most profoundly that Mary could keep his attention for at least long enough for her to enjoy the first part of the afternoon.

Mr. Wickham smiled. "I think we have some minutes before your cousin attempts to monopolise your attention. I heard your sister engage him in some difficult passage in Fordyce's Sermons."

Elizabeth tried not to show too much amusement. "I'm surprised you know about that text for young ladies, Mr. Wickham," she teased, and he laughed for a brief moment before looking concerned.

"I confess myself puzzled as to why your mother thinks Mr. Collins is preferable in her eyes to seek your hand. Is not Mr. Bingley a much better catch?"

Elizabeth nodded; he was quite astute. "Yes, I'm sure that is in her mind. Unfortunately she thinks by encouraging Mr. Collins to pay attention to me, it will harden Mr. Bingley's attentions, too, and encourage an early offer."

He smiled sympathetically. "Why do you say unfortunately, Miss Bennet? I think it might be a good plan."

Elizabeth felt exasperated. "If Mr. Bingley has not made an offer by now, then I do not think he will. His sisters and Mr. Darcy will prevent it." She shrugged. "I do not wish to marry him anyway — and I would certainly refuse Mr. Collins if he makes an offer." She glanced over at her mother. "Mama would be much better suited to push Kitty at Mr. Bingley, they would be well-suited — *if* he is inclined to matrimony. And Mary would accept Mr. Collins and save the entail. But I will not." She wondered if he would take offence at her sharp words. But when she looked at him, he seemed amused.

"I understand you are a difficult lady to please, Miss Bennet. But I hope we, at least, may have pleasant discourse."

Elizabeth felt rather embarrassed. "Of course, Mr. Wickham. Let us begin, before Mama realises that Mr. Collins should be talking to me!"

He laughed. "If he does, then perhaps we could be about to walk in the garden. Although the clouds are heavy, at least it is not raining."

"It would be enjoyable, Mr. Wickham, but I fear Mama will overrule us and say that the dusk has fallen too far for it to be proper." She smiled archly. "She will want to observe that I am paying him proper attention."

"Of course," he murmured. "So, if the weather is inclement in the next few days, what do you intend to do to occupy your time?"

She turned to him, more animated. "I wished to ask you about your studies at Cambridge. There must be something you think that will be new and interesting to me."

He shook his head. "I believe you have already outstripped me in knowledge, Miss Bennet. And I must also confess that my talents run in other directions."

"Oh?" Elizabeth could not control her eyebrows.

Mr. Wickham laughed at her response. "I enjoy watching people and their actions, Miss Bennet. It is why I feel I was destined for the church." His expression was sad. "I would be able to help so many more people in the parish."

Elizabeth gave a sympathetic murmur, but she wondered if there wasn't a calculating look behind his appearance, and suspicion of him began to take root. Why was he doing this, what did he wish to achieve? "So what do you like to discern when you observe people, Mr. Wickham?"

He smiled. "My concern for you, Miss Bennet, is that Mr. Collins will not accept you refusing his offer. He will believe that you must think his situation in life is irresistible."

She looked at him with more attention. It was an accurate thought, and one that had already occurred to her. "Thank you, Mr. Wickham. I have been considering how I can try and avoid receiving an offer at all, but I am not convinced it will be easy." She sighed. "I have been trying to tell Mama that she should assist him to move his intentions to Mary but she will not listen to me." She determined to leave the topic.

"Let us think of pleasanter things, Mr. Wickham. Have you heard that Mr. Bingley is holding a ball at Netherfield Park next week?"

"Why yes," Mr. Wickham followed her lead. "I am inclined to think well of him, Miss Bennet. He has extended an invitation to all the officers, so there is great happiness within the billet." His smile was sunny and guileless, and Elizabeth felt even more suspicious. But she prided herself on being able to hide her true feelings. He would never guess.

She thought of the ball, and Mr. Darcy came to mind. Her insides twisted, would he be able to discern her feelings?

CHAPTER 9

*D*arcy watched absently as Mr. Maunder moved around the room, setting out his evening wear. His valet was used to his master watching him, and knew that he was not really seeing anything, just deep in thought.

Why on earth had Bingley decided to give a ball here at Netherfield? Darcy jumped to his feet and went to the window. He thought it likely that Bingley was trying to impress Miss Bennet. The man was infatuated with her, foolishly so, in Darcy's view.

He'd been watching them whenever they were together, and he was certain her affections were not stirred. Bingley should be able to see it if Darcy could.

He smiled slowly; the last time they had called at

Longbourn, Miss Bennet had frequently drawn her younger sister into the conversation. She had encouraged Miss Kitty to participate, and despite the younger girl's reserve, Darcy could see what Miss Bennet obviously could; Miss Kitty was much better suited to Bingley's tastes and intellect.

"Are you ready for your shave, sir?" his valet asked quietly, and Darcy turned.

"Thank you, Mr. Maunder." He crossed the room and sat back in the chair as the man prepared the paraphernalia.

He could think while he sat here, and he closed his eyes. Why was he so sure that Bingley shouldn't pursue Miss Bennet? Every time he thought of it, he found himself scowling, wanting to intervene, tell Bingley to step back …

"I'm sorry, sir." Mr. Maunder's voice interrupted his thoughts, and Darcy blinked.

He'd scowled, just thinking of Bingley and Miss Bennet, and he was lucky that the servant had been aware of his movement.

He smiled slightly, it would be a fine thing if he appeared at the ball with a cut face. "No, it's my fault. I must clear my mind." He sat back again and closed his eyes. He would think of his business affairs. He would need to return to London soon, his solicitor had written to him, and he needed to arrange a meeting with the trustees of the estate.

They'd be able to complete the business he'd been working on ever since Ramsgate — a separate trust for Georgiana's fortune, so that no man could gain access to it unless she had married with the full consent of her guardians, and even Georgiana herself would not be able to dispose of more than a fraction of the income until she had attained the age of thirty-five years and had the approval of her brother or whichever of the Fitzwilliam family was overseeing her welfare.

He caught himself about to scowl again when the blade against his skin hesitated and forced himself to clear his mind. He would think of nothing, nothing at all.

"I have finished, sir." His valet proffered a towel, ad Darcy leaned forward, and wiped his face.

"Thank you. I'm sorry I was inattentive."

Mr. Maunder smiled. "You have many cares, sir."

Darcy nodded ruefully, and a few minutes later, the man returned to his side with a crystal glass.

"Just a small whisky, sir."

"Thank you." Darcy pondered how much better his evening would be, sitting up here with a decanter of whisky and a good book. For a moment, he considered the option, then he walked to the fire and leaned against the mantel. It would not do. He must ensure Bingley did not do anything foolish, he must see if the blackguard Wickham was there and attempt to warn Miss Bennet about the man without her suspecting his motives.

Perhaps he might ask her for the honour of a dance? Surely she would not refuse. Or she would have to sit out the remainder of the evening, and she wouldn't do that. Her vivacious manner and laughing eyes showed her enjoyment of such affairs.

He shuddered slightly, she was very different to him. But she was angry with him. He had been thoughtless to appear to insult her sister within their hearing, and he felt the flush steal round the back of his neck. The memory would live with him for a while. But he dreaded the thought of Wickham dancing with Miss Bennet, those hands touching hers. He gulped his whisky, he could not abide the thought.

If he could go to London, perhaps he could forget all these people here, it shouldn't concern him what a few country girls of humble birth thought of him.

HE WENT downstairs at the appointed hour and waited at the back of the hall to watch the guests arriving, while Bingley and his relations stood in the receiving line.

A tight sensation in his chest told him when Miss Bennet arrived with her family, and he watched her as they moved towards the receiving line. His gaze sharpened as he watched the clumsy-looking young clergyman scuttling obsequiously alongside Miss Bennet. He watched her carefully, sensing her embarrassment as the clergyman pressed closer to her than was quite acceptable.

But she stepped back so that her father introduced him to the Bingley ladies, and Darcy surmised that he was some sort of relation.

Bingley stepped out of the line and offered Miss Bennet his arm — well, it was his ball, of course. Darcy felt his lips twitch, and he moved round the hall toward the ballroom, trying to push away the odd feeling within him. He was not jealous of Bingley, was he? *No, it cannot be so.*

Many of the officers had already arrived, and Darcy was relieved not to have seen Wickham arrive. But he must ensure he had checked each and every redcoat in the room.

His attention was drawn back to Miss Bennet without his being aware of it. She looked delightful tonight. Tiny white flowers and thin ribbons twined through her dark hair, which was swept into an elegant updo, although he thought the errant curl that tumbled down by her ear was the most fascinating part of it. He wondered what it might be like to twine it around his finger …

He jerked to attention. He must not think like this! It is madness! He shuddered again. He must persuade Bingley to London. Then they could both forget her.

The orchestra struck up the music for the first dance, and Bingley turned to Miss Bennet with a ready smile, which turned to dismay as she shook her head, looking downhearted.

Was she refusing to dance with Bingley? Darcy stood, thunderstruck, as the little clergyman sidled up beside her with an ingratiating smile.

Bingley obviously noted the desperation behind her polite exterior — and so he ought. Darcy could see it from where he stood.

She gave Bingley a dazzling smile in response to his next words, and accompanied the clergyman to the dance floor, her expression fixed in icy politeness.

Darcy watched from the edge of the room. The man was an idiot. He was so wrapped up in his own self-importance that he was talking when he should be concentrating on the moves of the dance — which he didn't know. He bumped into the other dancers and his apologies were loud and offensive.

He'd thought he'd be amused by him, but Darcy saw the mortification and embarrassment of Miss

Bennet, and was dismayed on her behalf. He was even more discomposed when he saw the gloating, possessive expression on the man's face.

Disgusted, Darcy turned away. He quartered the room to look for Bingley. Perhaps he had the next with Miss Bennet, but he must know who this odious man was.

But Bingley was dancing with Miss Kitty Bennet, and she was talking much more freely than when he'd seen her at Longbourn. There was a rather arrested expression on Bingley's face, mixed with guilt. Amused, Darcy determined to wait nearby until the dance was finished.

As it drew to a close, he picked up two glasses of wine, and waited at the edge of the dance floor, and bowed to them both as they approached him. Miss Kitty looked at him nervously, curtsied to Bingley and fled. Darcy held out the glass to Bingley.

"We must talk."

CHAPTER 10

*B*ingley looked uncomfortable, but nodded.

"I cannot leave the room, Darcy."

"I am aware of that, but we cannot be overheard if we talk quietly." Darcy was implacable.

"Miss Bennet suggested I dance with Miss Kitty," Bingley spoke hurriedly, and Darcy blinked. Was that what the man was feeling guilty about?

"I do not think it a problem, Bingley. Of course you must dance with many of your guests." He was slightly amused to see Bingley's relief.

"But I thought Miss Bennet seems very uncomfortable with the clergyman. Who is he? And did he have a prior claim on her?" He hoped he didn't sound too abrupt. He almost smiled, Bingley was too naive to think of the reason Darcy would be concerned about it.

Bingley mopped his brow, and sighed. "He is a cousin, Darcy. And he had claimed the first two with her at their home when they first had the invitations." He looked wretched. "There seems to be some reason — I understand Mrs. Bennet is pushing hard for him to make an offer to Miss Bennet. I cannot for the life of me understand it."

Darcy couldn't understand it, either. He frowned, the very thought of the odious man having her in his power made him shudder. "Did you ask Miss Kitty about it?"

Bingley looked startled. "I wouldn't know how to say it to her, Darcy!"

"It seemed quite an amiable time you were having," Darcy commented, and was surprised when Bingley flushed and looked away. He hurried to repair the situation. "I meant nothing, Bingley, merely that I had not seen Miss Kitty so relaxed in company before."

"Ah!" Bingley looked relieved. "Of course, once he has had his two dances, he cannot bother Miss Bennet again," he beamed. "She has accepted the third and the supper dance with me, so she is safe then."

Darcy nodded. "With your understanding, perhaps I may ask her for the honour of one."

Bingley looked more cheerful. "Of course, my friend! If you are willing, it would be a great service to me."

Darcy turned and looked at her on the dance floor. A great service! If Bingley knew his inner turmoil, he would not call him friend.

In the dance, Miss Bennet was flushed with continuing mortification. The fool was still falling over his feet and treading upon her toes. Darcy winced. He could see a torn area around the hem of the gown that might be the best she owned.

Bingley groaned beside him. "I wish I could eject him, but as a guest staying with the Bennets …"

"No, of course you cannot do that," Darcy said absently. "But I am at a loss as to why Mrs. Bennet prefers him over you. As a potential suitor, there is no comparison." He would have to investigate. He swung round to his friend.

"You have the third with Miss Bennet, Bingley, and enjoy yourself. Then perhaps you might leave the floor and finish near me, and I might ask her for the fourth, and see what I can discover." Even if she was angry with him, she might be less likely to refuse him if Mr. Bingley seemed to approve.

When Bingley escorted her from the dance floor after the third, she seemed much more herself, and Darcy was pleased. He bowed to her.

"Miss Bennet, may I request the honour of the next?"

She looked startled, and glanced at Bingley, who nodded encouragingly. She looked back at him and her eyes were cold as she curtsied. "Thank you, Mr. Darcy."

He supposed it was about the best he could expect, and he wondered if he might need to apologise for that incident before she would talk to him on the subject of today's enquiry. He led her to join the couples on the floor. As he faced her, he was aware of the surprised gaze of many of the town's residents, and his lips tightened. Gossiping crows, all of them.

They danced the first few forays down the line in silence, Miss Bennet not seeming inclined to favour him with her usual vivacity. He wondered how to broach the topic of his insult to Miss Kitty. Or perhaps he should ignore it.

She glanced at him, and seemed to decide that she must say something. "I am happy the rain ceased yesterday, Mr. Darcy. It made the arrangements here very much easier for Miss Bingley, I suppose."

He nodded, and they continued the dance. She glanced reprovingly at him. "It is your turn to say something now, Mr. Darcy."

He raised his eyebrows. "Do you talk by rule then, while you are dancing?"

She smiled, "Sometimes. One must speak a little, you know. It would look odd to be entirely silent for half an hour together."

He huffed a laugh. "I suppose so." He seized on the moment. "I did think, however, that your first partner talked overmuch."

Her expression closed down. "Yes, sir." He was irritated, she wasn't being much help to him. As they turned away from each other in the dance, he drew a deep breath, he must not lose his temper.

When they returned closer to each other, he was better prepared. "I understand he is some sort of cousin, Miss Bennet, and that your mother seems to be encouraging your union." He tried to keep his voice gentle and it seemed to work, for she didn't appear to take offence. She met his eyes.

"Papa and Mama have five daughters and no sons. Longbourn is entailed away from the male line, and Mr. Collins is heir to the estate."

The dance took them away from each other to dance with their neighbours' partners for a moment, and Darcy went through the motions, not even noticing the lady opposite him, while he thought about what she had vouchsafed to him.

It was a great deal more than just the entail, of course. The implication was obvious to him. Bennet could have made arrangements that would make his wife and daughters worry less about the future, but he must be an indolent man, if even the catastrophe of five daughters had not stirred him to action.

It also seemed that Mrs. Bennet was beginning to despair of Bingley making an offer. That was good from his point of view, but it made Miss Bennet's situation rather more precarious.

He didn't have to try hard to keep his voice gentle when he spoke again. "What are your feelings on the matter, Miss Bennet?"

Her eyes flashed. "I will never accept him, never!" Her lips tightened. "But there will be much trouble at home." She sighed, before looking up at him again. "He thinks women have no brain, no intelligence, need to learn nothing, have no interests in life outside marriage!" Her bosom heaved with emotion. "I want to learn new things, I am not vacuous or stupid, and any man who cannot accept that would not be afforded a happy marriage with me!" Her low voice could not be heard by any other but Darcy, and he was bemused as she suddenly seemed to dissolve into laughter.

For a few moments, she continued to dance with her lips pressed together until she seemed satisfied that her laughter was under better regulation. "I'm sorry, Mr. Darcy, you cannot have expected such an outburst." Her lips curved and he drew his gaze away hurriedly.

"Not at all, Miss Bennet." He wanted to say *Bravo!* He wanted to say, *I would like you to meet my sister*, and more, but the dance was drawing to a close, and he escorted her off the dance floor in frustration. He still wanted to speak to her, but she curtsied, seemingly in a hurry to get away from him, and went to join her mother as if she knew he would not follow her there.

He scowled.

CHAPTER 11

The ground was still rather muddy, but Elizabeth was sure she could get to Shenley without getting her shoes too dirty, and Jane would want to hear all about the ball. She talked the cook into giving her a selection of pastries and her basket smelled heavenly.

But she wanted to be honest with herself. It was more to escape the house that she had decided to call on Jane, not telling Jane about the ball. Mama would be trying to engineer a proposal; she knew that, and dreaded it.

She was content about what had happened at the dance. Despite having to avoid Mr. Collins' feet during the first two, she had watched Mr. Bingley dancing with Kitty. Surely he had begun to realise that his affections were stronger than they were to her? She frowned a little, he'd feel obliged that he had been paying her some attention, she must convince him that she was most unsuitable.

She'd begun during the supper. Sitting beside him after the supper dance, she'd implied that she was a dutiful daughter and might have to consider her parents' wishes regarding Mr. Collins.

Mr. Bingley had seemed to be relieved, although she could tell he was puzzled. But he hadn't demurred.

But Elizabeth was protective of Kitty, she wouldn't mention anything to her, not yet.

She was vexed with herself, though, for telling Mr. Darcy about Mr. Collins and how she felt. He hadn't even apologised for offending Kitty, and she'd told herself she'd never dance with him, or speak to him. But he'd seemed sympathetic, and kind, and understanding.

She frowned. But what did he matter? He'd only tell Mr. Bingley and make him feel that he could not switch his affections to Kitty.

Then she smiled; Mr. Darcy was still very handsome, especially when he looked kind and concerned, rather than proud and disdainful. Very handsome indeed, and Elizabeth began to run, wanting to get away from the strange sensation within her.

IT WAS ALMOST lunchtime when Elizabeth neared Longbourn again. Her spirits were as confused as her steps were slow — as she so often felt after calling on Jane.

She didn't feel it was right that her sister was telling her that she ought to accept Mr. Collins to ease her parents' minds. Jane hadn't met Mr. Collins apart from when she and Mr. Lawrence had come to dinner last week, and she knew Elizabeth's ambitions and hopes.

Perhaps Jane thought she might never have a child and thus cause Mama to need to move all her hopes to Elizabeth.

Elizabeth smiled, Van Leeuwenhoek would have to wait again; Elizabeth needed to find a new tisane or herb that might aid her sister's childlessness.

As she turned into the driveway of Longbourn House, she could hear shrieks and lamentations from her mother, and her heart sank. Somehow, she knew that she was the object of her mother's ire.

She stopped for a brief moment and took a few deep breaths before walking round to the back of the house. Perhaps she'd see Papa first. He would support her, she knew that.

But it wasn't to be. Mama was crossing the hall. "Lizzy!" Her voice must have been heard throughout the house, and Elizabeth saw Kitty in the doorway of the sitting room, looking anxious.

"Mama," she kept her voice cheerful and untroubled. "I've been to see Jane and tell her all about the ball." Jane was Mama's favourite, surely she would ask after her.

"Don't try and change the subject, Lizzy! I needed you this morning, and now you can do as you are instructed. Go into the sitting room and hear Mr. Collins!" Her mother hurried behind her, shooing her along, and then took Kitty's arm.

"Come along, Kitty. Lydia, Mary, you all need to come with me — now!"

Elizabeth found herself in the sitting room, where Mr. Collins stood by the fireplace; a smug and satisfied air about him, and a tolerant smile upon his face. Elizabeth stood with her back to the door, wishing she could just run right out again.

But nothing would satisfy her mother until all this was over; and she knew, with a sinking feeling, that even then, the expectations would not cease.

She steeled herself and looked at her cousin.

"Dear Miss Bennet," her cousin didn't wait for her to be seated, or say that she was ready to receive his addresses; he had obviously decided to have his say at once. "You can hardly doubt the purport of my discourse, however your natural delicacy may lead you to dissemble; my attentions have been too marked to be mistaken." His smile was wide and patronising, and Elizabeth looked down.

Mr. Collins sounded as if he was delivering a well-practised sermon, and she wondered if his address would last as long. But she must try and listen.

"As soon as I entered the house I singled you out as the companion of my future life. But before I am run away with by my feelings on this subject, perhaps it will be advisable for me to state my reasons for marrying."

His whole bumbling speech was so extraordinary that Elizabeth was soon staring at him in astonishment. Even the single sentence he spoke about his affections sounded false and rehearsed. She felt sick.

"One moment, please, Mr. Collins! I — I thank you for the compliment of your offer, but I cannot accept it, it would be against all that I have ever believed in!"

He stared at her in astonishment, his pallid face slack and disbelieving.

"But, Miss Elizabeth! Your family security depends upon you accepting — and my situation in life, my connections with the family of de Bourgh, and my relationship to your own, are circumstances highly in favour of my offer." He had obviously not expected a refusal, indeed, he had been certain of her happy and joyful acceptance.

He tried again to persuade her of the necessity that she accept him. "Lady Catherine de Bourgh will receive you, you will move in the best of circles." He pressed home his advantage. "It is by no means certain that another offer of marriage may ever be made you. Your portion is unhappily so small …"

Elizabeth raised her hand. "You have said enough, Mr. Collins! My decision has been made, and made before today. My need is for me to be able to study extensively, and follow my heart to knowing more than may be acceptable to you, and to Lady Catherine." She smiled placatingly. "I would not wish your patroness to find your wife wanting."

"But Miss Bennet …" He was not about to give up, and Elizabeth had tried long enough. "My answer is *no*, Mr. Collins. I will not change my mind." She dipped a polite curtsy, in deference to his relationship to her father, then left the room, shutting the door behind her.

But she was not so fortunate as to escape further censure. Her mother had been loitering in the hall, probably even listening at the door, Elizabeth thought, resigned.

"Lizzy! You must go back and accept Mr. Collins! I insist you marry him!"

Elizabeth stared at her in amazement. She had been utterly convinced that Mama had only encouraged Mr. Collins to try and make Mr. Bingley bring forward an offer. She was utterly bemused by her mother's disapprobation.

"I will not marry Mr. Collins, Mama. I am sorry, but I will not." Elizabeth marched off towards the stairs. Life was going to be a little uncomfortable here until Mr. Collins went home.

"Lizzy!" her mother screeched up the stairs. "Your father wants to speak to you!"

Eyes heavenward, Elizabeth wondered why her mother even thought that Papa would back her up. She'd been married for twenty-five years, she must know that he wouldn't force Elizabeth to accept an unwanted proposal. She smiled, he'd made his opinion of Mr. Collins quite obvious, although the object of his derision was oblivious of it.

"Lizzy!" her mother cried out again, and Elizabeth called back.

"Coming, Mama!" This was not going to be easy.

CHAPTER 12

*D*arcy House was a haven of peace, and Darcy turned into his library with a sigh of relief. Two days since the ball at Netherfield, and he had managed to get the whole party to London.

Bingley's coach had turned off at Grosvenor Street and Darcy's had continued to Brook Street.

He was very satisfied to be home. Pouring a whisky, he relaxed back into his own great library chair, the worn leather familiar to him. He had to admit that he was also happy that Georgiana was at Matlock House with their aunt and uncle for the next few days. He was definitely more relaxed, knowing he would not have to face her just yet.

He leaned back and closed his eyes. The contrast between his sister's superficial interests and Miss Bennet's eagerness to learn new things had struck him forcibly. How could he encourage Georgiana to be curious about the world around her? He suddenly jerked forward — more like Elizabeth Bennet, in fact.

He found himself by the window. He must stop thinking about Elizabeth Bennet, must stop Bingley going back to Netherfield, and they must forget the Bennets — even if Miss Bennet had to face down that foolish cousin of hers; and he didn't doubt that she would.

He smiled through the window at the gardens wreathed in evening mist. It was a pity Miss Bennet was from such an unsuitable background, her intellect would have made her a fascinating conversational partner. He pushed himself away from the window and went to his desk; he didn't want to think further about her.

Richard,

    I have returned to Darcy House, and wonder if you would favour me with your company at dinner. I have much to discuss with you.

    Pray do not tell Georgiana, and she can remain at Matlock House for another day or so.

    Yours,

    Darcy

He rang the bell as he sealed the letter and gave

it to the butler to be sent to Richard. "Thank you, Mr. Jones. Oh, and tell the cook that Colonel Fitzwilliam will be joining me for dinner."

"Yes, sir." The butler bowed.

Darcy gulped down the rest of his drink and climbed the stairs to his chambers. He would not wait until it was time to change, he wanted a bath now to ease the stiffness in his shoulders.

Tomorrow, he would rise early and ride out before most of the city was awake. He would take up his usual routine of business matters and meetings with Richard. He anticipated it with pleasure. Perhaps he would soon be able to push Miss Elizabeth Bennet out of his mind. And in his mind, her eyes gazed back at him, steady and calm. He shook his head and turned away from the window. He must make greater efforts to erase her from his thoughts.

DINNER WAS RESTFUL. It was the word that came to his mind. Without Miss Bingley present to make him uncomfortable with her stare and her comments, and without Georgiana to consider, he and Richard dined quietly and well.

"So, tell me what Hertfordshire was like, Darcy."

Richard pushed away his plate, and stretched out his legs under the table.

Darcy shrugged as the servants moved round the table, quietly clearing the dishes. "Much as expected, Richard. Bingley fell for the nearest pretty girl, as always. I'm glad to have got him away from there before he made her an offer."

The table cleared, a servant placed the port by his hand and closed the door behind him as he left the room.

Darcy poured his port and passed the decanter to his cousin.

Richard took it absently. "One of these days you are going to have to accept that Bingley needs to marry, Darcy. You cannot prevent it forever."

"Not this young woman," Darcy said firmly. "He would not be happy." And neither would I, he continued under his breath.

"What is wrong with this one?" Richard was twirling his glass between his fingers, admiring the deep amber liquid within.

Darcy shrugged. "Her family are dreadful. The behaviour of the mother and youngest daughter are particularly disgraceful, and the girl is without fortune." He smiled slightly. "She's also much too clever for him, as well as too independent; I think he would find himself puzzled and bemused by her."

Richard raised an eyebrow. "You have been very

observant, Darcy. What is the name of this paragon of virtue, who is of unfortunate descent?"

"Miss Elizabeth Bennet," Darcy sighed. "I do wish Bingley good fortune in finding a wife, but the man does not think behind the pretty face. I wouldn't like to see him unhappy."

Richard leaned forward. "Or yourself. Darcy, are you enamoured of this young lady?"

"Certainly not!" Darcy jumped to his feet and went to the window, his back to his cousin. "It is as I said. She will not be able to make a suitable marriage, her background will not permit it. And she will not suit him. That is all."

"So why are you hiding your expression from me, Darcy?" Richard's voice was steady, and Darcy swung round, scowling.

Richard didn't look at him, still twirling the glass between his fingers. "I will not mention it again, Darcy, if it makes you uncomfortable. But I beg that you do not deceive yourself."

"As there are no ladies, we can be more at ease in the library with our coffee, perhaps." If he didn't mention her again, perhaps Richard would not return to the subject. "We need to talk about Georgiana, too."

"Indeed." Richard drained his glass and followed Darcy to the library.

THE FOOTMAN PLACED the tray down on the table and poured their coffee. The rich aroma, familiar as the smell of leather in this room, was inexpressibly comforting, and Darcy sat quietly for some minutes.

Richard seemed equally content to just sit in silence, but after a while, he sighed. "So what do we need to discuss about Georgiana, Darcy?"

Darcy glanced over. "How has she been, these past weeks? Has Aunt Alice been able to make her keep up with her studies?"

"What do you think?" his cousin growled. "Georgiana — in the mood she is in now — will not listen to anyone. All she wishes to do is go to places where she will be seen in public, and to modistes to have new gowns made."

Darcy made a face. "I suppose she had better come back here. Your mother must be very tired of her if she is behaving like that." He thought of something else. "Does her companion have any powers of persuasion?"

Richard nodded. "Mrs. Annesley is quite competent, but of course, if Georgiana doesn't wish to go somewhere, then she will not go."

Darcy nodded. "I will clear some time to take her to art galleries and the theatre — operas, too, perhaps. I must try and engage her mind, she is too clever to be happy as an empty-headed wife."

"And if she doesn't wish to go?"

"Then I will ensure her mind is completely occupied with extra studies from the various masters she has." Darcy hoped he didn't sound too hard.

Richard raised an eyebrow lazily. "For the record, I think you will not win any sort of conflict with her in that way."

"Then I pray you tell me how to proceed." Darcy was nettled, which was probably Richard's intention.

But his cousin shook his head. "I think she must find someone that she can look up to, someone who might inspire her to wish to emulate them." He glanced at Darcy. "Would your little Hertfordshire lady be a suitable friend and companion?"

Darcy glared at him. Not for anything would he have her here as a paid employee! "No, she is a gentleman's daughter. She is not looking for paid employment."

"A pity," Richard mused. He thought for a few more moments, while Darcy had to try and push thoughts of Miss Bennet away again. When Richard spoke again, he was ready.

"Well, perhaps if she discovers young men also appreciate intelligence in a lady, that might inspire a willingness to learn."

"And how should we find such young men," Darcy enquired, "given that Georgiana is not quite sixteen and not yet out?"

Richard waved his cup at him, and Darcy got up to replenish the coffee.

"Thank you." Richard frowned. "Well, I think that when you take her out, it should be to cultural activities as you said, and perhaps it will bear fruit. As for the other, leave it to me. Jonathan is up at Cambridge, perhaps he can bring some undergraduates for dinner here, once or twice a month. In fact, Jonathan is quite studious himself. If he is with friends, he might seem more outgoing in Georgiana's eyes."

Darcy considered the matter. Richard's younger brother was indeed a bookish young fellow. Perhaps too much so for Georgiana. "Would it be more appropriate if the dinners were at Matlock House? I'm sure your mother would assist us."

Richard shook his head. "If Georgiana wants to be so grown up, she can manage the dinners here. It will give her responsibility, and perhaps she will learn something."

Darcy nodded. "It is a good thought. We would have to find at least a few young ladies, or it will be an unbalanced table. And I would not wish that to have consequences."

Richard got up. "Leave it with me, Darcy.

Perhaps my sisters might help. I'll bring Georgiana home tomorrow after lunch, so that you have the morning to catch up on your business affairs."

Darcy rose with him. "Thank you, Richard. I'm grateful for your assistance."

As they waited a moment while the horse was led round, Richard eyed him. "You need to rest. Was Miss Bingley much of a nuisance?"

Darcy grimaced. "Not too bad. But I had to keep my wits about me."

Richard laughed. "Just make sure you do not end up compromised. She would prevent Georgiana using her brain at all!"

Darcy growled irritably, but fortunately his cousin did not raise the name of Miss Bennet again.

Not that it would prevent her disturbing his dreams, as she had on previous nights.

.

CHAPTER 13

For three days now, Elizabeth had taken a long walk in the woods above Meryton. Netherfield was empty, and on the day Mr. Collins had finally absented himself from Longbourn, she had discovered from Charlotte that he had made her friend an offer of marriage.

Not only had the shock of that been shattering, but Charlotte admitted that she had accepted his offer.

Elizabeth climbed over the stile, and dropped down on the other side. She took a deep breath of fresh air. The whole affair had added to the unsettled feeling she had.

She was unable to study, to concentrate on things that would have usually have occupied her mind. Being able to work would have prevented the last few weeks turning her thoughts all aback.

Why would Charlotte do something like that? Elizabeth had thought Jane accepting Mr. Lawrence was bad enough, but Mr. Collins was so much more foolish, so much more difficult to tolerate. Just being in the same house as he had been a trial, and for Charlotte to put herself in that position; why, Elizabeth could not imagine anything — security; the wish for her own establishment — surely *nothing* could be worth such a daily, unending trial.

Papa had told her again that she must not judge others by her own standards, and, with Charlotte; if she could not hide her feelings, she might not be able to maintain the friendship that he was sure she had long valued. So Elizabeth had tried to hide her thoughts on the matter, and as such, she and Charlotte were able to maintain cordiality.

But she thought the intimacy they had shared on so many of their opinions, and for so many years, would never recover to the state they had before.

Why did Elizabeth feel such a sense of betrayal? After all, she had refused her cousin, so she ought not to be disturbed by the matter.

She found a fallen tree trunk to sit against and stared out in the low afternoon sunlight. Was it that she had hoped to persuade Mama to try and convince Mr. Collins to make his addresses to Mary? Or was there still a disappointment within her that nothing more had been heard of Mr. Bingley, so all her hopes for Kitty were dashed?

It certainly wasn't because she felt there was some unfinished — something — between Mr. Darcy and herself. She closed her eyes against the light, and that gentleman's lean, dark features swam into her mind's eye. She remembered the look as she had last seen him, as they danced at Netherfield. He had been concerned for her, and his dark eyes had pierced her very being, as he'd quietly asked how she felt regarding the pursuit of her cousin.

She smiled a little, she had been surprised. She had thought Mr. Collins' actions would please him, because he quite certainly disapproved of his friend's pursuit of her. Elizabeth knew he would have been horrified if he had known of her feelings for *him*. She jumped to her feet, she must get home before dark.

But he would be the same as all other gentlemen, especially in proud aristocratic society. She knew they wished their wives to be decorative creatures, merely concerned with the management of their homes.

She wondered what he had thought of her outburst that she would never accept Mr. Collins because he disapproved of ladies who had a desire to learn new things.

Hurrying back down the path, she was sorry the dance had finished at that moment, she would never know what he had thought of her opinion. But she pushed thoughts of him aside. None of them would ever hear from the Netherfield party again, and there was nothing to be done about it.

But it was nearly Christmas, Aunt and Uncle Gardiner would be arriving at Longbourn this afternoon for the season, and Elizabeth was greatly looking forward to their arrival. The gathering at Lucas Lodge tonight was less welcome, but there was no escaping it, and at least she might be entertained by Mr. Wickham.

She arrived back at Longbourn just as her uncle's carriage drove round the corner of the lane, and broke into a run, a smile on her face. Aunt Gardiner would smile at her and not berate her, as Mama still did constantly. It would be refreshing not to sense disapproval around her.

LUCAS LODGE WAS full of people talking, moving from one group to the other, and some of the younger girls playing and singing Christmas songs.

Elizabeth smiled as Mr. Wickham bowed and

came towards her. His amiable smile and friendly expression was comforting to her, and she decided to enjoy herself. They both understood that marriage was out of the question because they were both without fortune. She could accept his company with pleasure and no expectations, and without feeling judged.

"Miss Bennet," he bowed. "I'm hoping for the pleasure of your company this evening."

She smiled happily. "I believe there may be the opportunity for some conversation, Mr. Wickham." Thus the evening proceeded happily until Elizabeth sighed a little.

"I'm sorry, Mr. Wickham, I believe I must go and speak to Charlotte for a few moments. I have enjoyed our conversation this evening, it has been quite restful."

He smiled. "I've seen that recent events have unsettled you, Miss Bennet. I'm happy to have been of assistance."

As Elizabeth threaded her way through the crowded room, she wondered at her earlier suspicion. It seemed to her that he was perfectly amiable, and she'd been wrong to think badly of him.

She stood beside her friend, and was able to make polite conversation, although she wasn't able to talk of her feelings about Jane, Mr. Wickham,

Kitty and all the other matters which so occupied her mind at present.

Then a further worry was added to her mind. She watched Lydia outrageously flirting with the officers — including Mr. Wickham. She chewed her lip, she must remonstrate with Papa again about limiting Lydia's ability to embarrass the family.

She sighed, Mama was here, and she ought to uphold Lydia's manners.

Charlotte touched her arm. "Don't be dismayed, Lizzy. We all know what Lydia is like, and the officers will be gone before too long."

Elizabeth nodded gloomily. "I suppose so." She wanted to go and sit with her aunt, but knew Mama was there, and her rude attitude to Elizabeth would make her temper against the Lucases too obvious.

Perhaps she would have the chance to talk privately to her aunt in the next few days.

CHAPTER 14

*H*er opportunity arose the next day. Mama was talking to Uncle Gardiner in loud and exhaustive tones how badly abused she had been to lose the entail on the house by the actions of her least favourite daughter.

Elizabeth took her teacup and a book into the small parlour. If she was out of her mother's sight, perhaps Mama might forget about Mr. Collins and be able to talk of other things. She suppressed a smile, it would certainly be more peaceful for her.

Ten minutes later, Aunt Gardiner put her head round the door. "May I join you, Lizzy?"

Elizabeth jumped to her feet. "It would be perfect, Aunt!" She cleared some of Papa's books off the other chair. "There, you can sit here." She moved a side table next to the chair. "And there's somewhere for your cup."

Her aunt sat down with a sigh. "Thank you, Lizzy. I can see why you sought some peace in here."

Elizabeth grimaced. "Events have made life rather a trial recently, Aunt. But I have told you that in my letters."

"Indeed." Aunt Gardiner looked at her. "I've felt for you as you wrote." She frowned slightly. "But I cannot see why you have been so affected by your friend having accepted an offer from your cousin."

Elizabeth sighed. "I suppose it is not so important, really. I think it is because I was hoping that he might make an offer to Mary. Then Mama would be consoled, and I know Mary would have accepted him."

"Would she?" her aunt mused. "After what you wrote about him, I would have been surprised."

Elizabeth laughed. "Oh, yes! Mary was so hurt that he paid her no attention. And I suppose he cannot be as bad as I thought, for even Charlotte, who I know you thought sensible, accepted him."

"Yes, I had that thought for a moment," Aunt Gardiner said, smiling. "But you know, she is past the age for a good marriage, and she might have seen no other option available to her."

Elizabeth nodded. "You're right. But I was hurt, especially that she did not tell us until after he had gone from here, and then — oh, I don't know!"

Her aunt regarded her steadily. "I think that your dismay is more that you have now lost another confidante, another you considered your intimate friend. And it is not so long after the loss of association of your sister. You now feel as if you have no-one with whom you can express yourself without risk of censure."

Elizabeth looked down. "You're right, of course." She looked up. "What should I do?"

Her aunt reached over and took her hand. "There are two things you must do, Lizzy. The first one is to maintain your relationships with your sister and your friend. No, I know there is little chance that everything will be as it once was between you, but I think you will be able to accept it with more equanimity if you can understand that everyone is different." She leaned forward. "People want different things from their life, Lizzy. Your friend must have wished to be able to make her life away from her family, have her own establishment and the chance of children of her own. I know that is not what you want quite yet, but you must be aware that Charlotte is seven years older than you, seven years of watching her chances, hopes and spirits fade."

Aunt Gardiner's face was stern. "She waited until you had rejected him. I think you would have been justified in your disappointment if she had taken his affections before you refused him. But I do not see that she has done anything wrong, Lizzy."

Elizabeth stared at her aunt, not having expected quite such a long speech. She swallowed. "You're right, Aunt; I should not have judged her so harshly. But Mama — I thought I had time to encourage him to Mary."

"No, I do not think you would have succeeded there, Lizzy." Aunt Gardiner shook her head. "Mary is still too young to be suitable for a clergyman's wife, especially your cousin, because I understand that his choice will be under the stern scrutiny of his patroness." She smiled. "I think you must be forgiving to your friend, Lizzy. Mr. Collins was never going to marry any of the Bennet girls once you had refused him."

Elizabeth smiled sadly. "I understand, Aunt. Thank you for your insight. She laughed. "Now, before you tell me about how I have erred with Jane, I will fetch two fresh cups of tea."

Her aunt was still amused when Elizabeth returned with the fresh tea.

"You are such a breath of fresh air. But I do want to talk to you about Jane, although I know you wrote to me what your father told you, so I'm asking first why you haven't been able to take his words to heart?"

Elizabeth tapped her feet, her hopes fading of a comfortable chat with her aunt. But she had needed to hear her views about Charlotte, and it had helped a little.

Aunt Gardiner smiled. "We will talk in a moment about your telescope, I promise, but I did just want to ask you one brief thing about Jane."

"Of course."

"Do you think Jane is content, and safe?"

"Of course I do! Mr. Lawrence is a kind man and I have no scruples on that store."

"And she is content?"

Elizabeth frowned. "I think so, if only Mama would keep from lamenting that Jane is not with child every time she visits."

Aunt Gardiner frowned, too. "That is unfortunate. I suppose Jane is very anxious about it, as well? That cannot help her, I am afraid."

Elizabeth nodded. "I have tried to explain to Mama that she ought not to distress Jane by talking about it, but it has done no good." She made a face. "I have been researching newer discoveries of tisanes and herbs that are rumoured to help with childlessness, and Jane is feeling more hopeful now."

Her aunt reached over and embraced Elizabeth. "Oh, I am so glad you have done that for her. Even if it is not effective, you have shown her that you still care enough about her to take the time to try and help her. Thank you, Lizzy." She sat back down. "And you still visit her regularly, I expect."

"Oh, yes. I am over there at least twice a week, Aunt. It is all Jane can really spare from her duties in the parish."

"So she has a busy and satisfying life, then?" Her aunt lifted an eyebrow.

"I suppose so," Elizabeth felt a little ashamed of herself.

Aunt Gardiner reached for her hand. "I don't think it is so much that you think Jane has given up wanting to learn things, so much as you feeling that she has abandoned you. You were so close, Lizzy. But marriage always changes things."

Her voice changed, and she sat up briskly. "Now I will change the subject. I hope you can make up a little of your felicity with Charlotte before she goes into Kent, and then you may maintain contact by letter with less resentment." She smiled kindly. "Now, tell me what you have learned about your study of the heavens."

Elizabeth rolled her eyes. "I've been so upset by everything that's been happening, Aunt, I have found it really difficult to concentrate recently. But when I've had a chance to think about what you've told me, it will be better, I can assure you."

"Good." Aunt Gardiner stood up. "It would be better if we joined the family now, or questions might be asked."

CHAPTER 15

*D*arcy tried to conceal his impatience as he waited at the foot of the stairs for Georgiana to join him. An evening at the theatre was not really his preference, but he was manfully attempting to allow Georgiana such time in society as he could, while showing her that culture and learning would make things more interesting.

Perhaps he should have waited in his library and waited to be called when she had come downstairs. But she was already a few minutes late. He would wait.

Fortunately he didn't have to wait very long. She descended the stairs, dressed in a beautiful silk gown, her hair piled high on her head.

As she reached the bottom of the stairs, he bowed and offered her his arm.

"You look beautiful, Georgiana. I'm so proud of you."

She blushed, her usual petulant expression in abeyance today. "Thank you. I'm looking forward to tonight."

"Good." Darcy led her to the door. "We're going to the Lyceum tonight. It's the Drury Lane Company, of course; they are based there after the fire."

As he assisted her into the coach, he thought of his feelings as he had watched her come down the stairs. His baby sister was no longer a child. She was a lovely young lady, on the cusp of womanhood, and, as such, in a very vulnerable position.

He sat opposite her. "Cousin Richard is joining us at the theatre." He smiled at her exclamation of pleasure.

Perhaps it would be tonight that Richard would be able to bring his plan to fruition. Darcy had not had a note from him about it, but he knew it was not easy to organise. He just hoped Georgiana did not suspect anything other than a coincidence, and, more profoundly, that she would be happy to see Jonathan and his fellow undergraduates.

Once this first, apparently chance, meeting had happened, Darcy could tell Georgiana that she might entertain them at dinner occasionally.

At the theatre, servants took her cloak and

Darcy's overcoat, and they waited in the foyer to see and be seen, as he knew Georgiana wanted. His own preference would be to retire immediately to his box and read the programme, but this evening was for Georgiana, of course.

"Darcy! And Georgiana!" Richard bounded up the steps towards them. He turned to Georgiana and bowed. "You look beautiful, dear cousin."

He stripped off his greatcoat and scarf and handed it to the servant. "Shall we go to your box, Darcy?"

He offered his arm to Georgiana, who looked engaged and pleased. Darcy followed them up the stairs to the first tier of the gallery, and they found his box; the richly coloured, heavy curtains, comfortably upholstered seats, and a good view of the stage.

Several servants stood ready to serve if required, and Georgiana sat down, looking forward as the audience began to filter in. The opposite boxes were filling up, and they had a good view of those.

Darcy sat down and leaned back, looking at his cousin behind Georgiana's head. He raised his eyebrows, and Richard gave a tiny nod.

At last! Darcy had waited what seemed like weeks, and his patience was wearing thin. He smiled tightly and silently mouthed, "where?"

Richard nodded to the box almost opposite

them, the other side of the Royal box, and Darcy suddenly understood. It was the Matlock box; Jonathan must have asked his father for permission to use it.

The box was empty at the moment, and his lips tightened. He hoped the young men were not tardy, careless individuals. If Jonathan brought young men like Wickham along, boys who cared nothing for learning, he would not be best pleased.

Richard didn't seem concerned, leaning back, reading lazily through the programme.

Darcy watched quietly, and noticed Georgiana stiffen slightly as she saw a group of laughing young men enter the box opposite. They seemed to be enjoying themselves and many of them held a glass.

Georgiana turned to him. "Is that Cousin Jonathan over there?"

Darcy leaned forward. "Where? Oh, in the box." He looked over. "Yes, I think it is. He must have brought some of his fellow students, I suppose."

There must be eight or nine of them, he thought, and the box was crowded. He smiled at his sister. "Perhaps we may meet him during the inter-mission."

She blushed a little, and lifted her fan in front of her face. "He might be too embarrassed to intro-duce his friends."

"Perhaps." Darcy pretended disinterest. He could sense Richard watching with amusement, and frowned.

Fortunately, the play was about to start. It was a comedy, not the sort of play Darcy would normally choose. But it had won critical acclaim, and it had been written by a woman. If Georgiana enjoyed it, Darcy was prepared to tell her those facts.

Georgiana turned to the programme. "Ourselves?" She read out the title. "What sort of play is it?"

It was fortunate that there wasn't time to answer as the curtains were drawn back. Darcy sat back to listen and watch his sister.

RICHARD JOINED them in the coach back to Darcy House, having given up the earl's conveyance to get Jonathan and his friends back to their lodgings and then to Cambridge the next morning.

Georgiana was excited and bubbly. "Wasn't it good of Cousin Jonathan to ask if we could meet him and his friends during the interval?" She was flushed with pleasure and he was enjoying watching her enthusiasm.

"It certainly was. They seemed to be pleasant young men, don't they?"

"Yes, they were very polite." Georgiana looked away.

They dined quietly that night. Georgiana was quiet and thoughtful, speaking only to change the subject when either of the men spoke of the theatre. Darcy decided to leave the topic, and he talked of society matters and the progress of the war.

For the first time, he felt optimistic that she might be beginning to understand the joy of an enquiring mind, and he felt quite grateful to young Jonathan Fitzwilliam.

When Georgiana rose and withdrew, he smiled at her. "We will not be long. Then we'll join you."

"Of course, William." She smiled at him, and then at Richard.

Once they were alone, Darcy glanced at Richard. "Thank you for arranging this evening. I am delighted with the way it proceeded."

"I admit I didn't think it would go so well," Richard mused. He cast a sideways glance at Darcy. "I did think she had more of an eye for Jonathan than any of the others."

Darcy made a face. "I suppose it was to be expected. But she never appeared to take much notice of him when they met at Matlock House."

Richard chuckled and helped himself to more port. "You need to drink this faster, Darcy. I see that I need to come here more often to assist you." He put the glass down. "No, I think his attractions improved once she could see he is respected by his peers." He sat forward. "But he is without fortune, as you know."

Darcy nodded, and grinned, feeling younger. "I think his family might be quite suitable, though." He ran his hand through his hair as Richard laughed. "They are both much too young, but they might continue the acquaintance for a while. I already think she was quite surprised that they seemed to include her in their conversation, expecting her to have the same knowledge that they did."

"It is very helpful to our cause." Richard nodded, and drained his drink. "Perhaps we should go through." He turned back to Darcy.

"And, of course, with the possibility of Jonathan calling there, she will be happier to go to Matlock House while we do our penance next month."

"Penance?" Darcy glanced at Richard.

"You have forgotten, my friend!" Richard clapped him on the back. "We have to go to Kent and visit our aunt. Lady Catherine will be delighted to see you!"

Darcy groaned.

CHAPTER 16

"Well, I believe this is Hunsford Parsonage." Sir William rumbled, as his coach turned into the driveway.

Elizabeth was particularly happy to arrive. While she wasn't really looking forward to her stay here, the journey had been quite insupportable.

She'd never had much to do with Maria Lucas, but on the journey, she'd proved herself to be without any conversation other than awe at the thought of meeting Lady Catherine.

"Charlotte says that Lady Catherine will undoubtedly invite us to take tea," she told Elizabeth for the fifth time since they began their journey. "Charlotte and Mr. Collins actually dine there twice every week!"

Elizabeth smiled faintly. The servile way in

which Mr. Collins had spoken about his patroness had quite convinced her that she liked overly respectful people about her, those who would not argue with her.

She stifled her smile, wondering how many days she might be able to show what her cousin thought of as due deference. She thought it could not be long. Then she reminded herself of what Papa and Aunt Gardiner had told her. She sighed, she must make every effort to fit in with the expectations around her.

But Maria Lucas had made her forget her resolve. The girl had so little to say. Elizabeth glanced over at Sir William. He was no help, his conversation was no better, in her eyes. She bit her lip to stop herself smiling — she could not imagine he'd ever read *The Gentleman's Magazine and Historical Chronicle* that graced his library monthly. He must subscribe to it merely for the sake of being able to boast about it. Still, Elizabeth had benefitted from it.

In fact, she'd found the details from that very periodical of the publication of a new herbal, and Papa had purchased it for her to study.

She was distracted from her thoughts as the coach drew up outside a very pleasant parsonage, and she saw her friend and her cousin both hurry out to meet them.

Despite her reservations, she was pleased to see Charlotte, and descended from the coach with great relief. First, of course, she had to suffer the very proper greetings from Mr. Collins, who declaimed how happy he was to welcome them to his very humble abode. Elizabeth could see he was inordinately proud of every aspect of it.

Just the first sight of the house and gardens told her that Mr. Collins was very fortunate indeed to have obtained such a valuable living as Hunsford for his first position. Lady Catherine must indeed have singled him out, for Papa had told her that their cousin had little to recommend him from his family situation.

She fixed the smile upon her face. Shenley was a much poorer living; she'd have been much happier for Jane had the Shenley parsonage been as well-favoured as this one.

Mr. Lawrence was a weak man, she thought, but he must be a much better clergyman than Mr. Collins, and a burning sense of outrage rose up in her again. She pushed the thought away, she was here to try and keep her friendship with Charlotte.

So she followed demurely and politely as Mr. Collins showed the visitors round, in exhaustive detail. Then she trailed behind them as they toured the gardens, finding that a great deal of energy was expended on them.

Charlotte dropped back and walked with her, and Elizabeth discovered that her friend had made a very comfortable routine for herself.

"Gardening is such a healthful pastime, Lizzy. I very much encourage Mr. Collins to be out here for several hours each day. I find it helps him to concentrate the rest of his mind on his sermons."

Elizabeth smiled. "Do you assist him with suggestions for the topics of his sermons, then?"

"Oh, no!" Charlotte laughed, and tucked her hand in Elizabeth's arm. "He must go to Rosings Park nearly every day. He takes a list of subjects that he feels appropriate for his next homily, and Lady Catherine tells him which to undertake." She smiled contentedly. "Then he goes into his own room to write the sermon that she has recommended to him. He is most diligent, poring through his books in order to make the best sermon that he can."

"I am delighted you're settled into such a pleasing routine," Elizabeth said. She smiled at her friend. "And what do you do, Charlotte? How do you occupy your time? I can see this home has had much attention lavished upon it, too. It seems you have made it very much your own. It has quiet good taste — so like you."

Charlotte flushed. "Thank you, Lizzy. It means a great deal to me to hear you say that." She looked round to see that they weren't being overheard. "I have had to change things very slowly and carefully. Lady Catherine had refurbished much of the house before Mr. Collins came to the parish, and he did not wish to change anything at all. So I have tried to ensure that he noticed nothing."

Elizabeth laughed quietly. "Well, at least I know it was you all along. But if you wish, I can praise the elegant taste of Lady Catherine when I congratulate him on your home."

"I think he would be in a very happy place were you to do that, Lizzy." Charlotte turned and smiled at her sister, who had dropped back to them.

"What are you talking about?" Maria wondered.

Elizabeth laughed. "I was admiring the house and garden, Maria. Now the only remaining wonder will be the chance to admire Rosings Park and meet Lady Catherine herself."

CHAPTER 17

*I*t was barely two days later when she had her wish, and they all repaired to Rosings, where they had been invited to dine with the lady herself.

Afterwards they all sat in splendour in an enormous, over-ornate drawing room. Elizabeth watched Maria as she gazed around in awe at the decoration, and she was amused to see that Sir William was also quite subdued at being in such exalted company.

Lady Catherine held court, leading the conversation completely. No one could say anything unless she had directed a question at them first.

Elizabeth amused herself by guessing at the identity of the next person to be spoken to, and was perfectly correct most of the time.

Soon it was her turn, and Lady Catherine put her lorgnette up to her nose and examined her minutely. Elizabeth submitted quite happily, perfectly sure that she could give great offence to the lady if she chose to do so, but also sure that she could hide whatever she wished.

"Hmmm." Lady Catherine concluded her assessment. "At least you are quite a genteel, prettyish sort of girl. Tell me about your father's estate, Miss Elizabeth Bennet."

"What is it your Ladyship wishes to know?" Elizabeth countered.

"Why, how you have been brought up!" Lady Catherine hadn't been prepared to be answered back, even though Elizabeth thought she had been quite polite.

Lady Catherine had gone rather purple, and Elizabeth did not wish to cause any trouble for Charlotte, so she smiled equably.

"I have received quite a normal upbringing, Lady Catherine. My father's estate of Longbourn is in a hamlet in Hertfordshire, about a mile from the market town of Meryton." She smiled reminiscently. "I am the second of five sisters, so you can imagine that we have all learned a great deal together." She glanced at Charlotte. "Mrs. Collins was a wonderful friend to me, too."

"Hmph!" Lady Catherine's eyes flickered

towards Charlotte and back again. She looked Elizabeth up and down. "So many of you must have proved quite a handful for your governess, Miss Elizabeth Bennet."

Elizabeth laughed. "We didn't have a governess, Lady Catherine. We were encouraged to follow our own interests and learn particular things in detail, if we wished to do so."

"What! No governess?" Lady Catherine leaned forward in agitation. "What if you, or one of your sisters, was of an idle nature? What would you learn?"

"I am sure something would have been done if that had happened, Lady Catherine. As it is, all of us are competent in basic skills and the requirements of a lady's life, and some of us have some further detailed knowledge, too." Elizabeth did not like to look at Charlotte, or her family members, and she trusted that they were still too much in awe of Lady Catherine to refute her statement — which was not quite true for her youngest sister.

"Do you play, Miss Bennet?" That lady sounded disparaging.

"Yes, your Ladyship."

"And draw?"

"No, ma'am."

"What? None of you draw?"

Not one, your Ladyship. If any of us had

expressed an interest in learning, our parents would have obtained the services of masters for us." Elizabeth smiled serenely. "As for myself, I am studying ancient literature in the original Greek, and also …"

"Cousin Elizabeth!" Mr. Collins interrupted her. "I recall I have had occasion before this to recommend you do not …" he stopped suddenly, as Lady Catherine raised her hand. She faced Elizabeth.

"Miss Bennet. You will never gain an offer from a gentleman if you think you are superior to him." She looked superciliously down her nose at her guest.

Elizabeth smiled slightly. "I understand, Lady Catherine. Thank you for your advice."

She heard a slight sigh from Charlotte; was it relief? Surely she hadn't thought her friend would be so rude as to disagree with someone so important to Mr. Collins.

As they rode home in her ladyship's carriage, Elizabeth smiled to herself in the dusk. She certainly didn't want an offer from a gentleman — or any other man, Mr. Collins included — if he felt himself superior to her. Of course she wanted marriage, but it must be a true meeting of minds; a truly equal partnership.

THE NEXT MORNING, Elizabeth rose early, and stole out of the parsonage to go for a walk and explore her surroundings.

It was just past dawn and the dew was thick on the banks. Thankfully, there was no frost, and she lengthened her stride down the path.

She looked round as she walked down the lane, towards the slopes leading to the woodland. Kent was a pretty county, she thought, though nothing compared to the familiar hills of home. But, if she was to remain here for six weeks, she would most certainly make the most of her stay.

She enjoyed her thoughts and being alone, for Mr. Collins rarely stopped talking. She shook her head in disbelief. How could Charlotte bear it?

But, at least, when Sir William returned to Meryton after a week, leaving the two young ladies here, life might return to a more normal routine for them.

Observing the hedgerows, Elizabeth noticed many familiar herbs and plants from home, and she wondered if she might find nothing new here to study.

She had reached the final few hundred yards before the woodland, and she slowed, looking more closely at what she could see. There! That was a plant she wasn't familiar with. She looked harder, but wasn't able to see any more plants of the same type. She fixed in her mind the location of the plant, and decided it would not be unduly harmed for the loss of a few leaves.

She plucked a small shoot, pleased that she was wearing gloves, and continued on, feeling encouraged that there might be things to learn here.

It was a pity that her drawing skills were so limited — although she would never admit it to Lady Catherine; she would have liked to have been able to sketch the plant. At least she would be able to press this shoot and be able to check it when she got home.

She wondered if Mr. Collins' library would possess a botany primer, at least. It would be helpful to identify the plant while she was still in Kent.

Depressed, she doubted Mr. Collins would own anything so frivolous. His texts would all be dry, religious texts, suitable for a clergyman.

Climbing up through the woods, her mood lightened. Perhaps Charlotte had a herbal, so that she might treat common ailments.

And for now, she could explore new places. And she had brought the telescope with her, despite her father's frown when he saw it beside her trunk. She smiled, she'd already found a nice corner in the garden, where there would be no slightest gleam of candlelight from the house.

But the moon was waning, it would be another

fortnight before it was worth observing again, reflecting enough light to be able to see and observe what she could. Hopefully the weather would be clear. She'd missed the last full moon completely because of the heavy cloud cover.

An hour later, as she was thinking she ought to turn for home; she crested a small hill, and gazed down into the next valley. An expanse of still water met her eyes, the trees growing close to the banks. She stopped and looked round. After tracing the banks with her eye, she decided it was a river, not a pond; but flowing so very slowly that it might as well be a pond.

Still waters run deep. The quotation dropped into her mind. She frowned in thought. Papa had used it once, hadn't he? She smiled slightly, it had been about a gentleman he hadn't trusted.

Elizabeth had looked up the origin, finding the Latin phrase in a history of Alexander the Great, though she couldn't quite remember the actual Latin just now. She turned and walked along the top of the bank, judging it just a little too steep to be safe to descend to the river's edge.

Of course, Shakespeare hadn't used the phrase as most people now did. But she liked Henry IV:

Smooth runs the water where the brook is deep,
   And in his simple show he harbours treason...

No, no, my sovereign, Gloucester is a man
Unsounded yet and full of deep deceit.

Quite unaccountably, Mr. Darcy's impassive features swam into view. Still waters, indeed.

She smiled, was he full of deep deceit? He'd seemed to ask for her views on the possibility of an offer from her cousin, when they were dancing together at Netherfield.

But looking at him from the opposite view, Mr. Wickham had told her that Mr. Darcy had refused to honour the expressed wish of his father's will.

She tried to push the image of his face from her mind. He had been there far too much, in her decided opinion. Just another aristocratic man, one from a place in society which looked down on the minds of women.

She turned back towards Hunsford, ready for her breakfast, Shakespeare quite forgotten.

CHAPTER 18

*I*n the first two weeks, Elizabeth had collected, and was pressing, several plants that were quite new to her. She smiled as she examined them that morning, between the pages of the heaviest book she could procure from Charlotte. The sheets of blotting paper would be all right for another day, then she must move the plants around again.

She was enjoying her stay more now that life had settled back to what seemed to be the routine here. She had discovered a pleasant walk through a quiet grove on the outskirts of Rosings Park, where she could be sure not to be disturbed.

Much of the time Mr. Collins left his guests to be entertained by his wife, while he sat in his office and watched the road in case Lady Catherine drove by, or else he was working in the gardens.

Elizabeth straightened up. It was time to go downstairs and join the others for breakfast. She thought Papa would be pleased with her, she'd worked hard to spend time with Maria as well as with Charlotte, and she thought the girl was actually beginning to become rather more interesting in her conversation, as well.

Elizabeth had even encouraged Maria to help her with the beginnings of developing her ability to sketch, and was beginning to learn how to draw the details of the plants she was collecting. She smiled; now she could see the benefit of learning, she could put her mind to it properly.

It had been a little mortifying when Lady Catherine had condescended to tell her that it was much too late to learn such things; that to become accomplished, she should have started many years ago. But Elizabeth had taken a deep breath, and agreed with her, keeping her eyes down. Anything was possible for a quiet life for her friend. And she cared nothing for what Lady Catherine thought — Elizabeth needed to learn this skill now, when she had not felt the need before.

Over breakfast, Mr. Collins was in an exalted mood. Yesterday, he had been loitering about the gatehouse of Rosings Park, for Mr. Darcy was imminently expected that day for one of his regular, but infrequent visits to stay with his aunt. And Mr. Collins had seen his coach turn into the Park yesterday afternoon.

Lady Catherine had told the party of his expected visit ten days before, and much time had been expended on her plans for the expected union of him to her daughter.

Miss Anne de Bourgh had barely come to Elizabeth's attention during these first two weeks, for she was a colourless, quiet little thing. Elizabeth felt very sorry for her; it must be terrible to live under the control of a mother like Lady Catherine, but she never had the chance to speak or converse with her, and doubted that she ever would.

She listened to Mr. Collins as she ate her breakfast, wondering that such a man as Mr. Darcy would agree to marry Miss de Bourgh. She would not be able to go out into society with him, neither would she be any sort of wife.

Elizabeth shrugged to herself. Perhaps that was what he wanted, and perhaps the opportunity of inheriting Rosings Park was too tempting to refuse. She glared at her plate. It would be just like him; he had kept the living that was rightly Mr. Wickham's, and had probably accepted a payment for it to be allotted to another.

But she wondered if his cousin would be

capable of bearing him an heir. It would be dreadful if Miss de Bourgh lost her life in attempting to fulfil her matrimonial duties.

Elizabeth's opinion of Mr. Darcy thus began to harden further against him; his perceived misdeeds joining with what Mr. Wickham had told her.

While any addition to their small company ought to be welcome, Elizabeth could not think of anyone she would wish to meet less.

She wouldn't let herself think of the reason why he had disordered her thinking ever since he had left Netherfield with Mr. Bingley.

When she sat with Charlotte and Maria after breakfast, all with needlework in their hands to allow for easy conversation, Elizabeth found she had little to say. But they knew each other so well, the silences were not uncomfortable.

Mr. Collins had hastened across the lane to Rosings Park to pay his respects to the honoured visitor. No doubt he would claim that prior acquaintance from the occasion of the Netherfield ball. Even at the memory, Elizabeth blushed, remembering how her cousin had approached Mr. Darcy to inform him that Lady Catherine was his patroness. The fact that Mr. Darcy had walked away from him had quite escaped his memory, and he was determined to glory in his closeness to such a high-born gentleman.

She stabbed her needlework with rather more ferocity than accuracy, and had to stop and suck her finger to stop it bleeding on her stitching.

She looked up at the knock on the door, and the Hunsford housekeeper looked in.

"Mrs. Collins …"

Charlotte put down her sewing, and unhurriedly left the room. Maria looked across at Elizabeth, who shrugged. They would soon know what it was about. An instant later, Charlotte came hurrying back into the room.

"Lizzy, Maria, Mr. Darcy and another gentleman are coming to the house with Mr. Collins! They are only a few minutes away."

Maria jumped up and looked as if she did not know what to do.

Elizabeth smiled at the sight, and tugged the girl to sit back down.

Charlotte looked at her. "I must thank you, Lizzy, for this piece of civility. Mr. Darcy would *never* have come so soon to wait upon me."

Elizabeth hastily shook her head. "You know that can't be right, Charlotte, for he always looks at me as if I am beneath his notice." She glanced at Maria.

"Be calm, Maria. Stay sitting beside me."

At that moment the doorbell sounded.

CHAPTER 19

*D*arcy wasn't sure quite how he had come to be here, at Hunsford Parsonage, the very first morning after his arrival at Rosings Park. But at least Richard was beside him.

He had been extremely disconcerted — no; he'd been completely dismayed — over dinner the previous evening, when Lady Catherine had mentioned that Collins was married and his wife seemed a very nice kind of young woman.

She married him!

Horror had filled him, and he had missed much of the conversation at table in the next ten minutes, and when he finally pulled his mind to attention, he was confused by the news that Mrs. Collins' sister and her friend were staying with her.

"… and Sir William Lucas stayed the first week,

too. Not the top drawer of course," Lady Catherine had said disparagingly. "But very much better than Mr. Collins could have hoped for, I'm sure."

"Hoped for what?" Darcy was utterly confused. He was aware of Richard across the table looking warningly at him.

"As a father-in-law, Darcy!" Lady Catherine looked at him impatiently. "You really must pay attention!"

Darcy had nodded silently, and attended to his plate. Perhaps, if he listened, he could glean what he had missed. His mind picked over what he thought he'd heard. If Sir William was the father of Mrs. Collins, then the man hadn't married Miss Bennet.

But that had most certainly been his intention. Darcy had smiled slightly, he had been certain she would have refused him. So, how had he come to marry Miss Lucas?

Over the port, Richard had enlightened him over what he had missed.

"You really looked as if you had seen a ghost, Darcy." His cousin had considered him. "I think the thought that Miss Elizabeth Bennet had married Collins affected you very much."

Darcy took a hasty gulp of the drink and grimaced. He must keep his wits about him while he was here.

Richard had grinned. "I will be interested to meet her, and since she is conveniently staying at Hunsford with Mrs. Collins, I have the opportunity."

Now, here they were. Collins was fawning obsequiously over them, and the house looked small but quite well-cared for.

His heart was pounding in his chest and his thoughts were behaving very strangely. He angrily tried to suppress them. He had managed to push this young woman to the back of his mind during these past weeks; yet a single mention of her, and he was in turmoil again.

The housekeeper announced them, and they entered a small, but comfortable sitting room. Darcy's eyes went at once to Miss Bennet, curtsying politely, her eyes demurely lowered. He bowed, and had to turn to Mrs. Collins to greet her.

He remembered her now, an ordinary-looking young woman, rather older than Miss Bennet, quite staid and placid. He knew at once that Collins would have an easier life than if he had succeeded in gaining Miss Bennet's hand.

He managed to stop himself smiling, but couldn't prevent his gaze turning back to her. The housekeeper brought in tea, and he sat down, not really hearing all that Collins was saying about his

delight that such eminent gentlemen had condescended to call at his house.

Richard had found a chair near Miss Bennet
and commenced an easy, cheerful conversation with
her and Mrs. Collins. *Fortunate man!* Darcy attempted
to listen to what was being said, without the appearance of it.

The two ladies appeared to be enjoying their
conversation with Richard; Darcy thought the talk
was of the weather and the local countryside. As he
listened, it seemed to Darcy that Miss Bennet was
somewhat distracted; her attention was not fully on
the conversation.

After he had drunk his tea, Darcy could not help
but draw near to them. Miss Bennet looked up at
him, her face tranquil but without a smile.

"Miss Bennet, might I ask if your family is in
good health?" He cursed himself inside for such a
trite remark and wondered if he might extend the
conversation more widely.

"Thank you, sir. They are all very well." Miss
Bennet was perfectly composed, although she didn't
seem inclined to elucidate.

"I'm glad to hear it." He looked round. Perhaps
there was a chair nearby he could take. Then he
might be included in the conversation. But he was
not so fortunate. He walked over to the window and
looked out over the well-kept gardens.

He wished most acutely that he had the easy manners and open, cheerful countenance of his cousin — and Bingley, too. But it was not his nature and he was unable to perform in such a way. Not that he wished to, he told himself firmly. Anyone who wished to talk to him must accept him for what he was.

But she *had* accepted him for what he was. He recalled their dance together at the Netherfield ball. She had been quiet to begin with, but she had started a polite little exchange with him, and had become quite animated when she declared to him that she would never marry Collins because he thought women were foolish creatures.

He smiled slightly, she had not been wrong. Collins was one of the most foolish men he had met, and his entirely misplaced confidence in his own abilities merely emphasised the fact.

He could hear Richard drawing the conversation to a natural conclusion and turned back into the room. Miss Bennet was smiling politely, but he was certain she was as distracted as he was.

He bowed politely as they took their leave, and then he and Richard were striding up the lane.

"No. Stop." He turned. "Richard, let's go the other way, and walk through the grove. We don't have to be back at the house too long before luncheon."

Richard nodded, and fell into step beside him, and they made their way up to the gate into the park. They walked much of the time in silence, and Darcy was glad of it, he was not convinced that he would be able to answer Richard if he began questioning him.

Ten minutes later; he could no longer wait. "What did you think, Richard?" He needed to know that his cousin approved of her.

"I'm happy she is not Mrs. Collins, if that is what you are asking, Darcy. She would be very unhappy if in that situation."

Darcy nodded. It was not quite what he had wanted to know, but he agreed very much with the sentiment.

Richard was striding out, and both had to watch the path ahead.

Perhaps Richard felt Darcy would listen with less embarrassment if he didn't have to look at him, but he was still uneasy.

"What are your feelings about her now?" Richard sounded a little offhand.

Darcy shrugged. "The fact that she is away from her family does not make them any more suitable, Richard."

Richard glanced sideways at him. "When you marry, Darcy, you will not be marrying the family. I think it is more important to look at the attributes and accomplishments of the young lady."

Darcy digested the comment in silence. He would not be pressured into anything.

Richard didn't say anything more, and Darcy was grateful to him. But he had a lot to think about, and it was likely he'd not sleep well tonight. He would do better to stay away from Hunsford Parsonage.

At dinner that night, Lady Catherine fixed him with a fierce stare. "It is about time that you united the estates of Pemberley and Rosings, Darcy!"

He raised his eyebrows, but could not help a brief glance at Cousin Anne. She appeared not to have heard her mother, and he decided it was better to shut down the conversation as fast as he might be able to.

"This is not the right moment for such a conversation, Lady Catherine."

He glanced at Richard, but he seemed to be not much help, concentrating on his soup.

His aunt sniffed, disdainfully. "Well, when will you talk about it? You always put it off."

Darcy took a slow, deliberate spoonful of soup. He was tempted to tell his aunt that it was his business alone, but perhaps it would be better to speak to her about the matter for once and for all. But he would not do so in front of Cousin Anne. It would be too cruel. His cousin usually retired with her companion before everyone else. Perhaps that would be a good time.

He looked up. "Later," he said, tersely. The silence that ensued allowed him to plan a little how to finally convince Lady Catherine that he meant what he said. Cousin Anne was not getting any younger, and by waiting for a union with him, her mother was preventing any other suitable marriage Anne might be able to make.

He hoped she could find a kind and respectful gentleman.

CHAPTER 20

*E*lizabeth cautiously began to relax over the next week. She thought Mr. Darcy must be avoiding the parsonage and its occupants, and that suited her very well. Colonel Fitzwilliam called every few days, and he was a pleasant, easy companion, even if he did seem slightly distracted on occasion.

"I'm sure he admires you, Lizzy," Charlotte said, as they strolled in the garden before lunch one day, just after that gentleman had taken his leave.

Elizabeth laughed. "And I am quite as certain that he does not, dear Charlotte. He comes because there is little else to do at Rosings Park, and because he likes amiable company, not because he prefers my company above yours, or Maria's. And, we must remember, he is a younger son, and therefore must marry a lady of fortune."

She hastened to change the subject, because it was true that he talked a great deal to her; and while she didn't know why, she was very sure that he had no personal interest in her.

She went up to her chamber to check whether she had any space in the blotters to pick some more plants to press. As she went, she puzzled over the colonel's calls at the parsonage, and also his slight distraction.

He must marry a lady of fortune. Her own words came back to her, and suddenly the thought of Miss de Bourgh intruded. But Lady Catherine intended her for Mr. Darcy, and Elizabeth immediately understood the gentleman's distraction. She shook herself out of her introspection. She might well be wrong, she had not even seen the couple in the same room together.

The next day was Good Friday, and the party crossed the lane to church. Elizabeth sat beside Charlotte and tried not to look at Mr. Darcy, sitting with his party in the pew reserved for the de Bourgh family.

She tried to stop her lips twitching. If the parsonage pew had been in front of theirs, she would have felt the heat of his gaze for the whole length of the service.

But she didn't want to see him any more than she had to, he had been less than honourable to Mr. Wickham, and she was sure he would be disparaging of her efforts to study. She wished now that she hadn't told the colonel so much of her study efforts here; perhaps he had told his cousin.

She tossed her head, and looked up at the great vaulted roof. It was of no import to her if he had told Mr. Darcy. That gentleman had stayed away from the parsonage, and she was perfectly content with that.

Mr. Collins' sermon was seemingly endless, and Elizabeth wished she could see through the roof to the sky beyond. For the last week the mornings had been sunny, but cloud had thickened each after-noon. She was beginning to long for suitable weather to use the telescope.

She looked down demurely. Perhaps she might take it out on her walk tomorrow. If she went to the west, there were fields, rather than woods, and she might try and see how far she could see. Yes, she could do that. If she looked at the map this evening, she would know where she was looking.

Elizabeth found her peace somewhat disturbed over the next week. On Easter Day, after church,

Lady Catherine invited them to join her during the evening. At least Colonel Fitzwilliam was there to make the occasion a little more interesting, and he and Elizabeth had a rather pleasant little conversation until Lady Catherine demanded their attention.

After dinner, he sat beside her while she played, and she really quite enjoyed not having to be part of the conversation which the rest of the party had to endure; Lady Catherine holding forth with her opinion as she always did.

She did try and observe how Mr. Darcy and Miss de Bourgh acted in company, but she saw no difference in either of them, neither did they speak to each other. She did notice how often the colonel's gaze turned to Miss de Bourgh, but that young lady was as apathetic as ever. Elizabeth hadn't ever seen her utter more than a few words, and those to her companion were in a whisper.

She jumped as she realised Mr. Darcy was standing by the instrument, but was relieved her fingers still played. She hoped her discomposure had not been apparent to either of the gentlemen.

She made herself smile. "You mean to frighten me, Mr. Darcy? There is a stubbornness about me that never can bear to be frightened at the will of others. My courage always rises with every attempt to intimidate me."

He gave what might have seemed to be a slight

smile, *if* she had been in the mood to be agreeable. "You could not really believe me to entertain any design of alarming you; and I have had the pleasure of your acquaintance long enough to know that you find great enjoyment in occasionally professing opinions which in fact are not your own."

She raised an eyebrow. Was he really inclined to be amiable? Perhaps he wished to impress his cousin. But she was not inclined to lose the colonel's good opinion, either, so she smiled again, and continued playing.

"You play with remarkable understanding of the composer's intentions, Miss Bennet." Mr. Darcy seemed determined to compliment her, and she could hardly spurn his remarks.

She smiled. "Thank you. I have discovered that playing with feeling can often cover any imperfections in technical skill." She was sure he was complimenting her only because playing the pianoforte was an accomplishment valued in ladies. What might he think of her more demanding studies?

But Lady Catherine and her demands intruded, and the moment passed.

SHE WAS VEXED over the next three days when, each day, her walks in the grove were interrupted by apparently chance meetings with Mr. Darcy. At first, he stopped only to pass the time of day with her. But on the third day, he turned and walked beside her.

"Are you enjoying your stay here in Kent, Miss Bennet?" His conversation was light and superficial, and she determined to keep it that way.

"I am, indeed, Mr. Darcy. I had not seen my friend since she moved to Hunsford, and it was ..." she could not, in all conscience say *enjoyable,* "... an opportunity to renew our friendship."

He looked as if he wished to ask about the circumstances that had led to Mr. Collins marrying her friend, but she did not wish to follow that path.

"I have very much enjoyed the opportunity to walk in a new countryside, Mr. Darcy. It may not be considered very far from Hertfordshire, but I have noticed the weather appears to be different enough to make the local plants somewhat different."

He nodded, seeming to have nothing much more to say, and after accompanying her back to the parsonage, he bowed and went away.

Elizabeth was left to defend herself from Charlotte's excitement at Mr. Darcy's attention to her.

AT LAST, the weather had cleared, and Elizabeth

had spent several hours the previous evening huddled over the telescope, looking at the moon. It was almost full, and so bright that she was able to see even quite small details. It was more difficult without the special supporting cradle for the instrument; that had been left at home, but she was able to get some help from the back of a garden bench.

Today, she was determined to improve upon the sketches she had made, certain that her depictions would be better than those in the old atlas at home. The telescope she had was much improved over the early lenses the author had had to work with. She just wished she had access to newer books.

So she was hard at work at the table in the sitting room when the gentlemen called. Resentful, she put down her pencils and rose and curtsied with Charlotte and Maria.

As they took tea, the superficial conversation was led mostly by Colonel Fitzwilliam, with assistance from Charlotte. Mr. Darcy was his usual silent self; and Elizabeth was still resentful of him, certain of his disapproval of her activities. Maria was still too overawed to speak much when the gentlemen were present.

After a little while, Elizabeth began to join in, feeling that she was, perhaps being rather unfair to Charlotte, and she ventured a few comments.

The colonel beamed. "I was wondering what you were sketching, Miss Bennet. Might I see?"

"Of course, sir." Elizabeth turned to her sketches. "The only astronomical atlas I have access to at home is very old and the lenses they had available then mean that there is little detail. But the one I have is wonderful." She pulled the sketches towards her. "At last, the cloud cleared and I have seen more craters than I ever have before."

He admired her work. "But, I must confess, Miss Elizabeth, that I now know why you appear fatigued this morning!"

She could feel her face heating, it was perhaps not the most tactful thing he could have said, and he saw her embarrassment and apologised at once.

"Of course, sir." She accepted his apology; he was properly gentlemanly.

Mr. Darcy rose to his feet and crossed the room to join his cousin. He observed her work in silence for a few moments, and she felt uncomfortable.

"I hope that you do not take unnecessary risks, Miss Bennet," he said, gravely. "Going out at night must cause you to put yourself in danger that ought not to be taken lightly."

She met his eyes. "I thank you for your concern, Mr. Darcy. But I do not go out in darkness. The telescope I have been loaned is a Navy issue. They are not good light collectors, so I go out at dusk, and only within the gardens. So you see, I am quite safe." Her chin went up. He must expect ladies to sit and do nothing at all when they were not needed to be decorative or there for them when needed.

His jaw tightened. Perhaps he had understood the censure behind her words. She told herself she didn't care, and anyway the gentlemen were due to return to London in the next few days.

She and Maria were also going back to Hertfordshire soon, and, for Elizabeth, it was not a moment too soon.

CHAPTER 21

The Hunsford party was invited to Rosings for dinner that night, but Elizabeth had spent much of the day going over and over in her mind the conversation of that morning, and by the evening, she had developed a headache such that she was certain she could not attend.

Mr. Collins was beside himself. "But, Cousin Elizabeth! Lady Catherine has condescended to invite us! It behoves you to force yourself to put aside your own wishes and comforts and respond humbly and reverently to her invitation."

But not for anything did Elizabeth wish to see Mr. Darcy again, especially not today. She was sorry to dissemble more than was actually needed, but it wasn't until she declined for the fifth time and went up to her bedchamber, that he hesitated. Charlotte urged him not to risk Lady Catherine's displeasure by also being late, and Elizabeth heard the door shut behind them with utter relief.

She waited a few minutes and then she took a small sheaf of letters from home, not being quite up to study.

Making her way downstairs, she reclined on the chaise longue and decided to read her letters from Papa first.

But it was not many minutes before the sound of the doorbell intruded, and she looked up; perhaps she ought to have stayed in her chamber.

Perhaps the colonel had called to enquire after her. She smiled, he was certainly braving the displeasure of Lady Catherine if she noticed his absence.

She was therefore surprised when Mr. Darcy was shown in, his expression disordered, and his manner distrait.

He bowed hastily. "Good evening, Miss Bennet. I wished to enquire whether you are feeling somewhat better?"

Elizabeth was even more surprised. She curtsied her greeting. "Thank you, peace and quiet cannot fail to help."

But he did not take the hint and she sat down collectedly. Surely he would not stay long.

But it seemed that he had more to say. He paced

the room, then took a seat across the table from her. She waited for him to speak, but he jumped to his feet again, seemingly at war with himself. She frowned.

"Mr. Darcy, are you well?"

He turned and stared at her, and she was so disconcerted that she looked down. Whatever ailed him?

He crossed the room and stood before her. "In vain have I struggled. It will not do. My feelings will not be repressed. You must allow me to tell you how ardently I admire and love you."

Whatever she had expected, it wasn't a declaration of love. She knew she blushed and wished she had not. Looking down, she bit her lip. What had led him to believe she had expected his attention like this?

Perhaps she ought to have spoken at once; her hesitation seemed to give him encouragement, and he stepped forward again.

"Miss Bennet, let me explain a little more why I have declared myself to you in this way, and I must apologise for not approaching you sooner; but you must of course not be insensible to the very great anger and distress I will be causing to all my relations and friends. Not only their opinion of your background and upbringing, but my own pride at my family name, must have quailed at the degradation which such a union must cause. Nay, such disappointment for the obstacle of your background and more so, the behaviour of your relations — your mother, your youngest sister — all that formed a determination that I must not permit you to be thus in my thoughts, nor those of Bingley."

He strode about the room, determined to have his say, and her indignation grew at his insult to her family, of which he seemed to be quite insensible.

He turned back towards her. "But I must conclude; inform you that the strength of my attachment has overcome the consideration of all such possible obstacles, and I hope that I might thus be rewarded by the honour of your acceptance of my hand in marriage." He drew breath to speak further, but Elizabeth rose to her feet.

"It is enough, Mr. Darcy. Pray allow me to speak." He bowed slightly and took a step back.

She faced him. "In such cases as these, it is, I believe, the established mode to express a sense of obligation for the sentiments avowed, however unequally they may be returned." She turned away slightly. "But I cannot. I have never desired your good opinion, and you have certainly bestowed it most unwillingly." Her temper flared. "You have expected me to listen to your insults to my family and background; and expected me to rejoice in their downfall compared to what my position would be if I *had* accepted you."

Her head was pounding more than it had been before the party left for Rosings Park, but she dare not show weakness. "I am sorry to cause you pain by refusing you, but I hope it will be of short duration. The feelings which, you tell me, have long prevented the acknowledgment of your regard, can have little difficulty in overcoming it after this explanation."

She moved back to the chair and sat down. Her legs were trembling so much, she might otherwise fall down.

She was astonished to see the lack of colour in his face, the clear effect her refusal had on him, despite his apparent impassive features. Perhaps he was a more passionate man beneath the stern exterior than she had thought.

The silence dragged out for a long moment, and she wished he would speak and remove himself from the house. Finally, he answered her.

"And this is all the reply which I am to have the honour of expecting! I might, perhaps, wish to be informed why, with so little endeavour at civility, I am thus rejected."

She wondered if he really wanted to know. But first she must answer his accusation of incivility. "I might just as well ask why, with so evident a design of offending and insulting me, you chose to tell me that you liked me against your will, against your reason, and even against your character? Was not this some excuse for incivility, if I was uncivil? But I have other provocations. You know I have." She looked away. "It was many months ago that my opinion of you was decided. Your character was unfolded in the recital which I received many months ago from Mr. Wickham. Can you deny that you treated him abominably?"

He was a most peculiar colour, she thought.

"And you would believe the words of a man without even considering that there might be another side? A side which might allow your opinion to be decided with full knowledge, instead of mere hearsay?" He strode to the mantel and stared into the dark fireplace, scowling. He did not look at her. "Could you expect me to rejoice in the inferiority of your connections? To congratulate myself on the hope of relations whose condition in life is so decidedly beneath my own?"

It was now impossible to stay in her seat, and Elizabeth jumped to her feet. "From the very beginning, from the first moment I may almost say, of my acquaintance with you, your manners, impressing me with the fullest belief of your arrogance, your conceit, and your selfish disdain of the feelings of others, were such as to form that ground-work of disapprobation, on which succeeding events have built so immoveable a dislike." She grasped the edge of the table, "I had not known you a month before I felt that you were the last man in the world whom I could ever be prevailed on to marry."

She was prepared to declare the sort of man she wished to know, the sort of gentleman who would encourage her intelligence, who would talk to her of learned things, but she hesitated a moment too long.

He straightened, still white with apparent anger, but his eyes were blank. "You have said quite enough, madam. I perfectly comprehend your feelings, and have now only to be ashamed of what my own have been. Forgive me for having taken up so much of your time, and accept my best wishes for your health and happiness." And without another glance, he hurried from the room.

Elizabeth sank into the chair, her mind in turmoil. Why had she not told him of the real reason why she would not marry him, the disdain with which he admired only suitable accomplishments for ladies and not others?

Slowly she got to her feet and gathered the letters from home. She could not face her friend tonight, she must go up to her chamber. Her throat was dry, but there was a carafe of water upstairs; it would be enough.

CHAPTER 22

*D*arcy hurried to his chamber, avoiding any enquiry from his aunt or others of the house. How could he have been so foolish as to abase himself to her, to expose himself to ridicule of the most intense kind?

He prowled round the room, watching the darkness fall. Embarrassment suffused his face with warmth, he knew he flushed. At least there was no one to see.

Wickham! What poison he had poured into her ears! And she had believed him, had thought the less of Darcy, without question — how could she think so ill of him?

He crossed the room and poured some water from the carafe. He was well to be out of it. He would not wish to marry a woman who could think ill of him without a thought for the truth.

His valet appeared an hour later. Darcy was still pacing around the room.

"Would you care for dinner up here, sir?" Mr. Maunder seemed incurious. He really was the ideal servant.

"No. Thank you, I am not hungry." And Darcy was alone again, reliving the intense embarrassment of earlier.

He dropped into a chair, his head in his hands. What ought he to do? His instinct was to sit and pour out the facts in a letter, put it into Miss Bennet's hand the next morning, try and make her feel less animosity toward him.

But he pushed away the thought. It would only be for him, to make him feel better. If he must forget her, it would not matter if she thought ill of him. And he must put all thoughts of her out of his head. At once!

He jumped to his feet and rang the bell.

"Mr. Maunder, you may begin to pack. Colonel Fitzwilliam and I will be leaving first thing tomorrow. Tell the coachman to be prepared."

"Yes, sir." His servant seemed unsurprised. He hesitated. "Might I recommend a light meal, sir? It will help you to sleep when you need to be about your business tomorrow."

"Very well. But first you must inform Colonel Fitzwilliam's manservant so that he can also pack — and inform the colonel, too, please."

"Yes, sir."

Darcy turned to the window. He was prepared to acknowledge to himself that he was running away. But he could think of nothing but escape — escape from the chance of meeting Miss Bennet, escape from anyone talking about her.

He shuddered, the mortification crept up on him again. He must not think of it, must not think of her.

But he had spoken the truth. His feelings would not be repressed. He did most ardently love her — and desire her. How could he live without her?

Yet he must.

He watched, as if from afar, as Mr. Maunder laid out his cold supper on the side table before going through to the dressing room and beginning to pack.

Darcy turned and stood at the window, listening to his valet's quiet movements. He was hungry, but didn't wish to eat.

After a few minutes, the man was beside him, a glass on a tray.

"Whisky, sir?"

"Thank you." Darcy took the glass and looked

at his servant. "Bring up a jug of hot water, if you please. Then you will not need to return tonight."

If he felt he could sleep, he would ready himself. Until then, he would stay beside the fire. He must plan for the future, try and imagine how he could live without her.

HE WAS glad to get into the coach the next morning. He hadn't gone down to breakfast, but had entered the room when he knew the coach was ready.

He knew Lady Catherine would be displeased, and reprimand him for his rudeness. But he was beyond caring.

Richard climbed in behind him, and sat back. He hadn't said a word to Darcy about his sudden change of plan to leave a day early — and in such haste.

But Darcy was sure Richard would not long stay quiet. He wondered what he could say to explain himself, without divulging what had happened. He couldn't bear that.

As the coach turned into the lane, he had a sudden fear that Richard would demand they call at the parsonage to make their farewell, but soon they turned north for London and he breathed a quiet sigh of relief.

"I sent a note this morning to Mr. Collins, conveying our apologies for taking our leave without calling on them," Richard watched him. "I ensured it will only just be arriving now, to prevent us seeing the man hastening up the road to bow the coach away."

Darcy nodded. His mind saw Miss Elizabeth Bennet listening to her cousin over breakfast, reading out the letter and knowing that Darcy was running away. He looked out of the coach window, knowing the flush was spreading down his neck and that Richard was aware of it.

"Are you able to tell me the sudden business need that has called you to London?" Richard sounded offhand. "I hope Georgiana is not causing my mother difficulties."

"Georgiana?" Darcy was puzzled. "Oh. No. I have not heard that there are any problems."

"Good." Richard settled back down. It seemed he was going to be a quiet companion today, and Darcy was grateful for it.

He stared steadfastly ahead. He might even sleep after the post stop, having not gone to bed the previous night. But he was no clearer in his mind what to do.

When the coach pulled in at the post inn at Bromley, Darcy glanced at Richard. "I would like to stop for coffee, if it is well with you, while they change the horses."

"We can do that, if you wish, Darcy." Richard shrugged. "But I had thought you in a tearing hurry to return to London."

"It will not be much longer than merely changing the horses." Darcy felt a little nettled at Richard's sly look; but he climbed down, knowing his cousin would follow him.

He waited as his servant jumped down, surprised that his master had left the coach.

"Book us coffee in the private parlour, if you please." Darcy turned and looked out across the road. This was a busy road, and the town was growing, seemingly each time he called.

He wondered if he would have felt better if he had written to Miss Bennet and waited in the grove this morning to deliver it.

It was no good agonising over his decision. It was too late, and he had made his choice. Now, he must not think of her, must make his life without her.

He turned to Richard. "Do you think Georgiana will want to stay in London? I am thinking of going to Pemberley."

Richard shrugged as they walked together towards the inn. The landlord bowed respectfully and the aroma of coffee already filled the private parlour.

"Thank you." Darcy crossed to one of the chairs by the fire. Richard closed the door and followed suit, sinking into the other chair with a sigh.

"I don't know how Georgiana will feel about that, Darcy." Richard glanced at him. "It might depend on how often she has seen Jonathan and his friends."

Darcy nodded glumly. He hoped he would not have to stay in London and be sociable.

"Do you want to talk about what happened?" Richard seemed to be intent on watching the flames leaping in the grate.

"No." Darcy hoped his cousin did not have any idea what he had done. "Thank you, but no. I am sorry to have brought you away early."

Richard chuckled. "I think Lady Catherine was displeased mainly because she was planning to assault your ears with her plans for your marriage to Cousin Anne." He smiled unrepentantly. "Next time she might begin the very day you arrive, so as not to lose the chance again."

"By the time she believes I will not marry Anne, she will be past marriageable age," Darcy grumbled. He glanced at his cousin and thought an expression of pain crossed his face.

But he didn't have time to think more of it. He'd had a sudden thought.

Miss Bennet was another week at least in Kent. If he called on Bingley, he could certainly persuade him to return at once to Netherfield. Darcy could join him and perhaps try to get to know the neighbourhood which had formed her.

Ruefully, he knew it was not the way to forget her. But it might be the only chance he had, while she was not there, of talking to some of the people she knew and seeing if he could glean any knowledge of her.

He must be mad to think of doing such a thing. But he might find out something that would assist him. As it was now, he had no idea how to win her — or how to live without her.

He must hope Georgiana would be happy to stay on at Matlock House. Richard could oversee her behaviour.

CHAPTER 23

*I*t was two days before Darcy could persuade Bingley to Netherfield, but at last he rode there beside him, following the coach. Bingley's sisters and brother-in-law were within, a necessary evil in Darcy's mind. He just wanted to get Netherfield available to him.

Those two days had firmed his determination to find out what Miss Bennet had heard from Wickham — preferably by asking someone what they had discovered. He could not countenance approaching the man himself.

It was unfortunate it was already after noon. He must endure the evening with the family, before he could persuade Bingley to call at Longbourn tomorrow.

At first, he had intended to wait at Netherfield,

and discover from Bingley what was said. But he was now determined to overcome his feeling of mortification and go to Longbourn with Bingley.

He might find out what he needed to know from Miss Kitty Bennet. But he prayed Miss Bennet had not written to her sister; told her of his proposal.

As he climbed the steps of Netherfield behind Bingley and his sister, he pondered on her accusation of his ungentlemanly behaviour.

In the three days since he had seen her, he had been able to think of little else. Her words had hurt him — hurt his pride, tortured his sense of his place as a gentleman in society. That first night at Rosings Park had been the longest night, as he'd paced in bitterness at the memories of her words. But by the time he'd reached London, he regretted what had passed, knew his words had been unpardonable.

He sat over afternoon tea in the drawing room with the rest of the party, barely hearing a word.

Though her accusations had been ill-founded, formed on a mistaken premise, he had to acknowledge that his behaviour to her at the time ought to merit the severest reproof.

The recollection of his words, his actions, were inexpressibly painful.

"Mr. Darcy, pray do not frown so!" Miss Bingley was standing in front of him, and he had to attend.

He looked at her. "Miss Bingley, I hope when

you are rested from the journey, perhaps you might play for us. I enjoy listening to music." *And I enjoy not having to make conversation with you.* But he must behave as a gentleman, must prove himself to Miss Bennet. He took a deep breath.

After dinner, over the port, he asked Bingley if he intended to call at Longbourn the following day.

Bingley looked wretched. "I would like to, Darcy, but I find I wish to call on Miss Kitty, not Miss Bennet; and yet — the family might expect me to pay my respects on Miss Bennet."

Darcy turned his glass between his fingers. "If you think back, Bingley, did Miss Bennet not encourage you to talk to Miss Kitty, suggest you dance with her?"

Bingley looked confused. "I thought it was merely to help Miss Kitty feel better."

Darcy remembered his casual insult on that first occasion, and winced. No wonder she thought so little of him. But he could not tell Bingley she was too clever for him. "I think perhaps she wondered if you might be better suited to Miss Kitty." He thought of something else that might tempt him. "And I understand Miss Bennet is still in Kent. She will not be at Longbourn tomorrow."

He acknowledged to himself that he had thought Miss Kitty much too young for Bingley, but there were only five or six years between them, whereas he was eight years older than Miss Bennet. That no longer seemed important.

By the time they left the dining room, it was settled that the next morning they would call at Longbourn. He smiled slightly; Hurst would be left to entertain his wife and sister-in-law.

But that night, the memory of her searing words tortured him again. Mortified, he could not prevent himself recalling them. But he pushed the thoughts aside; he was on the way to making amends. He must find out her hopes and her dreams. He must show her that he acknowledged the truth of her words and accusations, and prove that he could overcome them.

Somehow, he must prove to her that he was right for her. No longer could he expect to choose a wife that would suit him. If he wanted to marry Miss Bennet — Elizabeth — he must prove himself equal to the task of making her happy.

BINGLEY LOOKED cheerful and excited as they rode up to Longbourn the next morning. Darcy was not so comfortable. He knew Miss Bennet would not be there, but was not quite sure how the morning would go, how he could learn about her, now that the moment was so nearly here.

But he was not prepared for what they found. Three of the Bennet sisters were the only people there to receive them. The eldest sister — Darcy could not recall her married name — curtsied politely, and the others, Miss Kitty and Miss Mary, followed suit. All three had reddened eyes, and could not smile.

"Mr. Bingley, and Mr. Darcy," the eldest sister said. "I'm sorry we're not able to receive you properly this morning. I'm afraid our mother is too distressed to leave her room."

Bingley looked deeply concerned. He glanced at Miss Kitty, who gave him a watery smile.

"I'm sorry, Mr. Bingley. It concerns our sister, Lizzy."

Darcy's heart stopped. A roaring in his ears held him still, prevented him from rushing forward, demanding to know what had happened.

He forced control, took one step forward. "I apologise for troubling you at this distressing time, ladies, and I am sure you are desiring our absence. But could you tell us what has happened? Might we be of assistance?" He must find out what happened. Was Elizabeth all right?

The two younger looked at the older. Darcy had seen her before, she'd seemed a quiet, bland lady. But today, she seemed different, more in control of what needed to be done.

She sat down, so the gentlemen could sit, too. "Thank you, Mr. Darcy. Lizzy has been in Kent, staying with her friend, who married Mr. Collins before Christmas." She looked at him. "Oh, of course, you know that. You were staying there, with Lady Catherine."

He bowed. "I left there early on Friday, madam." He wished he could remember her married name. But he had not bothered to listen properly. Was that part of what Miss Bennet had resented so much? He jerked his attention back to her sister.

"Oh. Well, we got an express late on Sunday from Charlotte Collins." She grimaced. "Lizzy went out for a walk on Saturday and didn't return." She shivered. "They sent out servants to look for her, but no trace of her has been found." She didn't seem to realise that tears were running down her face. "Papa left at dawn yesterday to go and join the search, but we have heard nothing since."

Saturday. And it was Tuesday now. Miss Bennet — his Elizabeth — might have been lying out there for three nights. His heart went cold. Surely something terrible had happened.

He rose to his feet. "I am deeply sorry for the news, madam." He swallowed. "It is wrong to remain here at this time." He met her eyes. "I will return to Kent at once. I know the park quite well, and some of the surrounding countryside. I may be of assistance in the search."

She rose, too. "It would be a great kindness, sir. I am sure my father will appreciate your help."

BACK AT NETHERFIELD, Darcy hurriedly wrote a note to Richard. "Express, please," he barked at the servant, handing it to him. Then he turned to Bingley.

"I'm sorry to have brought you here, Bingley, and then leave in such haste. But I might well be able to help. I sometimes saw her in the distance when I was riding out, so I may know better than anyone where she walked."

"Of course, Darcy. The family will appreciate it very much." Bingley grimaced. "But I can't imagine this will have a good outcome; it is one of the coldest years we've had for a long time."

Darcy's lips tightened. "I will ride to London at once and go immediately to Kent with Colonel Fitzwilliam. Of your kindness, might you provide a conveyance for my servant and luggage to follow?"

"Of course." Bingley clapped him on the shoulder. "Now, while the horse is being got ready, have a small plate of something."

"No, thank you." Darcy smiled thinly. "I

ordered the horse be got ready when we first arrived. I will leave now." He hurried through the hall. "Please convey my apologies to the rest of the party, Bingley."

Within minutes, he was on his way to London.

CHAPTER 24

They had made good time. The express had arrived only half an hour before he had, but Richard was ready, and two fresh horses allowed for a fast journey to Rosings park.

Darcy was hungry and thirsty, but there was no way he would stop to eat. He needed to be there, find out if she had been found. She must have been found, must have been.

Richard had ridden hard with him, without asking questions. But at the post, when new horses were led out within moments, Darcy was able to say a few words.

"I called at Longbourn, with Bingley, this morning. They had news from Kent that Miss Bennet went for a walk on Saturday and has not returned. A search has found no trace of her."

Ten miles later, they picked up more fresh horses. Richard looked at Darcy. "I'm sorry this has happened, Darcy. I think she means a great deal more to you than you have admitted, even to yourself."

Darcy grunted, and swung into the saddle. At least Richard hadn't used the past tense, and he was grateful for that.

He wondered what Lady Catherine would say when they arrived so soon after having quit the place. His lips tightened, and he pulled up slightly.

"Richard, how do you think we should explain ourselves to our aunt?"

His cousin smiled. "I have been wondering what your plan was." He chuckled. "I am looking forward to it."

Darcy glanced over at him. "A pity I won't see it. I would like you to go and give our greetings to Lady Catherine — before the coach arrives." He smiled thinly. "I will go straight to the parsonage and see what is to be done. Mr. Bennet will be there. I am hoping against hope that she has been found safe."

Impatience struck again, and he urged the horse on, Richard following him. Not long now, and he might have his terrible fear relieved.

I T   W A S   H A R D L Y a good time to call, he knew that, yet nothing would prevent him. He rang the doorbell, and the startled housekeeper let him in and announced him to the astonished party in the sitting room.

Mr. Collins leapt to his feet. "Mr. Darcy! We are so honoured." He turned at once to his wife.

"My dear, tell the housekeeper at once to set an extra place for dinner."

"No. No, thank you," Mr. Darcy denied hastily. "I must go to Rosings at once. But I had to call here and speak to Mr. Bennet — just for a few moments."

Bennet was looking very much greyer and older. He rose to his feet. "Do you have news, Mr. Darcy?" He sounded anxious and fearful.

Darcy's heart sank. "I was hoping for news from you, Mr. Bennet. I called at Longbourn this morning and heard what had happened."

He looked down. "I came at once. I have ridden extensively in this region and I know the land well. I would like to offer my assistance."

Bennet sank into the chair. "Thank you, Mr. Darcy. How are they at Longbourn?"

Darcy tried to keep his voice gentle. "I saw only three of your daughters, sir. I understand Mrs. Bennet is too distressed to be downstairs. They are, of course, waiting for news."

The older man shook his head. "There is no news. I can only think she is lost. But no trace of her has been found." His expression crumpled.

"Very well." Darcy straightened. "I will take my leave now. Tomorrow, I will return, with your permission. Colonel Fitzwilliam has returned here, too, and we will bring a map and ensure every inch has been checked." He turned and looked at Mrs. Collins. "Madam, might you recheck her chamber tonight? There might be a note of what she intended to study, or something of the sort."

She nodded calmly. "I will see it is done, Mr. Darcy. Thank you."

He rose to his feet. "Thank you for your hospitality, Mr. Collins, and I am sorry to have kept you from your dinner." He bowed to the others and hurried out. Mounting his horse, he walked away, careful in the fast-falling dusk.

It would be difficult to sleep tonight, wondering where she was, if she was still out in the open, unprotected. He shuddered.

When he entered the dining room, Lady Catherine waved him to his seat.

"Sit down, Darcy, and explain yourself!"

He bowed to her, and then to his cousin Anne, before taking his seat opposite Richard, who raised his eyebrows.

Darcy shook his head, despondent that there was no news.

"I have explained to Lady Catherine the reason for our return, Darcy," Richard said. "It appears there is no news."

Darcy sighed, leaning back as the servant served him his food. "It is not good," he admitted. "I have said you and I will be there early tomorrow, and take charge of what appears to be a rather haphazard search so far." He raised his hand to wave the servant away.

"Enough, thank you."

"Of course." Richard laid down his fork. "Does Collins have a good map of the area, do you think?"

"I doubt it," Darcy looked at his plate with little appetite. Then he looked at his aunt.

"I would like to check for a quality map in your library, if you please, Lady Catherine."

She sniffed disdainfully. "I think they are too valuable to risk damage from it, Darcy." She met his gaze. "The girl is opinionated and stubborn. "She has probably run away."

"No." Darcy said firmly. "She would never do something like that, especially something that did not have the agreement of her family. As for the maps, I will undertake their replacement." He would need them, he knew that.

"Well, she is most careless," Lady Catherine

sniffed. "I loaned her an extremely costly botanical last week, with very expensive hand-coloured prints. She told me it would be useful to her, and now she has gone without having had the use of it."

Darcy's attention was caught. "Is the book still at the parsonage?"

"I certainly hope so!" his aunt snapped. "She should not have removed it from there."

"I'm sure she hasn't," Richard said placatingly. "I think Darcy is wondering if she has placed a marker sheet in there, showing what plants she might be looking for, and therefore the type of country she would be walking in."

Darcy nodded. "Indeed. I just hope the evidence has not been tidied away."

"Well, I think you are wasting your time, both of you. I have sent servants over, so that Collins can coordinate the search for his wife's friend. And since Mr. Bennet has appeared, there is quite enough supervision for the servants." Lady Catherine gave her usual well-practised sniff. "Darcy, we need to have a conversation about your marriage to Anne."

Darcy took a deep breath. "I have already told you, madam, dinner is not the right time to talk about it, especially as I have repeatedly told you that neither your daughter or I, desire the marriage."

"Of course you do! I have a determined resolution to carry my purpose. I will not be dissuaded from it."

Darcy pushed away his plate. He could eat no more. He felt a pang, was Miss Bennet hungry and cold? Had someone taken her?

"Madam, I will not discuss the matter any further." He looked across at Richard, surprising a look of relief on his cousin's face and wondered at it.

CHAPTER 25

The following morning, Darcy and Richard crossed the lane to the parsonage immediately after breakfast. Three servants followed them, carrying the maps that Darcy had selected from his aunt's library.

"With your permission, Richard, I will suggest that you plan the campaign, and ensure that everywhere is covered until we find her."

Richard glanced over. "How far do you think she may have gone?"

"I have no idea, although I think she may venture further afield than anyone could imagine."

Richard nodded. "I don't think Bennet ought to go out alone — to be honest, I would suggest he remains at the parsonage, but I expect he will insist on searching." He shook his head. "I would not consider Collins a reliable searcher, so three servants is not nearly enough. I might have to demand more from Lady Catherine later, when I see how far they have got before now."

Darcy felt desperate. "She has already been out four nights!" He took a deep breath. "We must find her today." They turned in at the gate. "Perhaps I ought to send for my London steward and he can bring down ten trustworthy men."

"Wait until we have discovered what has been done so far. I think it will be a good idea." Richard paused before ringing the bell. "Do not let Collins rile you, Darcy. If necessary, let me deal with him. We will not find your lady if there is dissent."

Darcy swallowed, but nodded. He couldn't tell Richard she was not his lady, couldn't tell anyone what had happened here last week. Somehow, inarticulately, he felt he must be to blame for what had happened.

AN HOUR LATER, he was tramping through the tangled woodland behind the grove in Rosings parkland. He was determined to search every square inch of the area he had been given. But his mind was with the other searchers. Would Richard or Bennet find her first? When would he know?

At least he now knew how ineffectual the early searching had been. It seemed Mrs. Collins had been the prime mover in getting anything done at all, and he had admired her this morning as she had made suggestions to her husband, making him think he had the ideas himself.

He smiled grimly to himself, as he peered off the paths, looking for footprints, or trodden-down plants. Mrs. Collins was a good friend to Miss Bennet. But for her, he was not sure that any search would have been made at all.

He followed a few small side paths, checking the sketches he had made from the maps. At least they knew she was not on any of the main paths or lanes within a mile or so of the parsonage.

But he was angry that neither of the other ladies had gone with her. Even if no servants were to be had to accompany her, she ought to have been more careful if she was on her own.

Even a minor injury, such as turning her ankle, could have led to a long exposure until she was found.

He shuddered, hoping against hope that it was something as simple as a turned ankle. In his imagination, he found her, used his cravat to bind that shapely ankle — no! He must concentrate, must search as fast as was possible.

He hurried forward, down a tempting-looking

path. "Miss Bennet!" Would she answer his call? He doubted that after so long, she would be in a fit state to hear him, but he had to try.

He could not let his terrible fears overtake his hopes. Drawing out a pencil, he crossed off the area he had just searched, and hurried on to the next. He must find her, he must.

AT DUSK, he had slowed down. Still a few more small areas to cover, but it was taking longer. The light was failing, and he had to be more careful not to miss a single clue.

Not long later, and he was hurrying back to the parsonage. Perhaps someone else had found her. He would be happy that it wasn't him, as long as she was alive.

But all faces turned towards him hopefully, as he hurried in, muddy, dishevelled, and alone. His heart fell.

"Nothing?"

"Nothing." Richard looked down grimly at his map and crossed off the area where Darcy had been searching.

Darcy turned heavily to Mrs. Collins. "Of your kindness, might I have notepaper and pen? I will send to Darcy House and call down my steward and more servants."

He looked at Bennet. "I will find her, sir. I will."

The older man looked even more exhausted and shrunken in grief than the previous evening. "I fear we are too late, Mr. Darcy. I have lost her."

Darcy had to turn away from the raw grief before him. He would not accept it, could not.

Mrs. Collins had laid out notepaper and pen on the table. "Here you are, Mr. Darcy. And my house-keeper is preparing a plate for you, since we did not see you at lunch."

"Thank you," he turned and sat at the table. The glass of water beside him made him realise just how thirsty he was, and he gulped it down. Was Elizabeth thirsty? His heart twisted in pain.

He folded and sealed the note, and looked up at Mrs. Collins. "Might it be sent express, please?"

Then he rose and crossed to the map. Richard was beside him. "I have instructed them to start at dawn, Richard. So we can expect them soon after eight." He bent over the map. So little had been covered. He shook his head. "I should have sent yesterday, not wasted a day."

He glanced at his cousin. "Will Lady Catherine accommodate them in the servants' quarters, or ought I to book rooms at the inn?"

"I will speak to her, Darcy. She will arrange it at Rosings for them."

Darcy ate hungrily. Richard looked at him and smiled. "Don't forget we must do justice to our food at dinner."

He chuckled as Darcy groaned.

THE FOLLOWING MORNING, he, Richard, and the servants presented themselves at the parsonage again. Collins fawned around them. "Welcome, welcome!" He talked incessantly, despite being rather ignored. Darcy was incensed at his apparent cheerfulness — his cousin was missing while under his protection — he seemed to have no sense of regret, of responsibility.

Richard gave him a warning glance. "It may be better if we use Rosings Park as the base for our searching," he looked round the room. "With more men joining us soon, the parsonage needs to get back to being the centre of the parish."

Darcy suppressed a smile, his cousin was the most diplomatic of men.

"I hope that will not be necessary," Bennet was polishing his spectacles, over and over again. Darcy was struck by how he appeared even frailer than the previous day.

"I assure you I will not give up until I know what has happened; until I find her, sir. If you feel you must return to Hertfordshire, I will ensure I send news by express each day until she is found." He felt acute compassion for the man.

"It is hard to leave," the man muttered. Then he looked up. "I am grateful to you, Mr. Darcy." There was suspicious moisture in his eyes and Darcy returned to the map. Out of the corner of his eye he watched as Mrs. Collins went and sat beside Bennet, her hand on his arm. Darcy couldn't watch longer.

"I will go and see if I can see my steward arriving." He strode out of the house.

Waiting outside, he felt the cold, frosty air, and then the despair. She could not possibly have survived outside, not in this coldest of springs. He stood, shoulders slumped, not knowing what to do, what to think.

"It is not looking good, Darcy." Richard was beside him, his voice heavy.

"No." Darcy could acknowledge it now. "I cannot see any hope." He turned to his cousin. "But I must know. I *must* know what happened to her." A dark place where his heart had been.

"I wondered why you left Kent so hurriedly on Friday." Richard sounded off-hand. "And in such a temper."

Darcy couldn't feel any of the anger he'd felt then. Nothing was important any more. "She refused my offer, Richard. I had to escape what I considered then my humiliation."

"But you went into Hertfordshire."

"I had to find out more about her, how I should change, be the sort of man she might accept."

Richard sighed. "I cannot tell you how sorry I am." He looked down the lane. "I think I can hear the coach." His voice strengthened. "I have decided. Go with the men at once to Rosings. I will get the map and join you there, with Lady Catherine's three men. Bennet has decided to return home." He shook his head. "He is a broken man. And I think listening to Collins is more than he can take."

"As I have found, Richard." Darcy straightened up. "One thing. Has every cottage, every home, been searched? Someone might have taken her in."

"They have not, Darcy. I am sorry, but that is what Bennet and Mrs. Collins did together yesterday. They have called at every house and cottage within two miles of here. No one saw her, no one has taken her in."

Darcy felt his shoulders sag. She was gone, she must be. With legs that would barely hold him, he walked out to the coach, and swung himself up beside the coachman.

"Rosings Park, across the lane." He pointed the

way, ignoring the man's astonishment and scandalised expression. It was quicker this way.

AT LUNCHTIME THAT AFTERNOON, he and his steward came across the river, deep and slow-moving; shaded by the close-growing trees.

"A dismal place, sir." His steward had caught his mood. He was loyal and discreet; Darcy trusted him absolutely.

"It is, indeed, Mr. Leigh." He stood up straighter and looked around. The path along the top of the bank was muddy and slippery, little sun got through to dry it. Surely Elizabeth would not have come this way? More than three miles from Hunsford, it had been almost too far to search, but Darcy was determined. He would not give in.

Grasping branches as they went, the two men continued on. Darcy could not imagine a young lady coming this way.

"Sir! Over there!" Mr. Leigh called back, and Darcy craned to see past him.

"What? What is it?" He couldn't push past him. "Hurry, man!"

It was a lady's reticule, her small bag, the long ribbons caught on a branch, the bag halfway down the slippery bank.

"Careful, sir!" Mr. Leigh flung his arm out. The path had broken away, the mud had slid down, signs of someone carried down with it. Branches that had been grasped and broken. And the river was there.

He stood, stupefied, on the bank. Then he stirred. Was there any sign that she hadn't fallen in, any sign at all that she had continued along the bottom of the bank?

"Wait, sir!" Mr Leigh sounded urgent. "We must not spoil the track. The dogs might get the scent."

"I know, but I must reach the reticule, see if it is hers."

Mr. Leigh looked as if he wanted to hurry off to get the dogs, but wanted to stay in case Darcy had need of him.

"It's all right, Mr. Leigh." Darcy forced a smile. "Go and get the dogs — and Colonel Fitzwilliam as well, if you please."

He watched as his steward pushed away through the trees. A good man. Then he turned, as if with a great effort. He must reach the bag, look inside, see if there was a clue in it as to where she might be. But he already knew.

It seemed very wrong to be opening a woman's reticule, utterly improper. But he had to know.

A small notebook, pencils.

He opened the book. Sketches, drawings of leaves, notations in a firm but feminine hand. He turned another page. An outline of the moon, familiar craters and shading — and — himself. A basic but recognisable sketch of his own visage.

He stared at it in shock. Why would she sketch him? He had heard her say that she could not draw; and indeed the sketch was unpractised, unskilled. But it showed a strong power of observation, and was recognisably himself.

But she was gone. He had lost her. He slid the notebook into his jacket pocket. No one must see it.

He sat there a long, long time. The dark, still water, no vestige of sunlight — all matched his mood, his sense of aching loss.

CHAPTER 26

*S*omeone was spooning a small amount of water into her mouth. She swallowed obediently. Her whole world was here in this place; this cot, this room that smelled small and cosy; full of people.

"All right, dearie. A bit o' gruel now." The voice sounded conversational; a little rough, but kindly.

"It's about time you opened your eyes, miss. You been restin' long enough."

She frowned, what did the voice mean? But she tried, and managed to open her eyes just a tiny bit.

"Good, very good," the voice encouraged her. The light was not too bright; she could see the window was very small.

Her eyes opened further. A plump, motherly-looking woman was smiling at her.

"My, you've been asleep for a long time, young lady." She offered her another spoon of gruel. "It's 'bout time you woke up and told us who we can tell that you're here."

She sipped from the spoon again and then tried to push herself up a little more.

"Wait a moment," the woman put the spoon down and then helped her sit up a little. "There." She plumped the cushion up a little behind her. "My name's Liddell — Susan Liddell. It's been nigh on a week since my husband an' another found you and brought you here. And we've not heard nuthin' about a lost lady." Her voice was questioning.

Who was she? Who? — "My name …" she rubbed her head with her hand — and it came to her. "My name's Lizzy."

"There, there," Mrs. Liddell patted her arm kindly. "Now you've woken up, you'll soon remember who you are and we can tell your family. They must be very worried about you."

Elizabeth bit her lip. Who was she? Where was she from?

"Now, you're not to go a worryin', miss. Everything will be fine, just you see." The woman got up and went to the table that formed part of the kitchen in the corner of the room. She returned with a fresh cup of water. "Let's get more water inside you, now you're awake. Then I'll get Jake —

that's my husband — to go and get the vicar, and we can send to your home."

"I ought to get up, I've troubled you for too long," Elizabeth protested, but as she put her weight on her wrist, she fell back with a cry.

"I think I've hurt my wrist," she rubbed it. "Do you know what happened to me?"

"No, miss. Just don't worry 'bout a thing." The woman bustled round the room, and Elizabeth rested back against the cushion, and closed her eyes, remembering what she had seen.

It was a small room, her impression had been right. A tiny cottage, only one room, for kitchen and living. Probably only one room upstairs, too.

"Did you really say I'd been here a week?" Elizabeth was mortified that she had been such a nuisance. "We must send to my family, I've trespassed on your kindness too long already."

"It's no trouble, Miss, not at all. But if you'll be all right there, I'll just go an' tell Jake to fetch the vicar an' he can write a letter for you." The woman hurried out of the cottage, and Elizabeth shut her eyes again. The light seemed very bright, although she knew it couldn't possibly be.

She felt quite weak, so the woman was probably right that Elizabeth had been here a week. So why wasn't she remembering what had happened, who her family were? She knew she had never seen Mrs.

Liddell before in her life. But she knew everyone round her home. She waited for the name of her home to drop into her mind, but it didn't. She screwed up her face, trying to force it, but nothing came.

How would the vicar be able to send to her home if she couldn't remember it? Perhaps she would know him.

SHE DIDN'T KNOW HIM, not the faintest recognition struck her. But he looked kind. A young man, very thin, with a bookish appearance.

He pulled up the chair beside the cot that Elizabeth was lying on.

"Good evening, madam. I'm happy you're so much better." He smiled. "Mrs. Liddell has been most helpful, allowing you to stay here, and caring for you." He frowned slightly. "I would have had you taken to the vicarage as a more spacious place to be looked after, but as I am not married, it was, of course, out of the question."

Elizabeth looked round at her hostess. "Thank you so much. I can see what disruption I have caused you." Then she turned her attention back to the vicar.

"All right. I'm Mr. Parks. I'm the clergyman here

at Copthorne, and I want to help return you to your family." He frowned slightly. "I have to say, I am puzzled that no one seems to have reported that there is a young lady missing, and I have enquired right up to my Bishop, so I am at a loss how to account for it."

She looked up at the window. Who was she, what had happened before she got here? Then …

"Copthorne? Where is that, Mr. Parks?"

"Copthorne?" He looked surprised. "It is between Crawley and East Grinstead, in the diocese of Chichester. Don't you come from here?"

There was a silence. Frantically she searched her mind. It cleared a little, and she was relieved. "Longbourn. My father's estate is Longbourn."

He smiled properly. "I'm glad you remember. I do want to find your family." He wrote the name down on a sheet of paper. "I'm not familiar with Longbourn. What town is it near?"

Elizabeth stared at him. "Isn't it near here?"

He shook his head, and reached down into a leather satchel. "Never mind, I brought an atlas, although it's not as detailed as we might wish."

Elizabeth waited quietly while he looked through the index. Finally he shook his head. "Longbourn isn't listed. It must be in quite a small hamlet."

"I'm sorry," Elizabeth didn't know quite what to

suggest. She closed her eyes, tried to force herself to remember what she could.

A warm sandstone building. Lawns. Not an enormous house. Another word, bursting into her mind. "Meryton! It is near Meryton."

"Wonderful!" Mr. Parks turned back to the index. "Oh!"

"What is it?" Elizabeth felt anxious.

"Meryton is in Hertfordshire, Miss ..." he hesitated. "Do you remember your family name?"

She shook her head reluctantly. The lack of memory of people was worrying her, and she had to blink away the sudden moisture in her eyes.

"Do not worry," he hastened to reassure her. "As you are remembering parts of what you need to, I am sure the rest will come back very soon. In the meantime, may I refer to you as Miss Elizabeth? I mean no offence."

"Of course. I would be happy for that."

"Good." He closed the book after making some more notes. "With your permission, I will write at once to the master of Longbourn estate, and ask him if he is able to shed light on who you are and why you are here in Copthorne."

Elizabeth nodded. She would like to know that, too.

CHAPTER 27

*T*wo days. Two days by that dreadful river. Darcy lay back in the steaming bath, as Mr. Maunder carefully poured another jug of hot water in. Two days since the dogs had stopped at the riverbank, followed the track no further.

Two days prodding under the surface with sticks, two days since Darcy had felt his way into the water, trying to feel for her, his heart in dread of finding her lifeless body. Two days since he had known he would never stop searching for her.

He had sent the men down along the riverbanks, as it had curved to the south, following it to see if there was any trace of her along the banks. The nearby track had no trace of anyone passing, and he had been told it was barely used. Nobody would have found her, heard her cries for help.

He needed this bath, but he hated being here. He needed to be there, there where she was lost. But Richard had forced him away each evening.

"You must come back to Rosings, Darcy. You must speak to your men, tell them what they need to hear from you." His nose had wrinkled. "And you need a bath."

So, here he was. He didn't want to get out, go downstairs for dinner. Dinner, where nothing seemed to have changed, and the only mention of Elizabeth was when Lady Catherine spoke disparagingly of her impertinence and desire to learn unsuitable subjects for ladies.

He had held his tongue with difficulty. He needed to stay here, stay close to where Elizabeth was. But it was not easy.

There was a loud hammering on the door, Richard was shouting indistinctly.

"Answer it, man!" Darcy was on his feet, climbing out of the bath, reaching for the towel; and his valet rushed to the door of the bedchamber. Richard came striding through, waving a sheet of paper.

"She's been found, Darcy! She's alive!"

"What?" Darcy snatched at the paper, the towel dropping to the floor.

"Dry your hands, man, or the letter will fall

apart." Richard laughed, his happiness evident in his voice. "She's all right, Darcy, she is not too severely harmed."

Darcy dropped into the chair, reached for the towel, and dried his trembling hands.

Relief washed through him. She was alive. He might see her again. He became aware that Mr. Maunder was holding out his robe anxiously, and he rose and donned it, before holding out his hand.

"Where is she, what happened to her?"

"You read it." Richard thrust the letter at him, and Darcy took it and turned away towards the window, reading quickly.

Longbourn

Saturday 18th inst.

Dear Mr. Darcy,

I write in haste that I have news of Lizzy. She has been found and I understand that she is not too severely ill.

I have copied the letter that I received and enclose it for your perusal. I cannot express my joy and happiness that this has happened and I thank you from the bottom of my heart for your help and determination in this matter.

Might I beg of you one more favour? You will see that the vicar appears to think that she might not be fit to travel into Hertfordshire for a few days yet. I would be most grateful if you could call on him and assess the situation and see what is best to be done. If she needs the care of an apothecary, then of course I will pay for whatever is needed, and also pay for any costs that have already been incurred.

I have been most grateful for your express letters, and hope that you will be able to keep me informed.

I am, sir, most grateful to you.

I can never repay your kindness to this family.

Yours, etc,

Thomas Bennet

Darcy turned eagerly to the other sheet of paper.

The Vicarage

Copthorne

Friday, 17th inst.

To the master, Longbourn Estate.

I am writing to you as I have been given the name Longbourn, by a young lady who was found injured last week, near here.

Darcy glanced up. "Copthorne? Where is it? How did she get there?"

Richard shrugged. "As soon as you are dressed, we will go and look at the map."

She has been insensible since she was found, but today, she roused a little. She has been able to remember her given name — Elizabeth — and eventually remembered the name Longbourn, and after a while, that it was near the town of Meryton. So I am writing to you immediately to ask if you know the young lady, and if you are able to inform me how to proceed in this matter.

A local farm worker's wife is caring for her at this time, but their cottage is very small and basic. I have been unable to arrange to have her cared for here, as I am unmarried. I can assure you again that Miss Elizabeth is not severely harmed, although I think it may take several weeks for her to recover from what has obviously been a significant shock to her.

I am sir,

Yours, etc,

Christopher Parks

He stood there, reading and rereading the letter. She was alive, she had remembered her name and the name of her home. He folded the letter, noting that his hands still trembled.

"I will dress, Richard, and come downstairs. Order the coach, we must go to Copthorne."

His cousin shook his head. "No. It is too late, Darcy. We will go in the morning."

He held up his hand as Darcy rounded on him.

"We cannot. It must be many miles away as we had not found her in our local search."

Darcy sat down suddenly. "How did she get so far?"

"I don't know," Richard laughed, "and she may never remember. But if there is some mystery, we might do better not to enquire too closely. If there was some poaching, then we must remember that they risked the threat of hanging or deportation to save her and not abandon her to her death."

Darcy smiled reluctantly. Richard could always be relied upon to know the ways of men of all types.

It felt strange to be smiling, his face was no longer used to the movement.

"Good," said Richard, observing him closely. "Now, when you're dressed, we might walk to the parsonage and tell Mrs. Collins. We will need to ask her if she will be able to take Miss Bennet in and care for her until she is well enough to take home to Hertfordshire."

Darcy threw his head back and laughed. He had thought he'd never laugh again. "Lady Catherine will be incensed if we are late for dinner."

Richard grinned appreciatively. "I doubt you care a great deal."

"We will take the coach with us tomorrow, Richard. Perhaps Mrs. Collins and her sister will need to come with us to escort Miss Bennet back to Hunsford." Darcy frowned. "Will Collins permit them to miss church?"

Richard scowled. "Of course, tomorrow is Sunday." He shrugged. "If he will not, perhaps we can take a couple of maids with us." He grimaced. "We might have to wait for the service at Copthorne to finish so Mr. Parks can take us to the cottage where she is."

Darcy growled under his breath, and Richard chuckled again.

"I will see you downstairs, cousin."

THE MAIDS RODE in his coach, piled high with blankets and pillows; everything Darcy could think of that might be needed. Mr. Leigh and a couple of his men were on the back, alongside the coachman and grooms.

He and Richard rode behind, as they trotted towards Copthorne. He shook his head. "I still cannot believe she was nigh on fifteen miles away."

"I think that is why we didn't hear, Darcy." Richard rode closer to him, so they did not have to shout. "Parks would have consulted his Bishop — but that is the diocese of Chichester."

Darcy nodded. The relief was still too new to

be real, the gnawing grief to recent to be forgotten. Until he could see her, assure himself with his own eyes that she was unharmed, he could not relax.

Richard leaned over. "You seem concerned. Are you perhaps thinking she will not wish to see you?"

"I do not know." He glared at him. "I will thank you to forget what I said to you that day. I will work this out, however long it takes."

Richard held out his hand, placatingly. "Of course, of course!" He looked puzzled. "What were we talking about?"

Darcy laughed. "You're a good friend, Richard."

They knocked on the door of the vicarage before nine o'clock, and the housekeeper looked askance at them, changing to servility when she saw their manner and dress.

Parks came out to the hall as they entered, a tall, lanky young fellow, but with a countenance of genuine goodness.

Darcy bowed at him. "I'm sorry to disturb you just before the service, Mr. Parks." He reached into his jacket pocket and handed the folded letters to him. "As you see, Miss Bennet's father has tasked me with finding out what needs to be done, and with recovering her."

Parks scanned the letter. "You have come very

quickly, sir. I will take you to Liddell's cottage. But I'm afraid it will need to be after the service."

Darcy bowed. "I understand Sunday is taken up with your parishioners, sir. Perhaps you might direct us to the cottage and join us there when you are free?" Nothing was going to keep him from Elizabeth. "I have maids in my coach to chaperone her. Mrs. Liddell might appreciate the chance to attend church."

Parks' face lightened. "It would be a very great kindness, sir. She is an excellent woman." He walked out to the road with them, and pointed out a whitewashed hovel halfway down the lane. "The one with the broken gate, Mr. Darcy. You see it?"

"I do." Darcy held his hand out for the letters, and tucked them securely back in his jacket. He needed them. He had woken in the darkness, the nightmare still upon him. Only reading the letters had slowed his heart rate and allowed him to rest again.

He beckoned his coach, and the groom holding the horses, to follow them; and he walked beside Richard down the lane. It was only a hundred yards or so, but long enough for his sense of urgency to be overlaid with nervousness. Would she recognise him? Would she remember the last words they had spoken? *You are the last man in the world whom I could ever be prevailed on to marry.*

217

He hesitated. Richard looked sideways at him.

"Courage, my friend," he murmured.

He drew a deep breath, raised his hand and knocked.

CHAPTER 28

*E*lizabeth was resting on the cot in the corner of the room. She had sat up for an hour the previous afternoon, and the resultant headache had driven her back to bed.

Mrs. Liddell was sitting in the armchair, darning a stocking, but she pushed herself to her feet and went to the door.

"Mrs. Liddell?" The voice was familiar, but Elizabeth didn't know why. "Mr. Parks has directed us here; I understand you have been looking after a young lady, Miss Elizabeth Bennet."

Bennet! That's my name.

She heard Mrs. Liddell answer something, and then that familiar voice again, unutterably comforting.

There was movement in the room, and she kept her eyes shut, suddenly afraid.

Silence. Then she felt Mrs. Liddell's hand on her arm. Feeling foolish, she opened her eyes. She couldn't look at the other figures.

"Miss Elizabeth, these gentlemen have come from Mr. Parks. He has suggested I might be able to go to church. There are maids here to chaperone you." She hesitated. "Would that be all right with you?"

"Oh! Of course! You have been so good to me, please go, if you would like to." Elizabeth struggled to sit up, favouring her right wrist, and Mrs. Liddell pushed the cushion behind her a little more.

"Thank you." Then she was alone with two gentlemen she wasn't sure if she remembered, and the maids trying to be invisible against the wall of the tiny parlour.

She wished she was sitting in the chair; she wished she wasn't wearing a borrowed, ill-fitting, tattered dress; and she wished very much that she'd had a little more time to prepare herself for this.

"Please do not discompose yourself, Miss Bennet," His voice was very gentle. "Might I sit down?"

"Oh, yes. Please do." Who was he, and why did her heart feel so tight?

He didn't look very comfortable on the narrow, upright chair which was the only one apart from the old and fraying armchair that Mrs. Liddell used; and the other man leaned against the far wall, unobtrusive.

"Miss Bennet, we're happy you have been safe here. We have been searching for you, and had begun to despair."

She looked at him. "I'm sorry. I know I have seen you before, but I cannot recall …"

He bowed his head, "Of course. Darcy. Fitzwilliam Darcy." He reached into his pocket. "I have a letter here from your father that I received last night, asking that I assist you until you are well enough to go home."

She accepted the letter, but only read the first few lines. Her eyes filled with tears, she recognised her father's writing. She kept her head down for a moment while she blinked hard.

"Miss Bennet?" He sounded anxious, and she shook her head.

"Reading is difficult for me at the moment. But I accept you're here on Papa's behalf." She took a deep breath. "If I live in Hertfordshire, why am I here? Mr. Parks tells me Copthorne is down in Sussex."

"Perhaps you do not yet recall it, Miss Bennet. But you were staying with a friend in Kent, just over the county border. You went out for a walk and were found and brought here."

She looked up. There were lines of strain round his eyes. But he smiled.

"I confess I do not know how you reached here, nearly fifteen miles from where you were staying."

She knew she looked surprised. But it was not important yet. "Do you know the name of my friend?"

He nodded. "Yes, she is fairly recently married to Mr. Collins, but the name you knew her by was Miss Charlotte Lucas."

"Charlotte!" The memory came back to her, along with the face in her mind. "I must have caused her so much worry."

He smiled again. "She was happy when I took her the news as soon as I heard." He was still speaking but exhaustion was creeping over her again, and she couldn't really understand what he was saying.

WHEN SHE WOKE AGAIN, Mrs. Liddell was sitting in her chair, darning. It was as if nothing had happened. Elizabeth frowned.

"Mrs. Liddell, did I have a peculiar dream, or was there a gentleman here sent by my father?"

The woman smiled comfortably. "You went right off to sleep, I hear, in the middle of talking to him. I told him off for tiring you out." She heaved herself out of the chair and went to the stove. "Let's have a cup of tea." Her back was to Elizabeth, as she said. "They're waitin' outside 'til you feel better. They're talking to Mr. Parks right now 'bout whether you be fit to move back to your friend's house."

A few moments later she bought the steaming cup over to the cot, and placed it carefully on the table. "Do you want to sit up in me chair fer a bit?"

Elizabeth glanced at the door. "I suppose it might look better — but then you haven't anywhere to sit."

"I kin use the other, Miss Elizabeth."

She helped Elizabeth walk slowly towards the chair and spread the blanket over her knees. "There you are. Look much better when you're sittin' up."

She carried the cup over. "Here's your tea. I think I heard them talking about askin' the apothecary to come over. So you'll be here another day, at this rate." She laughed comfortably.

"I'm very grateful to you for taking such good care of me," Elizabeth was conscious of how little space there was. "But I had better go soon. You must be so tired."

"You go only when you're ready, girl. There's

always a welcome for you here." The woman turned away, looking embarrassed. "A proper lady, you are, no airs and graces, that's what I say."

"Thank you." Elizabeth felt humble. But she wanted to go. She remembered Charlotte, now she had been reminded, and she wanted to see her; have a comfortable bed, and warmth, and her own clothes.

She sipped at her tea. She must say she was well enough, act strong.

CHAPTER 29

There was a knock on the door, and Mrs. Liddell opened it. A cold draught explored Elizabeth's bare feet and she bit her lip. *Be strong, Lizzy.*

Mr. Parks was almost too tall to get through the doorway, but he bent, anyway. Mr. Darcy, behind him, had to bend. Elizabeth smiled at that, and he looked relieved.

Mrs. Liddell backed away to make some room, and ended up sitting on the edge of the cot. Mr. Parks nodded acknowledgement at her, and then drew up the other chair beside Elizabeth.

"I'm glad to see you looking so much better, Miss Bennet." His eyes were kind. "I have been talking to the other gentlemen about the best way to proceed and I want to ask you what you would like to do."

She took time to think; she didn't wish to offend anyone. "Mrs. Liddell has looked after me wonderfully well, but I think it might be best if I go back to my friend's house, if she is willing to let me stay there until I feel better."

He nodded understandingly. "Now, I want you to think very carefully if you are well enough. Mr. Darcy has his coach here, and plenty of blankets and pillows." He looked serious. "But it is going to be probably two hours until you get there — two hours when you won't be able to rest from the movement of the coach. Would you be better for a few more days here?"

Elizabeth bit her lip. Two hours sitting up in a coach seemed a long time. But she had to be strong.

"I will be all right, Mr. Parks. Thank you for your concern. But if Mr. Darcy has his coach here, I would like to go back to Charlotte, if I may."

Mr. Darcy didn't say anything, but in some indefinable way, she knew he was pleased. He bowed his head.

"The seats are quite long, and you might wish to lie down along them, Miss Bennet. Or if you prefer, I can get some boards to make a litter for you to lie on across the seats."

She shook her head, and tried to smile. "I will be perfectly all right with what you already have, Mr. Darcy. But thank you." Her eyes wandered to the other gentleman. She recognised him, too, but he hadn't been introduced, and it didn't seem terribly important, anyway.

"Well, if you wish to travel, then perhaps we should start as soon as possible." Mr. Darcy straightened up. "If you will excuse me, I will call the coach."

The gentlemen left the room, and Mrs. Liddell bustled round. "Let me see. Yer boots is not fit for wearin'. Stockings, yes. I have this pair, Miss Elizabeth. Just darned 'em myself, an' they'll keep your feet proper warm."

"Thank you, Mrs. Liddell. I will make sure everything is properly cleaned and sent back to you."

"I know you will, dearie. A proper lady, that's what I said. A proper lady."

The light from the window dimmed, and Elizabeth saw that Mr. Darcy had certainly got the coach close to the cottage, the front of it was right in front of the window. She smiled, at least she wouldn't get too cold.

He seemed to take his mood from her, smiling in return. "Are you ready, Miss Bennet?"

She nodded nervously, and pushed herself to her feet, wincing with the pain from her wrist.

"What is the matter, are you unwell?" He'd seen.

"It is no matter. I forgot I had hurt my wrist, and foolishly used that hand. It is already better."

He seemed to realise that she would not relish further conversation, and offered her his arm.

But she turned first to Mrs. Liddell. "Thank you, again, for all you have done for me. I will make sure that the clothes are returned as soon as possible, and I hope, when I'm recovered, that I may come and thank you properly."

The woman bobbed slightly, more intimidated while the gentlemen were in the room. "You be always welcome here, Miss Elizabeth. I hope you feel well very soon."

Elizabeth tucked her arm in Mr. Darcy's, trying not to lean too heavily on him. One of the maids draped a blanket over her shoulders, and then climbed in, ready to reach out and support her in.

"But you have no shoes!"

Elizabeth wanted to laugh, had he really just noticed? "I am afraid my own are not fit to wear, Mr. Darcy."

The other gentleman was standing, watchful. "Perhaps we ought to wait a day, Darcy. If we came back tomorrow, then Mrs. Collins can accompany us with a few things for Miss Bennet."

She felt Mr. Darcy hesitate, and wondered why he seemed so reluctant. But she was up now, and had a will to get on with it.

"The coach is very near, sir. It will not be a problem."

Mr. Darcy lowered his head towards hers. "Please permit me, Miss Bennet."

Before she had understood him, he had lifted her in his arms, and sudden warmth spread through her. It was only two steps for him, then he was carefully easing her through the narrow, low doorway, and into the coach, only a pace away.

She reached out and grasped the doorframe as she steadied herself, and he was halfway in, supporting her, as she waited for the world to stop revolving.

Then she smiled, and sat back carefully.

He looked concerned. "We will go very slowly, Miss Bennet, so that we do not jolt you too much. Perhaps if you lie down, you will not get too fatigued."

"Perhaps in a little while; first I will begin like this."

"Very well." His gaze moved to the maids. "Colonel Fitzwilliam and I will be riding behind. If you need to stop, or anything at all, you must indicate out of the window. Do you understand?"

"I will ask them to if I need to, Mr. Darcy." Elizabeth felt a little nettled. She might be weakened from her illness, but she was still able to decide what was right and what was not.

"Very well." He bowed and closed the door.

CHAPTER 30

*E*lizabeth was very, very relieved to reach Hunsford during the afternoon. The coach had stopped after an hour, and Mr. Darcy had come to the door to see if all was well.

She had not wanted to stop. "I would prefer if we continued, Mr. Darcy."

"Very well," he'd bowed; but his eyes were guarded, and she spent the next hour wondering why.

As they drew up outside the parsonage, Elizabeth remembered it; and also that the coach could not get as close to the house as it had to the cottage.

She was dismayed at the sudden race of her heart as she imagined him lifting her into his arms once again, carrying her into the house.

"Lizzy! I'm so glad you're here. I've been so

worried." Charlotte was at the coach door. "But, my goodness, you're so pale and thin! You must go straight to bed and I will get you properly warm."

Mr. Darcy's eyes were still guarded, and distant, too. What had she done wrong? Elizabeth stood up, holding onto the doorframe.

He smiled slightly, and raised his eyebrows. She found herself smiling, a little foolishly, and his gentle look nearly undid her.

Then she was in his arms and being carried through the front door. *I wish this could last forever.* She pushed the thought away. *I don't even know him.* She crinkled her brows, trying to think. *But Papa does.*

"Cousin Elizabeth!" A pompous voice, doing closer. "It is fortunate that you were found and taken into safety. Now you must take care to recover and not cause such trouble for others."

Mr. Darcy ignored the other man, and carried her straight past him to the bottom of the stairs. "There, Miss Bennet, you will not have to walk far." Gently, he set her on her feet, not letting go until she had grasped the bannister.

"Thank you, Mr. Darcy." Charlotte intervened.

Then she was beside her. "Come on, Lizzy, let's get you into some clean things and then into bed."

Elizabeth slowly climbed the stairs, knowing he was watching her, and feeling bereft at the increasing distance between them.

Just as the stair turned, she glanced back. His expression was impassive, but there was something — but she was just too tired. Heavily, she dragged herself back up to the bedchamber she dimly recalled. Behind her, she could hear Mr. Collins voice expounding on her reckless acts which had caused so much disruption and the disfavour of Lady Catherine.

But she was too, too tired. Poor Mr. Darcy, having to listen to him.

MARIA LUCAS WAS SITTING with her in her chamber the next morning, as Elizabeth was resting in bed, trying to read from her journal. She wanted to know what she had been doing. Why had she walked so far?

But after only a few minutes, she laid it aside, her head aching acutely. When would that resolve?

She and Maria both heard the sound of heavy footsteps on the stairs. Elizabeth frowned, they didn't sound like Mr. Collins.

There was a knock on the door, and Charlotte put her head round the door. "Lizzy, Mr. Darcy has sent a physician to see you." She looked at her sister, who hastily got up, smiled at Elizabeth, and left the room.

Charlotte came in and fussed around Elizabeth, smoothing the blanket that covered her. "All right?" she whispered.

Elizabeth nodded, and Charlotte went to the door. "Come in, doctor."

He looked very distinguished, not at all how Elizabeth had expected a country doctor to look — not that she had ever seen a physician. Meryton only had an apothecary.

"Good morning, Miss Bennet." He put his bag down on the table, and bowed to her. "I am Doctor Moore, Mr. Darcy's personal physician from London. He's asked me to come down and see you." He paused. "Are you in agreement that I speak to you?"

Elizabeth nodded. "Of course, doctor. Though I'm sure Mr. Darcy needn't have gone to this expense."

He smiled. "I think he hopes to feel reassured that nothing has been forgotten that might further your recovery."

"I think I will be well soon enough, sir. Time is all I need."

He nodded, and sat on the chair beside her bed. "I have heard what your friends know about what happened. Can you remember, yourself, anything of what occurred?"

She shook her head, reluctantly. "I'm sorry. But

I am recalling some things. When someone tells me something, I know it. I just can't think of the words without being reminded."

"I think it is to be expected, Miss Bennet. Does it concern you?"

"No, sir." Not for anything would she admit to her fear that this might remain with her. She had been proud of her memory, she knew that much from her journal.

He was looking at her steadily. Then he nodded. "I understand your wrist was painful. Is that improving?"

"It is." Elizabeth felt unaccountably tearful. *I must not weep, I must not.* "I'm sorry, doctor, that you have had such a journey when it was not needed. There is nothing I need; nothing that will not get better with time."

"If you're sure?" he enquired, then he rose, and bowed, before leaving.

"Are you all right here, Lizzy?" Charlotte said hurriedly. "If I go down, too, I might hear what he says to Mr. Darcy."

"That's well thought of, Charlotte." Elizabeth nodded, and when Charlotte hurried out, Elizabeth could roll over. She wanted nothing more than the opportunity to cry and feel a little sorry for herself.

THE NEXT DAY, she was better. She sat out in her chair, looking leisurely through the great botanical book that Charlotte reminded her had been loaned by Lady Catherine.

A ring at the doorbell sent Charlotte hurrying apologetically downstairs; but Elizabeth hadn't expected her next visitor.

Neither, it appeared, had Charlotte. Suitably awed, she showed Miss Anne de Bourgh into the bedchamber, and departed to order them some tea.

"I'm honoured you've come to call on me, Miss de Bourgh," Elizabeth said, wondering at it. She tried to remember the times she had visited Rosings Park with the rest of the Hunsford party, and could not recall a single instance where Miss de Bourgh had opened her mouth to speak other than in a brief whisper to her companion.

"I was sorry to hear of your mishap, Miss Bennet." Her visitor's voice was quiet, but perfectly distinct. "Your friend was distraught at your disappearance."

Elizabeth shook her head. "I feel very guilty about it. I would not have wished to cause such concern, especially to those I hold dear."

Miss de Bourgh smiled. "Everyone is very pleased that you are back, and recovering so well." She glanced at Elizabeth, as if wondering whether to say something. But she didn't, and the silence drew out.

Elizabeth smiled, it was for her to break the deadlock. "I am glad you've called, Miss de Bourgh. I was wondering if I'd ever have the opportunity to get to know you."

The young woman smiled. "Please call me Anne — but only when we're alone together. I think your cousin might tell my mother if he thinks you so impertinent."

Elizabeth smiled, laughing would make her head ache. "And I'm Elizabeth."

"Well, Elizabeth, I know that many people think I am quiet and uninteresting. But if you really know my mother, you would know it is a much easier life if she does not think to make any demands on me."

"I think it very clever, Anne." Elizabeth smiled. "I believe you are a most accomplished actress."

Anne got up, and looked outside the door. Then she closed it and came back to sit down close to her.

"I wonder if I might ask you something in confidence, Elizabeth?" Her voice was low and hurried.

"Of course." Elizabeth was curious, but waited quietly.

"I have seen how much confidence you have in your own abilities, and a belief that you can control your own future." Anne looked round nervously. "I'm sure you know that my mother is trying to push through a marriage for me that neither I, nor the gentleman, wants." She shook her head. "I don't know what to do."

Elizabeth reached out and touched her hand. "It's hard, having a burden like that, and not being able to tell anyone."

"It certainly is." Anne nodded. "Can you advise me what to do?"

Elizabeth squeezed the hand she held. "I think you already know — but you are concerned as to what will happen when you do."

"I can't think of anyone who would not be concerned."

"Neither can I. But if you are to avoid the marriage, it will have to be done — unless the gentleman concerned is very convincing in his refusal."

Anne looked down. "I think you know who it is, don't you?"

"Has he told your mother that he will not?"

"He has. Every time they visit, every meal, she starts. I don't know how he is so patient."

"Anne." Elizabeth leaned forward. "Does he know that you are such an astute young lady as you have just proved to me?"

She watched a flush steal over Anne's face. "No," she whispered.

"Perhaps he would not be so much against the

marriage if he knew it." Why did her heart feel so heavy? Mr. Darcy was nothing to her, nothing.

Anne looked up. "But I love another."

Elizabeth was silent, nonplussed, and Anne laughed. "Please don't tell anyone."

"Of course I won't." Elizabeth thought for a moment. "Do you ever go away, Anne? Just with your companion?"

"No." Anne shook her head. "I don't think I could manage that."

"That's a pity. I was thinking that you might tell your mother you want to take the waters in Bath, or something like that. Get away, have time to think. Or even …" she looked sideways at her. "… as a place to get away when you have had your say, and you want to leave her to calm down."

Anne laughed. "I have never dared to think what might happen when I tell her."

"So you know you will need to tell her," Elizabeth commented. "And what of the gentleman who holds your affections? Are they returned? Does he know what you are really like?"

Anne drooped. "I think they are, but I think he feels pity, too. And in any event, he is without fortune. Mother will never accept him."

"That's up to your mother." Elizabeth suddenly wondered if her words were too harsh. "I don't mean any offence. But you are over the age of consent — and you have fortune enough for both of you. It is far more important that he loves you and will care for you."

Anne stood up. She looked suddenly determined. "You're right. I must make a decision, and be prepared to make my life as I want it to be." She smiled down at Elizabeth. "After all, we none of us know how long it might be." She touched her hand. "I'm so glad you are well."

Elizabeth pushed herself to her feet. "Thank you for coming, I'm glad to have you as a friend."

"And I, you. But please don't tell *anyone*." Anne looked at her earnestly.

"I won't," Elizabeth promised readily. "I'm hoping that Charlotte permits me to come downstairs tomorrow for a little while."

"That will please Mr. Darcy." Anne said slyly, and was at the door before Elizabeth could say a word more.

She dropped back into the chair, very glad to be on her own. What had Anne meant by that last comment?

CHAPTER 31

*E*lizabeth held onto the bannister tightly as Charlotte helped her downstairs a few days later. Her legs were not nearly as weak as they'd been yesterday and Elizabeth had decided she must push herself back to health. She didn't want to sit around and be treated as a fragile, frail person.

Anne had said that she'd seen Elizabeth as confident and self-reliant. Elizabeth wanted to believe it until she could remember it.

Sitting in a comfortable chair in the back parlour, beside a fire built up high for her comfort, Elizabeth decided that this was enough progress for today, and that she would stay up at least until lunch.

"There you are, Lizzy." Charlotte pushed a

241

small table close to her. "I've brought down some of the books you were reading, and your sewing, just in case you feel like doing anything." She gave her a long look. "But I think you might be better just to sit and rest." She smiled. "And back up to bed after an hour."

Elizabeth smiled lazily. "You're very good to me, Charlotte. Thank you." She would argue against the hour when it happened, she decided.

"Yes, Cousin Elizabeth, you must do as my dear Charlotte bids you. Your duty is to recover as quickly as you can and not cause as much trouble again as you have been." Mr. Collins looked as if he was ready to lecture her further, but Charlotte touched his arm.

"Of course, dear, but Miss de Bourgh honoured us with her presence quite early the other day. It might be better if you watch from your book room in case Lady Catherine calls today."

She looked back and smiled at Elizabeth as she shepherded him from the room.

Elizabeth looked at the books, but she didn't quite feel up to reading. Perhaps this first time she could just rest. She could push herself harder when she wasn't quite so tired.

She wasn't sure how long she'd been just sitting there, almost asleep, when she heard the doorbell. There was no excited chatter from Mr. Collins, so

Elizabeth surmised the caller was not Lady Catherine. She turned her head towards the door as it opened.

Charlotte entered, "Lizzy, Mr. Darcy is here."

The man himself was following closely on her heels, hat and gloves in his hand.

Elizabeth wanted so much to stand easily and curtsy, but somehow her feet got tangled on the footstool, and her efforts did not have quite the effect she wished.

"Please remain seated, Miss Bennet." He stepped forward. "I would not have you strain yourself."

"I am much better, thank you, Mr. Darcy." her voice came out rather more sharply than she intended. She untangled her feet, and rose to curtsy. Then she sat down hastily again.

His lips twitched. "You do seem more yourself, Miss Bennet, I admit."

"Hmph!" Charlotte turned for the door. "I'll order tea."

Mr. Darcy sat down in the chair opposite her. His regard was steady and warm. "I'm pleased you're well enough to be downstairs, Miss Bennet. I trust you had a comfortable night?"

"Thank you, yes. Charlotte is very solicitous."

He must have surmised more from that than she had supposed he would; he was unable to prevent a smile, and his normally impassive face was transformed. Elizabeth looked away hastily.

Charlotte had come back into the room, and she smiled, too, not having heard Elizabeth's comment. The housekeeper carried in the tea tray, and conversation became more general.

Mr. Darcy did not stay long; after he had drunk his tea, he rose to depart.

"Thank you for your hospitality, Mrs. Collins." He turned to Elizabeth.

"I hope you do not stay downstairs too long on this first day, Miss Bennet. You are very pale."

She pursed her lips. "Thank you for your solicitude, Mr. Darcy." She knew he would remember her earlier comment. She rose to her feet to curtsy, and his lips twitched.

At the door, he looked back, smiling. "I think you may have a difficult guest, Mrs. Collins."

Elizabeth sat down and looked away. Independent, self-reliant. She must do this.

"Oh, and I have asked the doctor to return to check on your progress, Miss Bennet. I hope that is in order."

"I don't think it necessary, Mr. Darcy. It is a long way from London." She knew she sounded tart. "If there is any concern, I'm sure the local apothecary can be called."

He bowed. "I trust you will indulge me in this,

Miss Bennet. I wish to ask him how long he feels you need to remain here, so that I might write to your father with his advice."

"Oh." Elizabeth was disconcerted. "Have you heard from Papa?"

He smiled slightly. "I write to him each day with whatever news I can glean, Miss Bennet. He writes in return. I have explained to him that you have sprained your wrist and that is why you haven't written home."

He looked a little anxious. "I have sent him your best wishes, even though I had not seen you here before today. I hope you are not offended."

"No, of course not." Elizabeth was dismayed. "Thank you, I ought to have thought of it myself."

"Not at all. Until you are recovered, there is nothing for you to do." He bowed again and was gone.

She was alone for a few moments to think on what had been said. Then Charlotte came back into the room, smiling.

"You must admit, Mr. Darcy is very concerned for your well-being, Lizzy."

Elizabeth merely shrugged; she didn't want to talk about him. "I suppose that as Papa has asked him to undertake to get me home, he feels responsible. But I cannot for the life of me think why. Papa could come here, couldn't he?"

"He *was* here, Lizzy." Charlotte came and sat in the chair on the other side of the fire. "He was staying here, searching for you." She reached across, and took her hand. "Lizzy, I will never forget how awful he looked, broken down with fear that he'd lost you." There was a short silence. "Mr. Darcy was so kind to him. He promised he'd never give up searching for you and that he'd write every day if your father went home to rest with your family."

Elizabeth stared into the fire. She would not weep, she would not — at least, not until she was alone. But the guilt would sit heavy in her heart for a long time, she knew.

"Charlotte, will you help me bind something round my wrist? I think I could write then. I must write to Papa and apologise for the distress I caused him." She looked over at her friend. "And I apologise to you, too. You're very good to me, and I've been such a problem."

Charlotte got up and embraced her. "You're my friend, Lizzy. Now, I will help you write to your father — after you've had a rest." She smiled. "Mr. Darcy was right. You are very pale."

All right, I won't argue today." Elizabeth struggled to her feet. "But I want to walk by myself. You don't need to support me."

Charlotte rolled her eyes. "That's my Lizzy back!"

CHAPTER 32

Two mornings later, Elizabeth was sitting downstairs again, this time at the table. Her wrist was improving; she was determined to be able to make notes, and wanted to work out a plan of study of her notes to see what she had forgotten.

But she hadn't had much time. Each day, Mr. Darcy called, sometimes accompanied the other gentleman, whom she now knew was Colonel Fitzwilliam, Mr. Darcy's cousin.

But Mr. Darcy was alone when he called that morning.

Charlotte showed him in. "Lizzy, might you be all right if Maria sits with you and writes her letters? I have arranged to see one of the ladies of the parish who is unwell."

Elizabeth smiled at Maria, who was still overawed by any visitors from Rosings Park. "Of course. It is perfectly all right."

The housekeeper brought in tea, and Elizabeth reached over to pour it. As she handed Mr. Darcy his cup, he thanked her, and the glint in his eye told her he was not going to say anything about her doing too much. Her lips curved, and she decided to try him further. She rose to her feet and picked up Maria's cup and saucer in her left hand. But when the cup rattled on the saucer, he rose to his feet.

"Please allow me." He reached over and took it from her.

She sighed, and he chuckled as he returned to his seat. "I can see that being an invalid has palled somewhat, Miss Bennet."

"Indeed. It feels a long time since I was even able to stroll in the gardens." She looked longingly outside. "It's such a lovely day."

He looked at her thoughtfully. "It is quite warm outside today; but do you think you are able to walk out without tiring yourself too much? If you wish, I could walk in the garden with you."

She knew her eyes brightened. "I would be very happy if we could do that."

"But, Lizzy, you can barely get up and down the stairs yet," Maria objected.

Elizabeth clenched her jaw and looked away. If

she did not, she might snap at Maria, and she must not do that. But disappointment weighed her down.

"Miss Bennet," his voice was very gentle. "I can see you're disappointed, and since there are no stairs outside, if you can bring yourself to take my arm, we might try a short walk outside."

How he had divined her feelings, she didn't know, but she would not decline the offer.

"Thank you, Mr. Darcy. I would enjoy taking the air." She turned to Maria.

"Perhaps you could fetch our coats."

IT WAS HARD NOT to lean too heavily on him as they walked very slowly along the path beside the house. But she was determined not to. She must demonstrate that she was well on the road to recovery — because she was. The problems she was having with her memory must resolve soon, she was determined. Each afternoon she pushed herself to remember more.

He looked behind; Maria was out of earshot. "Can you tell me what discomposes you, Miss Bennet?" He wasn't looking at her, as if it might be easier for her to speak if he seemed less concerned. "Doctor Moore is certain there is something you are reluctant to talk about, and it causes him some disquiet."

Elizabeth grimaced. Doctor Moore was an understanding man who seemed to know what was troubling her without her having admitted to anything. While she had confessed to having headaches, she had assured him that this was improving.

But she would not admit to him the anxiety that she could not recall facts in the way that she had been used to, or her fear that it might never improve. But it seemed that she had not been entirely convincing in her assurances.

"There is nothing that concerns me, Mr. Darcy. My only thought was when I might be able to go home."

He glanced down, and there was doubt in his eyes. "The two hour journey here caused you quite a setback, Miss Bennet. I would be worried were you to travel such a long way too early in your recovery."

She knew he was right, but she did want to go home. "I might be able to break the journey at my aunt and uncle's house in London, and then travel on a few days later."

"That way, you would not be home any sooner," he remarked. "Are you so anxious to leave this house?"

She smiled ruefully. "I suppose that is part of it. But you are right about not getting home any sooner." She looked round the garden; she might have to admit the need to go back indoors soon. "Did the doctor say when he thought I might be able to go home?"

He hesitated. "It might be managed if we could build up some sort of comfortable way for you to lie down in the coach for most of the journey. The roads are mostly quite good." He looked down at her. "Would you like me to make some plans for your early return?"

She stopped and looked out into the distance. "I would, Mr. Darcy, if you please." It would, at the very least, mean she was her father's responsibility once more, so this unsettling gentleman would not be able to say what she might, or might not, do.

"Very well. But I think it's time you returned to the parlour, Miss Bennet." He seemed thoughtful and distracted as they went back into the house.

Charlotte had just got home, and was hurrying through toward them. "Lizzy, I'm sure you're not well enough to walk out. Did you tell Mr. Darcy you were?"

Mr. Darcy chuckled. "I'm afraid I encouraged it, Mrs. Collins. Do not remonstrate with Miss Bennet, and I assure you we have not been outside many minutes." His arm tightened on her hand.

"But, perhaps you had better sit down, Miss Bennet. It is not beneficial for you to stand too long."

Charlotte looked a little mollified, but was still slightly disapproving as she took Elizabeth's other arm and hurried her through to the parlour.

It was not very long before Mr. Darcy took his leave and Elizabeth was rather dismayed that he did not talk to her friend about arranging her journey home.

As SHE ATE lunch with the others, Elizabeth forced herself to seem cheerful and involved. But behind her conversation, she began to ponder how she would work to improve. It had been quite long enough; and it was time she was well.

When they got up from the table, Charlotte came up to her.

"Let me help you upstairs, Lizzy. After your walk in the garden this morning, you ought to rest for a while."

Elizabeth smiled affectionately at her friend. "You're right, Charlotte, of course. But I will be able to climb the stairs, I'm sure."

She did climb the stairs without assistance, although her friend walked beside her.

"I sense a new determination within you, Lizzy." Charlotte's sly look made Elizabeth laugh. "Just do not climb out of the window for any midnight walks."

"I can safely promise you that." Elizabeth sat on the bed. "I can't thank you enough for looking after me so well."

"Your thanks will be better shown by not doing too much." Charlotte frowned at her. "I know that look in your eye."

They laughed together in a way that Elizabeth thought hadn't been that way for a while.

But Charlotte was relentless. "I think you might have forgotten what the doctor said when he came. That you had a number of days when you could not eat or drink anything because you were insensible, and that your body has a number of poisons within it that are the reasons you are still tired and weak. I hope you remember that he said you will recover more quickly if you do not try to do too much, too soon."

Elizabeth grimaced. "Thanks for reminding me, Charlotte." She hadn't even been able to remember that, and she wished she could remember the all the events of recent weeks.

She remembered some things — refusing Mr. Collins' offer of marriage, her dismay as Charlotte married him; but she didn't remember coming to stay here, nor the incident that had led to her current situation.

And why was Mr. Darcy so closely involved with the situation at all? Papa didn't even really know him, except as Mr. Bingley's friend.

Charlotte had explained that he was Lady Catherine's nephew on a visit to that lady. But what Elizabeth hadn't liked to ask was why he'd taken such a role after she was found. She was sure there was something — something, in her mind that she must unlock, must discover.

She decided that perhaps she might lie on her bed for a short while. She could think about him, then. Think about his intense, dark gaze; his unfailing courtesy. But surely he could remember their last meeting? That she had told him that he was the last person on earth she would ever marry? She had accused him of arrogance, conceit, and selfish disdain of others. Those moments had come back to haunt her, but he never alluded to them. Did he think she hadn't remembered?

She could hardly ask him. She knew she was smiling as she could feel sleep stealing over her. He was certainly being most gentlemanly now.

CHAPTER 33

*D*arcy leaned back in the chair in his bedchamber. Richard stood by the mantel, regarding him curiously. There was nowhere downstairs that they could talk without the risk of Lady Catherine intruding, and Darcy was heartily tired of it all. But he needed to be here.

He wondered how Richard occupied his time when he did not call at Hunsford with him. Perhaps he ought not to be so occupied with Miss Bennet.

"Why not sit down, Richard? We might have a whisky up here before going down for dinner."

"We can do that." Richard reached for the bell to summon Darcy's valet.

"You're looking out of sorts, Richard." Darcy stared into his glass. "I'm sorry, I have been too taken up by Miss Bennet and her recovery."

Richard shrugged. "Since you told me that you had made her an offer, Darcy, I understand your feelings. But has she not yet remembered that she refused you?"

Darcy shook his head, "I dread that happening. But I am trying to learn my lesson, and be more gentlemanly."

Richard laughed mirthlessly. "If you do wed, you will have an interesting time." He took a gulp of his drink. "But I will warn you, Darcy. Lady Catherine has had enough of your failure to pay Cousin Anne the attention she believes is due. She will have her say today."

Darcy regarded him thoughtfully. "What would you have me say?"

Richard shrugged a little. "It is not for me to tell you."

RICHARD HAD BEEN RIGHT. Lady Catherine began within a few moments of them sitting down for dinner.

"Darcy, I have written to your uncle about you spending so much time at Hunsford. I expect you will hear from him forthwith." She looked down her nose disapprovingly. "You will be causing expectations in a young woman and her family — a young woman who is totally unsuitable to marry in every single aspect."

Darcy watched the footmen moving round the table, serving the soup and bread. When it was completed, he took bread from the platter offered, and placed it carefully, neatly, on his side plate. Then he looked up calmly at his aunt. She was an interesting puce colour from having to wait for his answer, he noted dispassionately.

"I agree she is from a family that must very materially lessen her chance of marrying a man of any consideration in the world, Lady Catherine." He saw she was about to interrupt, and raised his voice slightly. "However, I have made an undertaking to her father that I would see her returned to her family once she is well enough." He bent a stern gaze on his aunt. "I hope you understand that I am a gentleman, and I will keep my word."

"Yes, yes!" She wasn't really listening, he knew. "But she will harbour ideas above her station if you continue to call there each day!" She favoured him with her most imperious stare. "But if your engagement to Anne is formally announced, and the date set, then Miss Bennet will not be able to plan to ensnare you!"

He almost laughed. Far from wanting to ensnare him, Miss Bennet had refused his offer. The shock and pain of it still made him disinclined to dwell on the memory, but Lady Catherine was very wrong about her.

Richard coughed, and he realised he had been silent for too long.

"I'm sorry, Lady Catherine, you appear to have forgotten that I have told you repeatedly that I will not marry Cousin Anne. I could not make her happy, and I think it unkind of you to keep raising the subject in your daughter's presence." He glanced at Cousin Anne, she was looking down, appearing not to listen; and he wondered what her feelings actually were.

"Yes, yes!" she repeated again. "But you are foolish, Darcy. You know very well that marriages can be built well from within family responsibilities. And, as you said, you are a gentleman; so of course you will ensure that Anne is happy." She leaned forward. "Just think, by uniting the great estates of Rosings and Pemberley, you will preside over probably the largest estate outside the aristocracy."

He stared at her. "What would I want with Rosings? I have Pemberley, and wealth enough, Lady Catherine." He was tired of saying it. "I repeat, I will not marry your daughter." He sighed. "Perhaps we ought to leave Rosings, we have been here for too long."

He glanced at Richard, surprising a peculiar expression on his face. He didn't see that Darcy was watching him, he was looking at Cousin Anne, and Darcy was thunderstruck to see them exchange a glance.

All through dinner, he remained silent, refusing to be drawn further by his aunt; pondering over what he had seen. Was Anne de Bourgh perhaps more able than he had even considered? Was she able to speak and converse? Remorsefully, he wondered why he had never bothered to get to know her, find out what her hopes and dreams were, too.

And, he had to acknowledge Miss Bennet had been right when she had accused him of *arrogance, pride and a selfish disdain for the feelings of others*. He kept his gaze on his dinner, feeling a flush of shame.

He would speak to Richard over the port. But if he was to be properly worthy of gaining Miss Bennet's trust, he must think of this cousin too. He thought back. Might Richard have some affection for Cousin Anne? If so, why did Lady Catherine not see it?

It was a great relief when the ladies rose to withdraw, and the butler placed the port at his side, and closed the door silently. He and Richard were alone.

He filled his glass, and passed the decanter to Richard. They sat in silence for some minutes, it seemed Richard was not inclined to be garrulous today.

Darcy wondered how to raise the topic. What would Elizabeth want of him? How did Richard feel? He knew he must consider his feelings, he was closer to him than a brother could ever have been.

"I must apologise to you, Richard." He glanced over. His cousin was turning the glass round and round in his hand. He didn't answer.

"You've helped me a great deal," he tried again. "Might I be able to assist you?"

There was a haunted look in his cousin's expression. "What could you do?"

Darcy took a deep breath. "What do you need me to do?"

Richard shrugged. "I don't know what is to be done," he shook his head hopelessly.

Could he speak delicately enough? Darcy knew he had to try. "Forgive me if I have been blind before, but I saw just now the way you looked at her." He drew a deep breath. "Does she return your affections?"

Richard looked at him without warmth. "She has been ignored by all the family, you included, Darcy. But, yes. She does."

"My felicitations, Richard." Darcy smiled thinly. "I would be delighted to assist you in …"

"Stop, stop!" Richard waved his hands. "It is impossible, we don't know how to proceed." His shoulders slumped. "Lady Catherine would never permit it." He looked up, a wry smile on his face. "She might say Miss Bennet has an unsuitable family, but who — who — would choose Lady Catherine as a mother-in-law?"

Darcy couldn't prevent a grimace. "You might live on the Matlock estate. She would not travel to Derbyshire often."

His friend looked desolate. "I could not ask her to leave her mother." He regained his humorous look. "Neither am I prepared to live here."

Darcy chuckled. That was Richard, indeed.

Richard looked up. "But it is all beside the point. Lady Catherine will never consent to our union."

"I don't see why not," Darcy argued. "You are more eligible than I, as the son of an earl. Fortune is not needed, Rosings is a wealthy estate in itself."

"Lady Catherine will not see it that way," Richard shrugged.

Darcy observed him thoughtfully. "I think we must make a plan, Richard. If I tell her that we will leave tomorrow, and that I will not return, then she must begin to accept it. Then in London, you may obtain a special licence — Anne is of full age, she does not need her mother's consent." He reached for the decanter. "We just need to find a way for you to speak to her before we leave tomorrow."

Richard followed his lead in pouring another drink. "If it is not too early, we can call at Hunsford to bid them farewell. I expect I can indicate to Anne to have called there to speak to Miss Bennet."

Darcy frowned. "Has she done so before?"

"Of course," Richard laughed. "She has called a number of times. She tells me that Miss Bennet is a very astute lady and has given her very welcome advice."

"Cousin Anne? And Miss Bennet?" Darcy was nonplussed.

"Yes, of course." His cousin was amused. "There's a lot you miss, Darcy, stuck in your own thoughts." He drained his glass. "We had better join the ladies. And I will thank you to keep Lady Catherine in conversation so that I might indicate to our cousin the plan for tomorrow morning."

CHAPTER 34

The next morning, Darcy and his cousin walked over to the parsonage. His steward and valet were loading up the second coach with their luggage, assisted by Richard's batman, and they would shortly leave for London. Darcy's coach would be brought round to Hunsford within the hour.

He was unsure how Miss Bennet would receive the news that he was returning to London without having arranged her return to Hertfordshire; and he was discomposed trying to think how to explain to her the new plan he was formulating in his mind, without having to tell her the reason behind it.

He wondered what Cousin Anne had been talking about with Miss Bennet. What did such ladies talk about? And surely his cousin could not hold a sensible conversation? That had been assumed by the family for as long as he could remember. He was overcome by shame that he had never questioned it.

The housekeeper answered the doorbell, and melted at the sight of Richard's smile, opening the door wide for them. The sound of laughter emanated from the parlour, and he found himself smiling too, as he followed Richard into the room.

His eyes turned at once to Miss Bennet; she had risen with the other ladies, and curtsied as he and Richard bowed. She glanced at Anne, caution in her eyes, and he wondered just what she knew.

With Mrs. Collins and her sister in the group, there would not be the privacy he craved to speak to her, tell her why he had to leave Kent, but he must try and explain in a way which would not distress her too much.

He approached the chair near her. "May I?"

"Of course, Mr. Darcy." She waited for him to take his seat, but her gaze was challenging. "I under-stand you and your cousin are returning to London?"

He hid a wince. Cousin Anne must have told her. He forced a smile.

"I trust you suffered no ill-effects from your turn in the garden yesterday, Miss Bennet. I wonder if you might care to repeat it this morning?"

"I think it is a good idea," Richard said heartily. "Would you join us, too, Cousin Anne?"

Darcy and Richard waited in the hall while the ladies donned their coats; then he offered Miss Bennet his arm, and Richard did the same for their cousin. Soon he was strolling with her along the path by the house in the most privacy they could obtain.

"Thank you, Mr. Darcy." Miss Bennet drew a deep breath. "The chance to walk outside is limited while I am here."

"I think Mrs. Collins is solicitous of your health, Miss Bennet." He must try and ensure she was reasonably happy to remain here for a few more days. "She was so distraught at your disappearance that I think she must be anxious that you remain well."

She sighed. "I understand." She glanced at him. "I also understand why you feel you must leave for London. I bear you no grudge, Mr. Darcy. I will write to my father, asking if he can make plans to send his coach for me."

Darcy shook his head. "Please allow me a few days, Miss Bennet. I intend to go to Hertfordshire tomorrow or on Thursday, and will speak to your father about the safest way to convey you to Longbourn without risking your recovery." He smiled down at her. "I was of the mind that my coach can be made comfortable, and that your sister and a maid might wish to come here with it to accompany you and Miss Lucas home."

She brightened perceptibly. "Oh, that would be very helpful. I was concerned that Maria might feel the responsibility of my welfare more than is appropriate for her years."

He nodded, quite happy that she had accepted his statement that he still intended to assist her. "Did my cousin tell you of our impending departure?"

She laughed musically. "Indeed she did! I think she is a little discomposed; but she understands the reason behind your decision."

He hesitated, he couldn't ask her what he really wished to. "I hope you and she have enjoyed each other's company."

"Oh, yes! I have learned so much from her strength and resilience," she mused. "And her stoicism, when things cannot be changed. I hope she has also gained something from our friendship, and we have promised to write to each other."

"I'm very glad. I think her chances at friendship are somewhat limited." *By me, as much as her mother.*

"I hope things can change soon for her." Miss Bennet glanced across at the other path, where Richard and Cousin Anne were in deep conversation.

Darcy felt acutely guilty. Why had he not seen;

not noticed? "Do you think there is any way in which I might be of assistance?"

Miss Bennet looked up at him. "I understand you have made an even firmer declaration to your aunt. That must help matters."

"And might you have thought of an even stronger way to convince my aunt on the matter?"

She smiled as she walked on. He must remember she was an observant young lady, she had quite possibly got the measure of Lady Catherine.

"I think you might need to wait — it will not be long — but when Anne is ready to stand up to her mother, she might appreciate both you and Colonel Fitzwilliam beside her." She grimaced. "And have somewhere ready where she might go and stay until her mother understands that Anne will make her own decisions."

"We could do that." Darcy wondered if Anne would ever actually be able to do it. He found Lady Catherine intimidating enough.

Miss Bennet looked up at him. "Might your uncle and aunt — the Colonel's family — welcome her? Or would they be against the match?"

He was silent, and she pressed on.

"I would not have spoken out, Mr. Darcy, and broken her confidence; but I can see from the way you are looking at them that you now know the situation. I think your cousin will also welcome your approval. He must feel himself unable to support a wife." She sighed. "I think I would like to return to the house, please. Maybe Mrs. Jenkinson can be outside so that they can continue their discourse."

"Of course." He was dismayed that he had not had longer to speak to her, but, if she was admitting fatigue, it must be significant, or she would try to hide it from him.

CHAPTER 35

*A*s the view of Rosings Park vanished behind the coach, Darcy glanced at Richard.

"I hope you were able to explain to Cousin Anne why I was taking you from Kent."

Richard didn't turn to face him, but he saw a dark flush on the back of his cousin's neck, and he couldn't prevent a smile.

"Do I understand that she is more hopeful of being able to accept your advances, Richard?"

His cousin smiled ruefully. "I am not as good an actor as I had hoped — even for your unobservant eyes!"

Darcy smiled, too. "I spoke to Miss Bennet, of course. She said she could see from my gaze that I knew your situation so she felt free to tell me that she thought it would not be long before Anne would appreciate us beside her when she stands up to her mother."

"Did she?" Richard's head jerked round.

Darcy nodded, startled by his cousin's surprise. But Richard seemed to force control.

"I would be glad of your support, Darcy," he said formally.

Darcy smiled tightly. "I'd like to atone somewhat for my unforgivable failure to see what was before my very eyes." He grimaced. "Poor Anne."

He remembered his discomfort as he'd approached her as she walked in the garden with Richard. Once Miss Bennet was seated in the parlour, she had suggested he join his cousins. Mrs. Jenkinson was sitting reading beside the backdoor and Anne and Richard were deep in conversation. It was then that Darcy realised they had been part of her support, keeping her secret to make her life easier for her. He had not been in their confidence — and had been too unobservant to see it.

But when he spoke to her he discovered Anne to be a generous-spirited young lady with a mischievous sense of humour. No wonder she and Miss Bennet had found much in common.

He pushed his thoughts away, and smiled at Richard. "It is an interesting puzzle when looked at from the outside, although I can understand the frustration for you."

"Yes," Richard almost groaned. "Do we tell my parents that she is more able than they have believed, and risk Lady Catherine finding out before Anne is able to leave Rosings? Or do we allow Anne to tell her mother first, and come to Matlock House with us, and risk them sending Anne back rather than risking a rift with Lady Catherine?"

"I was more concerned with what happens if Lady Catherine will not sanction your marriage, and therefore deprives Anne of her rightful allowances."

Richard shrugged hopelessly. "That is why we have done nothing for so long, Darcy."

"You must not let it concern you. If both of you wish to marry, then do so. Lady Catherine will come round, when she realises that you are both happy. Until she does, you can use the dower house at Pemberley if your father does not suggest you use the one at Hayden Hall."

The dawning hope in Richard's eyes was all the thanks he needed, and he brushed off his attempt to put it into words.

"It is nothing, Richard. You have been a good friend to me for long enough. I know that I can never repay you."

His mind turned to Miss Bennet. "Might you

permit me to visit Netherfield first and ensure that arrangements are made to convey Miss Bennet back to her home? Then I will be able to give you all my attention until you are settled."

Richard guffawed, and Darcy gazed at him in astonishment.

"You will not be able to give me all your attention, Darcy, as you will wish to court Miss Bennet." Richard sobered. "But I understand you will be happier when she is with her family, and then I will welcome your assistance for a few days until our cousin is away from her mother." He looked directly over. "Please ensure there is no possibility of my family finding out that Anne is more able than her mother realises, or her life may be more uncomfortable than it already is."

Darcy shook his head. "We must be quick. By Cousin Anne being generous enough to visit Miss Bennet, the occupants of the parsonage know — at least the ladies do. I have no confidence that young Miss Lucas might not let something drop to Mr. Collins and he will not fail to inform Lady Catherine."

His cousin's downcast expression was enough to inform him that the risk was known to be severe, and he was sorry that he'd brought him away.

"I understand, Darcy. How long must you be in Hertfordshire?"

Darcy thought quickly. "I believe Bingley is still at Netherfield. If I take you to London, you may then do what you need to regarding the special licence and other matters. I can go directly on to Hertfordshire and conclude my business at Longbourn. Then I can be on my way back to London at dawn tomorrow." He smiled, although he felt uneasy. "It means Miss Bennet might not get home as soon as she wishes, but Anne might find her support helpful while she remains in Kent."

Richard nodded. "Perhaps we can return to Kent tomorrow afternoon?"

Darcy's heart tightened. He wished very much to be back, calling on Miss Bennet, but return to Rosings Park so soon? "Perhaps early on Thursday might be better. Lady Catherine will feel triumphant if I return too soon."

Richard grinned, despite his urgent desire to return. "Oh, yes! I think if we return very early on Thursday, you could call directly at the Parsonage, and I will go to Rosings and suggest I accompany Anne to call on Miss Bennet. Then we might plan our attack."

"Is Anne as ready as that?" Darcy was surprised.

Richard slumped back against the seat. "I don't know. But I would not care for her to feel alone at Rosings if her mother finds out the truth."

"You might offer her the opportunity to stay at

Darcy House as a guest of Georgiana, if she is anxious about going to your parents immediately." Darcy tried to reassure Richard. "Georgiana would welcome her, she seems very happy at the moment — entirely due to you managing to engineer her encounter with Jonathan and his friends." He chuckled. "She tells me she is at the theatre or opera with Mrs. Annesley or your mother quite often."

It was the middle of the afternoon when Darcy presented himself wearily at Longbourn and asked to see Mr. Bennet. When he was shown into the library, Bennet rose to his feet and bowed respectfully.

"Mr. Darcy, I'm very pleased to see you. I wanted to thank you in person for your help in recovering Lizzy and ensuring her welfare." He turned to the decanter. "Whisky? Or would you prefer tea?"

Darcy smiled. "A small whisky would be welcome, thank you." He took the glass. "And there is no need to thank me. I gave you my assurance as a gentleman that I would find your daughter, and that is what I have done."

"As you wish." Bennet glanced at him. "But my gratitude remains."

They sat in quiet, comfortable silence for a few moments. Darcy was not even discomposed by the sound of Mrs. Bennet's piercing complaints through the closed door. He smiled slightly. If Richard was prepared to have Lady Catherine as a mother-in-law, then he could hardly baulk at this lady. A heavy feeling inside reminded him of his unconscionable words when he had made Miss Bennet an offer, and her stinging rejection. He dreaded the time she would remember, and her expression would turn accusingly to him.

Bennet was talking and Darcy exerted himself to attend.

"Lizzy appears to be recovering steadily, Mr. Darcy. She writes to me most days, although her letters are short — I think her wrist still pains her."

Darcy nodded. "I think you are correct, sir." He smiled reluctantly. "I think she becomes impatient that the improvement is slower than she wishes." He frowned. "I accompanied her in the garden this morning again — she likes taking the air — but she asked to return to the house within a few minutes, whereas yesterday she managed a little longer."

Bennet eyed him. "Lizzy was always impatient, Mr. Darcy. I am sure she is determined to be well enough to travel home soon." He shook his head. "I am more concerned that she seems so downcast about her memory. As you know, she prided herself

— overmuch, I thought — on her sharpness of mind and her learning. She is finding it difficult to recall facts she once knew, and relearning them is proving problematic. It seems to be causing her the most distress at the moment."

Darcy glanced over. "She has not mentioned it to me. But …"

"I did not expect her to have done so," Bennet interrupted. "She has it fixed in her mind that most gentlemen despise ladies who wish to advance their learning." He huffed a laugh. "I would have been happy if she had not recalled *that* after her accident."

Darcy smiled mechanically, unamused. Had that been part of her refusal to him? He must think about it. But Bennet was speaking; he must undertake his consideration later.

"I wonder how soon you might think it wise for me to send my coach for Lizzy, Mr. Darcy. I know she is impatient, but it is a long way, and I must plan for the horses to be spared from the farm and find …"

Darcy shook his head. "Do not be concerned about that, Mr. Bennet. I have a very comfortable coach which can be made available when needed. The physician I have called in tells me that when Miss Bennet is fit to move, it would be better if a bed was built up in the coach, so that she might rest.

I have that in hand already." He looked at him. "I was wondering if it might be possible that Miss Kitty and a maid can travel to Kent to accompany her home. I know she is concerned that Miss Lucas might be anxious about being solely responsible for her."

The man's eyes widened. "It is a point I had not thought of." He nodded thoughtfully. "I think it would be better if they did not travel until Lizzy is actually ready to come home, Mr. Darcy." His smile was a little sly. "Kitty might be reluctant to leave for an extended period while Mr. Bingley is at Netherfield."

"I understand." Darcy wondered if that meant Miss Bennet's attempt to get Bingley to transfer his affections to Miss Kitty had borne fruit. He smiled slightly, he would find out from Bingley tonight, no doubt. "I do not think she is quite fit yet, sir, even though she thinks she might be." He hesitated. "I am intending to stay at Netherfield tonight, and return to London in the morning. After a small business matter I need to attend to, I will return to Kent on Thursday morning. I will write to you when I propose to arrange matters and then I can send a maid with the coach to collect Miss Kitty."

Bennet rose and turned to the decanter. "Another?"

Darcy shook his head. "Thank you, no. I will

leave in a moment. I did wish to ask, though; Miss Bennet has referred to her aunt and uncle in London, and at one point suggested she might journey home over two days, resting at their home between. Might that be more appropriate to your thinking?"

Bennet's face lit up. "Now, that is a good thought. She might be able to travel sooner if she can take several days between." He looked at his guest. "I have the impression from her letters that she wishes to leave Hunsford parsonage as soon as possible."

A twinge of guilt hit Darcy. He could have speeded her transfer to London, he supposed. "Are you able to explain why, sir?"

Bennet glanced at him. "I don't suppose it is so very secret. Collins is my cousin, and heir to this estate under the terms of the entail. He made Lizzy an offer of marriage; encouraged, I may say, by my wife. Lizzy, as I expected, refused. Then, within two or three days, he made an offer to her most intimate friend, who accepted. I think Lizzy finds his company uncongenial, and her friendship with his wife more uncomfortable than before. I'm not surprised she wishes to come home. And if it means breaking her journey in London, then I will consent to that."

Darcy bowed. "If you might furnish me with the direction, I will make whatever arrangements Miss Bennet wishes — that the doctor approves of."

CHAPTER 36

*E*lizabeth woke to another morning at Hunsford. How many weeks had she been here now? *Far too long*. She shivered, when would she finally get home?

Mr. Darcy and the colonel had left on Tuesday morning. He had told her he would then go to her father the next day or Thursday. It was Thursday today. She was ashamed to admit to herself that she missed his calls. She knew that once he had secured her back to her family, she would not see him again; and though the pain of her heart was acute as she thought of it, she would welcome the chance to forget about him.

Having refused his offer with such vehemence and certainty, he was not going to renew his advances to her, she knew that with absolute conviction. That he had been kind and generous to her, she knew as well, and had all the time in the world when resting in her chamber, to regret most bitterly having poured such scorn upon him that day.

She rolled over and buried her face in her pillow. But he had not reminded her of his proposal and her refusal. She supposed it would be a difficult subject to approach, unless he were thinking of renewing his offer. She pressed the pillow over her ears, as if to shut out the taunting impossibility of it.

"Lizzy! Are you unwell?" she heard the muffled voice of her friend, and groaned.

Rolling back over, she forced a smile. "Do not be concerned, Charlotte, I am well. I just — was just enjoying waking up in a leisurely way, that is all."

"Hmm." Charlotte eyed her suspiciously. "Well, do you want to stay in bed a little longer? I can tell you that Mr. Collins is away from home today, visiting a neighbouring parish."

Elizabeth smiled, and sat up. "I am going to get up, Charlotte. But I would have anyway, not because of what you have just told me."

Charlotte laughed and nodded. "Of course." She turned for the door. "I will send Clare up to you."

"No need, Charlotte; if she brings some hot water, I can manage very well."

Two HOURS LATER, Elizabeth sat quietly in the parlour. Charlotte and Maria were industriously working at their needlework but Elizabeth had placed her book open on the table beside her.

Turning the pages occasionally so she didn't attract attention, she read not a word. Instead she pondered her feelings. How soon would Mr. Darcy arrange that his coach might take her home to Longbourn? Would Kitty be happy to come here and accompany her home? It would be much the best course, because she knew Maria's anxiety would mean Elizabeth had to shoulder the responsibility of controlling the journey.

She wondered if she would be able to do the journey in a single day, and bit her lip. It would be better if she stopped at Gracechurch Street, she confessed to herself, she couldn't imagine staying in the coach all day.

But Kitty wouldn't want to stay there. Her letters had been full of Mr. Bingley, and his calls upon her at Longbourn. Elizabeth was delighted and it confirmed that she'd been right to encourage him to transfer his attentions to Kitty. But if he was going to make her an offer, Elizabeth ought not to ask for her to come to Kent.

There was a ring at the doorbell. Elizabeth

looked up, not much interested. It could not be Mr. Darcy or the colonel. Perhaps it was Anne de Bourgh, if so, she would be pleased to see her. But she hadn't called yesterday, and she'd had no chance to talk to her after the gentlemen had called on Tuesday, when they had walked separately in the gardens with them.

The housekeeper opened the door to the parlour. "Mr. Darcy, madam."

To her startled eyes, he looked tired. But his eyes were on her at once, and she dropped her gaze, flushing; though she rose with the ladies and curtsied.

"Good day, Mrs. Collins, Miss Bennet, Miss Lucas," he greeted them with grave politeness.

"Sit down, Mr. Darcy." Charlotte stayed standing. "You look fatigued from your journey. I will order tea." And she bustled from the room.

Maria dropped her eyes to her needlework, overawed all over again at their august visitor. Elizabeth smiled secretly to herself, she doubted Maria's nerves would ever make her less tongue-tied in company. But as she was only fourteen, Elizabeth supposed there was plenty of time for her to gain confidence.

She was suddenly aware of the silence and looked over at him, seeing him regarding her with some concern. But before she could say anything, the sound of the door opening heralded Charlotte returning to the room.

"Did you return to Rosings Park last night, Mr. Darcy?" Charlotte enquired. "Mr. Collins will be sorry to have missed you."

Elizabeth was watching closely, but he was perfectly calm, able to contain the distaste which she was certain he must feel.

"No." He smiled courteously at Charlotte. "My cousin and I travelled from London this morning. He has gone on to Rosings to ask Miss de Bourgh if she would care to call here this morning with him."

Their conversation continued politely while Elizabeth sat and thought about what he had said. Why had they both not gone to Rosings? Had he been to Longbourn? Did the fact that the colonel was bringing Anne here mean that something was about to happen? And what did that mean for her chances of going home?

She knew he wanted to speak to her, but also that they were unlikely to have any privacy this morning. She must contain any impatience until he might have the opportunity. In the meantime, she ought to assist Charlotte in the conversation.

"I hope your business was satisfactorily completed, Mr. Darcy," she ventured at last.

His gaze was warm. "Thank you, Miss Bennet. It was, indeed. But I wished to return here and begin to plan your return to Hertfordshire when you are well enough."

He had remembered, she had begun to wonder if he would begin to resent the commitment once he had returned to his own life in London. She smiled happily. "I'm grateful for you taking the time for it, Mr. Darcy. I confess I am beginning to miss my sisters."

CHAPTER 37

"*I*t's a long way, Lizzy," Charlotte intervened. "I'm not sure you're quite ready yet." She gave her a worried look. "You're very welcome to stay here as long as you need to, I wouldn't like to see you have any sort of setback again."

"I'm sure I'll be all right, Charlotte," Elizabeth knew she didn't sound very convincing, but she did want to get away from here.

"As you know, Miss Bennet, I was going to speak to your father about the matter, and I went to Longbourn on Tuesday afternoon," he said, and her heart swelled within her. He had kept his promise.

She tried to stop her eyes shining as she looked at him, knowing that Charlotte was looking suspiciously between them. "And what did you and Papa decide, Mr. Darcy?"

He smiled at her impatience. "He is happy that Mrs. Collins is content to let you stay here until the doctor considers you well enough to travel."

"And …?" She knew there was something else.

"He agreed with your original thought that it would be helpful for you to break your journey for one or more nights at your aunt and uncle's home in London." He looked over at Maria. "And you, too, of course, Miss Lucas."

"Does that mean I can go sooner?" Elizabeth suddenly realised it might seem to Charlotte that she wasn't happy here and she turned to her in dismay. She wouldn't like to upset her.

"It's all right, Lizzy. I know you are impatient to return to your books and study." Charlotte seemed more amused than upset.

Mr. Darcy nodded. "Yesterday, on my return to London, I called upon your aunt." He smiled at Elizabeth's startled gaze. What on earth had he thought when he discovered where they lived?

But he was speaking again. "I have a note here from Mrs. Gardiner to you, Miss Bennet. I hope you get the change to peruse it soon." He came towards her, the letter in his hand. As he handed it over, his eyes met hers, an intensity lending more urgency to his words. He wanted her to read it as soon as she could, she knew that.

She nodded at him. "Thank you, I hope my aunt was well?"

But before Mr. Darcy could reply, there was a ring at the doorbell, and everyone looked at the parlour door.

"Miss de Bourgh and Colonel Fitzwilliam," announced the housekeeper.

"Thank you, Mrs. Mitchell. Please bring fresh tea and cakes." Charlotte was welcoming. "Good morning, Miss de Bourgh, and Colonel Fitzwilliam. Mr. Collins is from home today."

Anne came straight over to Elizabeth, while her companion also entered and sat discreetly in a corner.

"How are you today, Elizabeth? You look very fatigued." She looked round, and dropped her voice to a whisper. "I think things are about to happen at home. Please be thinking of me when I return there with my cousins."

Elizabeth reached out and grasped her hand. "Is there anything more I can do?" She, too, kept her voice very low.

Anne shook her head. "I don't think so. But I think the gentlemen are thinking I will need to return to London with them immediately after it happens."

Elizabeth's heart sank. If Mr. Darcy was assisting his cousins, then he would not be able to ensure her return at least as far as Gracechurch Street. But she could not show it. "Are you nervous about it, Anne?"

The other nodded. "I am. I know it must be done, and you have helped me to see that I cannot live my life until this is over." She took a deep breath. "But she is my mother, and I do not want to think of the distress I will cause her."

Elizabeth smiled tightly. "I understand. My mother can be — embarrassing, too, although fewer people take notice of her. But I do not underestimate the courage it will take for you to do this."

The gratitude in Anne's expression was almost embarrassing; and she squeezed her hand again. "I will hold you to your promise, Anne. You must write to me, and we will meet again as soon as it can be arranged."

She watched her new friend a short while later, as she left the room with her cousins and companion, to return to Rosings Park for lunch. Even with them beside her, she looked very alone.

Elizabeth made her excuses, and went up to her chamber for a few moments before lunch. Hastily, she broke the seal of her aunt's letter, wondering that Mr. Darcy had seemed so impatient for her to read it.

Three sheets of paper. Two from her aunt, and a single folded sheet with her name on the outside in a masculine hand she didn't recognise.

She frowned, weighing in her mind which to read first. Then she smiled, and sat down. Of course she would read the unidentifiable one first.

Miss Bennet

By now, you will have read your aunt's letter to you, and she has kindly waited to seal it so that I can enclose this note to you. I hope you are not offended that she knows.

Her eyes dropped to the bottom of the page

Yours, etc,

Fitzwilliam Darcy

She lifted the page to her nose and smelled the musky sage scent of it. Of course it was Mr. Darcy. But she must read her aunt's letter first.

Darling Lizzy,

I'm so pleased to be able to write this to you today, knowing that you might be coming to us soon.

Mr. Darcy has explained the situation, and that when you arrive, you might be accompanied by another young lady as well as Maria Lucas, and, although I don't know the reason, I have assured him that our door will always be open for her.

Elizabeth was puzzled as well as touched. Aunt Gardiner must mean Anne, there could not be anyone else. But why might she need to come to Gracechurch Street?

She scanned the rest of the letter, but it contained only a happy anticipation of seeing her niece very soon, and stern admonitions that Elizabeth must not do too much. She kissed the letter affectionately, and turned impatiently to the page written by Mr. Darcy.

She will have told you that you might have Miss de Bourgh returning to London with you, should the need arise. I have wondered if it might be better if her mother cannot easily find her for a day or two, until the situation has settled down somewhat.

Might it be possible for you to be ready to leave at fairly short notice? I hope it would not be necessary, but I am uncertain of the way forward and think it wise to plan for every eventuality.

Elizabeth glanced round the room. She knew what he was concerned about. If Lady Catherine's temper was roused, she would be a formidable opponent.

Certainly Elizabeth could pack within a very few minutes, her clothes could be folded, and her few books. Only the telescope in its case must not be forgotten.

Lunch. She must go down for lunch, and afterwards she would come back here, ostensibly to rest. Then she would ask the housekeeper to bring her trunks to her chamber. She folded Mr. Darcy's letter, and wondered whether Maria would be coming with them, and how to ensure she could pack at short notice, too.

As she descended the stairs to join the party at lunch, she wondered very much what was transpiring at Rosings Park, and whether she might ever know. But Anne probably cared for her mother, and Elizabeth knew that she would not wish ill of her own mother, and therefore resolved to hope that Anne's news would result in her mother's joy and pleasure.

But she had to smile at the thought. No, Mr. Darcy was right to plan for the more probable.

CHAPTER 38

*L*ady Catherine did not seem to notice the atmosphere as they sat over lunch. Darcy watched the others in turn. Anne seemed composed, but he could see the rapid pulse in her throat betraying her anxiety.

And he knew Richard's feelings from across the table. But Anne was always seated with her companion between them. It was as if his aunt was determined to keep her isolated.

But as they had walked back to Rosings alongside Anne's little phaeton, he'd been struck by the sense of determination radiating from her. And her companion had proved that she was more devoted to her charge than her employer — who would doubtless dismiss the woman for leading Anne astray. He must ensure she was secure; she'd been a loyal servant to his cousin.

He ate mechanically, listening to Lady Catherine hold forth about the various merits of Rosings Park and the responsibilities that needed the help of a gentleman if she were to continue to maintain it in its current grand state.

He glanced occasionally at Richard. He would make a good master of the estate, if he were but given the chance. He suppressed a smile. Even if Lady Catherine decided she would take the dower house, it was most unlikely that Richard would choose to live here while she was alive.

But it seemed they were all being careful not to cause any discord over the dining table. Darcy knew it could not stay unresolved over the coffee.

Soon enough, Lady Catherine rose. She swept regally in front of them towards the drawing room, and Darcy fell into step beside Anne. Richard was walking on her other side, and he leaned towards her.

"Are you sure?"

Anne straightened up. "I am. I could not bear it if Mr. Collins discovered me and told Mother."

Coffee was served and Lady Catherine sat up straighter. "I was perturbed, Darcy, when your cousin arrived this morning without you. When he told me you had gone directly to the parsonage to call upon the ladies there, I was incensed!" She glared at him. "Did you deliberately pay no attention to me? Did you forget I told you that *Miss Elizabeth Bennet* …" she spat the name out, "… would expect to receive an offer if you persisted in this unseemly amount of attention to her?" There was a slight silence. "Well? What have you to say?"

Darcy didn't look at his cousins. He regarded his aunt steadily. "I wonder that you deliberately paid no attention to what I said to you, Lady Catherine. I told you very clearly — to leave you without a shadow of a doubt — that I will not marry Cousin Anne. We would not be a good match, I could never make her happy."

He sipped his coffee, and waited. It would not be long.

It was not. Lady Catherine's eyes narrowed. She drew breath.

"So, why have you returned yet again, Darcy? And so soon?" She smiled triumphantly. "There can be no other reason for it!"

He carefully placed down his cup. "On the contrary. I have been to Hertfordshire, to speak to Miss Bennet's father." He watched as her face lost its colour — he might almost feel sorry for her, but he would not allow her misconception to last. "Having made arrangements for her return home, I am here to ensure her early return, to complete the promise I made to him."

Her colour returned, and with it her confidence. "So then you will be free, Darcy. Free to do your duty to your family and your mother, by respecting her last wish."

He shook his head. "You are mistaken, Lady Catherine. I was there. Her last wish was that I be happy and also that I look after Georgiana. I will fulfil both those wishes of hers, and no other."

He heard the scrape of a chair behind him, and his heart tightened. Had Anne summoned up her courage? Would she face her mother? It was a heavy burden.

Her voice was still unfamiliar to him. Did her mother also find it strange, he wondered?

"Mother, you have to accept it. I do not wish to marry Darcy. I never have, and you didn't seek my opinion before forming your own." Anne was standing, and he stood, hastily, as did Richard.

The colour drained from Lady Catherine's face once again, and she stared at her daughter. Anne stared resolutely back. After a long silence, Lady Catherine found her voice.

"Daughters must do their duty just as much as sons. You ought to know, Anne, that I am not to be trifled with. I know what is to be done; and you —

by your sickly constitution, have not the experience of the world to know what is best for you."

Darcy had to admire her determination, in the face of what must be a shattering discovery to her. But he admired his cousin more.

She seemed entirely unafraid, despite the enormity of the changes to her life which would inevitably ensue.

"I know what is best for me, Mother, and it is not marrying Darcy. Why would it benefit me to marry a man who is unwilling to wed?" The scorn in her voice was magnificent, and he watched her with admiration.

He wondered whether everything was ready, then shook his head. Of course it was. He was glad he'd brought his London steward with him. Mr. Leigh had spent the last few hours loading the coach with Anne's belongings, which had been discreetly packed by her maid. Without a doubt, the horses were in harness, and ready to convey them across the lane to collect Miss Bennet. His heart pounded. Soon, they would be on the journey. He knew Miss Elizabeth would summon the energy to be companionable to his cousin; he just hoped she would not suffer a setback, such as she had before.

He turned his attention back to the room. Lady Catherine was still regarding her daughter with astonishment, mixed with scorn.

"Foolish girl! How will you ever marry well if you do not take advice from your own mother, who must have in mind the best for you?"

"I do hope to marry well, Mother." Anne's voice had wobbled a little, but now it strengthened, as Richard moved closer to her.

"I know she will, Lady Catherine. I wish to inform you that I have made Cousin Anne an offer of marriage, and she has accepted me."

Darcy cheered inside. He had counselled Richard most sincerely on the journey this morning, only to inform his aunt; and not ask for her permission or her blessing. He was sure a refusal would put his cousins on the back foot. Richard had obtained a special licence, Anne was of full age; her mother's consent was not needed.

Once again the colour drained from his aunt's features. He began to be concerned for her, and stepped forward.

"Lady Catherine, please calm yourself, I …"

"Don't try and importune me, Darcy!" she hissed. "If you had done as I said, this would not have happened!" Her eyes bulged, she was in a rage not to be diminished, and he stepped stoically in front of his cousins. He would bear it.

"Lady Catherine, do you wish to discuss the future? If not, we will leave now. We will escort Cousin Anne to London."

She rose to her feet. "I forbid it! Anne's constitution will not allow such a thing!"

Anne appeared beside him. "Goodbye, Mother. I will write to you, and I hope you will wish me happiness."

She stepped back, and he felt Richard touch his arm. Then they were gone, as they had planned. He remained; his task now was to prevent Lady Catherine from following them to Hunsford, where they would collect Miss Bennet.

He smiled, she would be ready.

"Take that smile off your face, Darcy! I suppose you have been conniving with them all this time keeping me misinformed and all unknowing!" She raised herself to her tallest extent. "I am ashamed of you!"

Darcy shook his head. "I admit to being ashamed of myself, in that I did not discover the extent to which my cousin had to hide her true ability, her true nature; all in order to remain here without constant attacks by you." He shook his head as she attempted to interrupt. "No, you will hear me, Lady Catherine. Richard is eminently suitable. I may be a gentleman, but you know he is the son of an earl, a fully aristocratic family. I cannot conceive why you should find him unsuitable for Anne."

She glared at him. "But he is without fortune!"

He sighed. "Do you not have fortune enough?

Anne will inherit the whole of Rosings Park. You need someone within the family to take on the duties of the estate, to nurture it for their heirs."

He strode to the window, angry enough at her to forget himself. Almost. He could hear Miss Bennet's voice in his mind;

… you are the last man in the world whom I could ever be prevailed on to marry.

He winced, he must be a gentleman at all costs, be worthy of winning her hand.

He turned, trying to think of how he might placate his aunt. The clock hands showed that he was nearly done. In a few minutes, he would be striding out of here, to rejoin the others, travel to London.

His aunt would be left here alone. He spoke more gently. "Do not think too harshly of them, Lady Catherine. They would welcome your blessing, when you feel able."

Her snort of disdain proclaimed his failure, and he sighed again. "We will escort Anne to London, where she can be safe until they are wed. She will write to you, no doubt, with the direction to which you might reply."

He bowed, anxious now only to leave this gloomy place. How Anne had survived it here for so long, he could not imagine.

"I will come to London! I will not permit them to marry!" She pursued him through the hall.

He turned. "You will not, madam. You must have seen that Anne is not inclined to admit you. You must wait and reconcile by letter when you are able to be conciliatory." He tried to make his voice more gentle. "It would be regrettable for you not to be able to see your daughter happily settled."

She stepped back, looking suddenly diminished, and he wondered if she had finally really heard him.

He bowed his farewell and turned away.

But it seemed she had not determined to take his advice. "Hunsford! That is why you spent so much time there! I will summon Mr. Collins here! He will know what you are about. And I will charge him as to why he did not tell me what was happening."

CHAPTER 39

*E*lizabeth was tired before she even left her bedchamber that afternoon. And she was concerned as to how she might have to explain herself to Charlotte when her friend discovered that she would be leaving so precipitately.

Their friendship had only just survived her feeling of betrayal at Charlotte's encouragement of Mr. Collins' hand. Now Charlotte might feel betrayed by Elizabeth seeming to be part of a plan to conspire against Lady Catherine's wishes.

And it had all happened here, at Hunsford. Elizabeth tried to tell herself that she had not been the instigator of the situation; Anne had done that when she called on them and made her real self obvious.

She left the precious telescope carefully on top

of her two trunks in her bedchamber, and descended the stairs carefully. If she was indeed leaving this afternoon — if Anne and the gentlemen had confronted Lady Catherine — then she would be ready.

She had been upstairs barely an hour, and without her usual rest, but she dare not stay longer. If the gentlemen called and she was not downstairs, they might leave without her, thinking she didn't wish to upset her friend.

If she was to travel to London after this, then she knew she must be very strong and not show weakness or fatigue — but she wasn't convinced that she would be able to do that.

She turned into the parlour where Charlotte and Maria were calmly at their needlework. It seemed impossible that they had no idea of the drama that might now be taking place at Rosings Park, just across the lane.

There was a ring at the doorbell, and Elizabeth smiled to herself. Somehow, it had an imperious tone and she knew what it heralded. But her amusement abated quickly; soon she would know what had transpired. She didn't know what she wanted — well, she did want to leave here and go to Aunt Gardiner's. But she also hoped that Lady Catherine would welcome the news of her daughter's wish to marry.

Elizabeth shrugged. She could not imagine Lady Catherine being pleased about the news. The door to the parlour opened, and the housekeeper announced Anne and Colonel Fitzwilliam.

Elizabeth rose to her feet and extended her hands to Anne, who hurried forward.

"Oh, Elizabeth, thank you for your support. Without having met you, I would not have been able to face Mother."

Elizabeth embraced her. "I hope it was not as bad as you had imagined," she murmured. Anne pulled back and took a deep breath. Elizabeth saw she was blinking back tears, and she squeezed the other's hands.

Colonel Fitzwilliam bowed. "Miss Bennet. I see you have divined what has happened. We must accompany Miss de Bourgh to London at once." His eyes were telling her a different story, "Darcy is talking to Lady Catherine. He will be joining us very shortly — or we will stop in the lane for him." He turned to Charlotte.

"Mrs. Collins. I am sorry that this is sudden, but …," he paused as there was a further ring at the bell. The colonel didn't finish his sentence, but waited as Mr. Darcy was shown in.

He bowed to them all, but his eyes were on Elizabeth, warm and concerned.

He turned as the colonel spoke. "I have

explained to Miss Bennet that we must leave for London at once."

Mr. Darcy nodded, and turned to Charlotte. "I am sorry for the suddenness of this turn of events, Mrs. Collins. As you know, I called on Miss Bennet's aunt in London yesterday. It seems that it would be better if I conveyed Miss Bennet to London now, where she can be accompanied on the way by Miss de Bourgh until we drive on to Matlock House. Then she can gather her strength for the rest of the journey home." He smiled at Charlotte, appearing to understand her bewilderment. "I understand the information was in the letter from Mrs. Gardiner to Miss Bennet, so perhaps she has already arranged that her belongings are packed."

Charlotte looked questioningly at Elizabeth, who nodded slightly.

"I'm sorry, Charlotte. But I do think it's better if I go now, to save Mr. Darcy another journey. As I am ready, perhaps I can assist Maria to pack quickly."

"But …" Charlotte didn't seem to understand the haste that Elizabeth could sense from him. But he broke in.

"Mrs. Collins, there is some urgency. Please arrange that Miss Bennet's belongings are collected from her chamber and conveyed to my coachman."

He waited while she rang the bell. "If Miss Lucas wishes to stay with you a few days longer, I am sure I can arrange for her to be taken home then, with suitable escorts. Perhaps your mother will come for her."

Charlotte nodded, still appearing confused. "Perhaps that would be better. Mr. Collins is not expected back until later in the afternoon. He will be vexed that Lizzy is gone without taking her leave properly, and I cannot let Maria go without a proper farewell."

He bowed. "I understand." He hesitated and glanced at Elizabeth.

"Might you be ready soon, Miss Bennet? I think we need to be on the road before Lady Catherine appears here."

Charlotte's gasp tore at Elizabeth. She didn't wish to leave her friend in such dread. She crossed to her. "Charlotte, perhaps you and Maria would wish to walk to the village this afternoon for an hour or so. Or maybe you ought to send word to Mr. Collins that he might be needed by Lady Catherine."

Charlotte stood up straighter. "I do not understand, Lizzy. But perhaps it is better that I do not." She smiled faintly. "But I will send for Mr. Collins." She turned to the door where the servant was waiting.

"Take a servant upstairs to collect Miss Bennet's luggage, please. At once."

Elizabeth watched, stifling the urge to remind the servant about her telescope.

"You must take great care, Lizzy." Charlotte embraced her. "I don't think you can have had your rest this afternoon, and you'll be very tired by the time you get to London."

Elizabeth smiled. "I have nothing to do except sit in the coach, Charlotte. Thank you for your care and concern and your wonderful hospitality, and I will write to you tomorrow. Please extend my gratitude to Mr. Collins for permitting me to visit you, and convey my apologies for my precipitate departure."

She could see that both Mr. Darcy and the colonel were growing impatient, and she broke away from her friend.

"I am ready, Mr. Darcy."

CHAPTER 40

*D*arcy was impressed that Miss Bennet didn't cause any delay, but followed Cousin Anne to the coach. She only hesitated a moment, looking at the trunks packed at the back. He smiled, he knew what she was looking for.

"I ensured that the telescope was placed carefully in the box seat, Miss Bennet."

To his delight, she blushed. "Thank you."

His heart swelled, and he offered his hand to assist her into the coach. "Please take the far seat, Miss Bennet. I am sorry that there is not room to provide somewhere for you to recline, but there are cushions and blankets for your comfort."

"It will be quite sufficient, Mr. Darcy. Thank you for your concern."

He assisted Cousin Anne up the step, watching as Miss Bennet crossed the coach to the seat he'd suggested. She turned and spoke laughingly at Anne, and he found himself smiling at the sight.

Richard was beside him. "Miss Bennet is good at helping Anne to be at ease."

Darcy nodded, not quite trusting himself to speak. He hoped he was doing the right thing; Mrs. Collins' concern over her friend's health had pricked his conscience — he hoped he wasn't doing this for his own convenience.

He reminded himself that she had admitted she had wanted to leave Hunsford. His lips tightened, it could not have been comfortable for her, sharing a house with the odious Collins, especially as he knew she had refused his offer.

He looked down the lane, and frowned. Was Mr. Leigh having difficulty?

"What's the trouble, Darcy?" Richard was beside him.

"My steward," Darcy made up his mind. "You accompany the ladies, Richard. I will walk up the lane and find him. I want to start via the back roads. It would not do to tempt Lady Catherine to follow us."

Richard chuckled. "Indeed not." He turned. "I think I will start the coach at a walk that way, around the park. You can cross the grove with your man, and we will wait by the far gate." He pointed.

"The gate with the old wagon store beside it?" Darcy nodded. "I know the one." He clapped Richard on the shoulder. "We will endeavour not to keep you waiting too long."

Fifteen minutes later, breathless, the two men hurried towards the coach.

"Thank you, Mr. Leigh." Darcy swung into the coach, feeling the weight shift as his steward climbed up beside the coachman, and the servant closed the door, and climbed up, too.

His gaze went across immediately to Miss Bennet, he couldn't help himself. She was sitting, quiet and serene, in the corner of the coach opposite Richard. Anne was in the middle, with her companion sitting quietly beside her.

"Is all well, William?" Anne asked him quietly. She seemed quite composed, although he was well aware he had always misjudged her feelings in the past.

He nodded. "I have explained that you will write to her soon with the direction for her to reply." He wondered whether he should say exactly what had happened, and decided to wait and see if she asked him.

She looked at Richard, and he laughed. "I told

you Darcy would need you to ask what happened if you wish to know."

Darcy kept his face impassive. But he was comforted by the presence of Miss Bennet. Somehow he knew she was sympathetic. She reached across and took Anne's hand.

"I think you only wish to know if your mother is likely to come to London immediately. Is that right, Anne?"

"I do." Anne nodded at him.

He wondered how he could say what he must without causing her any distress. "Lady Catherine was, of course, inclined to come to London, dear cousin. But after I spoke to her, I managed to persuade her that it would not be the wise thing to do." He smiled slightly. "When I left her, she was intending to summon Mr. Collins to give an account of himself."

Both ladies looked at each other, and he wondered what he could say to relieve their minds. "We did hear Mrs. Collins say that she would send for him, didn't we?" he ventured.

He saw Miss Bennet squeezing the other's hand. "Indeed we did, and I would not be at all surprised to find that Charlotte and Maria have gone for a walk in the woods for the afternoon." She laughed lightly. "And if they feel it necessary, they will probably decide to escort Maria to Hertfordshire themselves, for a short stay."

Darcy hid a smile, he was sure they would indeed do that, and very soon — when Lady Catherine was angry, she was not to be trifled with.

Anne looked distressed. "Then she will be all alone."

Miss Bennet moved up the seat a little, and put her arm round her. It wasn't very correct, but Darcy could see that Anne appreciated her action.

"Write to her when we get to London, Anne. Then she will receive it early tomorrow. Perhaps you might even want to write a short note twice a day for a little while. I'm sure your mother will appreciate it."

Darcy exchanged a glance with Richard. "May I ask, Miss Bennet, does Lady Catherine know where your aunt and uncle live?"

She shook her head. "No, she does not. Charlotte and Maria do, of course; but if Lady Catherine goes to Matlock House, there will be a delay while she sends back to find the direction from them." She turned to Anne.

"You might want to make Matlock House the direction on your letters. I'm sure Colonel Fitzwilliam will have them sent on to you."

Darcy nodded. He had to be satisfied with that

for the time being. He wanted to speak to Richard, encourage the couple to marry as soon as possible, but he could hardly do that in front of Cousin Anne, so soon after she had defied her mother. He must think of a safer topic of conversation.

CHAPTER 41

*E*lizabeth roused as the coach turned into Gracechurch Street. Anne was talking softly to Mrs. Jenkinson, but the gentlemen were sitting in silence. She knew she blushed; that they had been quiet to allow her to rest.

She looked out of the window, determined to recover her poise. She must not worry her aunt. With good fortune, Mr. Darcy and Colonel Fitzwilliam would not stay very long, and she'd be able to relax now she was back with her family.

As she glanced round, she caught Mr. Darcy's gaze, concerned and thoughtful. She forced a smile.

"I am well, thank you, Mr. Darcy. You did not need to be silent on my behalf."

He bowed his head. "I hope you are not too

fatigued; I thought it might be better if the journey seemed to pass more quickly for you."

She nodded, she must not argue.

Anne turned to her. "Tell me about your aunt and uncle, Elizabeth. I hope they do not mind me staying with you for a few days."

Elizabeth smiled. "They will welcome you for as long as you need. I love them dearly, and the children are not so exhausting, once they have got over their curiosity."

Mr. Darcy smiled over at them. "Mr. and Mrs. Gardiner are elegant and kind people, Cousin Anne. Miss Bennet is correct, and you will be safer there than at Matlock House — certainly at first."

Elizabeth looked at him thoughtfully. Was this the same man who had so disdainfully insulted her family, her background? The same Mr. Darcy who had raised his voice in anger, icy cold:

Could you expect me to rejoice in the inferiority of your connections? To congratulate myself on the hope of relations whose condition in life is so decidedly beneath my own?

He must think she had not remembered. Surely, if it was otherwise, he would not say such things.

His features darkened and she looked away quickly. Was he embarrassed? Did he think he might have remembered?

The harnesses jingled and she heard one of the

horses snort as the coach drew to a halt outside number twenty-three.

The gentlemen descended from the coach first and Mr. Darcy turned to assist them out, the heat of his hand through her glove a warning to her. She must try and get back to Longbourn and away from him, must forget him and heal her heart.

Aunt Gardiner was there, her arms outstretched, and Elizabeth struggled to keep her composure. She must not weep, must not show her weakness.

"Lizzy, I'm so happy you're here at last!" Her aunt embraced her tightly. "We so nearly lost you!" She regarded her critically. "You're very pale, come inside at once." She turned to Anne and curtsied.

Mr. Darcy stepped forward. "Mrs. Gardiner, might I introduce my cousin, Miss Anne de Bourgh, and my other cousin, Colonel Fitzwilliam?" He bowed, and turned to his guests.

"Cousin Anne, Richard; Mrs. Gardiner, Miss Bennet's aunt."

His eyes swung to Elizabeth. "Miss Bennet, I think perhaps we should not keep you outside any longer, I think you need to rest."

Elizabeth was vexed with herself for having started to shiver. "I am well, sir." But she would be glad to get indoors, and the support of his arm was welcome as she climbed the two steps to the front door.

Aunt Gardiner looked at her critically. "Perhaps you ought to go straight upstairs, Lizzy."

Elizabeth steeled herself. This must be very hard for Anne, she must stay downstairs until her friend was more settled. "No, might I stay downstairs a little? I would relish some tea."

She could feel Mr. Darcy's amusement at her subterfuge, as her aunt gave her a sharp glance and nodded at the servant.

But she was very relieved to be able to sit down by the fire. She tried to prevent herself shivering — she must not show weakness.

Her aunt sat close beside her, obviously rather torn between her duties as hostess, and her need to assure herself of Elizabeth's well-being.

Elizabeth sat up straighter. She could do this. She must.

Anne was talking to Aunt Gardiner, and she heard her confide in her aunt brief details of what had transpired that day.

"Well, my dear, you may stay here just as long as you or your cousins think it right to do so. I have been pleased to hear from Lizzy that she has found a new friend in you, and I hope you will be able to assist me in ensuring she does not do too much."

Elizabeth heard the chuckles of both gentlemen, who rose to their feet.

"Thank you, Mrs. Gardiner, for your hospitality." Mr. Darcy bowed. "We will take our leave now, and hope that you will permit us to call tomorrow."

Colonel Fitzwilliam spoke quietly to Anne and then they were gone. Elizabeth sank back into her chair. At last, she no longer needed to act.

Her aunt came back into the room after accompanying the gentlemen to the door. "Lizzy, I think you need to go to bed at once. I'm going to send for the apothecary if you don't look any better by the morning."

Elizabeth smiled faintly. "I'm all right now I am here and resting, Aunt. We can't expect Anne to stay down here without me …"

Anne broke in. "I will be quite all right, Elizabeth. You know that. I'm looking forward to getting to know Mrs. Gardiner. I have Mrs. Jenkinson, and I'll take your advice and write to Mother today, so that she doesn't think I've abandoned her, and hopefully she will not come to London."

Elizabeth struggled to sit forward on the edge of her chair. "You are going to be careful to use a plain seal, aren't you?"

Anne laughed. "You are talking to me, not Maria Lucas!"

Elizabeth felt a little ashamed of herself, especially when her aunt laughed.

"Perhaps you will excuse me for a moment, Miss de Bourgh, while I make sure Lizzy goes up to her chamber and gets straight into bed." Aunt Gardiner sounded determined and Elizabeth knew better than to argue.

CHAPTER 42

Darcy hurried up the steps of Matlock House with Richard. He would much rather have driven directly to Darcy House, but he would support Richard when he confronted his father. And of course, he must see Georgiana. He hoped she was happy and content.

But his mind was back at the Cheapside house where Elizabeth would, he hoped, be resting. He'd been concerned on the journey from Kent as her pallor increased, and the fact that she hadn't stirred when the horses were changed at Bromley had disturbed him still more.

Tomorrow, he would gain Mrs. Gardiner's consent to call Dr. Moore back to see Miss Bennet. One thing was certain, she could not return to Hertfordshire for a number of days.

Richard was more concerned about Anne, of course. They'd had nearly twenty minutes in the coach as they drove towards the more fashionable west of town. He'd told the coachman to take them along the embankment; the great river ran turgid and grey beneath the many bridges and gave him something to look at.

But now they were at Matlock House, and Richard would be confronting his parents. Darcy clapped him on the shoulder.

"Let us be about it." He looked at the door. "I'm sure Aunt Alice will be on your side."

Richard groaned. "Father will not wish to upset his sister."

"Yes, but I'm sure your mother will talk him round."

His cousin sighed. "If Lady Catherine is not already here."

"She won't be." Darcy hoped he was right. He thought he was; she would have waited for Collins in order to berate him, and she would be very angry at having to wait while he was summoned from wherever he had been. He smiled wryly. Perhaps the earl would go to Kent to speak to his sister.

In the hall, they handed their hats and canes to the butler, and he was pleasantly surprised when Georgiana came through to the hall.

"William!" Her delighted cry warmed him. It had been many years since she'd been so pleased to see him.

"Georgiana; I'm pleased to see you looking so well." He bowed. She was indeed looking well and her features were without the petulant expression that had marred it in recent months. "I look forward to hearing all your news later. But now, will you come with us while we join the family?"

Georgiana took his arm and he walked through to the drawing room, knowing Richard was behind them. His aunt and uncle were sitting by the great fireplace, and he moved forward to greet them.

"Uncle Henry," he bowed and turned and bowed over his aunt's hand. "Aunt Alice."

"Mother," Richard was beside him and leaned forward to kiss his mother's cheek.

There was movement around them as footmen carried in trays of tea, but Darcy was watching his aunt. She was looking narrowly at Richard.

"Let us take tea, Richard, and you will tell me what has happened. It is important, I can see that."

He saw Uncle Henry's head jerk round, and could barely keep his impassive expression. Aunt Alice was a very astute lady. As Miss Elizabeth Bennet was; and he smiled.

Georgiana's gaze moved from him to Richard

and back again. She stood on tiptoe to reach his ear. "What is it?"

Darcy shook his head slightly. He was watching his aunt.

Aunt Alice nodded at the footman. "Shut the door, please, and tell the kitchen that dinner might be delayed."

Darcy moved towards Richard. "Courage, my friend. You have faced worse in battle." His back was to the family and he kept his voice low.

Richard's smile didn't reach his eyes. "I wish I knew how to begin," he murmured.

"Ask you mother to wish you joy?" Darcy suggested under his breath.

"Come on, Richard," Aunt Alice patted the sofa beside her. "I am becoming more curious each moment."

Darcy heard his cousin swallow. "Yes, Mother — and Father —" Richard looked over at his father before letting his gaze swing back to her. "I want to tell you that I have become engaged to be married."

Darcy stepped back as Aunt Alice rose to embrace her son. But the frown on his uncle's face told him that there would yet be some difficulty.

"Come and sit down!" Uncle Henry barked. "I presume, given that we have had no warning, and that you have not brought your intended bride here to introduce us, that you have made a foolish choice." His great bushy eyebrows were drawn together over his scowling face.

"I don't think so, Father." Richard seemed glad to have got the conversation started, although Darcy saw that he sat beside Aunt Alice where she had originally indicated.

"So, who is she, Richard?" Aunt Alice wasn't to be distracted, and Darcy wondered how she would react. He thought with amusement how they would greet his news when he announced his betrothal to Miss Bennet; then pushed the thought away. He had a mountain to climb to gain her acceptance and he must support Richard first.

"I have had the honour to be accepted by Miss Anne de Bourgh, Mother." Richard said quietly, but with pride.

"But …" Aunt Alice's face had fallen.

"You cannot marry Anne, Richard!" Uncle Henry interjected. "The girl is simple-minded!"

It was time to help his cousin out. Darcy stepped forward. "I confess I also thought that until recently, Uncle Henry. But now I have discovered it is just the way she has been forced to act all her life. She is the most delightful and intel-ligent young lady, who fully returns Richard's affections. I think they will be very happy together."

"Surely we would have seen through an act like

that at some time, Darcy." Aunt Alice was trying to keep her composure.

He shook his head. "I confess I have been remiss in not trying to get to know her better. And none of us have seen much of her. Lady Catherine has kept her secluded, and all around her have been too much in the control of her mother to see what they might otherwise have."

Uncle Henry was frowning. "Why would my sister have allowed it to continue?"

Darcy looked at him. "I don't know, Uncle, and I have only had a few days to think on the matter, but I think she finds it difficult not to be in command of every situation. As Anne grew into adulthood, the only way for her mother to stay in control would be to announce that Anne is unable to control her own affairs, and make the choices for her."

His aunt spluttered into laughter, and Darcy turned in surprise.

"I can't think you are right, Darcy. If she needed to retain control, she would not have chosen you as her daughter's intended husband."

Richard laughed, and Darcy was relieved that the atmosphere was more relaxed. But his uncle shook his head.

"Lady Catherine will not consent, Richard. She

is determined to unite the Rosings estate to Pemberley."

"Her consent is not needed, Father." Richard sounded determined. "This morning, Darcy told her again, very firmly, that he will not marry Anne, that he could not make her happy. Anne stood between us and also told her that she wouldn't marry him." He glanced at Darcy, before turning to his mother.

"I informed her that I had made Anne an offer and she had accepted me." He took a deep breath. "We had to bring Anne away, as her mother is so angry." He reached out a hand to his mother, and Darcy saw tears in her eyes as she listened to the son she could not openly admit to being her favourite.

"Mother, I have obtained a special licence, but I don't want to marry in secret. I'm not ashamed and I deeply wish to have your blessing."

Darcy watched his aunt. She looked bewildered. "But where is Anne? If you have brought her away, why did you leave her alone, and not bring her here? Is she safe?"

Richard looked at Darcy, who stepped forward.

"Aunt Alice, we were rather concerned that Lady Catherine might come to London and call here. We didn't wish to permit Anne to be distressed by it. She is staying with a friend in London, with that friend's relations, and she is safe there — at least for a day or two." He looked over at his uncle.

"Lady Catherine must come to accept it, Uncle Henry. But I think she will not, until the marriage has taken place. If she cuts off Anne's allowance, then I have said that she and Richard can use the dower house at Pemberley, until her mother perhaps becomes reconciled to the situation." He sat down. "I think the marriage must go ahead very soon."

Richard looked over gratefully, and there was a moment of silence.

Uncle Henry tried again. "You have obviously developed affection for Anne, Richard. Why did you not tell us before this?"

Darcy watched as Richard drew his hand across his face. "We didn't know quite what to do, Father. If you had known, it is inevitable that Lady Catherine would have heard of it. It would have been very uncomfortable for Anne to have continued living at home."

Uncle Henry looked at his wife. "It is too late to get her here to dine with us. But you must bring her to call on us tomorrow. When I have spoken to her, I will be able to say what I think."

Darcy shook his head. "I think Lady Catherine may come to London, Uncle. She will think Anne is staying here. I am not sure it is advisable for them to meet until after they have become reconciled by letter."

"Then we will call on Anne," Aunt Alice said firmly. "You will take us there tomorrow, Richard, as you know the family she is staying with."

Richard turned appalled eyes on Darcy, who considered his words. "The situation is not quite as simple as that, I am afraid. Perhaps I can explain a little over dinner?"

CHAPTER 43

*D*arcy rode behind his coach as he went back to Matlock House the following morning to collect the rest of the party.

He had been quite unable to dissuade his aunt from her determination to call on her niece, although Uncle Henry had agreed that he would stay away for this first call.

Darcy wondered despondently how Miss Bennet was this morning, how she and her aunt would feel when the Countess of Matlock appeared at their door. Perhaps she would be too unwell to leave her bedchamber today — he recalled the setback she had received just travelling the fifteen miles from Copthorne. His heart sank, he was relying on seeing her.

"I am concerned about Miss Bennet, too,

Darcy." Richard rode beside him as the coach carried Aunt Alice towards Cheapside.

"Yes." Darcy was terse, there was nothing to say.

"I hope Anne has not found it too uncomfortable, staying with people she doesn't know, with Miss Bennet too unwell to be with her." Richard was persistent.

Darcy shrugged. "She will not be alone. Miss Bennet will not agree to rest if she thinks Anne needs her support."

"I'm pleased to hear it, although I know that you'll be concerned if she suffers a setback." Richard leaned over. "I admit to being amused when Father realised we were not going to give him the direction, or his servants." He laughed.

It seemed to Darcy that despite the whole situation; the fact that Richard had been able to tell people about his affections, and that it seemed his marriage could go ahead, had seemed to lighten his spirits.

In contrast, Darcy found himself heavy-hearted. Miss Bennet was still unwell; the physician had been cautious as to her long-term recovery, although she had not admitted any concern about her memory to him. But Darcy knew she must be worried about the fact that her memory and ability to learn seemed impaired — or she would not have told her father. Darcy knew it made no difference to him, of course.

Even her physical health concerned him, although the doctor had repeated himself a number of times that she was likely to recover fully, although it might take many months. And since then, Darcy had moved her to London, in accordance with her wishes. He dreaded that it might have caused her another setback.

Every sign of her frailty tore through him. When she remembered her refusal of his offer, she might spurn him again. He would have to forsake his calls on her, wonder how she was, regret her absence — all from afar. He could not bear the thought.

As his coach halted at the door of Mr. and Mrs. Gardiner's house, he rode forward, wishing very much that he'd had the chance to let the family know his aunt would be with them. But he must make the best of it.

He assisted his aunt from the coach, before she took Richard's arm.

The servant announced them, and he craned to see past his relations to try and see if Miss Bennet was downstairs.

She was. Relief coursed through him, he would be able to assure himself of her well-being with his own eyes.

She sat down immediately after giving her curtsy, not waiting for Aunt Alice to be seated first.

He thought his aunt would not understand, but he hoped she would not say anything.

The atmosphere was slightly strained as they sat around tea. Darcy knew he had to do something about it. He put his cup down carefully.

"Mrs. Gardiner, I thank you again for your hospitality to my cousin. Might I ask if she and my aunt and cousin might walk in the gardens for a short while?" It would give them privacy to make whatever decisions were needed.

And he could perhaps have a brief conversation with Miss Elizabeth Bennet.

He thought she looked very ill indeed; her skin had a waxy, slightly yellowish pallor, and as soon as his relations were gone to the gardens, he approached her.

"I hope you are more comfortable here with your aunt, Miss Bennet, but I am sorry to see that you appear to look fatigued from yesterday." He turned to her aunt.

"Mrs. Gardiner, I called my London physician to attend Miss Bennet when she was in Kent. I wonder if you would consent to me summoning him here to see if there is anything else we might do to help her recover?"

"Mr. Darcy, I think that is an excellent idea. I have sent for the apothecary, but if you are willing to send your physician, I'm sure that would be better." She gave her niece a calculating glance. "I tried all I could to ensure she remained in her bedchamber to recover from the journey. But as you can see, I was unsuccessful."

He tried to stop his lips twitching. "Miss Bennet lacks nothing of determination, Mrs. Gardiner."

"And a will to speak for herself," Miss Bennet spoke up, rather tartly. But she didn't argue further, a more telling indication to him that she was very far from being her usual self.

She glanced at the window. "Do your cousins have the approval of your aunt and uncle?" She sounded wistful.

Mrs. Gardiner sat down, so he was able to pull up a chair. "It was a little difficult at first, Miss Bennet. As you can imagine, my uncle does does not wish to incur the anger of Lady Catherine. However, I am hopeful, very hopeful." He, too, glanced at the window. He wondered what they were talking about. Perhaps the marriage could take place in the next day or two. Then the couple could stay at Darcy House, if need be.

No. He would send them on tour for a week while things could be settled here. He smiled, and looked at Miss Bennet.

"I hope your aunt might be able to persuade you upstairs to rest when we are gone, Miss Bennet."

She smiled slightly, and turned her eyes to the

fire. "I am very comfortable here, and the chance to talk to Anne and my aunt is an opportunity not to be missed." She smiled at him. "I am grateful for your concern, Mr. Darcy, and that you're going to ensure I get home. But I'm quite all right sitting here."

A slight huff of disagreement from her aunt showed that lady disagreed, and Darcy was reassured that Miss Bennet would indeed retire to her chamber as soon as they were gone.

He turned to Mrs. Gardiner, and smiled. "Might I trouble you for writing materials, madam? I can send to Dr. Moore at once."

CHAPTER 44

*E*lizabeth roused herself when Anne re-entered the drawing room with her aunt and Colonel Fitzwilliam beside her. She looked much happier, and Elizabeth was reassured.

She held out her hand to Anne, who came over to her and took her hand.

Elizabeth took one look at her red-rimmed eyes. "Is all well?" she whispered.

Anne gave her a tremulous smile. "Oh, yes. Aunt Alice was really kind to me. But they are both convinced we ought to marry in the next few days."

"Don't you want to do that, Anne? It will mean you're safe." Elizabeth forced a smile. "Or do you want a society marriage, and show everyone who you really are?"

"Certainly not!" Anne grimaced. "No, I said I

wanted to wait until you are well enough to stand up with me, and Richard said that it might take a long time and asked if I was prepared for Mother to find me."

Elizabeth stared at her. "That seems as if — no, I will not say." She frowned across the room at the colonel, who was talking quietly to her aunt.

"I know what you're thinking, Elizabeth, and it's not like that at all." Anne sounded placatory. "He will do whatever I wish, including going to Rosings Park to ensure Mother doesn't try and see me before I am ready."

"Well, then, I suppose I will need to forgive him for what I thought him capable of," Elizabeth grumbled, and Anne laughed.

"I think you must be feeling a little better."

Elizabeth caught Mr. Darcy's gaze upon her. She felt herself blush and looked away hastily, turning her attention back to Anne.

"Anne, you do not need me to stand up with you, if you do want to marry soon. My thoughts will be with you, you know that."

"But I want you there," Anne said. "You were the one who made me think I could change my life and not wait for someone else." She smiled mischievously. "You're quite a fierce believer in yourself — do you know that?"

"Oh." Elizabeth would need to think about that.

"But, if you do want to marry soon, I will be well enough to stand up with you, if that is what you want. I will."

Anne looked doubtfully at her. "Well, if you stand up with me at the beginning, you could sit down in the front pew behind me for the main part of the service. Would that be possible for you?"

"Of course." Not for anything would Elizabeth let her new friend down. "I only hope you don't mind seeing me in a gown I have worn before, although perhaps Aunt Gardiner has something that will suffice."

Anne laughed. "I think I will be wearing a borrowed gown, too. Please say you will come. I'll wait as long as you need to feel well enough."

Elizabeth nodded. "This afternoon, then. I will ask my aunt about the gown when your relations conclude their call."

Anne's peal of laughter turned all heads their way, and Elizabeth felt herself blush again.

Mr. Darcy was on his feet. "I think it time to conclude our call this morning, madam," he said to Aunt Gardiner. "With your permission, may we call again tomorrow?"

"You will be very welcome whenever you wish to call, Mr. Darcy." Aunt Gardiner glanced at Elizabeth, and then back at him. "Would you care to come to dinner tonight?" She turned to the countess.

"Perhaps with your husband, Lady Matlock?"

"That is very kind, Mrs. Gardiner. But Darcy's sister would then be alone at Matlock House."

"I'm sorry, I don't know the family well," Aunt Gardiner said. "Miss Darcy would be very welcome, too."

Mr. Darcy bowed. "I am very grateful for your kind invitation, Mrs. Gardiner. But I am concerned that Miss Bennet is not yet well enough for such an occasion, and I doubt she would agree to …"

"Of course," her aunt agreed without hesitation. "But please feel free to call at any time to see Anne." She smiled warmly at her. "She is welcome to stay as long as is needed."

"You're very kind," Lady Matlock repeated. "Thank you for being so welcoming to my niece. I can see she is content to stay."

Not for anything would Elizabeth admit that she was glad there would not be a large dinner party tonight. As she curtsied with the others she saw a thoughtful expression on Lady Matlock's face and knew she must be wondering why Mr. Darcy was so solicitous of her.

She must get well soon. The sooner she was back at Longbourn, the better. Having made that decision, she did not even wait for her aunt to insist that she go up to her bedchamber, but excused herself.

ANNE HAD BEEN CONVINCED by Elizabeth's declaration that she was well enough; and the very next day, she found herself with her aunt and uncle in their coach, and driving to St. George's Church in Mayfair.

She smiled, her aunt and Mrs. Jenkinson had assisted Anne to get ready, and all Elizabeth had to do was suffer the ministrations of Aunt Gardiner to help her dress.

The Earl of Matlock and his wife had called in their coach to collect Anne, and Elizabeth could see the stately coach rolling ahead of them, the coat of arms on the doors glittering in the noon sunlight.

Matlock House was hosting the wedding breakfast, and Elizabeth envisaged quite a fight with her aunt afterwards. But she was determined to go. There would be so few there, and Anne deserved the very best.

At the church, she stood behind her new friend, who was on her uncle's arm. A frisson of nerves raised the hairs on the back of her neck and she knew Mr. Darcy was standing beside his cousin as groomsman. But he was looking at her. She knew that, and her head went up.

She looked good, she knew that. A touch of her aunt's rouge, and he would never see her pallor. Today was Anne's day, and no one should be tempted to turn their attention to Elizabeth.

She followed them down the aisle, looking interestedly around. It was designed in an ornate fashion, and she wondered how old it was. Perhaps she could look it up later.

She stood still, determined not to falter, while the first words were spoken. When the earl gave his niece's hand to the colonel, she stepped back and took a seat in the second pew, next to her aunt, who gave her a sharp look.

But Elizabeth wouldn't return her gaze. She watched as they spoke their vows. Mr. Darcy, grave and handsome, giving the ring when required from the clergyman. She glanced over at the other side of the nave.

Lady Matlock, beside her husband. A slender girl, about sixteen. Would she be Mr. Darcy's sister? A well-dressed couple in their thirties, and a younger man, who looked very like the colonel. She smiled. He must be a brother.

On this side of the church, Aunt and Uncle Gardiner, Elizabeth herself; and sitting quietly, self-effacingly, behind them, Mrs. Jenkinson, Anne's companion of so many years.

The ceremony did not take long, and Elizabeth stood to follow her friend and her new husband down the aisle.

Mr. Darcy was there, and offered her his arm, smiling. Of course, as groomsman, his duty was to the bride's attendant. She took his arm reluctantly, knowing she must hide her reaction to his touch.

Determined not to tremble, she walked beside him and out of the church.

CHAPTER 45

*M*iss Bennet was infuriating! Darcy travelled in his coach with Georgiana and his aunt and uncle, as they drove back to Matlock House; Richard and Anne being in the Matlock coach. But his mind was on Miss Bennet, travelling with Mr. and Mrs. Gardiner. All their efforts to persuade her to return to Gracechurch Street had been in vain; she was determined to join the wedding breakfast, even if just for a short while.

Mrs. Gardiner had looked ruefully at him. "There is a time when it is better not to argue, Mr. Darcy. I will undertake to persuade her home as soon as I can."

He had bowed, and turned to join Aunt Alice. But his mind was back at the exasperating, but extraordinary, Miss Bennet. He must win her soon, know that she was his.

The church was not far from Grosvenor Square, barely half a mile, and he expected little would be said. So his aunt had to say his name several times before he jerked his mind back to the present.

"We don't have much time, Darcy," she said, sounding tart. "So you need to listen. I shall say nothing today, of course, but once Richard and Anne are away and this unsettled time is over, I shall have some pertinent questions for you." She looked at him sternly.

He knew what she referred to, of course. He was not good at maintaining a disinterested distance from Miss Bennet, and a lady as astute as his aunt would undoubtedly have noticed the direction of his attention.

His lips tightened. "Yes, Aunt Alice." But he was safe for today. His aunt had too much to do.

But his uncle was eyeing him sternly, as well. Darcy hid a sigh. He must distract them somehow. He did not wish them to investigate the Bennet family. But, thankfully, they had arrived. As soon as the door opened, he climbed down, turning as his uncle descended, then his aunt. Georgiana followed, and she took his arm. In the coach behind, Richard's elder brother David and his wife Susannah, with Jonathan. They would be kind to Miss

Bennet in their own way, and were already trying to make amends with Cousin Anne.

He could see the Matlock coach being driven round to the stable yard; Richard and his bride had only arrived a few minutes ago.

He walked with Georgiana back to the final conveyance arriving at the house. Assisting Mrs. Gardiner and then Miss Bennet from their coach, he stood back and allowed Mr. Gardiner to climb the steps with a lady on each arm. Soon, he promised himself, soon he would have the right to offer Miss Bennet his arm.

It didn't feel like a wedding breakfast, of course, with so few people there, but Anne was radiant, and very pleased to see Miss Bennet there.

Darcy decided that she must have known that Anne needed her presence, and his displeasure at her stubbornness receded as he watched his cousin's delight.

He moved towards Richard. "My felicitations to you both."

"Thank you, Darcy." Richard didn't take his eyes off his bride. "I understand your concerns for Miss Bennet, but I am grateful to her. She seems to have an innate sense of what Anne has needed most, and was determined that our marriage should not be delayed."

Darcy nodded, his eyes on Miss Bennet. "I do

hope that she rests properly when she is home. I would like to see her back to her old self."

"Even if she remembers your final meeting before her accident?"

Darcy groaned. "Please do not remind me! I must be ready for her to remember." He grimaced. "Sometimes I think she already knows, when she looks at me in response to something I said." He sighed. "I can only be the best that I can, and earn her improved regard."

Richard nodded. "Perhaps you should not be too anxious to return her to Hertfordshire, Darcy. You can call on her here, in London, without having to contend with Miss Bingley as you would if you stayed at Netherfield."

"True," Darcy mused as he watched her. His gaze moved round the room and he saw Aunt Alice's steely look. He sighed again and turned his back, huffing a rueful laugh at Richard. "But your mother is determined to find out what I am about, and I do not want her to discompose Miss Bennet."

"Well, perhaps you ought to introduce Georgiana to her, and I will take Anne over to Mother." Richard straightened up and went over to join Anne and Miss Bennet. Darcy watched him, then turned to go to Georgiana.

An hour later, Miss Bennet and her relations climbed into their coach. Darcy ought not to have been there, ought to have left his aunt and uncle, as their hosts, to see them away. But he could not help himself. Even though Mr. Gardiner assisted her into the coach, he was ready in case of need.

"Thank you, Mr. Darcy, for your kind attention to my niece." Mrs. Gardiner was beside him. "I will ensure she rests now, to expedite her recovery."

He bowed. "I am sure she is in the best of hands, Mrs. Gardiner." He hesitated. "Is Dr. Moore going to call each day, as I instructed?"

She smiled. "He is, indeed. I think Lizzy feels it to be a needless expense, but I am insisting she complies with his recommendations — apart from today, of course."

Darcy smiled faintly. "When Miss Bennet has decided she must undertake something, she is determined not to fail at her task."

"Indeed." Mrs. Gardiner looked back at the house. "I wish Colonel and Mrs. Fitzwilliam all my felicitations for a happy marriage, Mr. Darcy." She turned to the earl.

"Thank you, my lord, for permitting us to accompany my niece — and for being understanding of us leaving so early."

Uncle Henry nodded acknowledgement. "Miss Bennet was very helpful to Anne when she needed it. We are grateful to her."

Darcy watched as the coach rolled away. He had

not stated his intention to call tomorrow, he could hardly do that in front of his uncle; but he was determined to go.

CHAPTER 46

Aunt Gardiner looked at Elizabeth. "I think you ought to go to your bedchamber and rest, Lizzy. It must have been difficult for you, standing for so long."

Elizabeth smiled tiredly at her aunt. "I think I will, although I didn't have to stand that much. Everyone has been very solicitous of me. But I am glad the marriage could go ahead."

"I think we're all happy about that, dear." Aunt Gardiner steered her towards the stairs. "Anne is a delightful lady and was a pleasant guest. But I think you were much too conscious of your responsibility towards her."

Elizabeth laughed. "You know me far too well!" She smiled at her uncle and aunt, and climbed the stairs, knowing that she would be glad to lie down.

Today, it did not distress her that she couldn't concentrate on reading. All she wanted to do was think about Mr. Darcy.

His intense gaze always on her; his care and concern — something must happen soon, and she didn't know what it was.

She had to acknowledge her feelings for him, but she didn't know what she wanted. He had been a gentleman personified these last few weeks. But once the memory of his offer had come to mind, she had been unable to forget what had been said.

He had been arrogant and rude, offending her about her background and upbringing. But thinking back about what she had said in return brought a hot flush of shame every time she thought about it. Knowing him as she did now, her stinging accusations must have hurt him very much. His escape from Kent the very next morning showed it.

But when he'd heard that she was missing, he had immediately returned to search for her.

She swallowed.

You must allow me to tell you how ardently I admire and love you.

His words were often in her mind, and his actions since then were more proof of their veracity than any fine speech could be.

She rolled over and buried her face in the pillow. How ashamed she was of her actions then. But why had he come back? Did he hope she would never remember the occasion? If he knew she had remembered, how could he ever make her another offer?

She rolled back over, unable to get comfortable. Did she want him to make an offer? She remembered clearly her opinion of ladies who married into wealth, just for security. Screwing her eyes shut, she wondered what he must have thought of her prideful attitude then — and what her family and friends must have thought.

A hot tear spilled out from under her lashes. Papa had warned her about her pride and her superiority. Now it was gone. Her memory was no better than theirs, her years of learning fragmented in a broken mind.

She had nothing left. Nothing to be proud of. No one would wish to ally themselves with a sickly young woman, with not even a small fortune to encourage them.

The sun shone into the window, somehow emphasising her dispirited mood. Elizabeth let the tears flow, nothing mattered now.

She knew that tomorrow, she would steel herself and be determined to hide her true feelings from the world, but just this moment, she needed to feel sorry for herself.

~

THE FOLLOWING MORNING, Elizabeth felt a little stronger, although there was still a deep ache in her heart.

An early caller was Dr. Moore, as he had been on the previous morning. Aunt Gardiner led him into the bedchamber, where Elizabeth was sitting quietly in the chair by the window, a pile of books beside her. She had been wondering if she would ever recover her enjoyment of discovering something new. She rose to her feet as her aunt bustled in to check that Elizabeth was prepared for the call.

Dr. Moore bowed. "May I sit down, Miss Bennet?"

She dipped her head. "Of course, Doctor. But I am well this morning. I'm sorry for your wasted calls each day."

He gave her a sharp glance, one that seemed to penetrate to her deepest thoughts. "Yet, to my eye, you seem rather dispirited this morning." His voice was gentle, and Elizabeth swallowed a big lump in her throat. She glanced at her aunt, studiously looking in another direction.

"It is nothing," she tried to keep her tone light. "I am just a little vexed that my strength is taking so long to return to me."

He nodded. "It must seem so, Miss Bennet. But

I must remind you that, while no one seems to know exactly what happened to you, you were insensible for about a week, which indicates you suffered a very grave injury." He smiled gently. "The length of time in which you could not be roused to take nourishment will have compounded that injury to a very great extent." He reached out and felt the pulse in her wrist. "You have a very strong constitution, Miss Bennet. Such a high level of harm would have not have been recoverable from for very many ladies."

He sat back. "You will recover fully, in my view, Miss Bennet. But you must be patient. It is not only the original injury you must recover from, but the damage that has been caused by the extended lack of nourishment that first week."

Elizabeth had to ask. She hoped her aunt would not repeat what she heard. "What about my memory, though? What about my ability to learn?"

He looked more serious, and her heart fell. "Thank you for sharing your concern, Miss Bennet. I think that has been at the heart of your anxiety, hasn't it?"

She nodded, not trusting herself to speak.

"Yes, well. My opinion is that you will also recover that love of learning," he said. "Your memory for what you learn may take a considerable time, though, and you will need to develop strategies for filing the notes you make, so that you can refresh your memory quickly." He smiled. "You are still a clever and resourceful young lady, and I have the fullest confidence in you."

He got to his feet. "I know it seems like a long time to you, Miss Bennet, but it is less than three weeks since you were recovered to Kent. You must not expect to see a complete improvement for many months."

"Months?" Elizabeth could hardly believe her ears.

He nodded. "You are making progress slowly; I have seen a steady improvement since I was first summoned to attend you. It is slow enough to be imperceptible to you, who lives with it each hour, and you have also had rather a setback each time a journey has been needed. But you are gaining in health, and you will be well." He picked up his bag, and moved to the door.

Before he left, he bowed to her. "Take the time you need to rest, Miss Bennet. I will be recommending that you remain here at least one or two weeks before you return home, maybe longer."

Elizabeth stared after him as he went down, followed by her aunt. Two weeks? *Two more weeks?*

When her aunt returned to her door, Elizabeth was at the table, writing.

"I see the doctor's words have galvanised you into action, Lizzy," her aunt laughed. "Please don't say you will be unhappy here. We can send for anything from home that you're missing."

Elizabeth pushed herself to her feet. "Dear Aunt Gardiner, don't even think that. I am writing to Kitty. I will need her to write to me very often with news of home, if I am to stay here."

CHAPTER 47

Darcy dressed with care after his early gallop. He would go to Cheapside this morning, and call on Miss Elizabeth Bennet. But first, he would wait for Dr. Moore to call, as he did each day to report on her health.

In the dining room, he stood with his coffee by the window, and looked out over the gardens. He was very pleased the wedding of his cousins was over, and hoped their week-long tour to Bath would allow them to relax away from Lady Catherine.

They was a sound at the door, and he turned, seeing Georgiana as she entered.

He crossed the room, and bowed over her hand. "Good morning, Georgiana. It is wonderful to be back home with you after so long." He hoped very much that the change he had seen in her at Matlock

House would stay with her, she'd been very good company. He shuddered at the memory of her petulant attitude a few months ago.

He smiled. "Let's have breakfast together, although I will have to leave you for a few moments when the physician calls after he has called on Miss Bennet."

"Thank you," she said as he waited for her to take her seat. He wondered what the glint in her eye meant, what she was going to say, and tightened his jaw. What was he prepared to say to her?

Perhaps she'd want to talk about herself, about Jonathan. He almost hoped so.

He tried to meet her inquisitive gaze with equanimity. "So, tell me about how you have been the last few weeks at Matlock House. I regret that I have had to be away so much."

She nodded at the footman as he poured her a cup of tea. "I'd like to talk about it, William, but not if we don't have a lot of time. Perhaps this afternoon, if you might be here?"

"Very well." He nodded. He would be back from his call by then.

She raised her eyebrows. "But I'm going to ask you about Miss Bennet. I'm sure you must have expected it."

He nodded, he wouldn't have to say everything, he thought. Just enough to satisfy her. "I wanted to thank you for being kind to her at the wedding breakfast yesterday. She has been of great service to Cousin Anne."

Georgiana took another slice. "Yes, Aunt Alice explained it to me." She glanced slyly up at him. "I think she is a very amiable lady. But I think that you agree with that."

He took a slow sip of his coffee, wondering how to deal with it. "I am grateful to her for what she has done for Anne. I also promised her father that I would ensure she got home safely after her accident." He smiled wryly. "It is taking longer than I might have thought."

His sister pursed her lips. "So, why did you make that promise to her father? You are not close friends — did you even know him before this?"

Darcy shifted uncomfortably on his chair. "I met him last year, when I was staying with Bingley, Georgiana. And I do not wish to talk about it further at present. I must fulfil my promise to him."

A small smile played around her lips as she spread conserve on the bread. "Of course."

He had to change the subject. "I have been very discomposed that I was not aware of Cousin Anne's wishes until very recently." He waved his coffee cup at the footman, who hurried over to refill it. "But I hope she and Richard are going to be happy."

"I don't think there's any doubt of that." She

glanced up. "What are you going to do about Lady Catherine?"

He breathed a sigh of relief that his young sister was not going to press him on the state of his heart. "Uncle Henry is going to Kent this morning, I understand. He will carry a letter from Anne, and will give her news of the marriage." He frowned slightly. "I hope very much they can be reconciled — although I do not think she'll be happy that Richard does not intend to live at Rosings while she is there."

Georgiana giggled. "I can't say I'm surprised."

He smiled reluctantly. "I agree, although I do hope she can moderate her position so that they may visit there occasionally." He looked up as the butler came to the door.

"Dr. Moore, sir."

Darcy put down his cup. "Please excuse me for a moment, Georgiana." He bowed and went to the hall.

"Good morning, doctor. Come to my library." He turned towards it. "Can I order you coffee?"

His favourite leather chair was the same as always. But Darcy could not be comfortable. He sat forward, on the edge, and when the coffee had been served, he spoke first.

"I hope Miss Bennet has not suffered too much ill effect from her exertion yesterday."

The physician frowned into his cup and Darcy's heart sank.

"No, I cannot make an statement either way, sir." Dr. Moore considered his words carefully. "Undoubtedly, her spirits would have suffered greatly had we forbidden her attendance at the marriage. So from that aspect, it was the right thing to do." He took a sip. "And she has suffered no real physical setback from the occasion." He sat back.

"But she did seem rather out of sorts this morning. It was, however, beneficial, in that she finally admitted to me what has been troubling her so much." He glanced up at Darcy. "It is as we thought; she is still very troubled as to her lack of memory and difficulty committing new facts to mind. I'm glad she was finally able to talk about it to me, and I hope I was able to reassure her that I believe her ability to learn will come back as her energy increases. I also assured her that full recovery of her memory may take many months, and that until then she can use her resourcefulness to file her notes in a way that makes referring to them simpler." He glanced sharply at Darcy. "I did not tell her that the longer it takes, the more likely it is that her quickness of mind might never be completely as it was before." He sighed heavily. "I do not think it will be helpful to inform her of it until she is much stronger in herself. And, of course, it might never be necessary, if she is to recover. It is only a few weeks, as yet."

Darcy nodded, trying to imagine how Miss Bennet — Elizabeth — might receive such news. He pushed the thought away, he would not consider it unless it proved necessary. "Thank you, Doctor Moore. I will hope that tomorrow you might find her in better spirits."

The other man rose to his feet. "Indeed, sir. I have emphasised to her that I would strongly recommend that she undertakes no further journey for at least a week, preferably two." He smiled faintly. "I think she was not very happy about it."

Darcy rose, too. "I will ascertain with her aunt that she is able to stay for that length of time. I'm sure there will be no difficulty."

"Good. I will call upon her tomorrow morning, then, and speak to you again afterwards."

CHAPTER 48

*E*lizabeth descended the stairs carefully. The doctor's visit had unsettled her rather, but she was determined not to stay in her chamber and be miserable. She smiled, she wanted to be downstairs when Mr. Darcy called, otherwise she was sure that he and her aunt would talk about her.

"Lizzy!" Aunt Gardiner hurried towards her. "I think you ought to have a day in bed to recover from yesterday, dear. The doctor did say that you must rest."

Elizabeth leaned forward and kissed her cheek. "Dear Aunt. Might I rest down here this morning, with you? I would relish your company."

She almost laughed at her aunt's suspicious look, but she didn't demur.

"All right, Lizzy. If that's what you need today."

She placed her in the comfortable high-backed chair beside the fire, and tucked a blanket over her knees. "There! Now, you don't need to move." She settled herself down on the sofa nearby with her needlework. "And there's no need to make conversation if you don't feel like it." Her rare smile helped Elizabeth to feel calmer, and she relaxed back against the chair and closed her eyes.

The doctor hadn't said it, but she was under no illusion that her memory was certain to return, and she tried to push the thought away, not yet ready to accept that she might never be specially favoured again.

She tried to push away the sad thoughts and think of something happier. Anne's marriage yesterday had pleased her very much. Her new friend had looked radiantly happy, even if she had whispered to Elizabeth on parting that all these new experiences were making her head spin.

Elizabeth had whispered back. "Tell him. Tell your husband that you need a slower pace than he is used to. He will be patient with you, I know." It pleased her very much that she'd been part of being able to help Anne find her freedom, and she contemplated the memory with considerable satisfaction.

The sound of the doorbell came faintly through the hall, and she hid a smile, trying not to blush.

"Hmph!" her aunt's quiet snort told her she hadn't succeeded, and she opened her eyes and looked guiltily at her aunt, who was waiting for their guest to be shown into the room.

But it wasn't Mr. Darcy.

"Papa!" Elizabeth couldn't help it, she surprised herself by bursting into tears.

"Lizzy!" Aunt Gardiner looked shocked, but Papa just hurried over to Elizabeth and embraced her. Elizabeth clung to him, feeling like a small girl again. He would take her home, make everything all right. Everything would be the same, this whole thing would never have happened.

"Papa, I'm so happy to see you."

"I'm the same, Lizzy. I know everyone was telling me you were well, and your letters, too. But I wanted to come and assure myself all was well." He pulled up a chair very close to her, and offered her his large handkerchief. It smelled of home.

Elizabeth mopped her eyes. "I'm sorry to be so foolish, Papa. Think nothing of it. Oh, it is so good to see you."

He patted her knee, his own eyes brimming. "Dear Lizzy."

Her aunt was staying back, out of their reunion, and Elizabeth reached out. "Aunt Gardiner, did you know Papa was coming, and didn't tell me?"

"No, I didn't tell her," Papa interjected. "I had

to wait until your mother was all right for me to leave, and I needed Mr. Lawrence to be able to spare Jane to stay and run the house. I caught the very early post." He smiled. "It is worth it to see you so much better than I had feared." But he still looked worried, and Elizabeth was sorry she had allowed her aunt to cover her with a blanket.

"Don't worry, Papa. I am well, really. Aunt Gardiner thinks I need more coddling than I really do."

Her aunt's snort was louder this time, and Elizabeth tried to stifle a giggle.

The doorbell rang again, and Elizabeth closed her eyes. What would Mr. Darcy think? Would he apologise and go away again?

Papa lifted his eyebrows at her aunt, who smiled placidly.

"Mr. Darcy calls most days, Thomas."

Papa's eyebrows rose further. "Ah!"

Elizabeth tightened her lips. "It means nothing, Papa. I …"

But the footman came to the door. "Mr. Darcy, Madam."

He bowed, his eyes at once seeking out Elizabeth, and the small line deepened between his brows.

Elizabeth forced a smile. "I am well, Mr. Darcy.

It is easier for me to submit to my aunt's ministrations. Then I am permitted downstairs."

The others all smiled appreciatively.

"I'm glad you are as astute as ever, Lizzy." Papa patted her shoulder.

"And I," Mr. Darcy dipped his head again. "I wished to assure myself that you had suffered no ill-effects from yesterday."

"Yesterday?" Her father looked bemused.

"Let's all sit down," Aunt Gardiner intervened, and nodded at the servant for tea. "We all attended a wedding yesterday, for the bride was insistent that Lizzy must stand up with her at marriage."

"A wedding!" Her father seemed even more confused. "Who was marrying? You didn't mention anything to do with it in your letters." He turned to Mr. Darcy.

"Or you, sir."

Mr. Darcy looked slightly abashed. "It was arranged at very short notice. I'm sure Miss Bennet will explain the details to you, but we wished my cousin to be safe as soon as possible; and she flatly refused to undertake the ceremony without her new friend beside her." He smiled at Elizabeth. "The family are indebted to Miss Bennet for assisting my cousin."

Papa looked from him to Elizabeth. "I'm not

sure I understand, but I expect I will find out at some point." He turned to Aunt Gardiner.

"I wonder if Mr. Darcy and I might take a turn in the garden before we take tea with you and Lizzy?"

"Of course, if you wish," she said calmly. "It's chilly outside, though, and I'm sure Edward will not mind if you use his library. He has a particularly fine malt there he is proud of."

Her father smiled. "I enjoy his whisky, certainly." He looked at Mr. Darcy.

"Library, or garden?"

Mr. Darcy was smiling too. "Library, if it is all the same to you, Mr. Bennet."

The two men left the room, and Elizabeth turned to her aunt at once.

"What are they going to talk about? I hope Papa is not …"

"You're not to worry, Lizzy," her aunt said firmly. "If you worry, and visitors excite you too much, I will send you to your chamber. Then will not know what is going on at all."

Elizabeth subsided a little. "But I wonder what they have to talk about?"

"I expect it is about when you will be fit to travel and other matters," Aunt Gardiner picked up her needlework again. "If they are going to enjoy a whisky, we will have to drink all the tea; it will not be fresh when they return."

"Of course." Elizabeth knew she would get no further. She sighed as the maid poured the tea and brought the cup over to the little table beside her.

"Take a pastry, Lizzy," her aunt urged. "You are still very thin."

CHAPTER 49

*D*arcy followed Bennet through to the library. It had to happen, he supposed, although he wished he'd had some time to prepare for it.

Sitting in the comfortable leather chairs with whisky in hand, he had to own that this was rather more comfortable than strolling in the garden, within sight of the drawing room windows.

He couldn't wait, though he ought to. "Miss Bennet appears to have been weeping. Do you know what might be the matter?"

Bennet shook his head. "I only preceded you by about ten minutes, Mr. Darcy. Lizzy was perfectly calm when I entered the room. I was surprised, as I think she was, when she burst into tears when she saw me." He huffed a laugh. "I think she felt like a

375

little girl again." His gaze flickered over to Darcy. "She was always my favourite daughter. We spent most of her childhood walking in the fields and woods, or exploring all the bookshops in Hertford."

Darcy nodded, more at ease now. She was all right. But Bennet obviously had something to say.

"I remain grateful to you, Mr. Darcy, for your care and concern for my daughter." He met his eyes. "I can never repay you. But I saw your expression when you entered the room just now, and I must ask. What are your intentions towards my daughter?"

Darcy took a deep breath, and his gaze wandered to the window. Perhaps he'd have been better outside. But he wanted to get this right.

"My immediate concern is for Miss Bennet's recovery, of course. I must see her well, and returned to you at home. Until then, I will say nothing." He smiled slightly. "After she is home, I will approach you and ask if I may court her." He stopped talking, his heart pounding.

"Why Lizzy?" Bennet's voice was neutral, and Darcy could discern no trace of approval or otherwise in his tone.

Darcy smiled thinly, hoping against hope that the circumstances of his first proposal were never aired to this family. "When I called at Longbourn with Bingley that day, and heard of her disappearance, I knew then my feelings for her could not be denied. I knew at once I could never be happy if I did not have her beside me, to keep her safe and happy to the best of my ability." He looked at Bennet, whose expression was unchanged. "I have to admit that before then, I tried to deny my feelings toward Miss Bennet, but even before I heard the news," he shuddered. "I had determined to call, find out what I could to help me to discover what she wanted for her life and prove myself worthy of her."

Bennet finally showed some reaction. His eyebrows rose. "Very informative, Mr. Darcy. And what have you discerned, since you have seen quite a lot of her in the last few weeks?"

Darcy wished the interview over, although he knew the man had the right to ask these questions. "My love for your daughter has only grown stronger, as I have watched her deal with her recovery, only really concerned for the effects on those around her, and her sorrow for causing such distress."

Bennet nodded. "She certainly caused much anguish." He looked up and sighed. "She will not have learned not to test the boundaries of what is possible, though. You will never be able to keep her completely safe, Mr. Darcy. She will fret against any attempt to prevent her from exploring the world around her, from enjoying occasional solitude, from

377

wishing to learn everything she can." He looked weary. "I would be very sorry if she married a man who wanted to keep her in the manner of most ladies."

It was what Darcy had expected, although he still dreaded it. The thought that he might yet lose her. "It is part of what makes her who she is. I will try my best not to stifle that eagerness to learn which is so exciting to find in a lady."

Bennet relaxed back in his seat. "Lizzy used to rail about gentlemen who refused to believe a lady could wish to learn, to improve her mind beyond what most would consider acceptable accomplishments for ladies. You would be well advised to desist in your courting if you cannot accept it, or she would refuse you."

Darcy smiled. He would not be deterred until he had her consent — although he would not wish to suffer another rejection. "I have spent many months trying to ensure my sister discovered a sense of pride in her learning; trying to discourage that shallow acceptance that she only needs to learn enough to gain a husband and security."

"Good." Bennet sat forward. "We understand each other, then. Mr. Darcy, I would encourage you to keep this conversation to yourself. I give my consent to you courting Lizzy, but only when she is fully well. I also warn you that you will be a fortu-

nate man if she accepts you. She has always had her
pride and disdainful thoughts about marrying a
man for his wealth. You may find your circumstances are not an advantage with her." He stabbed
a finger in Darcy's direction. "Even though I am
indebted to you, I will not give my consent if I think
she is not fully recovered and has only consented
because she feels indebted, which will mean she is
still affected by her injury."

He heaved himself to his feet. "But do not be
downhearted. I hope you gain your desire, sir. I
must just warn you that this might take much time,
even though I am sure you're impatient."

He turned for the door. "Now, they will be
wondering what we have been talking about. How
long should Lizzy stay here before she comes
home?"

"The physician called this morning, sir. He has
recommended at least a week, preferably two."
Darcy found himself smiling. "He told me that she
seemed vexed when he told her that."

Bennet laughed. "I'm sure she was."

DARCY FOLLOWED him back to the drawing room.
He was amazed and humbled at the strength of this
man and his daughter. He'd never considered

anyone would ever reject him, reject the wealth, comfort and security that he could offer. He knew he was a catch to be desired by all. No more. Elizabeth had rejected him, thrown his offer back in his face. Since then, he knew he must be the man she wanted, the sort of man she would accept. Now he knew he would have to gain the father's goodwill, too. He was determined to prove himself.

Elizabeth was smiling at her aunt. But she had discarded the blanket and footstool, and had some needlework beside her. Very like a normal call, then. He knew his lips twitched. He wondered whether the aunt had remonstrated. Perhaps he might venture a few words.

"I suppose being an invalid has palled for your niece, Mrs. Gardiner?"

She shook her head. "She is going to be hard work for the next two weeks, I know that, Mr. Darcy."

Bennet laughed, and took the chair next to Elizabeth. "I always suspected that would be the case, Madeline. Well, we have assisted Edward with the whisky, but I would relish some tea."

Mrs. Gardiner smiled, and reached for the bell. "I will order fresh tea for you." She nodded at Darcy.

"Do take a seat, Mr. Darcy."

Elizabeth looked at her father. "The doctor

said a week, maybe a little longer. But I'm sure it will be easier at home, I have been away for so long."

Mrs. Gardiner intervened. "The doctor said preferably two weeks, Lizzy. I heard him myself."

Darcy watched with amusement. Mr. Bennet leaned forward. "If you are a compliant invalid, Lizzy, perhaps you will be well enough after a week." He laughed. "We will have to see. But I am gratified, I must say, by your objections. You would not be my Lizzy if you agreed with everything without dissent." He sat back and crossed his legs. "Now, I have letters from you from home. Jane, Kitty, Mary and your mother have written, so you have much to keep you occupied." He looked slyly at her. "But I will give you my news of yesterday. Mrs. Collins called to see Kitty. Apparently, she and Mr. Collins have repaired to Lucas Lodge for a short time. I understand Lady Catherine is exceedingly angry about something, and displeased with Mr. Collins." He laughed heartily. "I think they feel that it is better to be away from Hunsford until Lady Catherine has calmed a little. And of course, they could take Maria home with them as an excuse for the journey."

Darcy leaned forward and caught Elizabeth's startled expression. Bennet noticed and looked between them.

"Do you know what it is all about, Lizzy? Pray elucidate."

"Oh, I'm so sorry that we caused Charlotte such trouble!" Elizabeth looked distressed. "Papa, it was Miss Anne de Bourgh, Lady Catherine's daughter, who married yesterday."

Bennet looked at Darcy, nonplussed. Darcy nodded ruefully. It had been inevitable, he supposed, that Mr. Collins would bear the brunt of Lady Catherine's anger once they had brought Anne to London, but it was regrettable that Elizabeth would feel the injury to her friend.

He leaned forward. "Miss Bennet, I'm sure there was nothing you could have done to make things easier for your friend. Perhaps she would welcome a letter sympathising with the upheaval caused by your departure. I would hope that Mr. Collins bore the brunt of Lady Catherine's displeasure, because she would have expected him to report what was under his nose at the parsonage."

He got to his feet. "But I am intruding on your time with your father. I will leave you now to tell him the story fully."

CHAPTER 50

*A*t last she was going home. The wait had seemed interminable to Elizabeth, and even though she would be in company with Mr. Darcy for the journey to Longbourn, she could accept it for the pleasure of being on her way home.

Her father had stayed two days at Gracechurch Street and she'd enjoyed his company, even though he had connived with her aunt to insist she spent each afternoon resting on her bed. So she had only seen him on those two mornings, and he hadn't explained what he had done with the afternoons, either, when she had asked him.

It was not much more than a week after he had gone back to Hertfordshire, though, that Doctor Moore had finally relented and agreed that she could travel home. She climbed into the coach with Aunt Gardiner's admonishments ringing in her ears. She was beside her now, leaning in through the coach door.

"Look, put those pillows behind you. Then you can raise your legs on the ottoman, can't you? It's beautifully padded. I think Mr. Darcy must have had it placed there. It's very thoughtful, and will mean you can rest quite well. Oh, look, there are lots of blankets."

"Yes, Aunt," Elizabeth tried to reassure her. "I'm sure I will be very comfortable." She leaned forward and kissed her again. "I'm so grateful for your care of me, and I'm sorry if I was difficult."

Her aunt wiped at her eyes with a scrap of lace. "You've been no trouble at all, Lizzy. I'm only concerned that you take good care of yourself. Longbourn can be noisy, so you must be sure to rest upstairs when you need to."

"I will," Elizabeth promised readily, rather embarrassed that Mr. Darcy was listening to this. He was standing by his horse, looking slightly amused, which irked her. "Goodbye, dear Aunt, and I promise to write tomorrow."

She smiled at Miss Georgiana Darcy, who was sitting in the coach already, and her companion was also seated quietly in the other corner. Elizabeth had readily agreed when Mr. Darcy had asked if he might bring his sister to call upon her at Gracechurch Street, and was pleased to discover a thoughtful young lady who was pleasant company.

She and Georgiana had struck up quite a friendship, even though she was sure the girl was keeping something from her. When she had discovered that Mr. Darcy intended to stay at Netherfield Park after taking her home, and asked if she would object to sharing the coach with Georgiana, she had been surprised.

"Of course not. I'm grateful that you're arranging my journey. I cannot object in any way to arrangements that you make." She'd smiled. "And I would not, anyway. Miss Darcy is a delightful young lady." His expression had lightened at her words, and her heart had jumped uncomfortably.

She needed to be at home, but she really didn't need him to be staying at Netherfield. He would undoubtedly continue to call upon her, and she ought not to see him so often, or she might never get over her feelings for him.

But here she was, for the next few hours, in company with his young sister. It was well that she was feeling so much better, or her heart would have been heavy at the thought of making light conversation. Through the coach window, she saw Mr. Darcy mounting his horse, ready to ride behind the coach. She made a face at the window. What did he think she was going to do? But she had to be pleased that he would not be travelling in the coach with them. That would have been uncomfortable for her.

She smiled at the girl as the coach jerked and started to roll. "It feels as if I have been away from home for far too long, Georgiana. I love the country, I think everyone loves the county where they grew up. But I understand it is your first visit to Hertfordshire."

Georgiana nodded. "I'm looking forward to seeing the country." Her expression belied her words; she seemed a little downcast.

Elizabeth cast around, wondering what the matter could be. "Do you know Mr. Bingley and his family?" She caught the barest flicker of a grimace on the girl's face.

"Yes, Elizabeth. They come to stay at Pemberley sometimes, and call on my brother at Darcy House, too."

That was at least part of it, Elizabeth was sure. "I'm sure Miss Bingley wishes to see more of your brother." She gave a knowing smile, and was pleased at Georgiana's resigned expression.

"I keep telling him he must be careful not to allow her to compromise him."

Elizabeth was startled. "I hope he takes you seriously. I don't think she could make him happy."

The girl made a face. "I don't know why he wishes to stay so long in Hertfordshire — well, I do, really, I suppose. He wants to assure himself you are well. But then I think he ought to be away from there until Miss Bingley gives up her pursuit."

"And when do you think she will do that?" Elizabeth raised an eyebrow.

Georgiana sighed. "She never will. Not with a prize such as Pemberley."

"Is it so grand a place as that?" Elizabeth was thoughtful. "Perhaps we could encourage her to set her cap at someone with a title. I'm sure she'd love to be part of the aristocracy."

Georgiana giggled. "You ought to write novels, Elizabeth. Something like that could only happen in fiction. No Earl or Duke would ever allow someone from trade to marry into their family."

"I suppose not," Elizabeth mused.

"Of course, I might persuade William to marry," Georgiana sounded off-hand, but she gave Elizabeth a sly look through her eyelashes.

"I doubt you could persuade Mr. Darcy to do anything he didn't want to do." Elizabeth was glad she managed to sound as casual as her friend. She wondered what Georgiana would think if she knew he had already made an offer to Elizabeth — an offer she had shamefully rejected.

Georgiana must have sensed something, she changed the subject. "While we are on our own, Elizabeth, I wanted to ask you something."

"Of course." Elizabeth tried to look encouraging.

The younger girl looked down and pleated her fingers through her skirts. "Well …" she seemed to be hunting for the right words. "Well — William said how you were a very astute lady, how you studied astronomy and the sciences as well as things that are normally deemed accomplishments for ladies." She looked up. "Did you ever worry that being so clever in these ways might lose you the approbation of gentlemen?"

Elizabeth thought for a moment. What did the girl really want to know?

"I think the answer would be different for every-one," she said, honestly. "For me, it didn't arise, because I started studying when I was very young. As you know, my father has no sons, so he encour-aged me." She reached over and took Georgiana's hand. "But I've always been certain that a gentleman who despises learning in a lady cannot be very confident in his own ability, and might make a very uncomfortable lifetime partner."

There was a moment or two of silence, and she

wondered if she'd said the right thing. "Does that make sense, Georgiana? Or have I misunderstood what you're asking?"

"Oh, it makes sense," the girl whispered. "I am just wondering what it means for me."

Elizabeth smiled. "Well, begin by thinking of a man you would never wish to marry and wonder if that is why, and then of a man you think you might like to, if it were possible and you were older. Do you think he would allow you to follow an interest, even if he didn't understand it and it was not a fashionable pastime?"

She watched a pleased little smile spread across the girl's face, and sat back. That would give her something to think about. She turned and looked out of the window.

She had much to ponder on, too.

At Longbourn, there was much fuss and bustling around. Jane was there, to her delight, as well as Kitty and Mama, and she barely had time to bid goodbye to Georgiana.

"Please call on me, Georgiana. I will want to see you very soon."

Then she went into the house, surrounded by

her family, quite unable to see Mr. Darcy, to thank him for bringing her home.

Jane was looking at her carefully. "Ought you to go straight upstairs, Lizzy?"

Oh, Jane!" Elizabeth looked at her reproachfully. "It's been so long since I have seen you all, and heard all the news. Please let me stay downstairs and hear all that has been going on."

The front door was still open, and she heard the coach drive away. She wouldn't let herself look round; her family surrounded her, so why did she feel suddenly bereft? She smiled grimly, it would be dishonest to tell herself it was concern that her telescope had been unloaded along with her trunks. No, the loss of Mr. Darcy was what felt so strange. But she didn't know why.

She enjoyed the company of her family, but fairly soon, she knew she would have to retire upstairs, the noise was indescribable after the peace and quiet of Gracechurch Street — even the little Gardiner children were not as noisy as Lydia and Mama.

But she was glad she'd not gone up to her chamber when her father came in, followed by Mr. Darcy. She hadn't known he had come in to speak to Papa.

He bowed. "I'm sure you're very glad to be home, Miss Bennet. I'm about to rejoin my sister at

Netherfield, and I hope you settle back happily with all your belongings with you." But there was a look of concern on his face and he looked expressively at Papa, before they both left the room.

Elizabeth conceded defeat a few moments later. "I'm sorry, Mama. I think I will go upstairs and lie down for a little while."

CHAPTER 51

*D*arcy waited impatiently for Bingley to finish his breakfast. He hoped Elizabeth had gone upstairs after he had left, the slight crease in her forehead had indicated that she had found the noise in the sitting room rather more than she could cope with.

He knew Bennet had seen it, too, and he'd reassured him as he was leaving.

"Don't worry, Mr. Darcy. I will see she goes up to rest."

Now he wanted to be there, to call upon her and find that she had not suffered from the journey.

Bingley hastily drained his cup. "All right, Darcy, I'm ready."

Darcy rose to his feet. "I will see you later, Georgiana." He was sorry to be leaving her this early, but at least she had her companion, and Miss Bingley had not yet appeared downstairs. He tried to think what might please her. "When I return, we might go out in the coach for a drive."

She beamed. "I'd like that, William."

He nodded at her, and followed Bingley to the hall. Accepting his hat and stick from his valet, he looked down the steps to where the horses were standing, shaking their heads at their enthusiasm for a gallop.

"I think we might go the long way round, Darcy." Bingley was looking at them, too.

Darcy nodded glumly, the horses did need more exercise than walking along the lane. "Not too much further." He supposed galloping round the field might be as quick as walking the lane. But he was impatient to see her.

He steeled himself as they rode along the driveway of Longbourn House, it really was the most raucous, vulgar place he'd ever been. If he had not seen her quiet serene manner at Hunsford and at Gracechurch Street — even her calm acceptance of Lady Catherine's appalling manners when they'd been at Rosings; he would never have considered her.

No. He had been enchanted with her as early as the first time he'd seen her at the Meryton assembly. He smiled to himself; he was bewitched by her, even then. So he would put up with whatever he had to, just to have her by his side. But he was pleased that Pemberley was so far from her home.

At the house, his eyes raked the room as they entered, and his heart went cold. She wasn't there. She must be very ill, or she would have insisted on coming downstairs. Only the three youngest sisters were present, it didn't appear that Mrs. Bennet was an early riser — or perhaps she was up with Elizabeth?

He bowed, and saw Bingley going at once to Miss Kitty. He followed.

"Miss Kitty, is your sister unwell?" He could not wait for the normal niceties of conversation.

She laughed. "No, Mr. Darcy, you may be at ease. Lizzy is sitting under the old apple tree in the garden. She insisted on going outside. Mr. Wickham escorted her." She was looking at Bingley, so she didn't realise what a blow she'd struck.

He turned at once to the glass door, wide open to catch the spring air. Miss Bennet would need a blanket to ward off a chill; but if Wickham was with her, she'd need more than a blanket.

He strode out to the garden, and saw her seated under the tree. To his anger, she had no chaperone, and Wickham was standing beside her, laughing down at her.

He turned blindly away, and hurried indoors.

"Bingley," he said, urgently. "Miss Bennet is unchaperoned. Miss Kitty, of your kindness, could you accompany us outside?"

Without waiting for an answer, he found himself striding over the lawns toward her. Had she sent for that reprobate? Was this why she had wanted to come home?

He ignored Wickham, whose face was a mask of shock, and bowed to her.

"Miss Bennet, are you warm enough? Would you care to return indoors?"

She looked up at him, and a look of puzzlement crossed her face. He had obviously failed to take the look of dark anger from his features. He took a deep breath, and sensed Wickham stepping back.

"I will leave you now, Miss Bennet, and see Miss Lydia."

Darcy looked up contemptuously. Of course he would make an approach to a young, innocent girl. But what had he been doing outside with Elizabeth?

"Be composed, Mr. Darcy." Her voice was quiet, she seemed to be quite calm. "Mr. Wickham merely walked outside with me. He came to see my sister, and volunteered to offer me his arm while I came out, seeking a little more peace than there is in the house at present."

Darcy swallowed. He dared not get too close, not until her sister was chaperoning her, but that she had not been accompanied outside while with that villain made dread settle around his heart.

With relief, he saw Bingley and Miss Kitty walking along one of the paths, well within view, and he could relax a little.

She was smiling. "It was all quite proper, Mr. Darcy. The doors are open, and we were visible from the house."

Of course, she didn't know that Wickham's story was merely a pack of lies; he had not explained after she had accused him at Hunsford.

He forced a smile, and dipped his head. "May I join you?" He indicated the seat.

"Of course. I do not wish to go inside just yet."

He smiled at that. "I know you like being outdoors, but I hope you will let me know if you require another blanket."

She nodded. "I will." She smiled ruefully. "I have an apology to make, Mr. Darcy."

He was surprised. "You do?"

"Yes, I had forgotten quite how noisy it can be here, and I'm sorry I didn't listen more politely to you and the doctor."

He laughed. "I expected nothing else from you. You have always known your own mind, and I'm sure that within a very few days you will tolerate the noise with more equanimity than you might imagine at the moment."

"Perhaps," she nodded.

There was a moment or two of silence. He must prevent himself from speaking before he had considered what she might remember. When she had refused him, it had been because she thought he had wronged Wickham. But did she remember? If she did not, he must not say.

"I was wondering if your memory is assisted by your being at home now, Miss Bennet. Do you find that things are coming more easily to mind?" He had to know, had to warn her somehow about Wickham.

She glanced up at him. "I am hoping it will, but it is too soon to know whether it will be so."

"Indeed," he murmured. What should he do? She would be dismayed if her youngest sister fell prey to the man, and yet he could not make reference to his connections with him without perhaps reminding her of her refusal of his offer.

He would speak to her father, he thought. Warn him of the sort of man Wickham was, and perhaps it would get back to Elizabeth, keep her safe.

CHAPTER 52

*E*lizabeth lay on her bed that afternoon, thankful that Lydia had walked into town with Kitty. Mama was not so loud when Lydia was out.

She pondered on the events of the morning. Mr. Darcy had obviously been angry that Mr. Wickham had been outside with her when he called. She laughed quietly to herself. He was so transparently unsure how much she remembered, and undecided how to find out what she thought of the other man without risking her sudden recall of his Hunsford offer.

She rolled over. It was obvious that he was interested in her — much more than just because he had promised to recover her to Kent. Yet she had refused his offer. Even if she didn't remember, he could not possibly live with the memory of her rudeness when she rejected him.

If he did wish to marry her, he ought properly to remind her of what had gone before and state that he was trying to make amends. His efforts in that regard were certainly considerable.

But he had still treated Mr. Wickham abominably. And this morning had merely underlined what that gentleman had said.

She rolled back and put her hands behind her head. What would have been the cause of such dislike? She wondered how she could find out. But she could not possibly say she had remembered what Mr. Wickham told her and not confess to also remembering his offer. No, she could never ask him.

What if she said Mr. Wickham had told her the story just now, realising she hadn't remembered? No, that would be wrong. And, after all her experience of Mr. Darcy these past weeks, she could no longer think ill of him. She wondered what reason Mr. Wickham might have to spread such stories, and for the first time she began to wonder at the man who said he respected the father too much to call out the son, yet spread the tales to people he'd only just met?

It was no good. Elizabeth rose and tidied herself. When she had slipped on her shoes, she made her way quietly downstairs and knocked on the door to her father's library.

"Come!" he called, and she turned the handle.

"Why, Lizzy!" He regarded her benignly over his spectacles. "I thought you were resting."

"I have too much to think about, Papa." Elizabeth sat on the chair by the table in the window, remembering with a pang the days she had sat there in previous years, surrounded by books and her notes. She could still remember the feeling of accomplishment when she had finally understood something she had studied.

Papa looked sympathetically at her; he must know what her thoughts were. "Well, ring for some tea, Lizzy, and we can talk about it — if you want to."

She got up and reached for the bell, before sitting back down. "What I am curious about is why was Mr. Darcy so angry this morning when he saw Mr. Wickham talking to me?" Her father's expression closed off, but she hurried on.

"And, all I have seen of him recently shows how honourable he is, so why would he do to Mr. Wickham what he accused him of?"

Papa laughed. "That's a fine sentence to have to untangle, Lizzy. But I think I know what you mean." He took off his spectacles and folded them neatly on the top of his book.

Hill answered the bell, and Elizabeth dispatched her for a tray of tea. When the door closed behind her, Papa sat back and sighed.

"It so happens that I know some of what concerns you, Lizzy." He glanced over. "He came in to see me after he had said his farewell to you this morning. He said he wanted to warn me about the sort of man Mr. Wickham was."

Elizabeth waited, her heart beating fast. Would she find out what Mr. Darcy's business here was?

Papa picked up his spectacles again, and Elizabeth smiled. She knew he needed them when he wanted to weigh his words carefully before speaking. He got out his large linen handkerchief and started polishing the lenses. She waited quietly.

"Well, he gave me the background of the story — how Mr. Wickham is the son of the late Mr. Darcy's steward. All that he told me was in accordance with what we had heard from Wickham himself. But then he told me how the man behaved at Cambridge, and what he has been like since." He looked up. "Apparently, he told Darcy that he had no interest in the church, and requested three thousand pounds in lieu of the living. This was granted him, in addition to his stated legacy of one thousand pounds. This fortune lasted him about three years, I understand, before it was all gambled away, and Wickham then demanded the living."

Elizabeth was sitting with her hands over her mouth. How could she have believed Mr. Wickham? How could she have accused Mr. Darcy of treating him with contempt and ridicule; flung his offer back in his face?

Her father was looking at her with some surprise. "I didn't think you would react like this, Lizzy. You did not confront Mr. Darcy about it, I hope. That would have been most unseemly."

"Was that all that he wanted to say about Mr. Wickham, Papa?" Elizabeth couldn't answer his question.

Her father gave her a sharp look, then sighed. "He also told me that he was concerned for the reputation of young ladies in the area, he said that although he was unable to offer the proof he had, he'd heard of unwelcome advances, heavy — and unpaid — debts, and other matters which I will not discuss with you, as a lady. He wished to warn me about the type of young man I was allowing into the house." He stopped while Hill brought the tea in, and they both watched as the housekeeper placed it carefully onto the table and left the room again.

"I was able to tell him that I had begun to hear rumours of that sort around the town." Papa looked at her steadily. "I had been inclined to forbid Wickham to enter this house again. But I am not sure how to prevent your sisters from engaging with him in the town, and, at least when they are here, they are under my eye." He shrugged, slightly helplessly.

"Papa, I'm sure I remember Kitty saying, in one of her letters, that the militia are moving on soon to their summer duties — Brighton, isn't it?" Elizabeth was anxious to keep the discussion from Mr. Darcy.

"Well remembered, Lizzy." Papa seemed pleased. "Yes, they are leaving in a few days, so I was rather hoping the situation would solve itself." He put the spectacles on his nose and reached for his book. "I'm just sorry that it appears to have caused Mr. Darcy some mortification. I owe him a very great deal, and I would not have wished to cause him any embarrassment while on my property." He opened his book, the conversation clearly over.

Elizabeth was left to drink her tea, gazing out of the window, and think about what she had heard.

Loud shrieks from the hall interrupted the peace of the library, and Elizabeth winced, caught by surprise. Her father sighed, and removed his spectacles.

"I rather think Lydia has arrived home." He gave her a sharp look. "Does the noise make your head ache? I'm sorry that it is likely to reach even the bedrooms." He chuckled. "Perhaps you ought to go outside again to escape it."

"Thank you, Papa. I will go to my room." Elizabeth frowned to herself, her headaches had been a great deal better lately — but that was at Gracechurch Street. Here at Longbourn, much as she loved her family, the noise was not conducive to a swift recovery.

CHAPTER 53

*D*arcy and Georgiana went for a drive in the countryside during the afternoon, and he decided to do his very best to concentrate on his sister. After all, she had been left with Miss Bingley for the morning, and she was uncomplaining. The petulance he had seen in her before seemed to have gone, and he marvelled at the improvement in her.

Was it staying with Aunt Alice, or had the opportunity to meet young men through their cousin Jonathan been an eye-opener to her? He must work the conversation round to the subject slowly.

"I'm grateful to you for staying at Netherfield this morning, while I called on Miss Bennet. It can't have been easy, making conversation with Miss Bingley."

Georgiana giggled. "I had to listen to a lot of questions about you," she replied archly, and he swallowed.

"Were they questions the subject of which I ought to know?"

She smiled. "It might be helpful if I know the answers, even if I then decide it is not Miss Bingley's business to know."

Darcy looked sideways at his sister. Perhaps he should change the subject.

"I've been happy, these last few weeks, that your letters indicate you are more content with things in your life at present, dear sister."

She giggled, and his heart lifted that she was not vexed by his question.

"William, before I permit you to change the subject, I really wish to remind you again how very important to me it is that you understand my concern about Miss Bingley's ambitions."

He swallowed; he knew that, but he didn't wish Georgiana to be anxious about it.

"I would not have you distressed about it, Georgiana. I am well aware of what she wants, and I can assure you that she will never be Mrs. Darcy."

She was serious now. "I know you would never

intend that, but I become more and more concerned that she will stop at nothing to compromise you." Her direct look scared him. "Even Elizabeth said in the coach yesterday that you must be careful. She said Miss Bingley could never make you happy."

"Eliz … Miss Bennet said that?" Darcy was startled. "Does she remember what she is like?"

His sister shrugged. "She must do. But she is right. I would urge you to be very careful while we are at Netherfield. She is getting increasingly desperate — I think it must be partly because of Mr. Bingley's very obvious partiality to Miss Kitty Bennet."

Darcy forced a smile. "He certainly talks a lot about her."

Georgiana frowned. "I cannot see why his attentions are on her. Surely he would be more likely to favour Elizabeth when they were first introduced?"

Darcy nodded. "I think he was. But Miss Bennet understood he would be better matched with her sister and was very adroit in steering his affections in that direction."

He was rather uncomfortable, the conversation was going to be difficult without revealing his full part in the whole situation.

"I like Elizabeth very much, William. May I call

on her tomorrow with you? Is she recovered enough?"

Darcy looked at her in consternation. What if Wickham was there? What if Elizabeth — Miss Bennet — spoke about him? This was a difficult place for his sister to be and it was all his fault for forgetting about Wickham being here in Hertfordshire.

"What is it? What's the matter?" Georgiana looked puzzled. "I only asked if …"

Darcy shook his head. He reached over and took her hand. He wondered if he ought to say nothing, take Georgiana at once back to London. But Bennet had, only this morning confirmed that Darcy could ask Elizabeth if he might court her, and he wanted to stay here.

But Georgiana was looking at him; he had to say something.

He squeezed her hand. "Georgiana, I don't wish to say this; I love to see you so happy, and I don't want to disturb your composure. It's my fault, I had forgotten he was here, and I ought not to have brought you." He frowned and wondered what he should say.

She went pale. "There's only one person you would be anxious about in that regard, William," she whispered. "Is he here? Might he be at Longbourn?"

Darcy nodded heavily.

"I'm sorry."

"But we ought to warn Elizabeth!" she said. "I wouldn't like to think he was welcome anywhere I had a friend."

"When I saw him this morning, I spoke to Mr. Bennet and explained what the man is like. So you can be reassured."

"But not about what happened to me?" She looked agitated, and he patted her hand.

"Of course not, Georgiana. I only mentioned the other things — which are bad enough." He knew he scowled, and made an effort to smooth his features.

Georgiana pulled her hand away and turned to the coach window, her face determined.

Darcy was relieved she didn't seem too distressed, although he wondered what she would say next. Her chin went up, and she turned back to face him.

"William, I am no longer afraid of him. I wish to call on Elizabeth tomorrow — and if he is there, well then, I will ignore him and he will be embarrassed, not me."

"Bravo!" Darcy wondered when she had grown up. "Very well, we will call tomorrow, if you still wish to." He wondered when he might get a little time to speak to Elizabeth with a little privacy.

He wanted to ask her if she might court him, and was feeling rather discomposed that she might refuse — or she might say she remembered his last offer at Hunsford. If that happened, he didn't know what he would do. But he must do this, or lose her. Perhaps he might call there this afternoon.

CHAPTER 54

"Y ou can't permit it, Papa! You must not!" Elizabeth couldn't believe he was even considering it. "Lydia is not to be trusted, and she will disgrace the family."

"Sit down, Lizzy, and please don't vex yourself so." Papa pointed to the chair.

Elizabeth sat down reluctantly. "Please reconsider, Papa. Lydia is so devoid of any propriety and is such a flirt, I cannot but think she will come to harm."

"You worry too much, my dear." He looked at her over the top of his spectacles. "She will be under the care of Colonel Forster and his wife. None of the officers will be so foolish as to take advantage of her."

"They won't have to take it," Elizabeth muttered to herself. "Lydia will throw it at their feet."

"If you want to talk about it, Lizzy, at least speak so that I can hear you." Papa sounded unusually stern. "Now, what did you say?"

She shook her head. "It doesn't matter. But you have seen the colonel and his wife. He is such a foolish man!"

Papa's eyebrows rose. "Are you feeling superior again, Lizzy? I was quite enjoying a rather less proud daughter."

Elizabeth clenched her jaw. "No, Papa. But you can see he was not thinking straight. He must be nearly fifty years old, do you not agree? And Mrs. Forster must be only a year or so older than Lydia herself." She tried to keep the disgust from her voice. "Such a man cannot be thoughtful of the need for careful control of Lydia. And Mrs. Forster is as empty-headed as Lydia." She jumped to her feet, unable to sit still. "How can she be a good example to her?" She turned to her father. "Lydia will cause shame on the family."

"You must sit down, Lizzy, or you will make yourself ill again." Papa waited until she had taken her seat again. "Lydia will never be easy till she has exposed herself in some public place or other, and there will not be such an opportunity for her to do it with so little expense or inconvenience to her family as this." He raised his hand, "No, do not say anything more. I am aware how noisy this house is, and I've already seen how much it affects you in your current fragile health. When Lydia goes to Brighton, this house will be a great deal more peaceful, and after a quiet summer, you will, I trust, be restored to health."

"Papa!" Elizabeth jumped to her feet again. "I will not allow you to use my health as an excuse to send Lydia with the officers! Our whole family will be affected; our importance, our respectability in the world, must be affected by lack of all restraint which marks Lydia's character." She knew that nothing was working, nothing she would say would make any difference to his decision, and she dropped dejectedly into the chair again.

He smiled benignly at her, reached forward, and took her hand. "Do not make yourself uneasy, my love. Wherever you are known, you will be respected and valued; and you will not appear to less advantage for having a very silly sister. And Kitty will be better without her. Jane is also of benefit to your reputation." He sat back complacently. "I think Lydia may learn a valuable lesson there." He smiled at Elizabeth's raised eyebrows. "The officers may enjoy her flirting, but they will never choose her as their wife, she is too poor and too silly."

"Just like Mrs. Forster," Elizabeth muttered rebelliously.

Her father frowned. "I will ignore that this time, Lizzy, as you have been ill. But I do not expect to have you answer me back in that fashion again, do you hear?" His voice was stern, but Elizabeth didn't have time to try and argue further. A knock on the door distracted them both, and the housekeeper entered.

"Mr. Darcy wishes to call on Miss Bennet, sir."

Papa smiled, his ill-temper forgotten. "Well, perhaps it is as well we have been interrupted." He looked at the servant.

"Show him in here, Hill, please." He heaved himself out of the chair. "You might as well stay in here, Lizzy. It'll be quieter than joining your mother — and Lydia."

He bowed at Mr. Darcy as he entered. "Stay in here, Mr. Darcy. You might have a little peace, and I will join the family."

Elizabeth had risen to her feet and watched her father leave the room. What was this all about?

She curtsied absently as Mr. Darcy bowed. He didn't smile.

"Are you well, Miss Bennet?"

She nodded. "I'm just surprised at Papa. He would never go and join the family and leave a caller here."

He smiled thinly. "Perhaps he thinks you needs some quiet. You look a little paler than this morning. Do you have a headache?"

She nodded. "It is not too bad, thank you."

He was waiting, she realised. "Oh, I'm sorry." She took her seat and indicated the other chair.

"Thank you." He placed his hat and cane on the table. He looked around for a moment, before seeming to come to a decision. "Forgive me, but I could not help overhearing the sound of raised voices. I do not wish to intrude, but is there any way in which I might assist you?"

Elizabeth sagged back in her chair. "I don't think so." She blinked away a tear that threatened to fall. "I suppose I should have known I wouldn't get Papa to change his mind."

His eyes were thoughtful as he nodded. "Yet it seems to be important to you."

"Yes," she sighed. "I suppose you will hear soon enough. My youngest sister, Lydia, has been invited by Colonel and Mrs. Forster, of the militia — I believe you have met them?" She looked up, and at his nod, continued. "She's been invited to go with them when they are posted to Brighton in a few days time, as the companion of Mrs. Forster."

She closed her eyes. "I do not think it's good for Lydia to go, I believe she will not be well supervised, and she is likely to cause shame upon the family."

There was a short silence, and she opened her eyes and looked at him. His gentle smile went straight to her heart and she looked away hurriedly.

"So, you were unable to persuade your father that he ought not to permit your sister to go?"

Elizabeth nodded glumly. "Not only that, but he said it was because of me, that he thought the house would be more peaceful and quiet for my recovery." She jumped to her feet, and began to pace around the room. "I will not have it! I will not have him using that as an excuse for his decision!"

She turned and saw he had risen to his feet.

"Oh, I'm sorry." Of course, he couldn't remain seated if she wasn't sitting down.

His smile was genuine and warm. "I imagine you made your feelings known."

Elizabeth smiled reluctantly. "I'm afraid I did."

"I would have expected nothing less." He hesitated. "Miss Bennet, the evening is quite warm. Would you care to take a turn in the garden? It might help relieve your headache."

She looked at him. Why was he here? He'd been here this morning already.

"Thank you. I'd like that." She tried not to see how his expression softened at her words.

CHAPTER 55

*D*arcy waited by the library door while Miss Bennet went upstairs to get her coat.

He knew he wanted to be open with her, ask if he may court her, so that she knew his intentions. What he really wanted to do, of course, was make her an offer. But the thought that she might refuse, give him no chance to return again, be in her company … he shuddered.

And she was not herself. He could see that, and knew that she knew it, too. Perhaps it would be wrong to trouble her with his request. Perhaps he ought to see if he could assist somehow, so that her mind was not unsettled by the behaviour of her youngest sister.

He stepped into the hall as she came down the stairs, and offered her his arm.

The heat of her touch, featherlight on his arm, took up all his concentration, and they walked out to the lawn in silence. He looked round.

"Are you content that we can be seen from the house, Miss Bennet? I would not wish you to …"

"That's perfectly satisfactory, Mr. Darcy. You may be at ease."

He nodded, and they strolled very slowly on. It was only a few moments until he realised she was leaning more heavily on his arm. "Would you care to take the seat under the tree, and rest? Or return to the house?"

"If it's all the same to you, I would like to sit under the tree." She smiled slightly, and they crossed the lawn to the tree.

He sat at the end of the bench, half-turned towards her, and wondered how to start the conversation. He had not the faintest idea what to say. At Hunsford, he'd blundered in, expecting her delighted acceptance. But, although she didn't recall that, he knew she was the same lady. So he must not use the same arguments. He'd been trying to become the sort of gentleman she'd accept, he could only hope it would be enough.

"Is there a reason you called this evening, Mr.

Darcy?" Her voice was neutral, and he couldn't tell if she was happy that he was here, or not.

It was time. He swallowed and took a deep breath. "My sister wishes to call here with me tomorrow to see you. I was concerned I might not get the opportunity to speak privately to you."

She sounded amused. "I think you have the chance now."

He laughed. "Indeed. But I find myself unable to begin."

"The beginning is often a good place." He could hear the smile in her voice.

"Very well." He stared up into the branches. "I spoke to your father this morning about this matter, and I have his consent to approach you." He stopped and took another deep breath. Surely she must guess what he was about.

He turned to face her fully. "Miss Bennet, I beg the honour of your consent that I court you in the hope that we can reach an understanding. When you are well again, I hope that we might be able to move forward together."

Now was the moment. Now she might fling his request in his face, tell him that she had refused him once and he was the last man she would ever marry. His heart constricted.

"Why?" her voice was quiet. "Why the route of a formal courtship between us?"

She hadn't refused, and his heart leapt. He smiled slightly. "My affections will not be denied, Miss Bennet. But I know your father's wishes, and he has told me that he will not consent to anything more than a courtship. Not until he believes you are fully well again."

She looked down at her hands as they rested in her lap. She seemed to be deep in thought.

He had to say something. "Please do not be too discomposed, we will take things very slowly. Your wishes are paramount in all of this."

She looked up. "Thank you. I've many questions, Mr. Darcy, and I will probably think of others. The first thing I want to say is that it is not because I am ungrateful that I am cautious of acceding to your request. But I, too, am aware that I am not fully recovered, and perhaps we ought to wait until I know whether I will ever be the same." She looked wistful. "It would not be right to hold you to any sort of understanding if I was not likely to recover further."

His hopes rose higher. She hadn't refused him. He reached out and took her hand, lifting it to his lips.

"When I heard that you were missing, I realised that my heart was lost to you. I'm happy that you are as well recovered as you are, and I would never think of regretting any further lack of improvement, except in that it made you unhappy."

Her expression was doubtful. "What would your family think?"

"To be honest, I think some of them will be discomposed, because they don't know you. But Georgiana and my cousin, Colonel Fitzwilliam — you have met them both, and they both would be delighted for us, should we wish to marry. They are the only members of my family whose opinion matters to me."

Her lips twitched. "It might be better to stay with the courtship, rather than move the talk to marriage." Her gaze turned pensive. "I'd be concerned for your reputation if I agreed to a courtship, but it didn't then proceed to marriage."

His heart twisted in pain at the thought, but she was still speaking.

"I confess I can't see the need for a courtship, Mr. Darcy. You have told me of your wishes, and so we understand each other. I think that would be enough, and would not lead to complications with your family."

"I would not wish any gossip that might adversely affect your reputation, Miss Bennet, by my extended attentions that did not appear to lead anywhere."

She smiled at that. "I think that Hertfordshire is

not the same as London as regards that concern, Mr. Darcy." She met his eyes. "If you really wish it to be a formal courtship, Mr. Darcy, then I will agree. But I don't think it's necessary — and I have much on my mind at present."

He forced a smile. "Well, let us not disagree." She hadn't given him any intimation of returning his affections, and he knew he must not press her further on the matter.

They sat in silence for a few moments, while he wondered what he could do to ease her mind. "Miss Bennet, I wonder if you would accept my assistance on the matter of your youngest sister? I'm sorry that it distresses you so much, and I'd like to help."

She glanced up. "Thank you. I don't think there is anything you can do." She sounded resigned. "If Papa will consent to her going, then nothing I can say will change her mind. Or Mama's." She shook her head. "If she does something foolish, then we will all carry her ruin with us, through no fault of our own. And I care about what she might do. I don't want her to ruin her life. I don't trust Mr. Wickham."

His jaw tightened. "I warned your father about Wickham and what he is like. Did he tell you?"

She nodded. "Yes, he did. But then he is letting Lydia go to Brighton. I cannot think he is taking it seriously enough."

Darcy considered the matter carefully. "Would you like me to go and see Colonel Forster in Brighton? I can tell him what I know of the man, so that at least he will be on his guard."

"Oh! Colonel Forster is a foolish man. He is as bone-headed as some of his men, I'm afraid. And Mrs. Forster is not a good role model." She looked up. "Brighton is a long way. I would not have you go to such trouble for me."

"Will it ease your mind, Miss Bennet? If so, then Brighton is not difficult." He would go to the end of the earth if he thought it would win him Elizabeth. "When do the militia leave for Brighton?" He must warn her about Wickham and Georgiana, although he didn't think it the right time to tell her the whole story.

She sounded vague. "I'm not sure. In the next day or two, I think." She thought a moment. "Perhaps you might find he can spare the time to see you before they go. That would save the journey."

"I will perhaps see. Although it may be better at Brighton. If I see him here, your father may think I am interfering."

She nodded sadly. "Perhaps you're right."

He could sit here with her all night, but she was looking tired. "I think I ought to escort you inside now. You look very tired."

She nodded. "I'm sorry, but perhaps it would be best."

He rose, and offered her his arm. "One small matter, if I might, Miss Bennet. I hope it is in order if my sister calls with me tomorrow, but I just wanted to request that you not mention Wickham's name in front of her."

"Of course." She seemed incurious, and he wondered at it. Perhaps she was just very tired. He ought not to have been so long with her outside.

CHAPTER 56

*E*lizabeth would never admit it to her father, but several days without Lydia in the house had indeed made a difference to her feeling of well-being. Slowly, but surely, she could feel her energy coming back to her, and she began to fret at Papa's protective behaviour.

Mr. Darcy called each morning, sometimes with Georgiana; but as nothing was said, she wasn't sure whether they were officially courting or not.

She was standing, staring out of the window, when Mr. Darcy called that morning. She turned and curtsied politely, and he bowed, smiling.

"Good morning, Miss Bennet." Then he frowned slightly. "Are you well, you look a little dispirited."

She raised her eyebrows. "I see I can keep

nothing from you." She turned back to the window. Did she welcome his calls, or was she feeling hemmed in because of them, as well as by Papa? She really didn't know.

He didn't say anything, and after a moment, she turned back to him. "I'm sorry, Mr. Darcy. I admit I am a little vexed this morning. What I would really have liked to do is have the freedom to walk over to Shenley and visit Jane." She shrugged. "I know I cannot, yet, but Papa says the horses can't be spared for the coach at least for the next few days, and I haven't been accustomed to have to wait for the coach to call on my sister."

He looked indefinably pleased. "Would you excuse me a moment, Miss Bennet? Perhaps I could have a word with your father."

Elizabeth sighed when he had gone. She knew very well that his coach would be made available to her, but she didn't want her visit there to be curtailed by knowing the coachman would be waiting. It would feel wrong.

But there was no other way she could call on Jane. She knew, deep within herself, that it might be many weeks before she would again be able to happily walk several miles over the fields.

She didn't have to turn round, she knew when he came out of her father's library. Somehow, she always knew when he was there.

He was smiling. "Would you care to take a turn in the garden?"

She smiled back, she was happy he was here, it must be that she was feeling restless. "I have my coat ready, Mr. Darcy."

Walking slowly on his arm, she ignored the seat under the apple tree, and walked further across the lawn. She was aware of his gaze on her, but didn't look up.

"Miss Bennet, we ought not to go out of sight of the house, unless a maid is nearby."

She sighed. "I suppose you're right, but I'm feeling — I don't know, rather out of sorts today. I'm sorry I'm not good company."

"I have been expecting it." His voice was full of suppressed laughter. "Anyway, I wonder if you would care to take the carriage out this afternoon with Georgiana and myself. We could take a hamper and you could acquaint us with a local landmark, perhaps."

She turned to him with pleased surprise. "Oh, I didn't know that was what you were speaking to Papa about!"

"What did you think I was asking him?" His slightly crooked grin made her heart jump, and she turned away.

She wasn't sure if she could bear to stay like this, not knowing whether they were courting, or not. "I supposed ... no, never mind." She knew her eyes shone as she looked up at him. "The chance to drive out is very welcome, I'd not imagined anything so good."

He looked indulgently down at her. "I know Georgiana will be pleased, too. She very much enjoys your company."

"She's a delightful young lady; it's been kind of her to call."

He chuckled. "She looks forward very much to coming here." He seemed to hesitate.

"I expect she is pleased to leave Miss Bingley behind," Elizabeth finished for him.

He nodded. "But it does not detract at all of the pleasure she takes in coming here." He turned. "But I wonder if I should not stay too long this morning. If I leave you, will you promise to rest before this afternoon?"

"No," she shook her head. "I am trying not to rest in the daytime now. I am much better than I was, Mr. Darcy, and I don't wish to be an invalid a moment longer than is necessary."

He threw back his head and laughed. "I think you are already progressing faster than the physician thought possible." His arm tightened on her hand. "Soon you will be well, and then ..." But he stopped.

She looked up at him and decided not to ask what he had been going to say. Somehow she knew he would make her an offer, and whenever she thought of it, her heart would do somersaults and make her head swim. She wished she could talk to Jane.

"After our drive this afternoon, I will not see you tomorrow, Miss Bennet," he said. "I am going to ride to Brighton and speak to Colonel Forster about your sister."

"Thank you. I appreciate your concern, and I'll feel much better if I know that he has been spoken to, even if he does nothing."

"Indeed." His voice was amused. "And, as I am going to ride, I'll not need my coach. So your father has agreed the loan of it, so that you can call on your sister." He looked down at her. "I know it is not exactly as you wish, because you would like to walk there, as you are used to. But it is the best that can be devised at the current time, I think."

"I agree. Thank you." Elizabeth looked up at him. It would be helpful for her to talk to Jane about her feelings. "I do want to see her."

"Good. Then I will leave you now, in the hope that you might rest, and make the arrangements for this afternoon." He smiled. "I will be interested to see where you decide to take us."

CHAPTER 57

*T*he next morning, Elizabeth climbed into Mr. Darcy's coach for the short ride to Shenley. She'd ridden in it before, of course, but she was struck again by the luxurious interior, and comfort it offered. If she accepted his offer when it came, this would be her life.

Mr. Bingley had accompanied the coach, to call on Kitty, and they waved her off, before turning to walk to Oakham Mount, Mary glumly walking behind them.

Elizabeth felt a little guilty. Perhaps she ought to have asked them to come with her to see Jane, so that Mary didn't have to trudge along with them. But Elizabeth wanted to talk to Jane, and if Kitty and Mr. Bingley were there, too, she would not be able to.

She smiled to herself. Her sister and Mr. Bingley were not formally courting, but it seemed they both knew that marriage was in their future. She wondered how soon they would formalise it. Perhaps Miss Bingley was trying to prevent her brother from marrying so far beneath what she wanted for him.

But she couldn't think of them for long, and her mind flew unbidden to Jane. Her sister would be happy that Elizabeth was so much improved.

It would be wonderful to be able to sit and talk in peace and quiet, without the rest of the family around.

She stepped eagerly down from the coach, the coachman offering a supporting hand, and embraced Jane, who'd hurried out.

"Lizzy! You're better!" The sisters embraced, and Jane drew back. "Come inside and I will ring for tea."

"I've been looking forward to calling, Jane, but may I ask when Mr. Lawrence will be back? I need to tell the coachman what time to call back for me."

Jane looked at her. "It is not that, Lizzy. I think you ought not to be too long out, this first time."

"Oh, Jane, I can rest here. In fact, I'm sure you will ensure I use the footstool just as much as Mama does!" Elizabeth turned to the coachman.

"Let us say two o'clock, then." He touched his hat, and climbed up to his seat.

Elizabeth heard the harnesses jingle, and the sound of hoofbeats behind her as she followed Jane into the small vicarage.

She looked round. Jane deserved so much better than this. Hunsford parsonage was much bigger and better. But perhaps Mr. Lawrence could obtain a better living? Elizabeth smiled to herself. She could ask Mr. Darcy how that might happen.

"So, Lizzy, how are you really feeling?" Jane hurried to move the comfortable chair nearer the fire. "Sit here, and I'll fetch you a blanket, and call for some tea."

"I'm well, Jane. Please don't be anxious for me, I so much want to get everything back to normal." Elizabeth sat obediently in the chair; she knew Jane would worry if she didn't.

She didn't say anything more as Jane fussed round her, moving the side table so that she could comfortably reach her tea, and placing a plate of little cakes at her side.

She smiled as Jane sat down opposite her, cup in hand, and sighed.

"That's a heavy sigh, Jane. Are you working too hard?"

"No, not at all. But tell me about yourself. Are

you recovering? You look rather anxious — as you always used to when something was disturbing you."

Elizabeth laughed. "You know me too well, dear sister. But I confess I was happy when I had the opportunity to call on you. I miss our heart-to-heart talks. They always helped me so much."

Jane pulled her chair forwards. "Then tell me what concerns you, and I'm sure we can sort things out." She gave a sly smile. "Would it have anything to do with the fact that you arrived in Mr. Darcy's coach?"

Elizabeth knew she blushed, and Jane laughed delightedly. "May I wish you joy?"

"Oh, no! Nothing like that, Jane! Please do not intimate to anyone else what you thought!" Elizabeth looked down. "I do think he might be going to make me an offer, though, Jane. But Papa told him he would not consent until he knows I am well enough to make up my mind without thinking I need to accept because I am grateful to him for assisting me after the accident."

Jane reached over and embraced her. "I knew it! He is a lovely gentleman, and you will be so happy." She sat back. "And you know that he appreciates your mind, and won't demur when you wish to study something."

Elizabeth bit her lip and looked down. "But it is

not that which concerns me — although I am glad he is so gentlemanly."

A puzzled little frown crossed Jane's features. "So what troubles you so much about it?"

"It's something I wanted to tell you about when it happened, Jane. But I was in Kent and I wouldn't dream of putting it in a letter. I was looking forward to talking to you about it — and then all this happened." Elizabeth sighed. "I didn't remember about it for a long time, but everything has come back to me."

She looked up at her sister. "I know Mr. Darcy thinks I still don't remember about it, and he hasn't reminded me. It doesn't seem very gentlemanly."

"So, what is it that happened?" Jane still looked puzzled. "Is it important?"

"Well, yes. I think so." Elizabeth felt embarrassed. "Oh, Jane. I wish I could remember exactly. But Mr. Darcy called on me at Hunsford, and made me an offer of marriage." She raised her hand to stop Jane interrupting. "Oh, I can barely think of it without shame. I know the manner of his offer was unpardonable, his insult to my family and background unforgivable. And I was angry. Offended and insulted, I was quite open in my rudeness to his offer and told him he was the last man on earth that I could ever marry."

She pushed herself to her feet, unable to stay seated.

Jane's hands were over her face. "Oh, Lizzy! I know how outspoken you can be when you're angry. I cannot believe he would ever forgive it." She reached out. "Sit down, Lizzy, I would not have you overtax yourself." She watched as Elizabeth dropped back into the chair with a sigh.

"So what did he say that offended you so much?"

Elizabeth shrugged. "Oh, I can't think of it, Jane! It was so embarrassing! He talked about the anger and distress he would be causing to all his relations, about the degradation to his family name that our union would cause. He railed against the behaviour of Mama and Lydia. He talked of not being able to rejoice in the hope of relations whose condition in life was so decidedly beneath his own." She felt her eyes fill with tears. "Oh, it was awful, and it is hard to think about, even now. He seemed to think I ought to be grateful for his offer, because it was despite my family."

Jane had jumped to her feet. "Oh darling Lizzy! How terrible you must have felt. And with no-one there to confide in." She sat on the arm of the chair and embraced her. "It was very wrong of him to speak thus, I can't imagine what he must have been thinking of, to think you wouldn't be upset."

Elizabeth suddenly felt she ought to defend him. "I suppose he thought he was complimenting me, in making his offer despite it all." She smiled for the first time while thinking of it. "I can only think he could not put himself in the thoughts of someone listening to it. And then I accused him of his abominable treatment of Mr. Wickham, and ... oh, Jane!" She buried her face in her hands. "I'm so ashamed of what I said. I think I hurt him very much."

"From what you're saying, it seems you have forgiven him." Jane's voice was quiet. "You do love him, don't you?"

Elizabeth nodded, her face still lowered. "But, if neither of us can forget what we said, how can we ever move forwards? How can he forget what I said to him?"

"But has he taken this second chance of caring for you as if he has learned from it? I don't think you should refuse him just on that alone — unless you want an excuse?" Jane sounded reasonable.

"No, I don't want an excuse. I just think he ought to remind me of it so that we can talk about what difficulties we may suffer with the difference in our social standings."

Jane tucked an errant curl behind Elizabeth's ear in her old big-sisterly manner. "But you love him, Lizzy. That's really all that matters. And the last weeks have shown you that he loves you; so he will want you to be happy, and that means encouraging you to learn, and helping you to get well. And if you really love him, are you prepared to forgive him that he didn't tell you about the time you refused him? He has taken your reproaches, and behaved in a really gentlemanly manner towards you — and to our parents." She smiled. "And the other part — Mr. Wickham's story? Well, I don't believe that gentleman's version any more. Why would he say and do what he did, unless it was to try and shame Mr. Darcy?"

Elizabeth looked up finally. "Thank you, you're so wise. I knew you would know what I should do." She turned the conversation away from her. "But are you happy? I cannot believe you would wish to …"

Jane smiled gently. "Hush. I am content. I knew what my life would be like and my Peter is kind and loving." It was her turn to blush. "Don't tell anyone, Lizzy, but I am increasing. It is too early to tell anyone else." She touched Elizabeth's arm. "I'll never forget how you helped me with those tisanes you researched. And now they have given me a child to love." She stood up and went to the window. "And I am determined that I will get your help to raise this child with great aspirations for the love of learning."

"Jane!" It was Elizabeth's turn to embrace her sister. "What wonderful news! When did you know? How long before you're ready to tell Mama?"

Her sister's face glowed. "You don't know how wonderful it is to be able to tell someone about it. I've been hugging the news to myself and it's been so difficult."

"Haven't you told Mr. Lawrence yet?"

"No." Jane shook her head. "I've thought it had happened before, several times — and I was wrong. I know now, but there is still so much that can yet go wrong, and I don't want him to worry." She sat up straighter, with a determined air to change the topic of conversation. "And what is Mr. Darcy doing today, that means he doesn't need his coach?"

CHAPTER 58

*D*arcy sat back comfortably in the coach. This was actually much better than riding to Brighton, and when Bingley had offered his coach for the duration, Darcy had accepted without hesitation.

He had started at dawn, and could stay overnight in Brighton. Then he would be back at Netherfield tomorrow afternoon; whereas if he was riding, he'd have to stop a night during the journey each way, probably at Darcy House.

Elizabeth hadn't seemed to have remembered that Brighton was nigh on eighty miles from Hertfordshire, and he hadn't been inclined to tell her, or she'd have objected to having the use of his coach.

He smiled. He hoped she would enjoy calling on her sister; he'd heard from Bingley that they had been very close before the oldest had married. And he'd heard from Bennet that Elizabeth had since been dismayed at the change in their relationship.

Perhaps today would bring her some comfort. She was definitely improved these last few days, and Darcy ascribed much of that to the more peaceful atmosphere at Longbourn since the youngest girl had left for Brighton.

He frowned, he must be careful not to discompose Colonel Forster so much that he sent her home. But he didn't want to think of the matter just yet. There were many hours driving before he got close to the south coast town. With good fortune, he might have time to walk along the promenade; the sea air would do him good.

He reached into the inner pocket of his coat and drew out the letters that had reached him yesterday. He shuffled through them and drew out Richard's to reread.

The Dower House, Pemberley.

   Darcy

   I am writing from our new home to thank you again for your very kind offer for us to live here. It seems strange to both Anne and I to be staying in a dower house, but we are very comfortable.

   Anne is somewhat tired after our tour, and as I told

you in my last letter, we cut it short and made our way here a few days ago.

But she is already stronger than she was before she left Rosings. We walk each day in the park, and delight in each other's company.

She has been writing letters to her mother each day. She has a delightful generosity of spirit, and her letters are light and cheerful, despite not having received a reply. That is, until yesterday, when a letter arrived from Lady Catherine.

It seems that several weeks to think about things, and also what my father said when he called upon her, have made an impression on her.

It was a very brief, stilted letter. However, it was cordial enough, considering its provenance, and Anne was happy to receive it.

I am, however, pleased that we are so far away from Kent, and that Lady Catherine appears to understand that it would not be politic to appear here uninvited.

Enough about that. I want to express my gratitude to you for the assistance you have provided to enable me to buy out my commission. I had not realised quite how much it would relieve Anne's mind. Her delight is palpable, and a pleasure to see.

I hope all is well with you, and that Miss Bennet continues to improve in health. I know Anne has been assiduous in her correspondence with her, and is delighted to receive letters back. She is a good friend to Anne.

Yours, etc.
Richard.

Darcy smiled at the words. Elizabeth would be a good friend to Anne, he knew that. And to Georgiana, too. He leaned back. Surely it meant that she would accept his family, not think him too proud and disdainful?

HE FELT REFRESHED after a long walk along the promenade that afternoon, before returning to the Rottingdean Club to prepare for dinner. He smiled wryly. Colonel Forster had returned his note with flattering speed, accepting the invitation to dine.

Darcy wondered what sort of a man he was. He knew he had been at the Netherfield ball, but he had to admit that he had taken little notice of those who did not concern him.

But he thought about what Elizabeth had said. A bone-headedly foolish man. A man who had taken a very young wife with little thought of suitability and companionship. He chuckled to himself, it would most definitely not be approved of by Elizabeth, he knew.

But it gave him an idea of how to approach the issue. First, he must ensure that Miss Lydia was under proper supervision, and Mrs. Forster was considered by Elizabeth to be a bad influence on her sister.

Secondly, he must warn the man about the presence of Wickham, tell him about the debts, the gambling, and the risk of ruin to young women and girls from all levels in society.

He would begin and see what the man was like, then he could tailor his words accordingly.

He relaxed in the chair by the fire of his chamber at the club when he was ready, a whisky in his hand, idly watching as his valet moved around the room, clearing away the paraphernalia.

Then it was time and he went downstairs, wondering if he'd even recognise the man if he was not in his regimentals.

He needn't have worried. Colonel Forster was resplendent in his gaudy uniform, and Darcy hid his smile. Richard had rarely worn uniform when off-duty; this man obviously needed the importance that his rank gave him. It was yet another clue to the way he needed to take the evening.

"Good evening, Colonel. Thank you for agreeing to dine with me." The two men bowed to each other, and Darcy led the way directly into the dining room. He watched with concealed amusement as the man looked around with satisfaction. It was perfectly obvious that he was unused to the quiet elegance and taste of a good club. The servants moved around the room quietly, and they were soon seated at a table in a small anteroom, the table laden with gleaming silver and crystal glassware.

"I was delighted to hear from you, Darcy." Forster looked over at him. "I was disappointed not to have the opportunity to meet you when we were both in Hertfordshire."

"As I was," Darcy lied, dipping his head in acknowledgement. "However, there are several matters I wished to draw to your attention, and it seemed better to me to wait until you had departed for Brighton and then dine here quietly and confidentially."

The man's gaze seemed quite astute, and Darcy knew he must be careful not to underestimate him. To have attained the rank of Colonel could not only be due to luck or patronage, he must be more able than he appeared. And, of course, the ability to avoid the sabre of an enemy was not to be thought of lightly.

The courses came and went, and they conversed of impersonal matters; mostly the progress of the war and the risk of invasion.

Darcy frowned; he ought perhaps, to consider what precautions he should take, should it appear more likely at some point. They discussed the issue, Darcy appreciating the insight the man could offer.

After dinner, they went to the club room, taking the great leather chairs each side of the great fireplace. The room was not crowded, and they could talk confidentially.

"They do a fine meal here, Darcy." The colonel looked round appreciatively. "But I cannot help but be curious as to the reason you summoned me here."

Darcy sipped his brandy. "Indeed. I wanted to talk to you about George Wickham, who has recently taken a commission in the Wiltshires." He saw the other man grimace. "You have concerns about the man already?"

"Who wouldn't?" Forster stared morosely into the flames. "I would be much happier had he chosen a different county to enlist in — preferably one about to undertake duties at the front."

Darcy grinned. They understood one another. "Well, I'm sorry I'm currently unable to assist you — although I suppose we might be able to think of something along those lines." He put his glass down. "I wished to tell you what I know of the man, so that you can try and mitigate any problems before they become too severe. I have known him many years, and in that time I have discovered him to be an inveterate liar and cheat. He cannot control his gambling, and thinks nothing of running up debts that he can never repay." He smiled thinly. "I don't think he has any intention of repaying them, either. His sense of entitlement to a better life than he could ever afford means he feels no guilt or shame about defrauding others." He waited.

Forster scowled. "It has been hard enough getting him to pay his mess bill," he grumbled.

"I'm certain he hasn't paid it, his latest creditor will have."

The colonel looked up. "There is something else about him, too. You would not have come just for this."

Darcy nodded ruefully. The man was no fool, whatever his lusts led him to.

"Yes. Wickham has also a long history of licentiousness. He has ruined a number of girls, including several young ladies, whom he has abandoned." He swallowed. "He has also attempted on more than one occasion, to gain the trust and affections of young girls of fortune, and persuade them to elope."

The colonel's face was dark with anger. "Thank you for telling me. It is required of my officers that they behave themselves." He glared at Darcy. "It is not always easy for them, there are young ladies who lack the slightest control of their behaviour, and some of my youngest men cannot easily think with their heads when a girl smiles winningly at them. But Wickham is old enough to be able to control himself."

Darcy remembered what Elizabeth had intimated, that Forster himself hadn't been in control of his feelings; but at least he had married the girl. Wickham was conscious enough of fortune to refuse to marry a girl he had taken advantage of.

"I have been asked as well to bring Miss Lydia Bennet's welfare before you, colonel," Darcy continued. "I know that she has little self-control and I am concerned that she may bring her family into disrepute, not just around Wickham, but any of your officers who pay her attention."

Forster nodded. "She is a foolish young flibbertigibbet, but my wife and she have a close friendship." He frowned at his glass, and Darcy signalled to the servant to refill it.

"But I thank you for the warning, Darcy, and if I feel her to be in danger, I will send her home. I will assure you of that." He nodded at Darcy. "I hope you feel reassured." He laughed humourlessly. "Now I just have to decide what to do about Wickham."

Darcy shrugged. "I could arrange orders from the War Office for him, and ensure he is posted to active service. It would not be possible for him to ruin young women when he is on the front line."

"I appreciate the offer, Darcy and I will bear it

in mind if I feel any young lady is in danger." He heaved himself to his feet. "Now I will take my leave of you." He bowed at Darcy. "Thank you for your hospitality, sir."

Darcy bowed in return. But when the colonel was gone, he shook his head. Young ladies would always be in danger from Wickham.

However, he could not spare the time to worry about him just now. Tomorrow, he could start at dawn, and be back in Hertfordshire during the afternoon. He might have time to call at Long-bourn. He would relish seeing Elizabeth.

CHAPTER 59

The journey home had been fast and uneventful. Darcy moved his shoulders uncomfortably in his jacket. Bingley's coach was not as comfortable as his own for fast journeys.

He bowed over Georgiana's hand. "It's good to see you, dear sister. But I pray you excuse me, I will be in a better temper when I have had the chance to rid myself of the stiffness from the journey."

"Of course, William." She smiled as if she knew he was having difficulty not asking about Elizabeth, and he hurried away.

Mr. Maunder was already preparing a bath for him, and he stood at the window as he waited, staring out towards Longbourn.

It was too late to call on her today. Two days, it was two days since he had seen her and he missed her most acutely. He would call there tomorrow, he must have the chance to speak to her.

The whole way home, he'd been free to think of his love and desire for her. The guilt was heavy in his heart that he had not told her of the time at Hunsford when he had spoken so reprehensibly of her family, of the shame the marriage he proposed would bring to his family. He shook his head despondently. Her stinging words had hurt him deeply, but over the last weeks, he'd come to accept that every single one was justified.

He hoped that his behaviour since then might be able to show that he had learned from her words, that he might be worthy of her.

But he must tell her, explain what had happened, and that he bitterly regretted what he had done. The shame at the thought of it sent the heat of a flush through him, and he turned irritably to see how long it would be before his bath was ready.

He smiled reluctantly; he had timed it well, the steam was coiling up from the jug Mr. Maunder was pouring in, and he could see there was enough depth.

Perhaps he would be able to stay in long enough to rid his body of the ache of the day before the water cooled too much.

He lay back in the water, a towel draped over

the bath rim to keep the heat in as long as possible. His valet appeared with a single whisky on a silver tray.

"Thank you, Mr. Maunder. It is much appreciated." He shut his eyes. He could take this time before he went downstairs.

The form of Elizabeth appeared through his closed lids, and he lay content, able to gaze unobserved, at her slender form as she danced at Bingley's ball, at her smile lighting up the room and the faces of whomever she was speaking to. He watched as the vision before him bent over her sketchpad, concentrating as she drew what she'd observed. His contentment shattered. How could he help her accept what had happened to her, assist her to devise a way of managing her notes to aid her memory?

And his mind went to Georgiana, then to Richard's letter. He wondered idly what subject young Jonathan was studying. Georgiana had confided in him her concern that he seemed to think he was expected to take a commission in the army. She was disturbed that he might be sent to the front and lose his life, or worse. Then Richard's letter had brought home to him how anxious a lady might be with a husband away at war.

Perhaps Jonathan could be found some

respectable appointment so that he did not need to take a commission.

But he didn't like to think of Georgiana married to anyone other than a gentleman. Perhaps he'd need to supplement her fortune, make sure their income would be adequate, so that he could manage an estate. It would be a heavy expense, even for an estate as wealthy as Pemberley. But something must be managed.

However, he must not act precipitously. She was still very young, this infatuation might not last.

HE DESCENDED THE STAIRS RELUCTANTLY. If it was not for Georgiana, he might have asked for dinner to be sent up to his chambers, but he must not shirk his duty.

He hoped she might be downstairs already, but when he reached the hall, he heard the loud, complaining tones of Miss Bingley from the drawing room.

No. He would not enter until he had to. He turned into Bingley's library. He would wait in there, where she could not follow. A slight prickle of suspicion, and he beckoned a footman into the room, and sank into one of the armchairs.

"Wait here."

The footman bowed, and stood against the wall. Darcy felt a little foolish. Of course she wouldn't come in here — she didn't know he had come down yet.

He leaned back, hoping for the vision of Miss Bennet to comfort him, but she wasn't there, just the hectoring tones of Miss Bingley.

He jerked forward.

"Oh, Mr. Darcy!" She was there, and he sprang to his feet in horror.

She was pulling at the neckline of her gown, her smile hungry. "I didn't know you would be all alone in here."

He recovered himself. "But I am not alone, Miss Bingley, and even if you were ruined, I would leave you so. I am promised to another," he said recklessly, and pushed past her.

"You!" He beckoned to the footman and they both hurried through the door, which he pulled to behind him, his heart pounding. Why had he said that?

"Darcy!" Bingley was just bounding down the stairs. "You look as if you have seen a ghost, man!"

"Worse than a ghost, Bingley." Darcy held the door closed. "It was fortunate I instructed a servant to be in the room with me." He scowled. "Your sister entered the library, believing me to be alone, and began adjusting her clothing." He shuddered.

"I will need to leave Netherfield." His heart sank.

"Not at all. I will not have it!" Bingley's normally sunny features were cold with anger. He crossed the hall and looked into the drawing room.

"Louisa!" He summoned Mrs. Hurst to him, and she came into the hall, looking wary.

"Thank you, Darcy. I will deal with this." Bingley beckoned his sister and turned to the library door.

Darcy knew himself dismissed and turned for the drawing room. Hurst was dozing on the sofa, and Darcy glanced at him. The man seemed to have heard nothing. He stood by the mantel, trying to hear what was going on in the hall.

He hoped Georgiana would not come down until it was all over. He wondered what Bingley had meant when he said that Darcy would not need to leave Netherfield.

The only way he could stay was if Miss Bingley was sent back to London, but he doubted Bingley was made of stern enough stuff for that.

BINGLEY TURNED into the drawing room, his expression cold. He was followed by Georgiana, looking shaken.

Darcy hurried over to her, and took her hand. "I'm sorry if you were disturbed, Georgiana."

Bingley joined them, shaking his head. "I can't tell you how sorry I am, Darcy — and that you had to witness it, Georgiana. But it needed to be done. Caroline will be dining in her chamber tonight. Tomorrow morning, Hurst will escort the ladies back to London — or Caroline can go on her own, with her maid." He looked stern. "I have permitted this to go on too long."

Georgiana looked between them. "What happened?" She looked fearful. "Did she …"

Darcy shook his head. "Please do not be anxious, I am all right. Miss Bingley was unaware I had kept a servant with me." He smiled down at her. "I took notice of what you said to me before."

"I was interested in what Caroline said to me, though," Bingley said delicately.

Darcy glared at him. "I had to say something to her," he said hastily, and offered Georgiana his arm and turned away. He certainly didn't want Bingley saying that he'd said he was promised to another in front of his sister.

Not that he was ashamed, he told himself. He was just unsure whether he and Elizabeth were really courting or not.

He was a little distrait over dinner. He doubted Miss Bingley would make the situation known, because she would materially damage herself in the opinion of others.

He had already decided he would call on Elizabeth tomorrow, and confess his errors at Hunsford. He wondered if she would wish to see him again. Was it possible that she would accept him? Might he be able to ask? He bitterly regretted being unable to say that he was engaged to Miss Bennet, be proud of the fact that she had accepted him.

He put down his knife and fork, smiling to himself. How he had changed. Before, he would have expected Elizabeth to be proud that he had chosen her. Now, he was the one who would be honoured beyond measure. Her circumstances were unchanged, it was he who had changed — changed out of all recognition.

He saw Georgiana was looking at him across the table, a slight smile playing across her lips. He looked away, embarrassed. Then his heart sank. He wanted time with Elizabeth tomorrow, but if Bingley's sisters were going to London, he could hardly leave Georgiana alone here.

At the end of the meal, Mrs. Hurst rose, sulkily, and Georgiana also rose to withdraw with her. Darcy's gaze followed her, worried; and he turned to Bingley.

"Perhaps we might not stay with the port for too

long. I am not sure that the ladies will be in good cheer."

Bingley nodded at the footman, who silently left the room, shutting the door behind him.

"I agree." He poured his port and passed the decanter. "I did want to ask you, though, about what you told Caroline. Might I soon be in a position to wish you joy?"

Darcy glanced at Hurst, who was concentrating on his drink. He supposed Miss Bingley would have told her sister, who would tell her husband. In fact she might be telling Georgiana even now.

He sighed. He could say nothing until tomorrow. "I merely meant that my heart is committed elsewhere, Bingley. There is nothing official."

"Oh." Bingley's face fell. "I understand."

Darcy nodded. He must be a gentleman. "I hope Miss Bingley is not too distressed."

Bingley looked at him in astonishment, and his lips twitched. "I think distress is not the term. Anger, perhaps. Mingled with rage for the embarrassment she believes you caused her."

Darcy put down his glass. "I'm sorry it happened, Bingley." He grimaced. "Perhaps we could rejoin the ladies."

CHAPTER 60

*E*lizabeth rose to bright sunshine the next morning. She smiled, sunshine always made her feel more cheerful. There was a feeling within her that something would happen soon. She welcomed the thought; currently the feeling of unfinished business had weighed heavily on her.

After breakfast, she sat at the table, and drew a sheet of notepaper towards her. She hoped Mr. Darcy might be back; she wanted to know how his business in Brighton had progressed. But she was an honest person, she must admit that she had missed his calls, had come to rely on his steady, calm presence, his reassurance that everything would be all right.

But while she waited and hoped that he would

call, she could write another note to Mrs. Liddell. It was always a little difficult to know what to say, for she knew the woman could not read, so she wrote a simple, bland little note, as the vicar would have to read it to her.

Dear Mrs. Liddell,

I hope this letter finds you well. I have been remembering your kindness to me when I was unwell at Copthorne and thought you would like to know I am continuing my recovery. I am able to walk in the gardens now, and hope soon to be able to walk in the lane near my home.

I'm sending this small gift in continuing gratitude to you, and hope you might find a use for it.

Yours, etc,

Elizabeth Bennet

She placed the note with the little parcel of heavy stockings that Kitty had bought from the milliners for her, and turned to write a little covering note for the vicar.

Pen poised, she made a sudden sound of annoyance. His name had escaped her. And her notes were upstairs. She put the pen down. Now she would have to go upstairs, and she couldn't be so careless about expending energy as she had before.

"What has vexed you so, Miss Bennet?" His

voice was full of amusement, and she turned suddenly. He was here! And she hadn't heard them arrive. Of course, they had been such regular visitors that Mama insisted they did not stand on protocol when they arrived — particularly Mr. Bingley.

Mr. Bingley was greeting Kitty with his usual extravagant bow. Mr. Darcy's to her was more restrained, but as his gaze burned into the depths of her soul, she felt it could not be less exciting.

She stood hastily. "Mr. Darcy! I didn't hear you enter."

He smiled, his eyes never leaving her features. "So I noticed." His chuckle warmed her through. "I reiterate, what has vexed you? Might I be of assistance?"

Elizabeth resumed her seat, and picked up her pen. "Indeed you can, Mr. Darcy," she said primly. "I have left my aide-memoire notebook upstairs, and I have forgotten the name of the vicar at Copthorne. Perhaps you might save me going upstairs to retrieve it."

His gaze wandered to the folded letter and little parcel. "Mr. Parks. He is a clever young man, and treats his parishioners well, I think." He smiled. "Mrs. Liddell is gratified that you send so often to her."

Elizabeth's eyebrows weren't under her control. "And you know that, because …?"

He looked a little embarrassed. "When you were first recovered, I wrote to him several times. He has maintained the correspondence, and has told me of her delight every time he reads your letters to her."

She smiled, a little sadly. "Without her generosity and kindness, I wouldn't be here."

He nodded, his eyes darkening as if in pain.

But she had thought of something else. "Have you discovered where I was found? How I got to that cottage?"

Mr. Darcy shook his head. "I'm sorry. We know that her husband and a fellow worker found you and brought you home." He looked a little discomfited. "Colonel Fitzwilliam thought it would not be politic to enquire further. He thought there might have been some poaching, and that they risked hanging or deportation to recover you, instead of leaving you where you were."

"Oh! I'm glad there was no investigation, and I will never speak of it again." She glanced at the parcel. "Do you think he objects to being constantly reminded of the risk?"

Mr. Darcy shook his head. "I doubt there will be any complaint. Where we think you fell is on a farm belonging to the Rosings estate." He smiled wryly. "Lady Catherine has other things on her mind. And in any event, Mr. Parks knows to contact me if there is any difficulty and I will deal with it."

"Mr. Parks." Elizabeth raised her hand. "One moment." She pulled the sheet of paper towards her and wrote the salutation of the note she would write. "There! I will not forget it now, and can complete the rest later." She tidied the little heap and pushed it to the side. "Now, I think the tea might be arriving. I hope your business to the coast was successful."

He nodded. "I think so, Miss Bennet." He glanced round as Kitty carried two cups of tea towards them.

"Good morning, Mr. Darcy."

"Good morning, Miss Kitty." Mr. Darcy stood and bowed politely. He nodded at his friend, close behind her sister.

Elizabeth smiled up at her sister. "Thank you, Kitty." She sipped her tea. When would Kitty become engaged to Mr. Bingley? She must ask her tonight why they seemed to be waiting, there seemed to be great affection on both sides.

She sighed. Would she ever be able to declare her love to Mr. Darcy, knowing that he was not disappointed by the loss of her acute memory and learning? Would he ever be able to forgive her for all the trouble she had caused?

She listened to the conversation. She could

hardly believe how gravely kind and considerate Mr. Darcy was to Kitty, given the anger in which he'd spoken of her family.

She put down her cup and at once Mr. Darcy turned to her.

"Might you care to take a turn in the gardens, Miss Bennet?" His gaze melted her heart.

"Thank you, Mr. Darcy. It would be very pleasant." In some indefinable way, he seemed pleased, and she looked down.

"That's a good idea, Lizzy!" Kitty bounced to her feet. "I'll get your coat for you."

As she hurried away, the gentlemen stayed standing, having risen when Kitty did. Elizabeth's lips twitched. What happened between married couples at that level of society, she wondered? Papa never rose when Mama did, but perhaps it was different in higher levels. How exhausting, trying not to disturb one's husband too much. She had to look down, it proving impossible not to smile. What a wonderful weapon, also, if one was displeased with one's husband, to keep jumping up and down for a forgotten spool of thread, and then a needle, then a pair of scissors, knowing he had to rise on each occasion.

His rich chuckle startled her, and she looked up. "I wonder if I will ever know the thought that caused such merriment." His amusement belied his words, and Elizabeth could barely contain her laugh.

"Someday I may be able to tell you."

"I look forward to it."

CHAPTER 61

*A*s they strolled along the path, Bingley and Miss Kitty some yards ahead of them; Darcy was conscious of little other than the heat of her hand on his arm.

She looked up at him. "Is your sister well, Mr. Darcy? Did she not wish to come with you this morning?"

He hesitated. How much should he tell her? She was bound to find out that Miss Bingley was no longer at Netherfield soon. No. If they talked about it, time would pass, and he would then have no opportunity to talk about — he swallowed — about Hunsford. She was looking a little puzzled, and he recalled her question. "Oh! No, Georgiana is having a quiet morning with her companion today." He thought she looked unconvinced. "Perhaps I might bring her with me tomorrow?"

What would tomorrow bring? Would he still be welcome here? He must know. He stopped, and turned to her. "Miss Bennet, I have an important matter I wish to speak to you about. Would it be agreeable to sit on the seat under the apple tree?"

"Of course."

He led her over to the seat, and waited while she settled herself. "May I?" He indicated the seat and she nodded. "Thank you." Once seated, though, he wanted nothing more than to be able to pace up and down. How ought he to begin? He raked his hand through his hair, and realised she was laughing at him.

"Forgive me, Mr. Darcy. I mean no harm." Her laugh was musical and lightened his heart.

"Miss Bennet, I must speak out. I have a confession to make to you. I'm aware that you have made great progress in many areas of your recovery, and your bravery and courage is without parallel." He glanced at her, she was listening calmly. He swallowed.

"I wish to repeat my declaration of a few days ago, that I have the deepest affection and love for you, but as you know, your father thought I ought to wait until you were fully recovered." He wanted to wipe his hand across his face. He pushed down the urge, and drew another breath.

"There is something else you need to know, Miss Bennet. I ... confess that I have been reluctant to tell you. But I can no longer live with the knowledge that I have kept these facts from you." He risked a look at her face again. Serenely beautiful, she looked unworried by his words.

He stared at her face. How could he ever lose her? His love burned stronger each day — but what did she think of him?

He drew breath, he must tell her. "You know that we were ... acquaintances, before your unfortunate accident." At her nod, he continued. "On the Thursday before it, I called on you at Hunsford Parsonage." He looked up and met her eyes. He would be honest, not matter what it cost. "I made you an offer of marriage, Miss Bennet." He couldn't prevent a slight smile.

"I will never regret the offer ... but the manner in which I made it was reprehensible. Since that night I have tortured myself with my unforgivable words, my arrogance and the assumptions with which I lived my life until then." He dropped his gaze, even though he could see nothing in her expression to indicate outrage, or sympathy. He had no idea what she was thinking. He could only continue.

473

"You refused my offer, you told me that my pride and arrogance meant that I was the last man you could ever be prevailed upon to marry." He tried to keep his voice level and unemotional, hide the pain the memory still brought.

He drew a final deep breath. If she rejected him, sent him away, he wasn't sure he could ever draw another. "Every word you spoke to me was justified. Your words, your refusal, they have tortured me ever since." He grimaced. "I left Kent, and travelled to Meryton to try and find out what you liked, what you wished for in a man you might learn to love." He wanted above all, to reach for her hand, but it would not be proper. "It was there I learned of your disappearance. I returned at once to join the search for you." He straightened up.

"I will acknowledge that you had every right and justification to refuse me. Although it caused me much heartache, I hope that I have not been too proud to learn from it, and that I've become the sort of man you might be able to learn to accept, to return his sincere affections, to make the happiest of men." He sighed. "I apologise most sincerely for keeping this matter from you; but I have been tormented by the thought that you might send me away — and I could not bear it."

There was a long silence, and he fought to get

his breathing under regulation. It seemed she was still ready to listen. "Miss Bennet, I beg that you might find it in your heart to permit me to prove to you that I have changed, that I can be the sort of gentleman you might be prevailed upon to marry."

Her lips twitched, and her eyes danced. His heart began to hope. If she was amused, she surely wasn't angry.

"Why, Mr. Darcy, what have you been doing these last weeks, but already proving that to me?" Then her features became serious. "But I would be anxious for you, that if I can never recover, remain the sort of lady whose mind is unable to recall what she needs to, you might then come to resent me."

"Never!" he declared. "Miss Bennet, you have already recovered so well — and even if you had not, I would beg the opportunity to care for you, whatever support you still needed. You need have no concerns that I would ever regret our union."

She leaned back against the tree, the gentle smile that he loved so much warming him through. "You may be at ease, Mr. Darcy. I can see you have changed — and I'm humbled that you should be willing to change — to do that for me." Her laugh made him smile, but her next words wiped it from his face.

She leaned forward. "Indeed, I have been

wondering for some weeks when you might raise the subject of that occasion. You see, I wish to apologise, too. Whether they were justified or not, my words were rude and unforgivable. That they were said in the heat of emotion doesn't detract in the slightest from the fact that, uttered, they rendered me unladylike and unworthy of your attention." She blinked hard. "I'm so happy you have finally spoken to me about it — I didn't have the courage to begin." She lifted her hand to him and he bowed over it.

"Please do not be distressed, Miss Bennet. It was my duty to speak of it, but I knew that at first, your return to health was of the greatest importance. Then I did not know how to begin." He knew his smile was rueful. "You must have been most amused by my efforts to prove myself to you without admitting to it."

"No, my concern was about why you still called on me, even though my words must have been so offensive to you that you would never wish to renew your addresses to me."

Hope flared within him. "Might I dare to hope that your feelings on that day are different now? That I might hope for the answer that I most earnestly desire?"

She looked a little wistful. "Do you think Papa would think I am well enough that he might give his consent? — and will Georgiana be happy about it? Perhaps you ought not to offer until you know the answers."

He found his fingers were entwined in hers, with no memory of it happening. "Dearest Elizabeth," he knew his voice was hoarse. "I will go and find out what you wish to know. But I beg that there be no confusion between us. I love you most dearly, and could never be happy unless I am able to make you my wife and have the chance to keep you happy, safe, and with all the books and study opportunities you wish to have."

He watched a rosy blush wash over her face.

"Thank you, Mr. Darcy. I accept, with delight that you have forgiven me my stinging words and the hurt I must have caused you."

"William. Can you call me by my given name?"

She smiled again. "William."

The sound of his name dropping from her lips was nectar such as he had never dreamed of, and he lifted her hand to his lips. "Dearest Elizabeth. Might I ask your father to consent?"

She looked dubious. "I hope he will not object."

"I will convince him," Darcy declared. He thought he knew how to do it, without expectations that he was a prize to any family, without pride, but with assurances that his care for Elizabeth would match Bennet's own. "I hope that we might be able to make the announcement to your family this very day." He looked sideways at her. "You might even need to rewrite your letter to Mrs. Liddell."

She laughed delightedly. "I think she'll be very pleased."

CHAPTER 62

*T*hat afternoon, Elizabeth lay on her bed, thinking. While she was trying not to rest regularly in the daytime, today she might be forgiven, she thought.

Tears filled her eyes as she recalled the events of the morning. Mr. Darcy — William — had gone in to see her father, while she waited outside; Kitty and Mr. Bingley still seeming to have endless topics of conversation.

Papa had returned with him outside to offer her his felicitations, his eyes embarrassingly moist.

"I always knew I would lose you, Lizzy, but this is a happy way, not the way I feared so very few weeks ago."

"Thank you, Papa." Elizabeth didn't know quite

what else to say, and William took her hand onto his arm.

"Perhaps you'd like to go inside, Elizabeth, and speak to your mother and Miss Mary?" He smiled over at his friend and Kitty. "I think they also haven't noticed anything has happened."

"Hmph!" Papa had exclaimed. "A fine chaperone she is, too!" But his tone was mild, and Elizabeth reached up and kissed his cheek.

"You're the best father in the world, Papa." Then she'd hurried over to speak to Kitty, and after her squeals of excitement, the whole party had repaired indoors.

She rolled over on her bed. It had been a memorable hour. William had borne Mama's excitement stoically and had listened seriously to Mary's admonitions, without the slightest sign of amusement or annoyance.

Kitty had been giving Mr. Bingley significant looks, and Elizabeth smiled to herself. She might need to ask Mr. Darcy — no, William — to give his friend his approval. Surely he would?

She put her hands behind her head and gazed up at the ceiling. She had to acknowledge that she didn't know him very well, didn't know what he would say when she asked for his help in encouraging Mr. Bingley. She smiled slightly, she would still ask him for his help in gaining a more valuable living for Mr. Lawrence. Jane deserved so much more. It wasn't far to Shenley, and she knew her express had probably arrived by now. Jane would know that she was engaged, and that her scruples about the first offer were all resolved.

Elizabeth squeezed her eyes shut, unable to stop a few tears gathering. He was so handsome, so thoughtful and loving. His intense gaze could burn into her heart even when she was just thinking about it; and warmth spread through her.

There was a soft knock on the door, and Kitty slipped into the chamber. "I thought you might not be asleep, Lizzy." She slipped off her shoes and climbed onto the bed beside her. "Oh, I'm so happy for you. It's perfectly obvious he loves you so very much."

"As Mr. Bingley does you," Elizabeth teased.

Kitty blushed. "And I him," she laughed. "If I did not think Mr. Bingley the better man, I'd feel quite envious of you!"

"The better man!" Elizabeth propped herself up on one elbow. "For that comment, I must rethink my whole idea of you as sensible and wise beyond your years!"

Kitty sobered up. "I can tell how much he loves you, Lizzy. But I have been concerned as to whether you return his affections. Are you sure you are not going to marry him merely for gratitude?"

"Of course not!" Elizabeth felt indignant. Kitty regarded her.

"I hope you don't mind me saying so, but I think you do not act to him as if you love him. Do you know him well enough? I mean, I know you have seen a lot of each other, but you have been so ill that it was all about getting well again, and having to accept his help." Chin on her hand, she looked away. "Don't be offended, dear Lizzy, but I'm not sure whether Mr. Darcy knows it either."

"He said he loves me!" Elizabeth felt the tears welling up again.

"Of course he does." Kitty embraced her. "I meant he is not sure whether you love him in return."

"Isn't he?" Elizabeth stared at her sister, she sat herself up on the edge of the bed.

"You'll have to excuse me, Lizzy, but I have been watching you both. I think your Mr. Darcy is unsure of himself. You might need to show him your love quite clearly, not just declare it. There is something that has been troubling him, and I can't think it would be anything other than that."

He had been concerned about Hunsford, Elizabeth knew. That Kitty had discerned its effects, without knowing about the cause … "You're a very astute person, Kitty, hidden in a very young lady's exterior. I think some people will lose arguments with you, by taking you at face value."

Kitty turned at the door and laughed. "And one of them was Miss Bingley. But at least she is gone. Did Mr. Darcy tell you about it?"

"No; what happened?" Elizabeth was puzzled.

"Oh, well, I expect he had something else on his mind," Kitty said slyly, and laughed as she closed the door behind her.

Elizabeth lay back and closed her eyes. She wanted to rest, William was bringing Georgiana to dinner tonight and Mr. Bingley would also ensure the party was a cheerful one. She had wondered why he'd been at pains to say there would only be three in the party, but if what Kitty had said was right, it meant his sisters had returned to London.

Perhaps she might find out this evening. As an engaged couple, they might have a little more privacy than would have been accorded them before today, and she was anxious to reassure him that his affections were certainly returned. She frowned a little, she must be careful not to make Georgiana think that she was usurping her brother's attention. What else did she want to ask him? She considered drowsily, perhaps it didn't matter, she'd remember after she'd had some sleep.

A SUDDEN SURGE in noise from downstairs woke her, and she glanced at the window. The sun had moved, perhaps she'd had an hour's sleep. She smiled, it would have to do. She would go down and see what her mother was so vexed about.

Mama wasn't vexed. She was delighted — and insulted — both at the same time. Harriet Forster and her maid had arrived in the colonel's coach, bringing Lydia home, along with a letter to Papa.

Elizabeth was pleased to see Lydia was unharmed, but the peace of home was shattered — what would William think? And poor Georgiana would have such a shock. She sat with her sisters as Mama fussed over Lydia, and railed against her having been sent home.

Her youngest sister slouched in the chair and sighed. "Oh, it's so dull here. At Brighton there were so many things to do. Balls and parties every night. There were even coffee houses where Harriet and I used to go to watch the soldiers marching past." She gave a dramatic sigh. "The town is full of soldiers and officers. It will be so dull tonight and every night."

"Yes, it will." No one had seen Papa in the doorway. His face was sterner than Elizabeth had ever seen it, and he was holding an open letter in his hand. Elizabeth took a glance at Lydia, who had gone ashen. What had she done? Hadn't Colonel

Forster supervised her as he'd promised William? Papa came further into the room and stood in front of Lydia. They were all silent — even Mama, who Elizabeth thought had been about to argue for Lydia to have the opportunity to return to Brighton with her.

Her father could be quite frightening when he was angry. Elizabeth thought it was unfortunate that he was usually so indolent — a sign of his sternness before this might have prevented whatever incident had happened. He loomed over Lydia. "Sit up properly, Lydia. You look like a common trollop like that."

There was a heart-stopping pause when Elizabeth thought Lydia would defy her father, but, with a sulky look, she complied. Papa nodded.

"At least it proves you can hear me." He waved the letter angrily in her face. "Colonel Forster has written to me of your utterly disgraceful behaviour. Now, what have you to say?"

Lydia looked around. Her expression was petulant, but underneath Elizabeth could see she felt hunted.

"Papa," Elizabeth interjected. "I'll take my sisters upstairs while you talk to Lydia, shall I?"

"No, Lizzy. You will stay there." His voice was implacable. "Your sister will wish to apologise to you."

485

"I will?" Lydia sounded dubious.

"You will. You have almost brought disgrace on this family. If Colonel Forster had not been so observant, you would have brought ruin upon all of us." Her father ignored Mama's gasp of shock, and continued to lecture her.

"Now, you will go up to your chamber within the next ten minutes. Tonight, you will not join us for dinner, you will have your plate sent up."

"Oh, but, Papa …" Lydia jumped to her feet.

"Sit down!" Papa snapped. "No, you will not dine downstairs tonight. We have guests, and I have no doubt at all that your selfish little heart hasn't even bothered to discover that your sister has become engaged today." He turned for the door. "I will write to your uncle. He may be able to advise me how a school for wayward girls is to be afforded. And …" he pointed at her, "you are not to leave this house until I say so." He didn't slam the door behind him, but it was very close to it, Elizabeth thought.

The room was silent for a long moment. Lydia looked defiant, then slouched down in the chair again.

"What did you do, Lydia?" Elizabeth was incensed that today had been ruined. Perhaps even her whole future. If William no longer wished to be allied to the family, she would not hold him to his offer, and a twist of pain told her that she would never be the same again.

"Nothing! I didn't do anything! Everybody lives like that in Brighton, and you're all just boring, insipid creatures!" Lydia was on the attack.

Elizabeth stood up. "It is yet for you to discover whether a school for wayward girls will be any less interesting than here. I will go to Papa. Perhaps he ought to send to Netherfield and warn our guests what has happened."

Her mother was galvanised to her feet. "You will not, Lizzy! I will not have it! Oh, all the preparation. And we have an extra ham, too!"

Elizabeth glanced at her, she must not be unkind, but she wanted Lydia to know how what she had done had affected them all. "Mama, you must be aware that Mr. Darcy may not wish to permit Georgiana to come here if what Papa has said is true."

"Oh!" Lydia gave a pronounced sigh and flounced off towards the stairs. Elizabeth watched her sadly. She turned to Kitty. "Do you want to come with me to speak to Papa?"

CHAPTER 63

$\mathcal{D}$arcy was enjoying the peace and quiet in the Netherfield drawing room that afternoon. It had been good of Bingley to send his sisters away, even though it meant he could not invite Miss Kitty to his home. He smiled — Bingley was quite comfortable at Longbourn. Darcy was manfully trying to be as stoic as his friend, for Elizabeth's sake, but he had to admit he was not looking forward to dining there tonight; except for the chance of seeing Elizabeth again.

He was ready to have a relaxed conversation with Georgiana, and he watched as she crossed the room towards him, her poise and grace a confirmation of how much she had grown up in the last few months.

He rose to greet her. "I'm glad you have joined

me, Georgiana, and I hope you will also enjoy dining at Longbourn."

She smiled sweetly. "I'm sure I will be all right. It is probably better that than the less formal times I have called."

She sat down, and watched as the footman brought in a tray of tea. "And I must offer Elizabeth my felicitations. I'm so pleased she's going to be my sister." She trembled. "When I think how nearly Miss Bingley achieved her objective …"

Darcy reached for her hand. "Do not distress yourself, it would never have happened. I would sooner lose the respect of the whole of society than marry Miss Bingley." He shook his head. "But it would not have come to that. By refusing to marry her, I have made it impolitic for her to make the incident public. She would only ruin herself. My *disgrace*, if it happened, would be transient. My wealth would mean it was all forgotten quite quickly, whereas ladies are treated very differently."

"I'm very happy that it doesn't seem to have affected your friendship with Mr. Bingley." Georgiana passed him a cup of tea.

"Thank you. Yes, I, too am glad of it. And if his attentions to Miss Kitty come to fruition, then we will be brothers."

"Oh, yes! And I'm going to have lots of sisters!"

Georgiana laughed, "including one or two you don't approve of!"

Darcy smiled reluctantly. He had to admit he was pleased that the youngest girl was still in Brighton, and had to admit that perhaps Forster was being careful. However, being fair, when he had dined once at Longbourn, right at the beginning of their acquaintance, she had been reasonably subdued, although most of his attention had been on Elizabeth, even then.

A footman entered, carrying a letter on a silver tray. He bowed. "An express, sir. From Longbourn."

Elizabeth! Darcy's heart almost stopped. He took the letter from the tray and nodded at the servant.

"Excuse me, Georgiana. I must read this." He broke the seal, trying to keep his fingers from trembling. She must be well, she *must* be. He could not lose her now.

Longbourn

> *Mr. Darcy,*
>
> *I apologise for disturbing you when we will be dining together shortly, but Elizabeth has asked that I inform you of the matter at hand.*
>
> *I would not normally be minded to accede to her request, but, given her recent infirmity, I have agreed.*
>
> *Be reassured, nothing has happened to Elizabeth.*

Darcy's heart began to settle to a more normal rhythm, and he read on rapidly.

She wanted me to inform you that my youngest daughter, Lydia, arrived back here from Brighton earlier this afternoon. I won't trouble you with the reasons given by Colonel Forster, suffice it to say that she is in no doubt of my displeasure, has been confined to the house and she will not be dining with us tonight.

But Lizzie was determined that you ought not to arrive with your sister tonight without knowing of the situation.

I can, however, assure you that Lydia will not defy me and come downstairs while you are here.

I do hope you will not feel unable to attend tonight, but I will understand, whatever your decision is.

Yours, etc,

Thomas Bennet, Esq.

Darcy thought for a moment, then made up his mind. He extended the letter to Georgiana.

"My decision depends upon what you think. Please don't mention that I have shown this to you."

She looked startled. But she smiled, and took the letter. "It is agreeable being treated like an adult." She looked down and started reading.

Darcy stifled a smile, and, while he waited, he recalled what he had read. So Colonel Forster had

had enough, had he? He wondered what the girl had done.

Georgiana smothered a giggle and held out the letter. "I don't see any reason not to go, do you? And, I think Elizabeth would be distressed if we sent our apologies."

Darcy folded it and tucked it into his jacket pocket. "You're correct. But I'm pleased she thought to send the news ahead, so that you were not surprised by it." He frowned. "I hope she isn't distressed by the thought that I might disapprove — I know she didn't wish their father to allow the trip in the first place, especially as Mr. Bennet said he would do it to make the house a more peaceful place for Elizabeth."

"I can understand that Elizabeth might feel this is all her fault." Georgiana nodded. "It will be good if you can show her it makes no difference to you." She looked directly at him. "Will it?"

Darcy shook his head. "Not in the slightest. Although I hope it is not so ruinous as to affect your standing in society. I will need to consider carefully what to do."

Georgiana rose to her feet and came round the table to sit next to him on the sofa. She turned slightly to face him, determination in her eyes.

"You must not do anything to jeopardise your union with Elizabeth," she said firmly. "Neither of you could possibly be happy with that." She reached out to his hand. "And remember," she whispered, "you saved me from something worse, at Ramsgate."

He nodded. "We will not think about that, Georgiana."

"All right, then." She took her hand back. "We know, of course, that all families have members who embarrass or shame them. Elizabeth might have Miss Lydia, but Mr. Bingley has his sister, and we have Lady Catherine."

"You make a very good point, Georgiana," he had to acknowledge. "I will see what I can perhaps do to assist."

Georgiana looked wistful. "It is at times like these that I regret very much that ladies have to withdraw after dinner. I expect you will hear exactly what has happened — and you won't tell me."

"Certainly not!" Darcy tried to quell her impish smile, but without success. He was only a little more fortunate with his own expression.

"I must say, Georgiana, that you are growing up very fast. I can barely keep pace with you."

She smiled wryly at him. "I would say you are not really keeping pace, William. But it is sweet of you to try."

"Sweet?" He was not sure whether to be amused or offended by her comment. But she merely smiled, and gave him a light kiss on the cheek, before rising and moving to the table beside them. "Do you think Mr. Bennet is expecting a reply, William?" she asked, refilling their cups.

He nodded. "I will thank him for informing us and say that we look forward to the evening there."

She leaned forward with his cup. "And when are you going to tell Aunt Alice? I wish I could see her face when she hears!"

"Perhaps I will write to her soon." Darcy nodded. "But I'm afraid there is no one to escort you back to London so that you might have your wish." He smiled. "I may be going back in a day or two, with Mr. Bennet, to arrange the marriage settlement. Perhaps Elizabeth will wish to return to her aunt and uncle in London, to arrange for her trousseau." He raised his eyebrows. "Perhaps you might wish to assist her with the task."

GEORGIANA CAUGHT his eye as she rose with Mrs. Bennet and her daughters to withdraw after dinner was finished, and gave him an expressive look. But he wouldn't hold her gaze, instead watching Elizabeth as she demurely followed her mother.

She'd been very pleased to see them arrive that evening, and he had found a moment of privacy to console her. "I do hope your headaches will not return if the house is less peaceful," he'd remarked. But there had not been time enough for anything more.

Bennet nodded at the housekeeper, the door was closed, and he poured his port, passing the decanter to Darcy, who followed suit and passed it on to Bingley.

Darcy wondered if Colonel Forster had inadvertently revealed that Darcy had been to see him in Brighton, and, if so, whether Bennet might comment. He must be cautious.

"I want to express my appreciation, sir, for your note this afternoon. It was helpful for my sister to be forewarned."

Bennet glanced at him, and sighed. "I'm glad you still dined with us. Lizzy was almost beside herself that you and your sister must be protected."

Darcy knew he must pick his words with care. "Have you had much time to think what must be done, Mr. Bennet? How might you assist your youngest daughter to overcome whatever harm she has caused herself?"

"And the family." Bennet sighed heavily. He glanced up. "I suppose you will find out what happened eventually." His expression darkened. "We're very fortunate that Colonel Forster was keeping a close eye on her. He discovered that she and Wickham were planning to elope, and immediately arranged a guard round the quarters, and sent Lydia home that afternoon, escorted by four officers. Mrs. Forster and her maid were not particularly happy." He smiled. "But I still turned the coach round and sent them straight back."

"It is fortunate that he was so observant," Darcy remarked. "It seems little harm has been done to her reputation."

Bennet nodded heavily. "But I cannot allow her to feel that she has gone unpunished. I have written to my brother-in-law to see if a school for unruly girls might be afforded — for a few months, at least."

"That is Mr. Gardiner?" Darcy clarified, and, when Bennet nodded. "Perhaps I might assist him and obtain a recommendation or two."

"I can recommend Darcy's assistance, Mr. Bennet." Bingley seemed glad to contribute to the conversation. "He is utterly discreet in his enquiries."

"I'm happy to hear it," Bennet replenished his glass and passed the decanter again. "I'm concerned that it is done quickly. I have confined Lydia to the house, but I can't do that for long without the rest of the family feeling the effects."

"I understand you cannot leave here while the situation is as it is, Mr. Bennet," Darcy regarded his host with sympathy. "Would it be of assistance if I went to see Mr. Gardiner tomorrow? Together we might find somewhere appropriate within a day or two. My sister has expressed a wish to return to Matlock House, so it is not an inconvenience to escort her."

Bennet brightened. "It would be a great service to me, Mr. Darcy, if it is not too much trouble for you." He smiled wryly. "I am aware the Bennet family troubles have weighed heavily upon you these last months."

"I am the fortunate one," Darcy replied formally. "I have the hand of the lady I love beyond measure."

"Get away with you!" Bennet gulped his drink. "If we're talking like this, we'd better go through to join the ladies."

CHAPTER 64

*E*lizabeth was pleased to see the gentlemen join them so soon. She glanced at Mama, and rose to ring for fresh tea.

William's gaze sought her out, where she'd been sitting with Georgiana. He bowed, and made his way towards them.

May I join you?"

Elizabeth glanced mischievously at Georgiana. "Certainly. Although, given what your sister has been telling me, you might be discomposed at the questions I will ask you."

His eyebrows went up, then he smiled. "We have no secrets, Elizabeth. I'll be happy to answer any and all questions that are safely asked in earshot of others."

She had to acknowledge the truth of what he

said. "Well, sit down then, and we might keep our voices down." She smiled guilelessly up at him. "Georgiana has been telling me about why Miss Bingley and the Hursts are not with us today."

She saw him glance sideways at his sister, who looked up at him with an innocent air.

"I'm not sure I can add much more to the story if you have already had the facts from my sister." He sat down, looking a little mortified, and she determined that it was wrong to embarrass him.

"It was not my intention to cause you discomfort, Mr. Darcy. It must have been a shocking experience."

He smiled, and she knew he was relieved. "I'm rather more concerned with the incident here today. I understand it has been a distressing time."

She sighed. Lydia always managed to spoil the nicest of days. "I was hoping that we could talk of other things tonight, if it is possible. I wanted to remember today with pleasure, not anxiety." She smiled wistfully. "It is not the sort of day I will ever live again."

Georgiana sighed too, but happily. "How romantic, Elizabeth. I'm sure we can talk of other matters. What about your wedding clothes, will you go to London to have them made?"

Elizabeth glanced at William. He seemed

relaxed with the topic, and was looking indulgently at his sister.

"I haven't really thought about it, Georgiana," she said. "But it might be fun. My aunt and uncle are lovely people — you were introduced at Anne's marriage, I believe — and I can stay with them." She sat up straighter. "I think it is a good idea of yours. I will suggest it to Mama."

William leaned forward. He glanced round, almost secretively, then reached forward and touched her hand for an instant. His touch burned as it always did, and she was reminded of Kitty's words that afternoon. Did he really not know that she loved him? But how could she declare it while Georgiana was with them? She tried to put all her feelings in her gaze, and an answer flared within his.

"I, too, think it an idea that will help to make the occasion special, but I'm afraid I have to say this now, as I will not have the chance tomorrow. After I have told you, we will talk only of the things you wish to." He smiled solicitously at her.

"Of course; if it's important, then we must talk of it."

"Very well, but I hope it does not come as too much of a surprise to you, or Georgiana in particular." Elizabeth watched as he glanced at his sister and then back at her.

"As you might have surmised, we discussed over

the port the difficulty your father had this afternoon." He sighed, "I was sorry to hear it; I know how you petitioned your father that he prevent your sister from accepting the invitation. However; it has happened, and I understand that he wishes to send Miss Lydia to a suitable school, even if it is only for a few months. Of course, with the need for her supervision, he is unable to leave Longbourn at present." He smiled. "So I have offered to go to town tomorrow, and see Mr. Gardiner. Together I hope we can find somewhere that will assist your sister to be able to take her place in society." He looked at his sister. "I thought you would like to go with me to Matlock House — you will indeed be able to see our aunt's face when I tell her I have had the honour of Elizabeth's acceptance of my hand."

Elizabeth blushed. "I hope she will not be too disappointed," she ventured.

"I'm sure she will be delighted," he returned. "I had always thought I would not care whether they approved or not; and Lady Catherine was certain to disapprove. The only opinions that mattered to me were Georgiana and my cousin Richard. But as my aunt met you when she called on Anne at your aunt's home, I know she will welcome you to the family." He hesitated. "I have a suspicion that she divined my feelings at that time, so she may not be much surprised."

There was a slight silence, then Georgiana rose to her feet.

"If you will excuse me, Elizabeth, I'd like to speak to Kitty and Mr. Bingley."

They weren't alone, of course, but they were together, and it was likely that no-one was listening. Elizabeth hoped he could not discern her disordered breathing. "Your sister is a very astute young lady." She gave him a little secret smile. "And I think she will be quite happy going to London." She raised her eyebrows. "And not just to see her aunt."

He looked at her sharply, then smiled ruefully. "I think it is my fault," he chuckled, and shook his head. "Colonel Fitzwilliam and I were concerned that she was being a little too — flighty, I suppose might be the word. At that time she didn't wish to continue learning anything more than superficial things, and so my cousin and I introduced her to his younger brother and some of his friends, who are at Cambridge." His smile was a little crooked. "It has worked very well, and she has grown up very fast, and enjoys much of more cultured society."

"Indeed, she is a delightful young lady to talk to, and very good company."

"Thank you. But it seems to have had the effect of securing her admiration of young Jonathan."

Elizabeth smiled. "A young man who is a member of the family, who is good company, and also a very clever scientist for his years — an almost irresistible attraction."

"When you say it like that, I suppose you are right." He ran his hand through his hair in his habitual way.

"Thank you for offering to assist Uncle Gardiner to find a place for Lydia," Elizabeth said quietly. "It will be a great help to him, and he admires you greatly."

"It is nothing." William touched her hand again. "I will do all I can to help your family — they will soon be my family, too."

She bit her lip. "I can still hardly believe it."

He chuckled. "It is regrettable that it is dusk, or we might walk in the gardens and talk of it without fear of interruption." He looked ruefully at the window. "And I suppose we must take our leave soon, or it will be full dark before we arrive at Netherfield."

She tried to keep her countenance cheerful, but it was difficult. "Please take care while you are away, I will be afraid for you until I know you are safe."

His eyes were dark and passionate. "I will write to you as soon as I arrive, Elizabeth, and each day thereafter."

She clasped her hands together. "It is wonderful to be able to write to each other now. Do I direct my letter to Darcy House?"

He nodded, his eyes dark with passion. "It would be an honour to receive a letter from you, Elizabeth. Darcy House is in Brook Street. Do you want me to write it down for your aide memoire book?"

She knew she blushed. "Thank you. I know it seems easy to remember, but I would be ashamed if I couldn't recall it and had to wait until I'd received a letter from you."

She had an idea, and glanced round the room. No one was looking at them directly, but she lowered her voice. "Might you move round a little, so your back is to the room?"

A tiny frown appeared between his brows, and he glanced round. His voice was little more than a murmur. "What troubles you, Elizabeth?"

She smiled secretly, he'd angled his body round. "Do not worry, I will watch for any untoward attention. Please close your eyes."

She almost laughed as he looked askance at her, but he did as she asked and her heart swelled. He trusted her.

She dropped her voice more. "All right, imagine you are in your library at Darcy House. A letter has just been delivered, and you break the seal. It is from me, and you begin to read.

Dearest William,

This is the first letter I have written to you since our betrothal, and I want to tell you how very dearly I love you; how honoured I am that I will become your wife.

I am impatient for our wedding day, and I will spend the rest of my life showing you my love ..."

"Enough," he whispered, and his eyes opened. He barely stifled a groan. "I need to be alone when I read those sentiments, dearest Elizabeth. If you are able to put those words on paper, I will treasure them forever." He drew his chair slightly closer, his smile slightly twisted. "But I cannot hear them without betraying my feelings for you." His hand touched hers. "And now I want to call on you in the morning, instead of going to London."

She smiled secretly at him. "I will write the letter tonight. I hope it will be in London almost as soon as you are."

He lifted her hand to his lips. "Now I see the need to hurry to London, Elizabeth." The heat of his lips burned the back of her hand and she brought it to her cheek before she saw his expression.

"I will be waiting here for you when you return."

CHAPTER 65

*E*lizabeth thought back over the last few whirlwind weeks as she sat in front of the glass, her newly appointed lady's maid carefully dressing her hair for her wedding, now only two hours hence.

After today, she would never think of this chamber as her own again; after today, she would be Mrs. Darcy, mistress of Pemberley and all the responsibility that entailed.

She smiled at her reflection. William had been kindness itself when she had expressed her fear that she might find herself unable to manage the estate in the way he would have wished.

"Dearest Elizabeth. I have excellent, loyal staff. They have run the estate for me for the last five years and they will continue to so so while you become accustomed to being mistress of the estate." He had raised her hand to his lips. "Then, when you see something you wish to change, you call the housekeeper and instruct her to make that change. One thing at a time, and you will make your mark on the estate."

He had leaned forward and whispered in her ear. "You don't have to do everything at once — in fact, it is better not to." His warm breath had fanned her cheek, his nearness had made her senses reel.

She lifted her hand to her cheek, the one warmed by his breath. After the ceremony and the wedding breakfast, she would leave this house, this place she had called home, and travel for more than two hours with William, to London.

Last night she had thought of him, had wondered what it would feel like to be alone with him, permitted to sit close, feel him perhaps embrace her. She pushed the thought away. It was important to her to retain her composure for the occasion, not to let him down.

The door to her chamber was slightly open, and she had been hearing Mama's voice penetrate up the stairs as she hurried round, berating the staff, trying to ensure everything was prepared for the wedding breakfast.

She grimaced slightly. Mama could indeed be

forgiven on this occasion. There would not just be family and friends who knew them well, but some members of William's family. Mama was beside herself to ensure everything showed that she was indeed a perfect hostess.

She could hear Jane and Papa's soothing voices; and it was only a moment later that Mama herself appeared in Elizabeth's chamber.

"Oh, Lizzy! Let me look at you. You must be the most beautiful bride they have ever seen."

Elizabeth turned. "Mama, you've done wonders." She tipped her face for her mother to kiss her cheek. "I cannot thank you enough for all your efforts to make everything go smoothly for us today." She indicated the chair in the window. "Why not take the opportunity to have a few moment's rest while Emily finishes my hair? Then you can help me into my gown." It was important that Mama was calm and unflustered, and she knew Papa had sent her up here.

"You're a good girl, Lizzy." Mama mopped her face with a scrap of lace. "I don't know what I will do without you. Especially as Jane has already gone."

Elizabeth looked at her through the glass. "You will be quite all right, Mama. Soon you will have only Mary at home — and Lydia, when she has finished at school."

"Oh, yes! I can hardly manage the excitement!" Mama fanned herself. The announcement of Kitty's engagement to Mr. Bingley last week had helped Elizabeth by taking some of the attention from her, and William had taken the opportunity of taking Elizabeth out for a drive with Georgiana on several afternoons.

They had visited Holywell estate, where William had just arranged for them to drive through the park, so Elizabeth didn't have to tour the house. They had driven past Oakham Mount towards the great woods of East Hyde, and on yet another day they had lunched at one of his favourite inns on the Great North Road. She knew it would soon be a familiar route as they travelled between London and Pemberley.

His strategy had worked, and Elizabeth felt much more herself. She could manage Mama for a few moments.

Jane arrived upstairs a few minutes later, and with Mama's help and loud protestations of happiness, Elizabeth slipped into the pale satin gown, embroidered with leaves and flowers all in the same thread. From a distance, it looked classically plain, but looking more closely, Elizabeth could pick out all her beloved plants of the countryside. She was truly surrounded by the companions of her childhood.

"Oh, Lizzy!" Mama fanned herself. "You look wonderful. And so calm!"

Jane smiled serenely, and reached for her sister's shoes. The shoe roses were already stitched on, and she eased her feet into the pretty slippers. "There, Lizzy," Jane examined her critically. "I'm wondering if you need a touch more rouge — just a touch, you don't want it to seem to overblown — but you don't want to seem pale."

Elizabeth turned back to the glass. "No, I think this is enough, Jane." She didn't know how she knew that William would prefer this, but somehow she did.

"Then let me assist you with your bonnet." Jane carefully lifted it it out of the box. Elizabeth looked at it happily. A light, delicate item, seemingly mostly lace, she knew it would set off well against her dark hair.

She smiled at her maid. "We'll be very careful not to disturb your careful work, Emily, so it will still look good at the breakfast."

Kitty appeared in the doorway. "Mama, are you nearly ready? The coach is waiting to take us."

"Oh, my goodness! And I'm sitting dallying here!" Mama leapt to her feet. "Oh, Lizzy, I will see you at the church." She bent over to kiss her, her eyes already full of tears.

"Jane will come down and assist you, Mama, as

I am ready." Elizabeth placated her. "Everything is prepared, you must just enjoy the occasion."

She was glad Jane was out of the room for a moment. She dismissed the maid and stood quietly at the window. William would be waiting for her, and her life would be bound to his. How fortunate she was, how blessed to be the recipient of his love.

"Lizzy!" Her father's voice echoed up the stairs. "Are you ready? Mr. Darcy's carriage is here for us."

"I'm ready, Papa," she called down, and turned to smile at her reflection. Then she left the room, to open the next chapter of her life.

CHAPTER 66

*D*arcy sat in the front pew, Richard beside him as groomsman. It seemed odd that he wasn't in his full army uniform on this formal occasion, but of course, having resigned his commission, he was in formal dress, as was Darcy.

The small Meryton church was already full to bursting. Darcy wondered how Longbourn would fit everyone into the wedding breakfast, and he hoped Mrs. Bennet had not disturbed Elizabeth's equanimity too much this morning.

Darcy was delighted the weather was favourable, he wanted Elizabeth to remember the day as perfect.

He leaned over towards Richard. "Thank you for telling Lady Catherine that you would go into Kent after the marriage. I'm pleased that she is waiting there for you and has not come here, where she may argue with your parents, and offend Mrs. Bennet, who wouldn't be able to take things quietly."

Richard nodded. "I think it will work quite well. Anne is confident that her mother will be amenable, and I have been writing to her regularly, asking if she might permit her steward to show me how she likes her estate to be managed. So she is thinking that I will not change everything, and that has relieved her mind somewhat."

Darcy nodded. "Will you stay long?"

Richard looked at him. "Several weeks, depending on how the visit goes. But, Darcy, you ought not to be thinking of it now. You must enjoy the marriage and taking Elizabeth to be your wife." His smile was almost imperceptible. "I think you are very well matched."

"I am fortunate indeed," Darcy agreed.

The muted noise in the church suddenly stopped, and a collective sigh told him Elizabeth had arrived at the door. Both men hastily rose to their feet, and Darcy moved out into the aisle. He turned and looked back — and all the breath left him.

He could never have imagined the sight of Elizabeth as she came towards him, and his heart bounded in his chest. Her slim body looked almost ethereal, her gown flowing round her like gossamer silk. Her father's arm seemed to be all that was anchoring her to the ground, and he saw her gaze, steady and unafraid.

She had come so far from the Elizabeth he had seen at Copthorne. He had loved her then, he had loved her before, and he loved her now.

He knew she was smiling at him, and knew his lips curved in response.

Soon, she was beside him, and the vicar opened his prayer book.

"Dearly beloved, we are gathered together …"

When he turned to face her to declare his vows, he felt her squeeze his hand very slightly. He bent his head to her.

"I love you, William."

He smiled back. "I am depending on it!" His murmur was for her alone, and he took her right hand in his, as the minister directed.

"I, Fitzwilliam George, take thee, Elizabeth Frances, to my wedded wife, to have and to hold from this day forward, for better for worse, for richer for poorer, in sickness and in health, to love and to cherish, till death us do part …" He had rehearsed the vows, determined to be word perfect, and her parted lips and luminous expression took all his attention.

Her own words were as sincere, led as they were

by the minister, but she didn't hesitate, and his heart swelled with love as he placed his mother's ring on her finger.

Then it was over, and he walked down the aisle, through the gathered friends and family, his wife on his arm. He leaned towards her. "You are most beautiful. Thank you for doing me the honour of consenting to become Mrs. Darcy." He knew his murmur would be heard by her alone.

She looked into his eyes. "I have always declared that I would only ever marry for love." Her eyes glowed. "I hadn't realised quite how powerful that love can be."

Warmth spread within him for a moment, and he pushed it aside with an effort. "We are as one, dearest Elizabeth."

Then he was assisting Elizabeth into the open landau as the rest of the party climbed into conveyances, and some of the villagers began walking towards Longbourn.

He climbed in behind her and settled himself on the seat next to her, instead of opposite. He heard her gasp and smiled at her. "You're quite safe. The journey is only a few minutes and I will not presume to allow you to arrive in a dishevelled state."

Her chin went up. "I refuse to permit myself to be disappointed."

He pressed his lips together. "Well, in that case,

madam, perhaps I ought …" His hand enclosed hers.

She turned to him in feigned alarm. "Oh, sir!"

He chuckled. "I see you are as light-headed with relief as I am. Do not worry, we have only to keep our heads for a few more hours, then we will be leaving for London."

Her fingers tightened round his, and they sat in silence for the few moments it took to drive to Longbourn.

As he assisted Elizabeth down from the landau, Darcy glanced round to see if he could see his sister.

"She's over there, William, with Lady Matlock." Elizabeth had divined his thoughts, and he smiled reluctantly.

"Might we speak briefly to her first? Or would your mother prefer us to go straight to the receiving line?"

Her light laugh was music to his ears. "We will soon hear if we are too long," and she set off towards Georgiana.

"Good morning, Lady Matlock. I'm honoured that you joined us today." He saw that she knew to address his aunt first, before she turned to his sister.

"Georgiana, I'm so pleased you're my sister now," she leaned forward and kissed the girl.

"My felicitations to both of you," his aunt said briskly. "I'm certain you'll be very happy." She looked towards the house. "I think you had better be about your duties, though. But Elizabeth, might you be certain to see me before you leave? I really want to look at the embroidery on your gown, it is delightful."

As he accompanied Elizabeth indoors, Darcy looked at the gown Elizabeth was wearing. For the first time he noticed the details of the stitching. He dipped his head to her ear. "I see what Aunt Alice means, your gown is exquisite."

She glanced up. "Thank you. I am surrounded by my old friends of the fields and hedgerows."

He thought about what she had said as they stood in the receiving line, but was soon exercised to ensure he said the names of all those he knew, so Elizabeth didn't have to hunt for their names in her mind. He was pleased that Jane was on her other side, doing the same for those whom Darcy didn't know.

Georgiana was safe with Aunt Alice and with Richard and Anne here as well, he wasn't concerned about her. He could stay with Elizabeth, which was his ardent wish. He set himself to bear the occasion with fortitude and ensure she enjoyed herself. But he acknowledged to himself that he wished for it to end. He wanted nothing more than to take Elizabeth to London, to enjoy the two days there he had planned before they left for Pemberley.

So much had happened recently; and he was determined that she would be able to rest properly and recover fully at Pemberley, before they took an extended tour next year.

Georgiana would be able to stay at Matlock House, or with Anne and Richard, and he would have nothing more important than to please Elizabeth for the rest of their lives together.

CHAPTER 67

*E*lizabeth embraced Jane before she climbed into the coach, and then turned to Kitty. "I'm sorry I won't be here to help you with your wedding preparations, but I'll write every day and give you my opinions; and, of course, we'll be back a day or so before your marriage to be with you."

Kitty laughed, and whispered in her ear. "There will not be many decisions to make, Lizzy. I have decided that everything will be just like today." She sighed. "It was perfect, and you look beautiful."

Elizabeth looked round, had she said goodbye to everyone?

William's low voice beside her was reassuring. "You've said all the farewells necessary."

"Thank you," she murmured back, and allowed him to assist her into the coach.

He climbed in behind her, and the groom closed the door. The coach rocked as he climbed up beside the coachman, and Elizabeth leaned out of the window to wave at her parents.

As Longbourn vanished behind them, she sat back, and smiled ruefully at William. "I'm sorry, it's just …"

"A very sudden realisation of all the changes you're making in your life," he finished for her, reaching for her hand. "I'm very conscious of the fact that, while I, too, am beginning a new period of my life; you have far bigger changes to surmount." His hand enclosed hers. "Pemberley and Darcy House — and their staff — are all familiar to me, and utterly new to you." Gently, he drew her closer. "And you have been very ill."

Elizabeth sighed and leaned against him. "I'm happy you understand me."

There was a smile in his voice. "I'm happy you've trusted me with your future."

Her heart was racing, and she struggled to keep her breathing under good regulation so he wouldn't know how she felt. She was alone with him. Privacy, for the next two hours, at least.

All that she had learned of propriety and decorum was different now. With her vows, she had given herself up to her husband and his wishes and desires. She smiled to herself. She trusted him, trusted him absolutely. She had nothing to fear.

"Elizabeth?" His voice was very gentle, and she looked round. His finger, under her chin, tipped her face up to his. His thumb traced the contour of her lips, which parted under his touch.

He groaned. "You don't know how long I've waited for you, how I have dreamed of this moment." His arm slipped round her and drew her closer still. His warm breath fanned her cheek and his mouth was close to hers.

"I love you, William."

"Your affections are returned, Elizabeth, beyond anything I ever imagined possible." His lips lowered to hers, and she yielded to his embrace.

It was only a few moments later that he lifted his head, and she relaxed onto his shoulder, but it felt as if everything had changed, yet again.

"No wonder people are not allowed to sit so close before marriage," she commented. "It is much too exciting."

She felt the rumble of his rich chuckle as much as she heard it. Warmth spread through her as she knew she'd hear it often.

There was a comfortable silence for a few minutes before he leaned forward and reached for the folded blanket opposite.

He seemed to find unfolding it and draping it over her knees rather difficult, because he wouldn't remove his arm from around her, but he managed it, tucking it round her warmly.

He saw her amusement. "No remonstrations?"

She shook her head. "I know it would be fruitless, you would not have stopped."

"You are beginning to know me, dearest Elizabeth. Now, I think you are fatigued. You may rest, I'm here." He moved slightly, so his shoulder was a more comfortable resting place for her head.

He was right; she was tired, but she pushed herself upright.

"No, it would be very rude of me to sleep. We have a long journey."

His arm tightened further and his other hand caressed her face. "Please rest, I will be exceedingly content with you here in my arms. I would not have you exhausted this evening when we dine at Darcy House."

She searched his face, and nodded. "Please don't let me sleep too long."

"I'll take the greatest care of you." His words sent a warm feeling through her and she didn't object further.

THE DUSK WAS JUST BEGINNING to draw in when William assisted her out of the coach in front of a large, gracious house of light stone.

She looked round with interest. Darcy House stood well back from the road, unusual for London. Black-painted railings and stately gates separated the road from a neat semicircular, gravelled drive, and the coach had stopped in the exact centre, outside the great oak door, which stood open.

"Welcome to Darcy House, Elizabeth." William took her hand on his arm, nodded at the coachman, and they turned to the door.

They climbed the two stone steps and entered the hall. He bent his head to her. "I have asked that only the most senior staff be here to be introduced today. The rest you will get to know later on."

She nodded. "Thank you." She stopped in front of them.

"Mrs. Porter is housekeeper here," William introduced them.

"Welcome to Darcy House, Mrs. Darcy. I hope everything is to your satisfaction." The woman curtsied deeply. Elizabeth nodded at her.

"Thank you." She turned to the man.

"Mr. Jones is the butler." William's arm tightened on her hand. "Like Mrs. Porter, he has been here many years."

"Good evening, Mrs. Darcy." The man bowed.

"Thank you."

Elizabeth looked at the second man. Stolid and imperturbable, he wasn't dressed as a house servant, but he looked very competent.

"This is Mr. Leigh, my London steward; he will be escorting your carriage if you ever need to go anywhere when I am not with you." William's voice didn't invite dissent.

The man bowed. "Welcome to London, Mrs. Darcy."

She nodded at him. "Thank you, Mr. Leigh."

William led her through to the drawing room. Large and imposing, it brought home to her, more than anything else had, the wealth and status of the man she had married today. Enormous fires flared in the great fireplaces, dozens of candles gave good light, portraits looked down at her, and, despite the size of the room, it still felt welcoming.

She didn't realise she had stopped dead in the doorway, until she felt William urging her forward.

"Come and sit down, Elizabeth. Mrs. Porter is arranging tea for us."

CHAPTER 68

*D*arcy didn't stay for the port, but accompanied his wife to the drawing room for their coffee immediately they had finished dining.

He was disinclined to be away from her a moment longer than he had to. He'd taken a few minutes to flick through the post waiting for him in his library, when she was still upstairs preparing for dinner.

But he didn't want to overwhelm her; he half thought he'd failed in that as he'd shown her their apartments, her chamber on one side of their private sitting-room, his own chamber on the other. She'd gazed round, wide-eyed.

He'd requested that she remain in the same

gown as she had worn for their marriage, and she'd smiled.

"Of course I will. I'm glad you like it." She hesitated. "Georgiana convinced me that it would be all right to incur the extra expense."

"And she was right to do so. You were the loveliest bride I could imagine — and if the plants and flowers of the countryside comforted you, then I'm happy you didn't omit them."

They sat beside each other on the sofa while they took their coffee. "You look better than you did when we left Longbourn," he remarked. "I'm glad you slept in the coach."

"It was certainly beneficial," she smiled. "Thank you for suggesting it."

He glanced at the clock. It was much too soon to retire, and he wondered how to pass the time without the tension becoming difficult.

"William?"

"Yes, dearest Elizabeth?"

"May I play to you a little? The pianoforte looks a much better one than I have ever had the opportunity to try before."

He'd been inclined to refuse to let her tire herself, but her reason disarmed him completely. "Permit me to sit beside you while you play."

She played; quiet, gentle tunes from memory, requiring little energy, and he recalled the first time he had heard her — at Rosings, with Richard sitting beside her; and he'd walked over to the instrument and ventured a few words to her.

But now, all misunderstandings were past, they were sitting close together, and she turned to him, still playing, her gaze luminous in the flickering light from the candles.

"It has been the most wonderful day, William. I will never forget the moment I saw you standing at the front of the church, waiting for me." She paused, thoughtful. "The sunlight shining through the stained-glass windows, and making rainbows of light on the flagstones." She sighed. "And I thought Mama did well, she remained reasonably dignified throughout, although I know her behaviour is not quite as you prefer. And your aunt was kind to her."

He nodded. "It went very well indeed. I will write to your father tomorrow to thank him for his hospitality, and ask him to congratulate Mrs. Bennet on an excellent occasion."

"Oh, Mama will be so happy with that!" she exclaimed. "She will carry it all round the town to show everyone."

She turned to concentrate on the fingering of the next piece, and he found himself noticing the delicate stitching on her gown as it flowed over her lap.

"So, when did you want to have this design stitched on your wedding gown, Elizabeth?"

She laughed. "It was just a childish fancy. When we were quite young, Jane and I drew pictures of our weddings, and I sketched out the designs on my drawings." She played a few more bars. "I was studying botany at the time, and I was never happier than when I was wandering the fields and woods, discovering where they liked to grow." She glanced at him. "And when the seamstress suggested she embroider a design on it, and Georgiana said the cost would not matter, I said what I wanted. But I didn't want too many people to notice, so I told her to make sure she used thread from the satin itself, so they can only be seen when you're close."

"It is exquisite." He touched the raised texture of a leaf on her sleeve. "Exquisite, yet understated. Beautiful."

He glanced at the clock. "Would you like some tea to refresh yourself? Then it will be time to retire."

AT LAST THEY were climbing the stairs to their apartments. At the door to her chamber, he bowed. "I will attend you shortly, Elizabeth."

She looked down, perhaps a little shy. "Thank

you," before she slipped through the door. He could see her maid waiting to attend her, and he closed the door behind her, turning to his own chamber.

His valet was moving quietly about the room, laying out his nightshirt and robe. Beyond him, water steamed in the china bowl, and he allowed the man to assist him out of his tailcoat and boots, before going to wash.

"Thank you, Mr. Maunder. I will manage now."

The man bowed. "May I offer my congratulations on your marriage, sir?"

"Thank you. Please check the stables are not expecting me for an early gallop in the morning."

Once alone, he crossed the room and pulled aside the heavy curtain. Looking out onto the quiet street, he wondered how long it would be correct to wait until he joined Elizabeth in her chamber. He didn't wish to disturb her preparations for the night, but nor did he wish to keep her waiting.

He let the curtain drop back, and went to finish his own preparations.

CHAPTER 69

*E*lizabeth stood at her window to wait for him. She drew the curtain aside and gazed down into the darkened street. Little points of candlelight indicated some of the uncurtained windows of the houses opposite, but there was little moonlight to illuminate the street.

She concentrated on trying to see more outside, not being quite sure how she felt inside. She trusted William absolutely, but she didn't know what to expect when he came to her, and Mama's little lecture yesterday had left both Elizabeth and Mama embarrassed, and Elizabeth more confused than before Mama had come into her chamber.

All the events of today had begun to blur into her mind as she could think only of the coming night.

There was a quiet knock on the door that connected the apartment to her bedchamber. Her hand went to her mouth as the handle turned.

He was there. A few quick strides and he was taking her into his arms.

"Don't be afraid, Elizabeth. I couldn't bear it if you're afraid of me."

His arms were round her, his heart beating steadily against hers through the thin layers of fabric.

"I'm not afraid, just — unsure of what you expect of me."

"Oh, dearest Elizabeth. Let me show you." His lips sought hers, and she turned her face up to his, her legs going weak with his nearness. His arms tightened round her, and he picked her up and carried her to the bed.

He lay beside her, gazing into her eyes, his finger tracing the line of her throat, and the weakness she'd felt in her legs spread through her body. Then his arm moved round her and he drew her into a close embrace, his lean body hard against her, the heat of his touch spreading even through the fabric of her night shift. His mouth descended on hers and she felt her desire rise as her lips parted, yielding to him.

SHE WOKE as his arms tightened round her in the middle of the night, knowing he was restless. She couldn't see his face in the dimness, but she lifted her hand to find it.

"I'm here, William," she murmured.

He shuddered. "I'm sorry, did I disturb you?"

"It doesn't matter, you were dreaming, I think."

His hand was behind her head, tangling in her hair, drawing her closer.

"It's the endless nightmare, knowing you are lost, and I cannot find you."

She put her arms round his neck. "I caused everyone so much distress. But I'm here now, beside you always; you can rest."

His lips touched her cheek. "I love you, and I'll care for you always."

Her lips touched his. "Please allow me to care for you sometimes." Greatly daring, she slid her hand into the front of his nightshirt and pressed it over his heart. "Now you know I'm near."

His hand covered hers. "My own Elizabeth."

She snuggled next to him. Unused to sharing a bed, she knew that she might not sleep again, but he needed her close, so that was the most important thing.

SHE WAS BEING WATCHED, and daylight was bright on her closed eyelids as she stirred sleepily. Looking over, she saw he was awake and regarding her with slight amusement.

"Waking with you in my arms is going to be the best part of my days now." His voice was warm and caressing.

She sighed with happiness. "I think all parts of my days with you are going to be agreeable."

He huffed a laugh and drew her closer. "I've been thinking this time alone together in the mornings with you will be a wonderful time to talk through the coming day and deal with any problems of the days before."

She rested her head happily on his chest. "I don't have a problem from yesterday, but I still want to talk about it. I want to remember it for ever and ever."

He was silent for a moment. "We didn't get a lot of opportunity to talk to Georgiana, but I'm very satisfied that she is happy to stay with my aunt and uncle in London while we go to Pemberley."

She smiled contentedly. "I think a great deal of her happiness was due to you having told her that your cousin Jonathan will be down from Cambridge for the summer."

His chuckle rumbled through her. "Indeed; and

that I told her I would see what is to be done about him not needing to take a commission."

"Mmm. Do you think she is very much in love? I confess I'm not entirely convinced." She smiled to herself. "I know that at that age, I was in love with the thought of being in love."

"My thoughts are in accord with yours," his voice held a hint of laughter. "I thought a summer when they would see a great deal of each other would either cement their affections — or not."

"A very sensible thought," she laughed. "But is your young cousin Jonathan a suitable match if they are in love?"

"Mmhm." She could feel him nodding. "Although I will have to supplement her fortune, perhaps, or make one of my properties available for them to live in. I would not like to see her married to a man who is always at work."

"How would that be afforded, William? I know Georgiana said I ought not to be concerned as to any expense I might incur, but I would not like you to feel that I was too extravagant for the estate, especially as you'll still wish to be of assistance to others."

He was twisting tendrils of her hair round his fingers. "I've wanted to do this since I first saw you — dancing with Bingley," he muttered. Then he gave the tendril a little tug. "You're not even to think about the cost. When you see Pemberley, you'll understand."

"Well," she said doubtfully. "You must get people asking you all the time for money or favours."

He nuzzled into her throat. "And what favour did you wish to ask me? It is yours. Whatever you want, you may have."

Her whole being was dissolving again in that strange way as he touched her. "But you don't know what I am going to ask!"

"It doesn't matter. Whatever you wish for, I will make sure you have it."

She smothered a giggle. "Even if I wanted — I don't really — but even if I did, you'd let us live near my mother?"

She heard the smile in his voice. "It is because I know that you will only want what is good for us, Elizabeth, that I say it." He propped himself up on one elbow and gazed down at her. "So what was it you do wish to ask for?"

She looked at him. "If you really don't mind me asking — so soon after we're married, then I was wondering if you might see your way to finding a better living for Mr. Lawrence — Jane deserves so much more than the vicarage at Shenley. It isn't urgent, of course," she hurried on. "But having seen the parsonage at Hunsford, and that Mr. Collins has it — why, Mr. Lawrence is better than him. And Jane, well, nobody knows yet, but I know you will keep my confidence. Jane believes she is increasing, so they will do better with somewhere larger and more gracious."

His hand smoothed over her hair, and his lips touched her forehead. "A salute to my dearest Elizabeth. So anxious about asking for a favour, and yet it is not for you, but for your sister. You are generosity itself." He looked up at the ceiling for a moment. "I think the clergyman at Kympton is retiring in a year or so. So your sister would be closer to her mother for the birth of their child, and then they would be living not ten miles from Pemberley. Does that sound as if it might be something that they would like? It is a valuable living, and an agreeable parish."

"So we would be neighbours! Oh, William, you have the most wonderful ideas." Elizabeth leaned up and pulled his face towards her. "You've been thinking about this already. You had it far too clearly in your mind!"

"You've discovered me," he laughed, and pulled her closer.

CHAPTER 70

Epilogue

*E*lizabeth closed her book and glanced at Georgiana. "I think I'm finished with this until after Christmas, do you agree?"

Her sister laid down her pencil. "I think so, too. Mr. Laidlaw has gone away now until later in the year, so we have plenty of time to study before he is back to teach us again."

She looked at her notes rather critically. "I think I want to draw that again, I'm not completely content with it." Then she looked at Elizabeth. "I'm so pleased you love studying. It is more interesting with two of us — and you must be glad that your memory is improving all the time."

"I am. Doctor Owsley was convinced that the more I studied, the better I would be at remembering things." Elizabeth smiled. "And it's working."

"William's so pleased," Georgiana commented. "But it will be good to have a rest from it all over Christmas. And our guests are arriving soon, aren't they?"

Elizabeth jumped to her feet. "Oh, I had forgotten! The Bingleys will be here before lunch, I think."

Georgiana followed her. "Mrs. Reynolds has everything in hand, Elizabeth. Don't fret."

Elizabeth hurried down the stairs. William was sure to come to the drawing room when it was time for their tea, and she wouldn't wish to miss a moment.

But he was there before her, and as she hurried in, he came towards her, and lifted her hand to his lips. "Elizabeth." But he stepped away from her then, and they sat down to take tea together.

Elizabeth missed the closeness they'd had when they first came to Pemberley. But they had agreed that when Georgiana joined them, they would keep signs of overt affection from the public rooms so they didn't embarrass her. And a month after their wedding, Georgiana had joined them, journeying up with her uncle and aunt, who opened Hayden Hall at Matlock for the summer, returning when

Parliament reopened.

The girl had fretted somewhat during the autumn, and Elizabeth had worked hard to keep her occupied. But the Michaelmas term was now over, and Jonathan would be travelling back for Christmas in Derbyshire with his parents. They would dine at Pemberley tomorrow. Georgiana was glowing.

Elizabeth caught her husband's eye, and he turned to his sister. "How did your studying go, and did you manage to keep Elizabeth from fretting about her sister's journey?"

Georgiana glanced at Elizabeth from the corner of her eye. "I think I succeeded, didn't I, Elizabeth?"

"You did indeed," Elizabeth answered, "but let's take tea. I'm ready for refreshment."

Half-an-hour later, she and William walked out onto the terrace for a moment alone. The air was chill, but Elizabeth didn't mind. She lifted her head and breathed deeply of the wild air, straight from the crags and peaks of the country she'd come to love so well.

William draped his arm over her shoulder, and drew her a little closer. "The change in Georgiana has been remarkable. You have worked wonders, dearest one."

"I cannot take the credit. Now she has seen that

Jonathan and his friends value learning, she has been eager to prove herself to him." She thought for a moment. "But I have been the greatest beneficiary. Having her with me as I studied kept me working, and learning again how to learn has made me happy."

"And that has made me the happiest of men." He looked down at her. "To have you here with me, to know you will always be with me — I ask for nothing more."

"I'm sorry you have to share me over Christmas — it was generous of you to allow the Bingleys to come and stay for the season."

He smiled. "Just Mr. and Mrs. Bingley. His sisters will not leave London now the season is almost begun."

"And we're all going to Netherfield together after Christmas, so we'll be nearby when Jane has her baby." She shivered in delight. "I can't imagine what it's going to be like to be an aunt."

He turned and they walked together to the end of the terrace, out of sight of the drawing room windows. There, he took her in his arms. "To me each day lasts an eternity, Elizabeth, until we can retire to our chambers and be as close as we were before Georgiana joined us."

Elizabeth lifted her face for his kiss. "I miss that time, too," she whispered. "Perhaps we might steal a short while before lunch each day — we could stroll in the gallery, perhaps. Georgiana is growing up, I'm sure she will be astute enough to remain in the drawing room with Mrs. Annesley; just for that little while."

His lips seared her skin as they trailed the length of her throat and she gasped. "Or perhaps we ought not. Knowing we cannot have long for privacy will be an exquisite agony."

At that moment he lifted his head, listening. Then he sighed. "I will have to bear it in silence for the rest of the Christmas period, Elizabeth. "I believe that is Bingley's coach."

They turned and walked along to meet her sister, Elizabeth on his arm, determined not to show an unseemly haste.

Standing with William and Georgiana as the coach drew up, Elizabeth waited until Mr. Bingley turned to assist Kitty from the coach, then she drew her hand from William's arm, and went to her sister.

"It's wonderful to see you, Kitty," she embraced her. "And you look so well! I hope to hear all the news from home."

"You look very well, too, Lizzy." Her sister stood back and regarded her. "I'm pleased your appearance matches the opinion I formed from your letters."

Elizabeth smiled at her and turned to greet Mr. Bingley.

A few minutes later, she was climbing the steps, arm in arm with her sisters, the gentlemen following behind, conversing in low voices.

THE CONVERSATION WAS general until William and Mr. Bingley decided to walk round the lake before darkness fell.

Elizabeth smiled at Kitty and Georgiana. "I'm going to order more tea and then we can catch up more easily with all the news."

Kitty was looking fatigued, she thought. "It's been a long journey for you, Kitty, has it not? Are you well?"

Her sister smiled, looking a little embarrassed. "If you promise not to talk about it in front of the gentlemen, Lizzy, and Georgiana, I will tell you. But I don't want Charles to know just yet — he'll make such a fuss."

"Oooh!" Elizabeth jumped to her feet. "I'm so pleased for you, you must be so happy!"

Georgiana looked puzzled for a minute, then her face cleared as she understood. "My felicitations, Kitty."

Kitty looked a little embarrassed. "I'm so

pleased I can talk about it at last. I don't want to tell anyone at home, and take everyone's attention away from Jane — she only has six or seven weeks to go, now. And I have been embarrassed that it has been so quick for me, when it took her so long."

Elizabeth embraced her tightly. "But it is such good news. Oh, you're going to be a wonderful mother!"

"But you must be certain not to talk about it, or behave any differently to me when the gentlemen are here," Kitty said anxiously.

"Of course I won't," Elizabeth promised readily. "Now, Kitty, I want to hear all the news that didn't seem quite real in the letters I get. First of all, you said Lydia has been allowed home, but that she has a companion sent by the school as well."

Kitty laughed. "I'm so happy I'm not living at Longbourn any more, Lizzy. The day after she arrived home, Mary walked over and called on us. She stayed right up until we left for Derbyshire — and then Charles let me take the coach and take her over to Shenley. She's staying with Jane now."

Elizabeth knew she was staring at her. "What did Papa have to say?"

"I don't think he's pleased, although Mary wasn't sure what he really thought. But he did say to Lydia that if she didn't behave better he would send her back to school before Christmas." Kitty shrugged ruefully. "But Mama is determined that she'll stay — and Lydia made such a fuss about Wickham not being in the Wiltshire militia any more …"

"He isn't?" Elizabeth struggled to keep up with everything.

"Well, no! Didn't I say in my letters? Sir William said that Colonel Forster had written to say that he could no longer pass on creditors details, because Wickham has been transferred to a regiment and was going to France to fight in the war." Kitty prattled on. "Papa said it was good riddance, but Lydia decided to play the martyred almost-widow, though I know she cared nothing for him, really …"

"Poor Papa!" Elizabeth decided to speak to William tonight. She thought he might know more than Kitty seemed to. But for now, she must change the subject.

"I'll call for more tea, I think, before it is time to change for dinner. Anne and Richard are joining us. I think you will enjoy getting to know Anne better, Kitty. I saw you talking to her at our wedding breakfast."

"OH, IT'S BEEN A WONDERFUL DAY!" Elizabeth crossed the room as William opened the door to her bedchamber and she sighed with satisfaction as his arms enclosed her.

She rested her head against the steady beat of his heart. "But this part of the day will always be the most magical for me, this time together."

She closed her eyes as he rested his chin on top of her head and his hand came up, tangling in her hair.

"Elizabeth," he groaned. "It is good to see everyone, but it seems so long since we were together this morning."

"We're here now." She lifted her face to his, gazed into his eyes and waited for his kiss. Even now, months later, his touch had the power to turn her legs so weak as to barely be able to support herself. But he knew that and his arms tightened round her, and she huffed a quiet laugh.

"Amusing, hmm?" His mouth left hers and nuzzled his way down the side of her throat and along her shoulder, pushing aside the soft linen of her night shift.

She breathed in deeply as her senses fled beneath her rising ardour. "William."

He picked her up. "Come." He carried her over to the bed. The warming pans had only just been removed and Elizabeth snuggled down happily.

"Thank you, and goodnight!" She let her eyes dance mischievously, and saw his expression lighten.

"So, you're tired are you — Mrs. Darcy?"

"Well — maybe not so very tired," she qualified, and extended an arm toward him. "I think I have the energy for a short conversation."

His eyebrows rose in an unspoken question.

"Well perhaps not quite as short as all that," she qualified.

"Well, we'll have to see." He climbed in beside her, and she smiled. He could refuse her nothing, she knew that.

He mumbled something in her ear and she frowned. "What was that?"

His hand was tracing down her arm, sending a line of fire through her. "I was just saying if you're too tired for anything but a short conversation, then we had better have the conversation last." His chuckle warmed her and turned her emotions upside down.

"No arguments from me," was all she managed before his hands drew her closer and she placed her hands each side of his face and kissed him back. "I love you, William."

Later, they lay, sated, in each other's arms. His finger traced its way leisurely up her arm. "There is so much to talk about — yet we've all the time in the world. Our time to hold each other is more curtailed, so I thought …"

"I think you're right," she picked up his hand

and turned it over, bringing his palm to her mouth. "I'm yours forever."

"As I am yours," he murmured, "always. I will never let you go."

Harriet Knowles is a mature Englishwoman who loves reading everything Pride and Prejudice related. She enjoys exploring the wild countryside and coast that Jane Austen's characters loved. Harriet lives in Kent, close to Ramsgate, so familiar to readers of the book.

She is the author of a number of other novels and novellas, including:

- Mr. Darcy's Stolen Love
- The Darcy/Bennet Arrangement
- Compromise and Obligation
- The Darcy Plot
- Hidden in Plain Sight
- Her Very Own Mr. Darcy
- Love Changes Everything
- A Life Apart

- Tug of Love
- A Rare Ability

Harriet Knowles' books can be found in paperback and ebook formats in online stores.

Printed in Great Britain
by Amazon

77830022R00318